FOR THE FIRST TIME
I SAW A MAN
OF THE DORSAI
IN ACTION

Across the meadow, directly in line with the table, four figures came forward. One of them was Jamethon Black.

Kensie and Jamethon saluted each other.

"Commander Graeme. I am indebted to you for meeting me here," said Jamethon.

"My duty and a pleasure, Commandant."

"I wished to discuss the terms of a surrender."

"I can offer you," said Kensie, "the customary terms extended to troops in your position under the Mercenaries' Code."

"You misunderstand me, sir," said Jamethon. "It was your surrender I came here to discuss."

"Look out!" I shouted at Kensie—but I was far too late.

GORDON R. DICKSON

BEGINNINGS

BAEN BOOKS

BEGINNINGS

Copyright © 1988 by Gordon R. Dickson

A Baen Books Original

Baen Publishing Enterprises
260 Fifth Avenue
New York, N.Y. 10001

First printing, August 1988

ISBN: 0-671-65429-2

Cover art by Greg West

Printed in the United States of America

Distributed by
SIMON & SCHUSTER
1230 Avenue of the Americas
New York, N.Y. 10020

F
DTC

TABLE OF CONTENTS

544228

ACKNOWLEDGMENTS

"The Brown Man," and "untitled," both copyright © 1984 by Gordon R. Dickson. Excerpted from The Final Encyclopedia.

"Danger—Human!" copyright © 1957 by Street & Smith Publications, Inc. Copyright renewed 1985 by Gordon R. Dickson

"Cloak and Stagger," copyright © 1957 by Columbia Publications, Inc. Copyright renewed 1985 by Gordon R. Dickson.

"Three-Part Puzzle," copyright © 1962 by the Conde Nast Publications, Inc.

"Seats of Hell," copyright © 1960 by Ziff-Davis Publishing Co.

"Listen," copyright © 1952 by Fantasy House, Inc. Copyright renewed 1980 by Gordon R. Dickson.

"Soldier, Ask Not," copyright © 1964 by Galaxy Publishing Corp.

"Strictly Confidential," copyright © 1956 by King-Size Publications, Inc. Copyright renewed 1984 by Gordon R. Dickson.

"Powerway Emergency," copyright © 1972 by Northern States Power Company.

"Idiot Solvant," copyright © 1961 by Street & Smith Publications, Inc.

"On Messenger Mountain," copyright © 1964 by Galaxy Publishing Corp.

FOREWORD

In the late part of the 1940s and the early '50s, I rented a room in a family house in North Minneapolis. The room next to mine was also rented, to someone who is an old friend of mine to this day: Poul Anderson.

Poul had established himself already in the magazine sf market—in those days the only steady market for science fiction—several years before I sold a first story to one of the magazines, too. (Although I had had scattered publications in other areas, as far back as poetry in newspapers in the '30s.)

But in the time of the rented rooms we were still both young, Poul and I, and the magazine market was all there was. (The paperback book was not yet on the scene in any useful numbers.) That meant most of the work consisted of trying to turn out short stories, novelets—and the occasional short novel; although we talked and thought of those only as possible serials—we were bound by the magazine format.

Making a living out of short fiction requires a steady production of different stories, and a writer trying to do that cannot afford to linger lovingly over his work, no matter how strong the urge to do just that. Rather, the main part of our work was the hunt for new ideas—story ideas, which to the professional writer means more than just a notion about a situation, a character, or a setting; it's a package that involves all of these, in potential. The idea is a story in miniature.

So Poul and I, spending a lot of time together, talked

about these things a lot. This was usually in the evenings, because both of us were still—for the early part of that period, at least—students at the University of Minnesota. I was resuming an education that had been interrupted by three years in the Army during World War II, and Poul was finishing up his degree in Physics.

Our studies affected our lives to different degrees. I had only an occasional class or two, generally in the mornings; so that I was in the habit of working on my writing in the afternoons. Poul, with a heavier schedule of classes and laboratory work, had longer days. So about the time I had finished my day's work at the typewriter, eaten something that was midway between a snack and a single man's version of dinner, and laid down for a nap, I would hear the opening and then closing of the door to Poul's room. It came well through the wall between us. And as I dozed off, I would begin to hear through that same wall the clicking of the keys of Poul's typewriter—tentatively at first, and then becoming more and more steady as he, in his turn, settled down to his writing.

About 10 PM I would awake and, if the sound of the typewriter next door had ceased, get up and wander over to his door. Or sometimes he would rouse me on having finished his work; and we would walk a couple of blocks to the nearest neighborhood drinking establishment, which served only beer. We would sit down there with the tall, cool glasses in our hands, facing each other across the dark top of a table in a booth, and talk of ships and shoes and sealing wax and many other things—always including story ideas.

It was the time of the day's relaxation; but also the time of brainstorming for ideas to feed into the shapes of stories from our typewriters. Sometimes we would talk through particular story problems, although that was a much lesser part of the program.

But we would throw notions at each other, and receive them thrown back with additions, changes, and suggestions—never workable as they were, to the mind of the originator, but acting as fuel for further inspirations, alterations and developments.

"I'd like to do something like this . . ." I'd say to him.

"In that case, how about your trying . . ." he would respond.

"No, no!" I'd say. "That wouldn't do. But you've given me a notion: suppose I . . ."

Or vice-versa.

In the end, if we were lucky, both of us would walk back home later, refreshed and with heads humming with further developments that we might never, or only much more slowly, have arrived at on our own—eager to be back at work tomorrow.

Some of the stories in this volume, in different ways, date back to those days. The mists of almost forty years have thickened enough that I can't tell you which did and which did not—and the copyright date of the story doesn't really tell, because sometimes an idea took years to gel. . . .

There was another reason why memory fails on this point. Of course we were both trying to write large numbers of stories in those days, to keep the rent and food bills paid. But these days people don't understand that, back then, a story was expected to see the light of day only once, in a single magazine publication. Then it would be gone forever—nobody thought of reprints, in their various forms.

So once we had written and sold a story, we effectively put it out of our minds with all other past things.

Nonetheless, since I can't identify specific stories in connection with specific evenings from those many late hours of hot discussion, tall glasses often forgotten in our hands, all of them have come to be illuminated to some extent by the amber lights and echoes of those evenings. Let those of you who find them enjoyable make your own best guesses as to which were which.

—*Gordon R. Dickson*

THE BROWN MAN

No one is so plastic-fine
That he lacks a brown man.
Twisted core of the old-wood roots,
In blind earth moving.

Clever folk with hands of steel
Have built us to a high tower,
Pitched far up from the lonely grass
And the mute stone's crying.

Only, when some more wily fist
Shatters that tower uplifted,
We may yet last in the stone and grass
By a brown man's holding.

DANGER—HUMAN!

The spaceboat came down in the silence of perfect working order—down through the cool, dark night of a New Hampshire late spring. There was hardly any moon, and the path emerging from the clump of conifers and snaking its way across the dim pasture looked like a long strip of pale cloth, carelessly dropped and forgotten there.

The two aliens checked the boat and stopped it, hovering, some fifty feet above the pasture, all but invisible against the low-lying clouds. Then they set themselves to wait, their woolly, bearlike forms settled on haunches, their uniform belts glinting a little in the shielded light from the instrument panel, talking now and then in desultory murmurs.

"It's not a bad place," said the one of junior rank, looking down at the earth below.

"Why should it be?" answered the senior.

The junior did not answer. He shifted on his haunches.

"The babies are due soon," he said. "I just got a message."

"How many?" asked the senior.

"Three, the doctor thinks. That's not bad for a first birthing."

"My wife only had two."

"I know. You told me."

They fell silent for a few seconds. The spaceboat rocked almost imperceptibly in the waters of night.

"Look—" said the junior, suddenly. "Here it comes, right on schedule."

The senior glanced overside. Down below, a tall, dark

form had emerged from the trees and was coming out along the path. A little beam of light shone before it, terminating in a blob of illumination that danced along the path ahead, lighting its way. The senior stiffened.

"Take controls," he said. The casualness had gone out of his voice. It had become crisp, impersonal.

"Controls," answered the other, in the same emotionless voice.

"Take her down."

"Down it is."

The spaceboat dropped groundward. There was an odd sort of soundless, lightless explosion—it was as if a concussive wave had passed, robbed of all effects but one. The figure dropped, the light rolling from its grasp and losing its glow in a tangle of short grass. The spaceboat landed and the two aliens got out.

In the dark night they loomed furrily above the still figure. It was that of a lean, dark man in his early thirties, dressed in clean, much-washed corduroy pants and checkered wool lumberjack shirt. He was unconscious, but breathing slowly, deeply and easily.

"I'll take it up by the head, here," said the senior. "You take the other end. Got it? Lift! Now, carry it into the boat."

The junior backed away, up through the spaceboat's open lock, grunting a little with the awkwardness of his burden.

"It feels slimy," he said.

"Nonsense!" said the senior. "That's your imagination."

Eldridge Timothy Parker drifted in that dreamy limbo between awakeness and full sleep. He found himself contemplating his own name.

Eldridge Timothy Parker. Eldridgetimothyparker. Eldridge TIMOTHY parker. ELdrIDGEtiMOthyPARKer. . . .

There was a hardness under his back, the back on which he was lying—and a coolness. His flaccid right hand turned flat, feeling. It felt like steel beneath him. Metal? He tried to sit up and bumped his forehead against a ceiling a few inches overhead. He blinked his eyes in the darkness—

Darkness?

He flung out his hands, searching, feeling terror leap up inside him. His knuckles bruised against walls to right and left. Frantic, his groping fingers felt out, around, and about him. He was walled in, he was surrounded, he was enclosed.

Completely.

Like in a coffin.

Buried.

He began to scream. . . .

Much later, when he awoke again, he was in a strange place that seemed to have no walls, but many instruments. He floated in the center of mechanisms that passed and repassed about him, touching, probing, turning. He felt touches of heat and cold. Strange hums and notes of various pitches came and went. He felt voices questioning him.

Who are you?

"Eldridge Parker . . . Eldridge Timothy Parker. . . ."

What are you?

"I'm Eldridge Parker. . . ."

Tell about yourself.

"Tell what? What?"

Tell about yourself.

"What? What do you want to know? What—"

Tell about. . . .

"But I—"

Tell. . . .

. . . well, i suppose i was pretty much like any of the kids around our town . . . i was a pretty good shot and i won the fifth grade seventy-five yard dash . . . i played hockey, too . . . pretty cold weather up around our parts, you know, the air used to smell strange it was so cold winter mornings in january when you first stepped out of doors . . . it is good, open country, new england, and there were lots of smells . . . there were pine smells and grass smells and i remember especially the kitchen smells . . . and then, too, there was the way the oak benches in church used to smell on sunday when you knelt with your nose right next to the back of the pew ahead. . . .

. . . the fishing up our parts is good, too . . . i liked to fish but i never wasted time on weekdays . . . we were presbyterians, you know, and my father had the farm, but he also had money invested in land around the country . . . we have never been badly off but i would have liked a motor-scooter. . . .

. . . no i did not never hate the germans at least i did not think i ever did, of course though i was over in europe i never really had it bad, combat, i mean . . . i was in a motor pool with the raw smell of gasoline, i like to work with my hands, and it was not like being in the infantry. . . .

. . . i have as good right to speak up to the town council as any man . . . i do not believe in pushing but if they push me i am going to push right back . . . no it isn't any man's business what i voted last election no more than my bank balance . . . but i have got as good a right to a say in town doings as if i was the biggest landholder among them. . . .

. . . i did not go to college because it was not necessary . . . too much education can make a fool of any man, i told my father, and i know when i have had enough . . . i am a farmer and will always be a farmer and i will do my own studying as things come up without taking out a pure waste of four years to hang a piece of paper on the wall. . . .

. . . of course i know about the atom bomb, but i am no scientist and no need to be one, no more than i need to be a veterinarian . . . i elect the men that hire the men that need to know those things and the men that i elect will hear from me johnny-quick if things do not go to my liking. . . .

. . . as to why i never married, that is none of your business . . . as it happens, i was never at ease with women much, though there were a couple of times, and i still may if jeanie lind. . . .

. . . i believe in god and the united states of america. . . .

He woke up gradually. He was in a room that might have been any office, except the furniture was different. That is, there was a box with doors on it that might have been a filing cabinet, and a table that looked like a desk in spite of the single thin rod underneath the center that supported it. However, there were no chairs—only small, flat cushions, on which three large, woolly, bearlike creatures were sitting and watching him in silence.

He himself, he found, was in a chair, though.

As soon as they saw his eyes were open, they turned away from him and began to talk among themselves. Eldridge Parker shook his head and blinked his eyes, and would have blinked his ears if that had been possible. For the sounds the creatures were making were like nothing he had ever heard before; and yet he understood everything they were saying. It was an odd sensation, like a double image earwise, for he heard the strange mouthnoises just as they came out and then something in his head twisted them around and made them into perfectly understandable English.

Nor was that all. For, as he sat listening to the creatures talk, he began to get the same double image in another way. That is, he still saw the bearlike creature behind the desk as the weird sort of animal he was, while out of the sound of his voice, or from something else, there gradually built up in Eldridge's mind a picture of a thin, rather harassed-looking gray-haired man in something resembling a uniform, but at the same time not quite a uniform. It was the sort of effect an army general might get if he wore his stars and a Sam Browne belt over a civilian double-breasted suit. Similarly, the other creature sitting facing the one behind the desk, at the desk's side, began to look like a young and black-haired man with something of the laboratory about him, and the creature farther back, seated almost against the wall, appeared neither as soldier nor scientist, but a heavy older man with a sort of book-won wisdom in him.

"You see, Commander," the young one with the black-haired image was saying, "perfectly restored. At least on the physical and mental levels."

"Good, Doctor, good," the outlandish syllables from the one behind the desk translated themselves in Eldridge's head. "And you say it—he, I should say—will be able to understand?"

"Certainly, sir," said the doctor-psychologist—whatever-he-was. "Identification is absolute—"

"But I mean comprehend . . . encompass. . . ." The creature behind the desk moved one paw slightly. "Follow what we tell him. . . ."

The doctor turned his ursinoid head toward the third member of the group. This one spoke slowly, in a deeper voice.

"The culture allows. Certainly."

The one behind the desk bowed slightly to the oldest one.

"Certainly, Academician, certainly."

They then fell silent, all looking back at Eldridge, who returned their gaze with equivalent interest. There was something unnatural about the whole proceeding. Both sides were regarding the other with the completely blunt and unshielded curiosity given to freaks.

The silence stretched out. It became tinged with a certain embarrassment. Gradually a mutual recognition arose that no one really wanted to be the first to address an alien being directly.

"It . . . he is comfortable?" asked the commander, turning once more to the doctor.

"I should say so," replied the doctor, slowly. "As far as we know. . . ."

Turning back to Eldridge, the commander said, "Eldridge-timothyparker, I suppose you wonder where you are?"

Caution and habit put a clamp on Eldridge's tongue. He hesitated about answering so long that the commander turned in distress to the doctor, who reassured him with a slight movement of the head.

"Well, speak up," said the commander. "We'll be able to understand you, just as you're able to understand us. Nothing's going to hurt you, and anything you say won't have the slightest effect on your . . . er . . . situation."

He paused again, looking at Eldridge for a comment. Eldridge still held his silence, but one of his hands unconsciously made a short, fumbling motion at his breast pocket.

"My pipe—" said Eldridge.

The three looked at each other. They looked back at Eldridge.

"We have it," said the doctor. "After a while we may give it back to you. For now . . . we cannot allow . . . it would not suit us."

"Smoke bother you?" said Eldridge, with a touch of his native canniness.

"It does not bother us. It is . . . merely . . . distasteful," said the commander. "Let's get on. I'm going to tell you where you are, first. You're on a world roughly similar to your own, but many . . ." he hesitated, looking at the academician.

"Light-years," supplemented the deep voice.

". . . light-years in terms of what a year means to you," went on the commander, with growing briskness. "Many light-years distant from your home. We didn't bring you here because of any personal . . . dislike . . . or enmity for you, but for . . ."

"Observation," supplied the doctor. The commander turned and bowed slightly to him, and was bowed back at in return.

". . . observation," went on the commander. "Now, do you understand what I've told you so far?"

"I'm listening," said Eldridge.

"Very well," said the commander. "I will go on. There is something about your people that we are very anxious to discover. We have been, and intend to continue, studying you to find it out. So far—I will admit quite frankly and freely—we have not found it, and the consensus among our best minds is that you, yourself, do not know what it is. Accordingly, we have hopes of . . . causing . . . you to discover it for yourself. And for us."

"Hey. . . ." breathed Eldridge.

"Oh, you will be well treated, I assure you," said the commander, hurriedly. "You have been well treated. You have been . . . but you did not know . . . I mean you did not feel—"

"Can you remember any discomfort since we picked you up?" asked the doctor, leaning forward.

"Depends what you mean. . . ."

"And you will feel none." The doctor turned to the commander. "Perhaps I'm getting ahead of myself?"

"Perhaps," said the commander. He bowed and turned back to Eldridge. "To explain—we hope you will discover our answer for it. We're only going to put you in a position to work on it. Therefore, we've decided to tell you everything. First—the problem. Academician?"

The oldest one bowed. His deep voice made the room ring oddly.

"If you will look this way," he said. Eldridge turned his head. The other raised one paw and the wall beside him dissolved into a maze of lines and points. "Do you know what this is?"

"No," said Eldridge.

"It is," rumbled the one called the academician, "a map of the known universe. You lack the training to read it in four dimensions, as it should be read. No matter. You will take my word for it . . . it is a map. A map covering hundreds of thousands of your light-years and millions of your years."

He looked at Eldridge, who said nothing.

"To go on, then. What we know of your race is based upon two sources of information. History. And legend. The history is sketchy. It rests on archaeological discoveries for the most part. The legend is even sketchier and—fantastic."

He paused again. Still Eldridge guarded his tongue.

"Briefly, there is a race that has three times broken out to overrun this mapped area of our galaxy and dominate other civilized cultures—until some inherent lack of weakness in the individual caused the component parts of this advance to die out. The periods of these outbreaks have always been disastrous for the dominated cultures and uniformly without benefit to the race I am talking about. In the case of each outbreak, though the home planet was destroyed and all known remnants of the advancing race hunted out, unknown seed communities remained to furnish the material for a new advance some thousands of years later. That race," said the academician, and coughed, or at least made some kind of noise in his throat, "is your own."

Eldridge watched the other carefully and without moving.

"We see your race, therefore," went on the academician, and Eldridge received the mental impression of an elderly man putting the tips of his fingers together judiciously, "as one with great or overwhelming natural talents, but unfortunately also with one great natural flaw. This flaw seems to be a desire—almost a need—to acquire and possess things. To reach out, encompass, and absorb. It is not," shrugged the academician, "a unique trait. Other races have it—but not to such an extent that it makes them a threat to their coexisting cultures. Yet, this in itself is not the real problem. If it was a simple matter of rapacity, a combination of other races should be able to contain your people. There is a natural inevitable balance of that sort continually at work in the galaxy. No," said the academician, and paused, looking at the commander.

"Go on. Go on," said the commander. The academician bowed.

"No, it is not that simple. As a guide to what remains, we have only the legend, made anew and reinforced after each outward sweep of your people. We know that there must be something more than we have found—and we have studied you carefully, both your home world and now you, personally. There *must* be something more in you, some genius, some capability above the normal, to account for the fantastic nature of your race's previous successes. But the legend says only—*Danger, Human! High Explosive. Do not touch*—and we find nothing in you to justify the warning."

He sighed. Or at least Eldridge received a sudden, unexpected intimation of deep weariness.

"Because of a number of factors—too numerous to go into and most of them not understandable to you—it is our race which must deal with this problem for the rest of the galaxy. What can we do? We dare not leave you be until you grow strong and come out once more. And the legend expressly warns us against touching you in any way. So we have chosen to pick one—but I intrude upon your field, Doctor."

The two of them exchanged bows. The doctor took up the talk, speaking briskly and entirely to Eldridge.

"A joint meeting of those of us best suited to consider the situation recommended that we pick up one specimen for intensive observation. For reasons of availability, you were the one chosen. Following being brought under drugs to this planet, you were thoroughly examined, by the best of medical techniques, both mentally and physically. I will not go into detail, since we have no wish to depress you unduly. I merely want to impress on you the fact that we found nothing. Nothing. No unusual power or ability of any sort, such as history shows you to have had and legend hints at. I mention this because of the further course of action we have decided to take. Commander?"

The being behind the desk got to his hind feet. The other two rose.

"You will come with us," said the commander.

Herded by them, Eldridge went out through the room's door into brilliant sunlight and across a small stretch of something like concrete to a stubby, egg-shaped craft with ridiculous little wings.

"Inside," said the commander. They got in. The commander squatted before a bank of instruments, manipulated a simple sticklike control, and after a moment the ship took to the air. They flew for perhaps half an hour, with Eldridge wishing he was in a position to see out one of the high windows, then landed at a field apparently hacked out of a small forest of mountains.

Crossing the field on foot, Eldridge got a glimpse of some truly huge ships, as well as a number of smaller ones such as the one in which he had arrived. Numbers of the furry aliens moved about, none with any great air of hurry, but all with purposefulness. There was a sudden single, thunderous sound that was gone almost before the ear could register it, and Eldridge, who had ducked instinctively, looked up again to see one of the huge ships falling— there is no other word for it—skyward with such unbelievable rapidity it was out of sight in seconds.

The four of them came at last to a shallow, open trench in the stuff that made the field surface. It was less than a foot wide and they stepped across it with ease. But once they had crossed it, Eldridge noticed a difference. In the five hundred yard square enclosed by the trench—for it turned at right angles off to his right and to his left—there was an air of tightly established desertedness, as of some highly restricted area, and the rectangular concrete-looking building that occupied the square's very center glittered unoccupied in the clear light.

They marched to the door of this building and it opened without any of them touching it. Inside was perhaps twenty feet of floor, stretching inward as a rim inside the walls. Then a sort of moat—Eldridge could not see its depth— filled with a dark fluid with a faint, sharp odor. This was perhaps another twenty feet wide and enclosed a small, flat island perhaps fifteen feet by fifteen feet, almost wholly taken up by a cage whose walls and ceiling appeared to be made of metal bars as thick as a man's thumb and spaced about six inches apart. Two more of the aliens, wearing a sort of harness and holding a short, black tube apiece, stood on the ledge of the outer rim. A temporary bridge had been laid across the moat, protruding through the open door of the cage.

They all went across the bridge and into the cage. There, standing around rather like a board of directors viewing an addition to the company plant, they faced Eldridge, and the commander spoke.

"This will be your home from now on," he said. He indicated the cot, the human-type chair and the other items furnishing the cage. "It's as comfortable as we can make it."

"Why?" burst out Eldridge, suddenly. "Why're you locking me up here? Why—"

"In our attempt to solve the problem that still exists," interrupted the doctor, smoothly, "we can do nothing more than keep you under observation and hope that time will work with us. Also, we hope to influence you to search for the solution yourself."

"And if I find it—what?" cried Eldridge.

"Then," said the commander, "we will deal with you in the kindest manner that the solution permits. It may be even possible to return you to your own world. At the very least, once you are no longer needed, we can see to it that you are quickly and painlessly destroyed."

Eldridge felt his insides twist within him.

"Kill me?" he choked. "You think that's going to make me help you? The hope of getting killed?"

They looked at him almost compassionately.

"You may find," said the doctor, "that death may be something you will want very much, if only for the purpose of putting a close to a life you've become weary of. Look,"—he gestured around him—"you are locked up beyond any chance of ever escaping. This cage will be illuminated night and day, and you will be locked in it. When we leave, the bridge will be withdrawn, and the only thing crossing that moat—which is filled with acid—will be a mechanical arm which will extend across and through a small opening to bring you food twice a day. Beyond the moat, there will be two armed guards on duty at all times, but even they cannot open the door to this building. That is opened by remote control from outside, only after the operator has checked on his vision screen to make sure all is as it should be inside here."

He gestured through the bars, across the moat, and through a window in the outer wall.

"Look out there," he said.

Eldridge looked. Out beyond, and surrounding the building, the shallow trench no longer lay still and empty under the sun. It now spouted a vertical wall of flickering, weaving distortion, like a barrier of heat waves.

"That is our final defense, the ultimate in destructiveness that our science provides us—it would literally burn you to nothingness if you touched it. It will be turned off only for seconds, and with elaborate precautions, to let guards in, or out."

Eldridge looked back in, to see them all watching him.

"We do this," said the doctor, "not only because we may discover you to be more dangerous than you seem, but to impress you with your helplessness so that you may be more ready to help *us*. Here you are, and here you will stay."

"And you think," demanded Eldridge hoarsely, "that this's all going to make me want to help you?"

"Yes," said the doctor, "because there's one thing more that enters into the situation. You were literally taken apart physically, after your capture, and as literally put back together again. We are advanced in the organic field, and certain things are true of all life forms. I supervised the work on you myself. You will find that you are, for all practical purposes immortal and irretrievably sane. This will be your home forever, and you will find that neither death nor insanity will provide you a way of escape unless we allow them to you."

They turned and filed out of the cage. From some remote control, the door was swung shut. He heard it click and lock. The bridge was withdrawn from the moat. A screen lit up and a woolly face surveyed the building's interior.

The guards took up their patrol around the rim in opposite directions, keeping their eyes on Eldridge and their weapons ready in their hands. Outside, the flickering wall blinked out for a second and then returned.

The silence of a warm, summer, mountain afternoon descended upon the building. The footsteps of the guards made shuffling noises on their path around the rim. The bars enclosed him.

Eldridge stood still, holding the bars in both hands and looking out.

He could not believe it.

He could not believe it as the days piled up into weeks, and the weeks into months. But as the seasons shifted and the year came around to a new year, the realities of his situation began to soak into him like water into a length of dock piling. For outside, Time could be seen at its visible and regular motion, but in his prison there was no Time. Always the lights burned overhead, always the guards paced about him. Always the barrier burned beyond the building, the meals came swinging in on the end of a long metal arm extended over the moat and through a small hatchway which opened automatically as the arm approached; regularly, twice weekly, the doctor came and checked him over, briefly, impersonally—and went out again with the changing of the guard.

He felt the unbearableness of his situation, like a hand winding tighter and tighter day by day the spring of tension within him. He took to pacing feverishly up and down the cage. He went back and forth, back and forth, until the room swam. He lay awake nights, staring at the endless glow of illumination from the ceiling. He rose to pace again.

The doctor came and examined him. He talked to Eldridge, but Eldridge would not answer. Finally there came a day when everything split wide open and he began to howl and bang on the bars. The guards were frightened and called the doctor. The doctor came, and with two others entered the cage and strapped him down. They did something odd that hurt at the back of his neck and he passed out.

When he opened his eyes again, the first thing he saw was the doctor's woolly face, looking down at him—he had learned to recognize that countenance in the same way a sheepherder eventually comes to recognize an individual sheep in his flock. Eldridge felt very weak, but calm.

"You tried hard," said the doctor, "but you see, you didn't make it. There's no way out *that* way for you."

Eldridge smiled.

"Stop that!" said the doctor sharply. "You aren't fooling us. We know you're perfectly rational."

Eldridge continued to smile.

"What do you think you're doing?" demanded the doctor. Eldridge looked happily up at him.

"I'm going home," he said.

"I'm sorry," said the doctor. "You don't convince me." He turned and left. Eldridge turned over on his side and dropped off into the first good sleep he'd had in months.

In spite of himself, however, the doctor was worried. He had the guards doubled, but nothing happened. The days slipped into weeks and still nothing happened. Eldridge was apparently fully recovered. He still spent a great deal of time walking up and down his cage and grasping the bars as if to pull them out of the way before him—but the frenzy of his earlier pacing was gone. He had also moved his cot over next to the small, two-foot square hatch that opened to admit the mechanical arm bearing his meals, and would lie there, with his face pressed against it, waiting for the food to be delivered. The doctor felt uneasy, and spoke to the commander privately about it.

"Well," said the commander, "just what is it you suspect?"

"I don't know," confessed the doctor. "It's just that I see him more frequently than any of us. Perhaps I've become sensitized—but he bothers me."

"Bothers you?"

"Frightens me, perhaps. I wonder if we've taken the right way with him."

"We took the only way." The commander made the little gesture and sound that was his race's equivalent of a sigh. "We must have data. What do you do when you run across a possibly dangerous virus, Doctor? You isolate it—for study, until you know. It is not possible, and too risky to try to study his race at close hand, so we study him. That's all we're doing. You lose objectivity, Doctor. Would you like to take a short vacation?"

"No," said the doctor, slowly. "No. But he frightens me."

Still, time went on and nothing happened. Eldridge paced his cage and lay on his cot, face pressed to the bars of the hatch, staring at the outside world. Another year passed, and another. The double guards were withdrawn. The doctor came reluctantly to the conclusion that the human had at last accepted the fact of his confinement, and felt growing within him that normal sort of sympathy that feeds on familiarity. He tried to talk to Eldridge on his regularly scheduled visits, but Eldridge showed little interest in conversation. He lay on the cot watching the doctor as the doctor examined him, with something in his eyes as if he looked on from some distant place in which all decisions were already made and finished.

"You're as healthy as ever," said the doctor, concluding his examination. He regarded Eldridge. "I wish you would, though—" He broke off. "We aren't a cruel people, you know. We don't like the necessity . . . that makes us do this."

He paused. Eldridge considered him without stirring.

"If you'd accept that fact," said the doctor, "I'm sure you'd make it easier on yourself. Possibly our figures of speech have given you a false impression. We said you are immortal. Well, of course, that's not true. Only practically speaking are you immortal. You are now capable of living a very, very, very long time. That's all."

He paused again. After a moment of waiting, he went on.

"Just the same way, this business isn't really intended to go on for eternity. By its very nature of course it can't. Even races have a finite lifetime. But even that would be too long. No, it's just a matter of a long time as you might live it. Eventually, everything must come to a conclusion—that's inevitable."

Eldridge still did not speak. The doctor sighed.

"Is there anything you'd like?" he said. "We'd like to make this as little unpleasant as possible. Anything we can give you?"

Eldridge opened his mouth.

"Give me a boat," he said. "I want a fishing rod. I want a bottle of applejack."

The doctor shook his head sadly. He turned and signaled the guards. The cage door opened. He went out.

"Get me some pumpkin pie," cried Eldridge after him, sitting up on the cot and grasping the bars as the door closed. "Give me some green grass in here."

The doctor crossed the bridge. The bridge was lifted up and the monitor screen lit up. A woolly face looked out and saw that all was well. Slowly the outer door swung open.

"Get me some pine trees!" yelled Eldridge at the doctor's retreating back. "Get me some plowed fields! Get me some earth, some dirt, some plain, earth dirt! *Get me that!*"

The door shut behind the doctor, and Eldridge burst into laughter, clinging to the bars, hanging there with glowing eyes.

"I would like to be relieved of this job," said the doctor to the commander, appearing formally in the latter's office.

"I'm sorry," said the commander. "I'm very sorry. But it was our tactical team that initiated this action, and no one has the experience with the prisoner you have. I'm sorry."

The doctor bowed his head; and went out.

Certain mild but emotion-deadening drugs were also

known to the woolly, bearlike race. The doctor went out and began to indulge in them. Meanwhile, Eldridge lay on his cot, occasionally smiling to himself. His position was such that he could see out the window and over the weaving curtain of the barrier that ringed his building, to the landing field. After a while one of the large ships landed and when he saw the three members of its crew disembark from it and move, antlike, off across the field toward the buildings at its far end, he smiled again.

He settled back and closed his eyes. He seemed to doze for a couple of hours and then there was the sound of the door opening to admit the extra single guard bearing the food for his three o'clock midafternoon feeding. He sat up, pushed the cot down a little, and sat on the end of it, waiting for the meal.

The bridge was not extended—that happened only when someone was to enter his cage. The monitor screen lit up and a woolly face watched as the tray of food was loaded on the mechanical arm. It swung out across the acid-filled moat, stretched itself toward the cage, and under the vigilance of the face in the monitor the two-foot square hatch opened just before it to let it extend into the cage.

Smiling, Eldridge took the tray. The arm withdrew; as it cleared the cage the hatch swung shut and locked. Outside the cage, guards, food carrier, and face in the monitor relaxed. The food carrier turned toward the door, the face in the monitor looked down at some invisible control board before it, and the outer door swung open.

In that moment, Eldridge moved.

In one swift second he was on his feet and his hands had closed around the bars of the hatch. There was a single screech of metal, as—incredibly—he tore it loose and threw it aside. Then he was diving through the hatch opening.

He rolled head over heels like a gymnast and came up with his feet standing on the inner edge of the moat. The acrid scent of the acid faintly burnt at his nostrils. He sprang forward in a standing jump, arms outstretched—and his clutching fingers closed on the end of the food arm, now halfway in the process of its leisurely mechanical retraction across the moat.

The metal creaked and bent, dipping downward toward the acid, but Eldridge was already swinging onward under the powerful impetus of his arms from which the sleeves had fallen back to reveal bulging ropes of smooth, powerful muscle. He flew forward through the air, feet first, and his boots took the nearest guard in the face, so that they crashed to the ground together.

For a second they rolled, entangled, then the guard flopped and Eldridge came up on one knee, holding the black tube of the guard's weapon. It spat a single tongue of flame and the other guard dropped. Eldridge thrust to his feet, turning to the still-open door.

The door was closing. But the panicked food carrier, unarmed, had turned to run. A bolt from Eldridge's weapon took him in the back. He fell forward and the door jammed on his body. Leaping after him, Eldridge squeezed through the remaining opening.

Then he was out under the free sky. The sounds of alarm screechers were splitting the air. He began to run. . . .

The doctor was already drugged—but not so badly that he could not make it to the field when the news came. Driven by a strange perversity of spirit, he went first to the prison to inspect the broken hatch and the bent food arm. He traced Eldridge's outward path and it led him to the landing field where he found the commander and the academician by a bare, darkened area of concrete. They acknowledged his presence by little bows.

"He took a ship here?" said the doctor.

"He took a ship here," said the commander.

There was a little silence between them.

"Well," said the academician, "we have been answered."

"Have we?" the commander looked at them almost appealingly. "There's no chance—that it was just chance? No chance that the hatch just happened to fail—and he acted without thinking, and was lucky?"

The doctor shook his head. He felt a little dizzy and unnatural from the drug, but the ordinary processes of his thinking were unimpaired.

"The hinges of the hatch," he said, "were rotten—eaten away by acid."

"Acid?" the commander stared at him. "Where would he get acid?"

"From his own digestive processes—regurgitated and spat directly into the hinges. He secreted hydrochloric acid among other things. Not too powerful—but over a period of time . . ."

"Still—" said the commander, desperately, "I think it must have been more luck than otherwise."

"Can you believe that?" asked the academician. "Consider the timing of it all, the choosing of a moment when the food arm was in the proper position, the door open at the proper angle, the guard in a vulnerable situation. Consider his unhesitating and sure use of a weapon—which could only be the fruits of hours of observation—his choice of a moment when a fully supplied ship, its drive unit not yet cooled down, was waiting for him on the field. No," he shook his woolly head, "we have been answered. We put him in an escapeproof prison and he escaped."

"But none of this was impossible!" cried the commander.

The doctor laughed, a fuzzy, drug-blurred laugh. He opened his mouth but the academician was before him.

"It's not what he did," said the academician, "but the fact that he did it. No member of another culture that we know would have even entertained the possibility in their minds. Don't you see—he disregarded, he *denied* the fact that escape was impossible. *That* is what makes his kind so fearful, so dangerous. The fact that something is impossible presents no barrier to their seeking minds. That, alone, places them above us on a plane we can never reach."

"But it's a false premise!" protested the commander. "They cannot contravene natural laws. They are still bound by the physical order of the universe."

The doctor laughed again. His laugh had a wild quality. The commander looked at him.

"You're drugged," he said.

"Yes," choked the doctor. "And I'll be more drugged. I toast the end of our race, our culture, and our order."

"Hysteria!" said the commander.

"Hysteria?" echoed the doctor. "No—*guilt*! Didn't we do it, we three? The legend told us not to touch them, not to set a spark to the explosive mixture of their kind. And we went ahead and did it, you, and you, and I. And now we've sent forth an enemy—safely into the safe hiding place of space, in a ship that can take him across the galaxy, supplied with food to keep him for years, rebuilt into a body that will not die, with star charts and all the keys to understand our culture and locate his home again, using the ability to learn we have encouraged in him."

"I say," said the commander, doggedly, "he is not that

dangerous—yet. So far he has done nothing one of us could not do, had we entertained the notion. He's shown nothing, nothing supernormal."

"Hasn't he?" said the doctor thickly. "What about the defensive screen—our most dangerous, most terrible weapon—that could burn him to nothingness if he touched it?"

The commander stared at him.

"But—" said the commander. "The screen was shut off, of course, to let the food carrier out, at the same time the door was opened. I assumed—"

"I checked," said the doctor, his eyes burning on the commander. "They turned it on again before he could get out."

"But he *did* get out! You don't mean—" the commander's voice faltered and dropped. The three stood caught in a sudden silence like stone. Slowly, as if drawn by strings controlled by an invisible hand, they turned as one to stare up into the empty sky and space beyond.

"You mean—" the commander's voice tried again, and died.

"Exactly!" whispered the doctor.

Halfway across the galaxy, a child of a sensitive race cried out in its sleep and clutched at its mother.

"I had a bad dream," it whimpered.

"Hush," said its mother. "Hush." But she lay still, staring at the ceiling. She, too, had dreamed.

Somewhere, Eldridge was smiling at the stars.

CLOAK AND STAGGER

First it was just a haze of light. Then it was something distant and white, with a dark blob swimming against it. Then it all cleared; and the white was the ceiling and the blob was the face of a medician.

"Hello, Torm, boy," said the medician. "Easy, now. How's the head?"

Torm Lindsay reached up and felt a skullcap bandage smooth and tight under his fingers. "Whuzzat?" he said.

"I'll take it off now," said the medician. His hands went to Lindsay's head, and Torm could feel the bandage being peeled and rolled back. "Now how does it feel?"

"Feels fine," said Torm, his voice strengthening.

"Fine. Not the best operating conditions here, you know. How d'*you* feel?"

"Feel?" For a long moment Torm just lay silent, puzzling over this last question. Feel? How *did* he feel? He certainly felt different than he had ever felt before. Or had he once—a long time ago . . . ? The memory, if it was a memory, slipped from his mind's searching fingers and was gone.

"I feel fine," he said.

"Ataboy." The medician helped him up off the long, narrow table with its white cover. "Take it slow and easy now; the aliens have the oxygen up around the embassy again. Breathe slowly and naturally. Don't try to move too fast."

Torm tried it. The room and everything in it began to settle around him once more. "Now what?"

25

"Room 243," said the medician. "She's waiting for you."

"Who's waiting?"

The medician peered at him. "Don't you know?"

Suddenly Torm remembered. It all blossomed out inside of him at once; and it seemed to him suddenly that it was the best, the most wonderful, and the funniest thing he had ever known. He started to laugh and his laughter mounted until he was leaning helplessly on the medician and whooping in his ear.

"I'm a *spy!*" he yelped delightedly.

The medician's face went white. He glanced frantically around him. "For . . . Torm, you crazy fool! Keep it down! *Keep your voice down!*"

Turning the corner of the corridor leading to room 243 of the Human Embassy to the alien Federation of Peoples, on Arcturus Five (there was a peculiar feeling of dizziness accompanying the action, as if he had been turning corridors all morning—but not an unpleasant feeling at all; Torm Lindsay could hardly remember ever having felt so good) he came face to face with a mirror. From it, his own image beamed back at him, pug nose, blue eyes, all the normal attributes. He was wearing, he noted, his formal, one-piece suit of diplomatic black with the Green Earth emblem on the chest. A pleasant sight.

"Hi, me," said Lindsay.

Looking beyond the mirror, down the corridor, he saw the doorway he was seeking and went on to and through it. Inside was an office with a tall, shapely brunette in the gold and white of a research medician, standing with her back to him, searching through the spools of a filing cabinet.

"Rrrufff!" Coming up behind, Lindsay gathered her in his arms. For a moment it was touch and go; but then she managed to break away from him.

"No, Torm," she said, getting a desk between them. "Not now. You sit down over there."

"But I love you," said Torm. "I love you madly, Selagh."

Selagh Maron, who had been about to say something, closed her mouth and swallowed a little convulsively. "*This* is no time to break the news to me."

"You mean I haven't told you before?" said Torm, frowning. "That's odd."

"Oh, is it?"

"Of course. I've loved you ever since they first sent you out from Earth."

"Torm, will you *please* sit down?"

Torm sat down. "Now," said Selagh, briskly, seating herself in turn behind the desk, "I want you to answer a few questions."

"Carry on."

"Name?"

"You know my name."

"Name?"

"Torm Alexander McTavish Lindsay."

"Age?"

"Twenty-eight."

"Position?"

"Junior attaché, diplomatic, Embassy to the Federation, Arcturus Five."

"Present duty?"

"To reach by any possible means the planetary center of government, and bring our case to the attention of the higher authorities."

"And what is our case?"

"Ha!" said Torm. "We haven't one."

"Torm!" cried Selagh, sitting up in her chair.

"Well, what do you think? They've got umpteen thousand races and half the galaxy. If they don't like us, how can we make them? If they don't want us, what can we do about it?" Torm scratched the tip of his nose. "Seems silly to me."

"Torm, that's not the point," retorted Selagh, swiftly. "The Representative they've assigned to deal with us is just being obstructionistic, that's all. Your job is just to find someone else that Ambassador Coran and Admiral Natek can take our case to."

"Ah, well . . ." Torm shrugged.

Selagh looked at him severely. "Got it?"

"Yup!" said Torm, with a yawn. "Makes no difference to me, anyhow."

"That's right." Selagh got up. "Come on now."

The guard at the entrance stood to one side, stiff in his maroon and gray uniform, and they went in. The office of the Human Ambassador to Arcturus was long and wide, lit by the same bright sourceless lighting that illuminated the

whole interior of the embassy building. Around a table at
the far end of the room sat three men.

No—not quite three. One had a curiously crippled look
about him. On closer inspection, it could be seen that he
did not have the outjutting shoulder bones that belong to
the human skeleton. In their place was something like a
large double ball-and-socket joint into which his arms fit-
ted at the top, but the details of which were hidden by the
sort of loose smock he wore. This structural peculiarity,
and the unvarying stillness of his expressionless face, tagged
him as an alien of one of the races which together made up
the humanly unknown numbers and extent of the Federation of Peoples.

"Oh, there you are," said Ambassador Coran, looking
up, his thin, lined face under its gray hair alertly upon
Selagh and Torm as they came up to the table. He turned
to the alien. "This, Representative, is the young man
we're sending out."

The Federation Representative turned his unmoving
face to Torm. His eyes were dark and lustrous, and seemed
to burn with a deeply hidden light. He stared at Torm.

"Reading my mind?" asked Torm, cheerfully.

"Lindsay!" snapped Coran.

The Representative raised one hand, slowly. The hand,
too, was very human, though somewhat long and fragile
looking.

"It's all right, Ambassador," he said, in words lacking
the faintest trace of any accent. "I've seen you before;
you're Torm Lindsay, aren't you?"

"Right."

"I thought so. No, Torm, I wasn't reading your mind; I
can't. We in the Federation, even the best of us, can
receive only what is consciously projected to us. You people are not telepathically dumb, you know. Merely deaf—or
rather, lacking in proper education. Now, Torm, you've
been warned that going outside of the Embassy may be—to
my mind, certainly will be—dangerous for you?"

"Check," said Lindsay.

"And you're going out of your own free will?"

"I am."

The alien's hand disappeared into the long sleeve of his
smock and came out holding a small, metallic-looking cap-

sule. He handed it to Torm. "Break this with your thumbnail."

Torm did; and a silver mist seemed to rise from the broken capsule, to flow about him and disappear.

"What's that?" asked Coran.

"Roughly the equivalent—but I should say a great deal better than one of your space suits," answered the Representative. "It will ensure a constant physical environment for him. His own atmosphere, temperature, pressure, gravity, and so on."

The eyes of stocky Admiral Natek lit up eagerly, then the glow faded resignedly. He had tried prying loose technical improvements from the Representative before this; and with no success.

"Selagh," said Ambassador Coran, "will you take Lindsay to the door and start him out? Then come back here. We're going to . . . just come back."

"Yes, sir," said Selagh.

She led Torm back out the door, down several levels and along a corridor that ended in a small door. At her touch it slid back, revealing a short ramp sloping down to a walkway that curved past the embassy building, and curved off to lose itself among further buildings of the great city—of which the humans, imprisoned in their embassy, knew next to nothing.

"There you are," Selagh looked up into his face. "Take care of yourself." Suddenly she threw her arms around him and clung to him. "Oh, take *care* of yourself!"

"Hey . . ." began Torm. But before he could respond, she had kissed him quickly and pushed him out onto the ramp. The door closed between them; and Lindsay was left staring foolishly at it.

"Well . . ." said Torm. "Well . . ." After a moment he shrugged his shoulders and turned away. He went down the slight slope of the ramp and turned to his right on the walkway.

II

As he stepped onto it, it seemed deserted. Aliens of all types, observation from the Embassy's windows had informed its human staff, seemed to prefer the simplicity of disappearing from one place and appearing in another, to more ordinary and personal methods of locomotion. However, Torm Lindsay, being only human, was finding an actual pleasure in stretching his legs; he strode along, whistling to himself.

He had, however, covered only a short distance before he discovered that the walk itself was moving him along. When he stopped and looked down at his feet, they seemed to be firmly planted upon an immovable surface. When he looked at the low walls edging the walkway, he saw, however, that he was undeniably in motion. By way of experiment, Torm sat down; he proceeded as easily and comfortably as before.

"Marchons!" This reminded him of the Marsellaise, and he sang a couple of verses. *"Allons,"* he said. *"A l'estacion. Aus den bierstube. Rrrrapido—"* he said, liking the sound of the rolling r's *"corrrrem los carrrros del ferrrrocarrrril."*

The walk, apparently puzzled, slowed down and stopped. Torm patted it reassuringly. "That's all right, boy. Just take me to the nearest transportation center."

The walk picked up speed again.

"Faster," ordered Torm.

It went faster.

"Faster!" cried Torm.

The edging walls began to blur with the speed.

"Faster!"

The walk stopped abruptly—and somehow without snapping Lindsay's head off at the neck. But at the moment he was not so concerned with that as with its evident disobedience to his command.

"What is this farce? I said—*faster!*" The walk did not stir. "How will I ever get to . . . oh."

He had just noticed that he was halted opposite a towering building that stretched impossibly up out of sight beside him.

"I am there? You are there!" he told himself. He got to his feet with another charitable pat for the walkway. "Thanks—and pardon my misunderstanding."

He turned and headed for the building's wide entrance. Just inside the shadow of it stood a tall, bipedal alien with several extra joints in each of his arms and legs. It looked at him with large, spaniel-like brown eyes set in a high, bony forehead that was seamed with wrinkles.

"Hi," said Tom. "This the transportation center?"

The alien continued to stare at him. Torm produced a small cube of plastic. "My identification." The alien looked down at it. "Torm Lindsay, Human Embas—" The cube abruptly disappeared. Torm stared at his empty fingers in some surprise.

The alien unexpectedly produced another pair of eyes from the wrinkles above the first pair. These four now surveyed Torm Lindsay with interest, then closed, one at a time, almost in cadence, from left to right, from top to bottom. Apparently blind, the alien turned and walked unerringly toward a small booth inside the doorway. Torm followed.

The door to the booth opened; the alien stepped inside; the door closed. Torm waited. After a few minutes he knocked.

The door opened. The booth was empty.

"Hmmmm?" Torm stepped inside the booth himself.

Behind him the door closed. In the opposite side of the booth, another door opened. Torm stepped out and found that he was no longer in the lobby of the tall building. He was possibly on the top of it—at any rate, in some large, open area with what seemed to be a curtain of white light shimmering by itself off at some distance from him.

The many-jointed alien was not in sight; but nearby was what appeared to be an oversize Gila monster, or something very like it, with bushy black whiskers. The whiskers were just now in the process of being retracted; as Lindsay watched, the alien split down the back.

A second later, the essential creature began to struggle out through the crack, leaving the heavy, discarded skin behind.

"Need a hand?" asked Torm politely.

The alien did not answer. It was almost completely out of the old skin now, revealing a pink, semitransparent new skin through which an assortment of organs could be seen dimly in palpitant motion.

"My congratulations," said Torm. "And now I wonder if you could direct me . . ." The alien abruptly disappeared. A moment later the old skin disappeared also.

"Ah, well," said Torm, philosophically, "it takes all kinds." He looked about him and saw at some distance away the shimmering wall of luminescence. A number of aliens of all descriptions seemed to be coming and going from it.

"When in doubt," Torm Lindsay advised himself, "follow the crowd." He commenced to stroll off in the direction of the shimmering wall.

The walk to it was uneventful. Occasionally, he had to sidestep to avoid aliens of various shapes and sizes who appeared in his path. He was almost trapped once, and was forced to detour, by a large hole that appeared before him for no apparent reason, and then as suddenly closed up again. And he stopped to watch what appeared to be a couple of twelve-foot grasshoppers fighting. It was a close match for a couple of minutes; then one of the grasshoppers got the head of the other between his enormous, bony jaws, and crushed it.

"The winnah, and new champeen!" applauded Torm. The winnah, however, like so many winnahs, appeared to have let success go to his head. For he ignored Lindsay and stalked off into the distance with a lordly air. The loser, as might have been expected, disappeared.

Torm shook his head and continued on. As he approached the wall of luminescence, he discovered that it was not a solid unit—as it had seemed to be from a distance—but a long line of glowing capsules of light, in continuous movement from left to right. Every so often, one of the aliens standing in front of it would plunge forward into an empty capsule; the alien would then be carried off, fading as he went, until by the time the capsule he had entered had covered a dozen feet or so, it was once more empty. Occasionally, other aliens would appear in an otherwise-empty capsule, ride along for a short distance until they had acquired full solidity of definition; and then pop out onto the floor. It was a busy scene.

"Eureka?" said Torm. "It doesn't look like an ordinary transport system. Still . . ."

Talking it over with himself, he stepped up to the line of capsules. A good share of them, he saw, were filled by aliens either dissolving or resolving. Occasionally there was an empty, however. He finally spotted one coming along between a capsule holding something that looked like a small, leafless bush, and another containing a sort of tuskless walrus.

"Heigh-ho, and here we go."

The capsule slid opposite.

"To the governing center of the planet, driver," said Torm, stepping into it. "And don't spare the . . ."

The lights went out.

Torm Lindsay was having a dream. He was dreaming that he was his own ancestor back on the border marches between Scotland and England. Appropriately dressed in kilt and broadsword, he was arguing with the Earl Douglas. His Scots accent was impeccable.

"Douglas," he was saying. "I gi' ye fair warning. Dinna let yersel be cozened into gaein' tae Bannockburn. Yon Percy have a lean and hungry look."

"Hoot, awa wi' ye, Lindsay!" the Douglas retorted. "Wi' sic as yersel' and Montgomery beside me, there's nae danger. Danger! Hoot. Hoot! Hooooot! Hooooooo . . ."

Torm blinked his eyes open and sat up shakily. A few feet in front of him, the walrus-shaped alien was doing push-ups on his front flippers and hooting distressfully. As Torm Lindsay sat up, the other sank down, closed his eyes as if exhausted, and became silent.

Torm shook his head—in gingerly fashion. It had been a trifle sore to begin with; now, it had picked up a pounding ache. Moreover, to top it all off, he had the dirty, ragged-nerved feeling that follows on a case of severe shock; and he was most outrageously thirsty.

He looked around in search of something drinkable. There was no such something in sight. In fact, little less than what he saw could have been in sight. Besides himself and the walrus-shaped alien, (which Torm, in his own mind, nicknamed "the monster") there was to be seen only the plant-shaped alien that had occupied the adjoining bubble of light on Torm's other side; and some evidently damaged contrivance of metal lying sprawled about. Elsewhere, as far as the eye could reach, there was nothing—nothing at all except a dead and level plain of sand. A blinding double sun burnt brightly overhead.

"Well," said Torm thoughtfully. "Well!"

"Hoot!" said the monster, suddenly. "Hoot. Hoot, hoot!"

Torm looked back at the fat alien and discovered him doing push-ups again. As far as it was possible to tell about such things, he seemed to be eyeing the plant. Torm got stiffly to his feet and went over to inspect this other companion in misfortune.

Unlike Lindsay himself and the monster, the plant appeared to be either still unconscious, or else done for altogether. It lay sprawled out on the sand, looking like something weeded from a garden and thrown on a rubbish heap for burning. Torm supposed that the monster was urging him to give it some kind of aid. At least, that was the natural assumption. But how do you go about—say—giving artificial respiration to a plant?

Torm scratched his head and fell, rather than sat, down on the sand beside it to look at it. There was nothing in the way of clues about its anatomy. Generally speaking, it appeared to resemble a small scrawny bush, a little over a meter in height. Its limbs were leafless, short and sparse, sticking out straight from its body and ending in sharp, but delicate tips. At its base, several of what Lindsay took to be roots sprawled out limply. And just above these, at the base of the stem, there was a bulge of about the same size as a small grapefruit. Torm touched the bulge dubiously with one forefinger, in the rather forlorn hope of running into something resembling a heartbeat. But the bulge was hard and silent.

Torm went back to the monster. His knees felt shaky and he dropped onto the sand facing it.

"Well, I guess something went wrong."

"Hoot," said the monster, companionably.

"Sorry to drag you two into it."

"Hoot. Hoot!"

"Look here," said Torm, "we're obviously all stuck someplace we didn't intend to be; and our friend over there doesn't seem to be in any too good shape. Now, I think the first thing we better do is work out some kind of a code for communication purposes. To start off with, if you can understand me, hoot twice."

"Hoot. Hoot!" hooted the monster.

"Fine. Marvelous. Now—is our friend over there alive?"

"Hoot. Hoot!"

"Is there something I can do to him?"

"Hoot. Hoot!"

"Good," said Torm, pushing himself painfully to his feet. "I'll just go get him and bring him to you . . ."

"Hoot! Hoot! Hoot! Hoot—" the monster went off into a frenzy of trumpeting.

Torm paused, astonished. "*Don't* bring him over?"

"Hoot—"

"Leave him where he is?"

"Hoot! Hoot!"

Torm goggled at the monster. "But shouldn't we—"

"Hoot!"

"But you just said—you know," said Lindsay thoughtfully, "I'm beginning to wonder if you understand me after all."

"Hoot! Hoot! Hoot!"

"Oh, fine; that explains everything." Torm glanced over at the plant. It was beginning to stir feebly. "Wait here," he told the monster. "I'll go see if I can't make a little more sense out of him than I can out of you."

Ignoring the busy hooting that the monster set up the minute he turned his back on it, Torm Lindsay walked over to the plant, which was making weak efforts to stand upright. He gave it a hand up; it pushed out with its roots, rocked dizzily for a moment and found its balance. Now that it was once more animated and erect, a lot of the scrubbing of its appearance seemed to have vanished. Vibrant and alive, it marched away on its roots for a few feet, turned and marched back, looking a little like a strutting dandy out of medieval Europe.

"Well, now," said Torm. "That's better. Can *you* understand me?"

The plant regarded him. Its top bent toward him and its limbs quivered slightly. It took a couple more steps toward him and quivered again. It came on and started to climb up his leg.

"Here!" said Torm, detaching it—the root and limb ends were a little on the sharp and thorny side. "No. Stay down." The plant was evidently anything but amenable to suggestion—it was trying to climb his leg again. "No, I say! Stay on your own—er—base."

He slapped it gently for emphasis. The plant retreated a few steps, dug its roots firmly into the sand, and began to quiver violently, as if with indignation. It occurred to Torm that possibly he was being told off.

"Well, I'm sorry," he said, soothingly. "Very probably you're one of the leading lights of the Federation. The point is, how am I to know? And I don't like you climbing on me like that. Gives me a prickly feeling."

"Hoot!" put in the monster.

"Another precinct heard from." Torm glanced over at the larger alien. "Now"—he turned back to the plant—"let's see if I can get into some kind of communication with you. At least one of the two of you ought to be telepathic."

The plant waved a few limbs and quivered expressively.

"I don't know what that's supposed to mean, but I'll take it for agreement. Now . . ." Lindsay sat down on the sand again. He found himself a trifle dizzy, and the dizziness seemed to subside a bit when he was closer to the ground. "Here's the situation as I see it. When I stepped into that—er—bubble, it threw something or other out of kilter. And as a result we're all both lost and stranded. Right?"

"Hoot," said the monster. Torm looked over at him; but it was impossible to tell whether the fat alien was agreeing, or merely felt like hooting. Torm inclined to the latter opinion. The monster was not a particularly impressive looking being; he looked like a grounded sea-cow, and his hoot resembled the note of a querulous fog horn. Torm turned his attention back to the plant, whose continual nervous movement seemed to augur a more alert and intelligent nature.

"At any rate," he wound up, "the point is we're stuck here. And the question is—what to do about it? Any suggestions?"

The plant quivered and did a little one-two step.

"Well, don't either of you have any notion of how to get out of this fix?"

His two auditors preserved their uninformative attitudes.

"Now look," said Torm. "We can't just stay here indefinitely. For one thing, I'm thirsty; and there's no water in sight. And whatever you two eat or drink—"

The plant turned and began to move away, abruptly. It marched over to the damaged-looking metallic contrivance and began to climb over it.

"Hey," said Torm, getting to his feet, "is this the gimmick that does the transporting?" He walked over to the "gimmick." The plant retired about the distance of a meter and quivered busily at him.

"I wish I knew what you were trying to tell me." Torm looked down at the gimmick again. "It makes sense, though. This is the transporter, or whatever it was. And it's been damaged." He looked at the plant. "Are you trying to tell me we can fix it?"

III

The plant stamped twice with its roots, marched in a half circle around to Lindsay's flank; as he turned to face it, the plant quivered once again. Torm looked over at the monster. "What do you think?"

The monster was lying still with its flippers limp on the sand and its eyes closed. It did not answer.

"Our friend yonder," said Torm to the plant, "doesn't seem to be mechanically inclined."

The plant turned half around, as if discovering the monster for the first time. For a second it merely quivered in the other's direction. Then, abruptly, it began to march toward the monster.

"That's right; wake him up."

The plant continued on its way, trundling along stiffly like a Napoleonic soldier on parade. When it was halfway to the monster, the latter suddenly opened his eyes. He took one look at the advancing plant and began to hoot violently, waving his flippers. His eyes were on Lindsay.

For a moment, Torm hesitated. "This doesn't make sense," he said. But the plant continued to advance and the monster continued to hoot.

Torm shook his head, walked over and caught up with the plant, and picked it up from behind. The monster's hooting abruptly ceased. The plant craned itself around in his hands, quivered energetically, and tried to climb his arm. It was unsuccessful.

Torm looked from it to the monster. "What's wrong between you two?"

Neither answered. Torm Lindsay shook his head and put the plant down. It immediately lit out once more in the direction of the monster.

"No," said Torm, going around and getting in its way. "Whatever there is between you two, we're all in this thing together and we can't afford to take picks at each other."

The plant was not convinced; it tried to go around Lindsay. Remembering a technique that had worked before, he slapped at it a couple of times, lightly. It retreated half a meter, dug itself perhaps twenty centimeters into the sand, and quivered violently for a good minute.

"Consider me told off again," said Torm. The plant drooped rather limply. "You shouldn't excite yourself that way. *He*"—Lindsay glanced over at the monster—"isn't doing any harm, just lying there that way."

"Hoot," said the monster.

"Of course, he isn't doing *us* any good either."

The monster closed his eyes and relaxed. The plant continued to droop.

"Perk up, son," Lindsay said to the plant, "and let's get back to business. You, at least, were making yourself useful on this gimmick business. Let's go back and see what can be done about getting it working again, eh?"

The plant made no response. After a minute, Torm dug the sand away from its roots, picked it up, and carried it back to the gimmick. It gave a couple of half-hearted quivers on the way over.

"Cheer up," said Torm. "Nothing is impossible. Now . . ." He sat down and placed the plant in front of him, between himself and the apparatus. "Let's see what we have here."

The plant walked off a meter's length or so and stood still. Lindsay poked interestedly at the gimmick.

In appearance, it was so simple as to appear easily understandable. There were several plates spaced along a narrow rod, which seemed to have been twisted somewhat out of plumb. There was a long coil of fine wire, attached to the bottom plate and trailing loosely off to one side. And there was a fine, colorful little object that would have made an excellent child's marble back on Earth if it had not been for the fact that it was ellipsoidal in shape, rather than spherical.

"Hmmmm." Torm lifted the long coil of wire. It draped nicely in length. "Where do you suppose this goes?"

It was a good question. The coil was too long to fit between the plates—unless Torm didn't mind having a lot left over. But the loose end had an uncompleted look about it, as if it were supposed to fit somewhere.

"Hey!" Torm called, looking over at the plant. "Give me a hand, here."

The plant ignored him.

"Fine thing! I draw one alien who spends all his time snoozing when he isn't hooting his head off; and another who's a little bundle of temperament." He reached over and poked the stem of the plant, gently. "Hey—"

The plant quivered briefly. That was all.

"Now look," said Lindsay, "what good's it going to do you to sulk? If this thing is completely unfixable, just wave your top back and forth a couple of times. If something can be done, just move a little closer to me."

This request got him nowhere. The plant refused to stir.

"I wouldn't bother you," said Torm. "But our friend yonder seems a little too bovine to be helpful. I've got a hunch you're the one with the brains in this crowd."

He waited; but flattery, it seemed, would also get him nowhere.

"Very well," said Torm, rising. "You force me to take my trade to the opposition." He gathered up rod and plates, coil and marble; and went over to the monster. He poked it in the region where in any reasonable scheme of bodily organization, it should contain its ribs.

"Pardon me; but about this gimmick . . ."

The monster opened one eye, suspiciously.

"How do I fix this?" demanded Torm.

"Hoot, hoot, hoot, hoot, hoot," said the monster and apparently went back to sleep.

"Much obliged. But couldn't you be a little more explicit?"

The monster lay quiescent.

"Ah well." Torm Lindsay sat down and resigned himself to fiddling with the apparatus alone. He tried wrapping the coil around the rod; he tried attaching it to the various plates; he searched for some evidence of a broken connection point. He picked up the marble and examined it.

"You wouldn't know this," he said confidentially to the motionless and silent monster, "but I'm supposed to be rather good at intuitive reasoning, according to the aptitude tests. Even with good intuitive reasoning, however—" he caught sight suddenly of the plant which was working around in a wide arc so as to come up behind the monster. He put the equipment down, struggled to his feet, and walked wearily over to confront the plant.

It stopped. "Son," said Torm, "this is unworthy of you." The plant quivered.

"I know. He's probably one of your own trail herd; or maybe he broke out of the pasture once and ate your uncle Otto by mistake. But I've already told you I can't take chances on one of you doing something to the other. I'm just about positive I'm responsible for this situation we're in; and if I don't get both of you back in top shape, I can just imagine what kind of reaction I'll get from the authorities—whoever they happen to be. Now, will you go back a reasonable distance and sit down?"

The plant took half a step toward him.

"All right," said Lindsay, "you asked for it." He looked around for some way of immobilizing the plant without hurting it. With the exception of the monster and the equipment, nothing presented itself as providing a possible restraint. Finally, an idea occurred to him. He took off his one-piece suit of embassy black, and tied a leg of it around the plant's stem just above the bulge.

"There," said Torm. The plant swayed and struggled against the weight of the suit. Dragging on the ground, the tangle of cloth made an effective hobble. Torm went over and got the equipment. He brought it back and sat down on one arm of the suit to work on it. The plant was neatly tethered. It quivered violently at Lindsay.

"Fortunes of war," said Torm, and got back to work.

It was a little hard to concentrate, he found. His headache was getting worse, and the desert seemed to shimmer and dance in the distance. When he tried to focus down on the metallic objects in his hands, these too seemed to waver and bend out of focus. It occurred to him, somewhat belatedly, that the contents of the capsule the Representative had given him to pop with his thumbnail, while "good as a spacesuit," might be somewhat lacking in protective qualities where the possibility of sunstroke was concerned. He looked over at the plant, which had dug itself into the sand and was, apparently, sulking again.

"You should grow some shade leaves," he told it.

The plant, however, showed no signs of obliging; and Torm Lindsay went back to fiddling with the coil of wire. He tried it in every way he could think of—without success; wadded up, wound around the rod, fastooned from the plates. No results.

He turned his attention to the marble again. He tried it against both ends of the rod and against all of the plates, unsuccessfully. His eyes were seeing dots by this time; and he stopped to rest.

He would probably not make it, he thought. In a little while, he would pass out from sunstroke; the plant would get free and eat the monster—or vice-versa, which was more likely. The survivor would keel over in due time; and eventually sometime in the galactic future, a passerby would find them all, three bleached skeletons, in the sand. *Alas, poor Lindsay, I knew him well . . .*

Torm squeezed his eyes shut, shook his head to clear it and opened his eyes again. *Concentrate*, he told himself.

"Hoot, hoot, hoot, hoot, hoot," hooted the monster, suddenly waking up and doing an energetic series of push-ups.

"And a happy New Year to you," said Torm, looking over at him. He picked up the equipment and bent once more to his task.

Sometime later, quite by accident, he got his first break. He was twisting the coil around aimlessly, and without any great enthusiasm, when it suddenly clung to the rod, as if a sort of magnetic force had abruptly asserted itself. Torm rubbed his eyes and looked at it. Through the swimming dots, he made out that he had looped the coil in an arc; and the middle of it was apparently glued to the top tip of the rod, while the far end had caught and frozen itself tight to the near end, where it fastened to the rod's base. The whole thing now looked something like a directional antenna.

"Hey!" said Torm, pleased. He set the contraption upright on the sand and stared at it.

"Let's see now; suppose it is directional. Suppose it taps some kind of channel of power; and then when you think of where you want to go—" Torm Lindsay closed his eyes and thought devoutly of the spot he had last seen back on Arcturus Five.

He opened his eyes again. The desert still surrounded them.

Undiscouraged, he kept his eyes closed, thought of the Arcturian station, and carefully rotated the device in a circle, on the sand.

No results.

He tried rotating it vertically.

No results.

He pondered the situation somewhat woozily for a few seconds; and then remembered that he'd forgotten the marble. He hunted for it among the sand and swimming dots before him and finally found it.

"All right, little marble," he told it. "Where do you go?"

Shakily, but methodically, he set out at the top end of the rod, and commenced to run the marble over every possible inch of the apparatus. He progressed down the rod, and over the three plates, with no success. However, the moment he touched the wire coil where the two ends joined together against the rod, the marble stuck.

"Hallelujah!" Torm bent down to take a closer look at the marble and found to his surprise that it was not merely sticking to the wire; in some mysterious fashion, it had melted around the wire so that it was now strung on it like a bead on a string. Torm poked it with his finger. It slid freely on the wire.

"Well, whither now?" Torm slid the marble around the coils, moving it up along the rod. At the very tip, the marble froze, making, it seemed, a connection between the tip of the rod and the wire.

"What a clever little old diplomat you are, to be sure," said Torm, admiringly. "Subspatial transporters repaired, rebuil . . ." The sentence trailed off, uncompleted. He became conscious of the fact that the effort involved in finishing it was not worth the trouble. He swayed a little, where he sat on the sand. It was taking most of his strength now just to remain upright. In fact, thought Torm, looking affectionately at the inviting bed of sand stretching off to the horizon, why stay upright, anyhow? A little nap . . .

A slight tugging sensation brought him back for a moment to his full senses. With a great effort, he turned his head to look behind him—and stared blankly for a moment at the sight of his suit still and empty upon the sand. For a moment he gazed at it stupidly; then he remembered what it should, instead, have been occupied with.

He swiveled his head toward the monster. Sure enough. There was the plant, loose from the suit, already well on its way toward the rotund alien.

"Hey!" cried Torm, in a cracked voice. The plant paid no attention. Lindsay made a spasmodic effort to get to his feet and found that his legs were like strips of unbaked dough, with neither substance nor muscle to them. The plant marched on.

"Wait—wait—" mumbled Torm. Gazing around, his eye fell on the apparatus. Dizzily he fumbled for it.

"Now—" he said. "Got to—" He made a mighty effort with his mind. "Station—"

Nothing happened. He fumbled with it.

"*Got* to work—" he muttered. "Push? Pull? Something—button to push? Button—" through waves of dizziness and swimming specks, and the nightmare marching of the plant bearing down on the silent monster, his attention was caught by the glitter of the marble.

"Button—" he mumbled; and, sliding his hand up the length of the rod, touched marble, wire, and rod, all at once.

There was a sort of colorless flash; and a black wave rose up over Torm Lindsay and swallowed him entirely.

IV

This time, he was very cautious about opening his eyes.

He lifted his right lid no more than a fraction of an inch and peered carefully through the tiny aperture. He saw a portion of white ceiling and the face of Selagh. Relieved, he opened both eyes.

Not only Selagh, but Ambassador Coran, Admiral Natek, and the alien Representative were standing looking down at him. He was lying in the same recovery room where it had all started.

"Uh . . . hello," he said.

"Hello, Torm," said the Representative.

Torm Lindsay decided to sit up. He swung his legs over the edge of the narrow couchlike affair he was lying on and pushed himself up with his hands. Selagh hurried to help him. He was back in his suit, he noticed with some relief; and the medician that he had first talked with was hovering in the background. Ambassador Coran noticed the direction of Torm's gaze.

"You can go now, Hartlye," he said. With an air of something very like relief, the medician nodded, went across to the door, and slipped out, closing it behind him. Coran turned back to Torm. "How do you feel?"

"Rocky," answered Torm. His head had come to life when he sat up; and now it seemed to be full of shooting pains.

"Anesthetics all out?" asked Coran, looking over at Selagh.

"Yes, sir."

"Well, then," said the Ambassador, turning to the Representative, "I think we've proved our point. Lindsay has certainly returned unharmed; and since you were watching his progress on that screen of yours along with the rest of us, you must admit that he behaved successfully in his contacts with other members of your Federation."

"Perhaps, Mr. Coran, perhaps," replied the alien. "But you may have settled one point of objection only to raise another. Torm was operated on by your people before being turned loose. Suppose you explain that operation to me."

Coran nodded at Selagh. "Commandress . . ."

"A refinement of the old operation of prefrontal lobotomy," said Selagh.

"I don't understand."

"On our home planet, back in the days when psychiatry was young," explained Selagh, "it was found possible to relieve cases of chronic tension, by, in essence, cutting off a certain portion of the brain from its normal connection with the rest of it. The tension would be relieved. Unfortunately, the patient normally suffered a loss of will power at the same time. He would start eating, say, and keep at it until the food was all gone, or someone stopped him. Or he might start doing something like chopping wood; and once started, keep at it until he was ordered to stop."

"Go on," said the Representative.

"Well, over the years, the technique was improved. The last innovation was a development of my own—the basis of my surgical thesis, in fact. What we did on Torm Lindsay was what you might call a selective topectomy, except that instead of cutting, we merely anesthetized to block off certain parts of his brain. When we finished, we hoped that we'd made him emotionally immune—that is, incapable of reacting emotionally to outside stimuli."

"I see," said the Representative, thoughtfully. He turned back to the cot. "You know about this, Torm?"

"Yes," said Lindsay, as cheerfully as he could with invisible little men probing through his head with white hot needles. "I volunteered."

"And how did you feel—after the operation?"

"Oh . . . fine, I guess. Good. Yes, I felt good."

"I see," said the Representative.

"Well?" demanded Coran. "You claim we humans aren't ready yet for contact with the rest of the races in your Federation. You offer to let us prove this to ourselves by sending a man out. You say that he will find contact psychologically unacceptable." He waved a hand at Lindsay. "Here's our answer."

The alien looked at him. "My dear Ambassador, you insist on misunderstanding my objection to allowing your people to join our group of races. It is not that you are a young people, or a primitive people, for those are minor points. It is simply that you must be able to rise above all barriers of mistrust and prejudice. Now, just recently, Torm here did very well. He was not shocked by a being with double the number of eyes he had himself, and a different skeleton, nor by the sight of alien viscera in the case of the being changing his skin. He made no attempt to judge between the two members of the same race which he saw fight until one was killed at the transport center. But that was the result of your operation. While now . . ."

He turned abruptly, and put an impossibly fragile hand on Lindsay's shoulder, at the same time bringing his inhumanly still face up against Torm's. In spite of himself, Torm started, and shrunk back slightly.

"You see?" said the alien, sadly, letting go. "Prejudice. Fear, suspicion, and disgust toward the strange and unfamiliar."

"I—" began Torm, miserably.

"Never mind," said the Representative. "Don't feel that

you have to apologize. I was merely proving a point where your race as a whole is concerned. I do not blame you for your fault, but you must see why it bars you from acceptance by the rest of us."

"But why isn't Torm's operation the answer?" asked Coran.

"Because," sighed the Representative, "your cure is more crippling than your disease. It is no solution to stop a man scratching his nose by cutting off his nose. In the case of Lindsay, you rendered him immune to emotional upset over something he might see or hear or experience. But the moral sense in all beings is based upon emotion; by removing emotion, you destroyed this, too. You created, in fact, a psychopathic personality.

"I grant you he did not immediately act like one, but that was because his habit patterns reacted for him out of sheer momentum. Given time, he would have behaved very badly, indeed. He would have become a danger to any community. You remember I noticed something odd about him, when he came in to meet us before leaving. His actions and his speech—even then—showed evidence of a complete nonmorality, and a complete unconcern for others." His glance singled out Selagh. "You," he said. "You noticed it."

Selagh blushed, and nodded.

"So you see," wound up the Representative, "by rendering yourself acceptable in one sense, you immediately render yourself unacceptable in another. In the galaxy, no race may judge another; but also no race may harm another. It is live and let live with a vengeance. If it had occurred to Torm to do damage to another individual, or to any thing, there would have been nothing within him to hold him back."

He looked around the room at the unhappy faces of the humans.

"Now wait," said Torm, suddenly. "Wait a minute—"

The Representative turned to him.

"If I'm so nonmoral," he said, "why was it that I had to be the one to keep the plant and monster from each other? They certainly weren't living and let living!"

He stared demandingly at the alien. He did not notice the looks of slight embarrassment on the faces of the other humans.

"Now, Torm," said Ambassador Coran, clearing his throat, "you jumped to the wrong conclusion about those two."

Torm Lindsay stared at him in surprise.

"Wrong conclusion?"

"My dear Torm," said the Representative. "The gadget was not what you thought it was. The monster was not—what you thought he was—but a rather nice old gentleman taking a botanical specimen home to his private laboratory."

"Specimen—oh," said Torm. "You mean, the plant—"

"Exactly," said the alien.

"But—but—"

"Yes, Torm?"

"But look here. How did it happen he was so helpless and frightened of the plant? Why did it have to be me who fixed the gimmick and got us home?"

"But you didn't," replied the Representative. "You were picked up by a transport rescue crew, summoned by me, when we saw on our viewer what had happened; and also by the old gentleman himself, who sent out a mental call the moment he discovered what had happened to the three of you."

"But the gimmick?"

"It had nothing to do with the mechanisms of transport, Torm. It was a device for restraining the plant." He shook his head at Lindsay's puzzled face. "The plant," he explained, "requires moisture to live. On its native planet, it gets it by sucking the juices from other flora and fauna native to the place. Because it's actually rather a weak, slow-moving creature, it has developed a weapon. It is capable of broadcasting a rather limited mental stimulus that induces a paralyzing fear in its victims. The gimmick inhibited this capacity in it and kept it immobilized by a counter field. The gimmick was set up in a center capsule to keep the plant under control; and it was that capsule you stepped into with conflicting directions of destination, just as the unit of three capsules was about to discharge for the old gentleman's home planet."

"I see," said Torm. There was a short silence. "But why didn't the plant affect me?"

The alien chuckled. It was an odd sound to hear coming from his still face.

"How could it?" he answered. "You were anesthetized.

Remember?" He chuckled again. "The plant has relatively little intelligence; but what it has must have been rather sorely tried by the way you reacted to its best attempts to immobilize you. You do deserve congratulations for putting the restraint back together though. It protected the old gentleman until the rescue squad arrived."

"Thanks," said Torm.

"Don't be bitter," replied the alien, kindly. "You did the best you could under the circumstances, and it turned out to be very good indeed, even if you were acting on false premises."

Off to one side, Ambassador Coran cleared his throat. "All this . . ."

"Yes." The Representative turned toward him with regret in his voice. "All this is beside the point. The situation stands that you cannot be accepted into the Federation of Peoples, for the reasons I have given you. You are still too rigid, too bound with prejudice; and Torm's operation is not an acceptable way of mending that fault. You must be all that you are normally; and, in addition, be free of the tendency to judge from your own small basis of experience."

"I must again request," said Coran, stiffly, "that we be allowed to take this matter to higher authorities."

"There *are* no higher authorities," replied the alien. "From the day when your interstellar ship first entered this system, from the day of my first meeting with your people, you have been unable to accept the fact that I am literally what I call myself. I represent the Federation. I speak not for myself, but for every member of every race included in it. Believe me, if you could question each one individually, he would say only what I say."

"I feel I must doubt that," said Coran.

The Representative sighed. "This embassy building is yours. Free passage to this world, and to this spot, is yours. But the rest of the Federation is closed to you. You will not be allowed in any of its solar systems, or on any of its worlds. If you approach them, you will be turned back." He looked about at them. "But don't give up hope. Don't be discouraged. This fault is one that time will inevitably mend; and the scale is larger out here in the galaxy. What are ten, fifty, a hundred thousand years, if they have to be?"

"We can't stand still," cried Coran, desperately. "It isn't in us. We aren't built to stand still."

"I am sorry."

The Representative was turning and going away toward the door, his strange form oddly pyramidal under the robe he wore. Torm Lindsay felt a choking sensation in his throat, as if from something huge and desperate, clawing to get out. He opened his mouth, but no words came. Frantically, he tried again. "Wait . . ."

The Representative, almost to the door, paused and turned.

"Wait," said Torm, chokingly. "Listen . . ."

"I am listening."

"We aren't all prejudiced. We aren't all like this. What would you say if we produced some people with an open mind? I mean—open completely?"

"Torm," said the alien, softly. "You don't understand. They must be without a single prejudgment; and yet unspoiled. And none of you are like that."

"But that's just it!" Torm cast a frantic look around at his fellow humans. "We're all alike here. But I noticed something. It was the way I felt, after the operation; I couldn't put my finger on it until just now. You see, it wasn't the first time I'd felt that way—and for a while I couldn't remember when."

"What are you talking about?" demanded Coran, harshly.

"What I remembered," said Torm. "I remembered that once I was free and unbound. Once I could look at anything new and accept it, and take it for granted as being just what it seemed to be and nothing else. You see? You understand?"

"No," said Coran.

"*I* see," said the alien. "And I should have seen before. But there is something about you people that is different from all us others. You would say your answer lies in the untouched minds of your children."

"Is that it? Am I right?"

"Perhaps . . ." In the alien eyes of the Representative, it seemed that a distant fire dimmed as something in him went away, and far far away, until nothing but the shell of a being stood before them. For a moment it stood, unguessable, and unknowable, facing them; and then slowly, gradually, he began to come back. The light kindled again, and the Representative was once more with them.

"Yes," he said. "It will be a long road for them and a hard one. And you will have to let them travel it alone and apart from you. But I think you have found your answer."

His eyes moved from Torm and took them all in. And they stood, the four humans and the one inhuman; caught then in a single crystal moment of a hope of peace and final brotherhood, and dream of greatness, future, ever-lasting. . . .

3-PART PUZZLE

The Mologhese ship twinkled across the light years separating the human-conquered planets of the Bahrin system from Mologh. Aboard her, the Mologh Envoy sat deep in study. For he was a thinker as well as a warrior, the Envoy, and his duties had gone far beyond obtaining the capsule propped on the Mologhese version of a desk before him—a sealed message capsule containing the diplomatic response of the human authorities to the proposal he had brought from Mologh. His object of study at the moment, however, was not the capsule, but a translation of something human he had painfully resolved into Mologhese terms. His furry brow wrinkled and his bulldog-shaped jaw clamped as he worked his way through it. He had been over it a number of times, but he still could not conceive of a reason for a reaction he had observed among human young to its message. It was, he had been reliably informed, one of a group of such stories for the human young. —What he was looking at in translation was approximately this:—

THE THREE (Name) (Domestic animals) (Name)

Once upon a time there was a (horrendous, carnivorous, mythical creature) who lived under a bridge and one day he became very hungry. He was sitting there thinking of good things to eat when he heard the sounds of someone crossing the bridge over his head. (Sharp hoof-sound) —(sharp hoof-sound) went the sounds on the bridge overhead.

51

"Who's there?" cried the (horrendous, carnivorous, mythical creature).

"It's only I, the smallest (Name) (Domestic animal) (Name)" came back the answer.

"Well, I am the (horrendous, carnivorous, mythical creature) who lives under the bridge," replied the (horrendous, carnivorous, mythical creature) "and I'm coming up to eat you all up."

"Oh, don't do that, please!" cried the smallest (Name) (Domestic animal) (Name). "I wouldn't even make you a good meal. My (relative), the (middle-sized? next-oldest?) (Name) (Domestic animal) (Name) will be along in a minute. Let me go. He's much bigger than I. You'll get a much better meal out of him. Let me go and eat him instead."

"Very well," said the (horrendous, carnivorous, mythical creature); and (hoof-sound)—(hoof-sound) the (Name) (Domestic animal) (Name) hurried across the bridge to safety.

After a while the (horrendous, carnivorous, mythical creature) heard (heavier hoof-sound)—(heavier hoof-sound) on the bridge overhead.

"Who's there?" he cried.

"It is I, the (middle-sized?) (Name) (Domestic animal) (Name)," replied a (deeper?) voice.

"Then I am coming up to eat you up," said the (horrendous, carnivorous, mythical creature). "Your smaller (relative?) the smallest (Name) (Domestic animal) (Name) told me you were coming and I let him go by so I could have a bigger meal by eating you. So here I come."

"Oh, you are, are you?" said the (middle-sized) (Name) (Domestic animal) (Name). "Well, suit yourself; but our oldest (relative?), the big (Name) (Domestic animal) (Name) will be along in just a moment. If you want to wait for him, you'll really have a meal to remember."

"Is that so?" said the (horrendous, carnivorous, mythical creature), who was very (greedy? Avaricious? Gluttonous?). "All right, go ahead." And the (middle-sized) (Name) (Domestic animal) (Name) went (heavier hoof-sound)—(heavier hoof-sound) across the bridge to safety.

It was not long before the (horrendous, carnivorous, mythical creature) heard (thunderous hoof-sound)—(thunderous hoof-sound) shaking the bridge overhead.

"Who's there?" cried the (horrendous, carnivorous, myth-ical creature).

"It is I!" rumbled an (earth-shaking?) deep (bass?) voice. "The biggest (Name) (Domestic animal) (Name). Who calls?"

"I do!" cried the (horrendous, carnivorous, mythical creature). "And I'm coming up to eat you all up!" And he sprang up on the bridge. But the big (Name) (Domestic animal) (Name) merely took one look at him, and lowered (his?) head and came charging forward, with his (horns?) down. And he butted that (horrendous, carnivorous, mythi-cal creature) over the hills and so far away he could never find his way back to bother anyone ever again.

The Mologhese Envoy put the translation aside and blinked his red-brown eyes wearily. It was ridiculous, he thought, to let such a small conundrum bother him this way. The story was perfectly simple and obvious; it related how an organization of three individuals delayed conflict with a dangerous enemy until their strongest member arrived to deal with the situation. Perfectly usual and good Conqueror indoctrination literature for Conqueror young.

But still, there was something—a difference about it he could not quite put his finger on. The human children he had observed having it told to them at that school he had visited had greeted the ending with an entirely dispropor-tionate glee. Why? Even to a student of tactics like himself the lesson was a simple and rather boring one. It was as if a set of young students were suddenly to become jubilant on being informed that two plus two equaled four. Was there some hidden value in the lesson that he failed to discover? Or merely some freakish twist to the human character that caused the emotional response to be dispro-portionate?

If there was, the Envoy would be everlastingly de-stroyed if he could not lay the finger of his perception on what it was. Perhaps, thought the Envoy, leaning back in the piece of furniture in which he sat, this problem was merely part and parcel of that larger and more wide-spread anomaly he had remarked during the several weeks, local time, he had been the guest of the human HQ on Bahrin II. . . .

The humans had emerged on to the galactic scene rather

suddenly, but not too suddenly to escape notice by potentially interested parties. They had fanned out from their home system; doing it at first the hard way by taking over and attempting to pioneer uninhabited planets of nearby systems. Eventually they had bumped into the nearest Conqueror civilization—which was that of the Bahrin, an ursinoid type established over four small but respectable systems and having three Submissive types in bondage, one of which was a degraded Conqueror strain.

Like most primitive races, the humans did not at first seem to realize what they were up against. They attempted at first to establish friendly relations with the Bahrin without attempting any proof of their own. Conqueror instincts. The Bahrin, of course, recognized Conqueror elements potential in the form of the human civilization; and for that reason struck all the harder, to take advantage of their own age and experience. They managed to destroy nearly all the major planetary installations of the humans, and over twenty per cent of the population at first strike. However, the humans rebounded with surprising ferocity and speed, to drop guerrilla land troops on the Bahrin planets while they gathered power for a strikeback. The strikeback was an overwhelming success, the Bahrin power being enfeebled by the unexpected fierceness of the human guerrillas and the fact that these seemed to have the unusual ability to enlist the sympathy of the Submissives under the Bahrin rule. The Bahrin were utterly broken; and the humans had for some little time been occupying the Bahrin worlds.

Meanwhile, the ponderous mills of the Galactic social order had been grinding up the information all this had provided. It was known that human exploration ships had stumbled across their first contact with one of the Shielded Worlds; and immediately made eager overtures of friendship to the people upon it. It was reported that when the Shielded peoples went on about their apparently meaningless business under that transparent protective element which no known Conqueror had ever been able to breach; (and the human overtures were ignored, as all Conqueror attempts at contact had always been), that a storm of emotion swept over the humans—a storm involving the whole spectrum of emotions. It was as if the rejection had

had the equivalent of a calculated insult from an equivalent, Conqueror, race.

In that particular neighborhood of the galaxy the Mologhese currently held the balance of power among the Conqueror races. They sent an Envoy with a proposal to the human authorities.

—And that, thought the Envoy, aboard the returning spaceship as he put aside the problem of the translation to examine the larger question, was the beginning of an educative process on both sides.

His job had been to point out politely but firmly that there were many races in the galaxy; but that they had all evolved on the same type of world, and they all fell into one of three temperamental categories. They were by nature Conquerors, Submissives, or Invulnerables. The Invulnerables were, of course, the people of the Shielded Worlds; who went their own pacific, non-technologic ways. And if these could not be dominated behind the protections of their strange abilities, they did not seem interested in dominating themselves, or interfering with the Conquerors. So the situation worked out to equalities and they could be safely ignored.

The Submissive races, of course, were there for any Conqueror race's taking. That disposed of them. But there were certain elements entering into inter-Conqueror relationships, that were important for the humans to know.

No Conqueror race could, naturally, be denied its birthright, which was to take as much as it could from Submissives and its fellow-Conquerors. On the other hand, there were advantages to be gained by semi-peaceful existence even within the laws of a society of Conqueror races. Obvious advantages dealing with trade, travel, and a reciprocal recognition of rights and customs. To be entitled to these, the one prime requirement upon any Conqueror race was that it should not rock the boat. It might take on one or more of its neighbors, or make an attempt to move up a notch in the pecking order in this neck of the galactic woods; but it must not become a bother to the local community of Conquerors as a whole by such things as general piracy, et cetera.

"In short," had replied the Envoy's opposite number—a tall, rather thin and elderly human with a sad smile, "a gentleman's agreement?"

"Please?" said the Envoy. The Opposite Number explained.

"Essentially, yes," said the Envoy, feeling pleased. He was pleased enough, in fact, to take time out for a little dissertation on this as an example of the striking cultural similarities between Conqueror races that often produced parallel terms in completely different languages, and out of completely different backgrounds.

". . . In fact," he wound up, "let me say that personally, I find you people very much akin. That is one of the things that makes me so certain that you will eventually be very pleased that you have agreed to this proposal I brought. Essentially, all it asks is that you subscribe to the principles of a Conqueror intersociety—which is, after all, your own kind of society—and recognize its limitations as well as its privileges by pledging to maintain the principles which are the hard facts of its existence."

"Well," said his Opposite Number, whose name was Harrigan or Hargan, or some such, "that is something to be decided on in executive committee. Meanwhile, suppose I show you around here; and you can tell me more about the galaxy."

There followed several weeks in which the Envoy found himself being convoyed around the planet which had originally been the seat of the former Bahrin ruling group. It was quite obviously a tactic to observe him over a period of time and under various conditions; and he did not try to resist it. He had his own observations to make, and this gave him an excellent opportunity to do so.

For one thing, he noted down as his opinion that they were an exceedingly touchy people where slights were concerned. Here they had just finished their war with the Bahrin in the last decade and were facing entrance into an interstellar society of races as violent as themselves; and yet the first questions on the tips of the tongues of nearly all those he met were concerned with the Shielded Worlds. Even Harrigan, or whatever his name was, confessed to an interest in the people on the Invulnerable planets.

"How long have they been like that?" Harrigan asked.

The Envoy could not shrug. His pause before answering fulfilled the same function.

"There is no way of telling," he said. "Things on Shielded

Worlds are as the people there make them. Take away the signs of a technical civilization from a planet—turn it all into parkland—and how do you tell how long the people there have been as they are? All we ever knew is that they are older than any of *our* histories."

"Older?" said Harrigan. "There must be some legend, at least, about how they came to be?"

"No," said the Envoy. "Oh, once in a great while some worthless planet without a population will suddenly develop a shield and become fertile, forested and populated—but this is pretty clearly a case of colonization. The Invulnerables seem to be able to move from point to point in space by some nonphysical means. That's all."

"All?" said Harrigan.

"All," said the Envoy. "Except for an old Submissive superstition that the Shielded Peoples are a mixed race sprung from an interbreeding between a Conqueror and a Submissive type—something we know, of course, to be a genetic impossibility."

"I see," said Harrigan.

Harrigan took the Envoy around to most of the major cities of the planet. They did not visit any military installations (the Envoy had not expected that they would) but they viewed a lot of new construction taking the place of Bahrin building that had been obliterated by the angry scars of the war. It was going up with surprising swiftness—or perhaps not so surprising, noted the Envoy thoughtfully, since the humans seemed to have been able to enlist the enthusiastic co-operation of the Submissives they had taken over. The humans appeared to have a knack for making conquered peoples willing to work with them. Even the Bahrin, what there were left of them, were behaving most unlike a recently crushed race of Conquerors, in the extent of their co-operation. Certainly the humans seemed to be allowing their former enemies a great deal of freedom, and even responsibility in the new era. The Envoy sought for an opportunity, and eventually found the chance to talk to one of the Bahrin alone. This particular Bahrin was an assistant architect on a school that was being erected on the outskirts of one city. (The humans seemed slightly crazy on the subject of schools; and only slightly less crazy on the subjects of hospitals, libraries, museums, and recreation areas. Large numbers of these were going up all over the planet.) This particular Bahrin, however, was a male who had been through the recent war. He was middle-aged and had lost an arm in the previous conflict. The Envoy found him free to talk, not particularly bitter, but considerably impressed emotionally by his new overlords.

". . . May your courage be with you," he told the Envoy. "You will have to face them sooner or later; and they are demons."

"What kind of demons?" said the Envoy, skeptically.

"A new kind," said the Bahrin. He rested his heavy, furry, bear-like forearm upon the desk in front of him and stared out a window at a changing landscape. "Demons full of fear and strange notions. Who understands them? Half their history is made up of efforts to understand themselves—and they still don't." He glanced significantly at the Envoy. "Did you know the Submissives are already starting to call them the Mixed People?"

The Envoy wrinkled his furry brow.

"What's that supposed to mean?" he said.

"The Submissives think the humans are really Submissives who have learned how to fight."

The Envoy snorted.

"That's ridiculous."

"Of course," said the Bahrin; and sighed heavily. "But what isn't, these days?" He turned back to his work. "Anyway, don't ask me about them. The more I see of them, the less I understand."

They parted on that note—and the Envoy's private conviction that the loss of the Bahrin's arm had driven him slightly insane.

Nonetheless, during the following days as he was escorted around from spot to spot, the essence of that anomaly over which he was later to puzzle during his trip home, emerged. For one thing, there were the schools. The humans, evidently, in addition to being education crazy themselves, believed in wholesale education for their cattle as well. One of the schools he was taken to was an education center for young Bahrin pupils; and—evidently due to a shortage of Bahrin instructors following the war—a good share of the teachers were human.

". . . I just *love* my class!" one female human teacher

told the Envoy, as they stood together watching young
Bahrin at play during their relaxation period.

"Please?" said the Envoy, astounded.

"They're so quick and eager to learn," said the teacher.
One of the young Bahrin at play dashed up to her, was
overcome with shyness at seeing the Envoy, and hung
back. She reached out and patted him on the head. A
peculiar shiver ran down the Envoy's back; but the young
Bahrin nestled up to her.

"They *respond* so," said the teacher. "Don't you think
so?"

"They were a quite worthy race at one time," replied
the Envoy, with mingled diplomatic confusion and caution.

"Oh, yes!" said the teacher enthusiastically; and proceeded to overwhelm him with facts he already knew
about the history of the Bahrin, until the Envoy found
himself rescued by Harrigan. The Envoy went off wondering a little to himself whether the humans had indeed
conquered the Bahrin or whether, perhaps, it had not
been the other way around.

Food for that same wonderment seemed to be supplied
by just about everything else that Harrigan let him see.
The humans, having just about wiped the Bahrin out of
existence, seemed absolutely determined to repair the
damage they had done, but improve upon the former
situation by way of interest. Why? What kept the Bahrin
from seething with plans for revolt at this very minute?
The young ones of course—like that pupil with the teacher—
might not know any better; but the older ones . . . ? The
Envoy thought of the one-armed Bahrin architect he had
talked to, and felt further doubt. If they were all like that
one—but then what kind of magic had the humans worked
to produce such an intellectual and emotional victory? The
Envoy went back to his quarters and took a nap to quiet
the febrillations of his thinking process.

When he woke up, he set about getting hold of what
history he could on the war just past. Accounts both
human and Bahrin were available; and, plowing through
them, reading them for statistics rather than reports, he
was reluctantly forced to the conclusion that the one-
armed Bahrin had been right. The humans were demons.
Or at least, they had fought like demons against the Bahrin.
A memory of the shiver that had run down his back as he

watched the female human teacher patting the young Bahrin on head, troubled the Envoy again. Would this same female be perfectly capable of mowing down adult Bahrin by the automatic handweapon clipful? Apparently her exact counterparts had. If so, which was the normal characteristic of the human nature—the head-patting, or the trigger-pulling?

It was almost a relief when the human authorities gave him a sealed answer to the proposal he had brought, and sent him on his way home a few days later. He carried that last question of his away with him.

"The only conclusion I can come to," said the Envoy to the chief authority among the Mologhese, a week and a half later as they both sat in the Chief's office, "is that there is some kind of racial insanity that sets in in times of peace. In other words, they're Conquerors in the true sense only when engaged in Conquest."

The Chief frowned at the proposal answer, still sealed on the desk before him. He had asked for the Envoy's report before opening it; and now he wondered if this traditional procedure had been the wisest move under the circumstances. He rather suspected the Envoy's wits of having gone somewhat astray during his mission.

"You don't expect me to believe something like that," said the Chief. "No culture that was insane half the time could survive. And if they tried to maintain sanity by continual Conquest, they would bleed to death in two generations."

The Envoy said nothing. His Chief's argument were logically unassailable.

"The sensible way to look at it," said the Chief, "is to recognize them as simply another Conqueror strain with somewhat more marked individual peculiarities than most. This is—let us say—their form of recreation, of amusement, between conquests. Perhaps they enjoy playing with the danger of cultivating strength in their conquered races."

"Of course, there is that," admitted the Envoy. "You may be right."

"I think," said the Chief, "that it's the only sensible all-around explanation."

"On the other hand—" the Envoy hesitated, remember-

ing. "There was the business of that female human patting
the small Bahrin on the head."

"What about it?"

The Envoy looked at his Chief.

"Have *you* ever been patted on the head?" he asked.
The Chief stiffened.

"Of course not!" He relaxed slowly, staring at the Envoy. "Why? What makes you ask that?"

"Well, I never have either, of course—especially by
anyone of another race. But that little Bahrin liked it. And
seeing it gave me—" the Envoy stopped to shiver again.

"Gave you what?" said the Chief.

"A . . . a sort of horrible, affectionate feeling—" The
Envoy stopped speaking in helplessness.

"You've been overworking," said the Chief, coldly. "Is
there anything more to report?"

"No," said the Envoy. "No. But aside from all this,
there's no doubt they'd be a tough nut to crack, those
humans. My recommendation is that we wait for optimum
conditions before we choose to move against them."

"Your recommendation will go into the record, of course,"
said the Chief. He picked up the human message capsule.
"And now I think it's time I listened to this. They didn't
play it for you?"

The Envoy shook his head.

The Chief picked up the capsule (it was one the Envoy
had taken along for the humans to use in replying), broke
its seal and put it into the speaker unit of his desk. The
speaker unit began to murmur a message tight-beamed
toward the Chief's ear alone. The Envoy sat, nursing the
faint hope that the Chief would see fit to let him hear,
later. The Envoy was very curious as to the contents of
that message. He watched his Chief closely, and saw the
other's face slowly gather in a frown that deepened as the
message purred on.

Abruptly it stopped. The Chief looked up; and his eyes
met the Envoy's.

"It just may be," said the Chief slowly, "that I owe you
an apology."

"An apology?" said the Envoy.

"Listen to this—" The Chief adjusted a volume control
and pressed a button. A human voice speaking translated
Mologhese filled the room.

"The Committee of Control for the human race wishes to express its appreciation for—"

"No, no—" said the Chief. "Not this diplomatic slush. Farther on—" He did things with his controls, the voice speeded up to a gabble, a whine, then slowed toward understandability again. "Ah, listen to this."

". . . Association," said the voice, "but without endorsement of what the Mologhese Authority is pleased to term the Conqueror temperament. While our two races have a great deal in common, the human race has as its ultimate aims not the exercises of war and oppression, plundering, general destruction and the establishment of a tyranny in a community of tyrants; but rather the establishment of an environment of peace for all races. The human race believes in the ultimate establishment of universal freedom, justice, and the inviolable rights of the individual whoever he may be. We believe that our destiny lies neither within the pattern of conquest nor submission, but with the enlightened maturity of independence characterized by what are known as the Shielded Worlds; and, while not ceasing to defend our people and our borders from all attacks foreign and domestic, we intend to emulate these older, protected peoples in hope that they may eventually find us worthy of association. In this hope—"

The Chief clicked off the set and looked grimly at the Envoy. The Envoy stared back at him in shock.

"Insane," said the Envoy. "I was right—quite insane." He sank back in his seat. "At any rate, you too were correct. They're too irrational, too unrealistic to survive. We needn't worry about them."

"On the contrary," said his Chief. "And I'm to blame for not spotting it sooner. There were indications of this in some of the preliminary reports we had on them. They are very dangerous."

The Envoy shook his head.

"I don't see—" he began.

"But I do!" said the Chief. "And I don't hold down this position among our people for nothing. Think for a moment, Envoy! Don't you see it? These people are *causal!*"

"Causal?"

"Exactly," replied the Chief. "They don't act or react to

practical or realistic stimuli. They react to emotional or philosophic conclusions of their own."

"I don't see what's so dangerous about that?" said the Envoy, wrinkling his forehead.

"It wouldn't be dangerous if they were a different sort of race," said the Chief. "But these people seem to be able to rationalize their emotional and philosophic conclusions in terms of hard logic and harder science. —You don't believe me? Do you remember that story for the human young you told me about, about the three hoofed and horned creatures crossing a bridge?"

"Of course," said the Envoy.

"All right. It puzzled you that the human young should react so strongly to what was merely a lesson in elementary tactics. But—it wasn't the lesson they were reacting to. It was the emotional message overlaying the lesson. The notion of some sort of abstract right and wrong, so that when the somehow *wrong* mythical creature under the bridge gets what the humans might describe as his just deserts at the horns of the triumphing biggest *right* creature—the humans are tremendously stimulated."

"But I still don't see the danger—"

"The danger," said the Chief, "lies in the fact that while such a story has its existence apparently—to humans—only for its moral and emotional values, the tactical lesson which we so obviously recognize is not lost, either. To us, this story shows a way of conquering. To the humans it shows not only a way but a reason, a justification. A race whose motives are founded upon such justifications is tremendously dangerous to us."

"You must excuse me," said the Envoy, bewilderedly. "Why—"

"Because we—and I mean all the Conqueror races, and all the Submissive races—" said the Chief, strongly, "have no defenses in the emotional and philosophic areas. Look at what you told me about the Bahrin, and the Submissives the humans took over from the Bahrin. Having no strong emotional and philosophic persuasions of their own, they have become immediately infected by the human ones. They are like people unacquainted with a new disease who fall prey to an epidemic. The humans, being self-convinced of such things as justice and love, in spite of their own arbitrariness and violence, convince all of us who lack convictions having never needed them before. Do you remember how you said you felt when you saw the little Bahrin being patted on the head? *That's* how vulnerable we are!"

The Envoy shivered again, remembering.

"Now I see," he said.

"I thought you would," said the Chief, grimly. "The situation to my mind is serious, enough so to call for the greatest emergency measures possible. We mustn't make the mistake of the creature under the bridge in the story. We were prepared to let the humans get by our community strength because we thought of them as embryo Conquerors, and we hoped for better entertainment later. Now they come along again, this time as something we can recognize as Conqueror-plus. And this time we can't let them get by. I'm going to call a meeting of our neighboring Conqueror executive Chiefs; and get an agreement to hit the humans now with a coalition big enough to wipe them out to the last one."

He reached for a button below a screen on his desk. But before he could touch it, it came alight with the figure of his own attaché.

"Sir—" began this officer; and then words failed him.

"Well?" barked the Chief.

"Sir—" the officer swallowed. "From the Shielded Worlds—a message." The Chief stared long and hard.

"From the Shielded Worlds?" said the Chief. "How? From the Shielded Worlds? When?"

"I know it's fantastic, sir. But one of our ships was passing not too far from one of the Shielded Worlds and it found itself caught—"

"And you just now got the message?" The Chief cut him short.

"Just this second, sir. I was just—"

"Let me have it. And keep your channel open," said the Chief. "I've got some messages to send."

The officer made a movement on the screen and something like a message cylinder popped out of a slot in the Chief's desk. The Chief reached for it, and hesitated. Looking up, he found the eyes of the Envoy upon him.

"Never—" said the Envoy, softly. "Never in known history have they communicated with any of us. . . ."

"It's addressed to me," said the Chief, looking at the

outside of the cylinder. "If they can read our minds as we suspect, then they know what I've just discovered about the humans and what I plan to do about it." He gave the cylinder a twist to open it. "Let's see what they have to say."

The cylinder opened up like a flower. A single white sheet unrolled within it to lie flat on the desk; and the message upon it in the common galactic code looked up at the Chief. The message consisted of just one word. The word was:—

NO.

THE SEATS OF HELL

"—The Seats of Hell," the drunken young Englishman with the straw-colored hair was saying. "You never heard of them?"

"No," said Bart Dybig. He was watching his own square-knuckled rock of a fist enclosing his whisky glass. He lifted the glass, drained it, and stood up from the bar. "I've got to meet someone."

He went off down the bar. Behind him he could hear the Englishman, Peter Toupil, saying something more. But he did not bother to puzzle out what it was. Funny about the English, Bart thought, with his hand on the door. They could turn out some of the best people you could ever hope to meet. And then, as if in compensation, they would occasionally produce someone like Peter. . . .

Bart stepped through the door of the bar, into the asphalt street. The South Pacific sunlight struck him like a blow as he turned right toward the market. He did not particularly want to go to the market, but it was the only place on the island where a man might occupy his time if he did not want to drink, make love, or sleep. To his left, over the tops of the low buildings as he went, the greenly forested cones of The Greater and The Lesser, the two extinct volcanoes that had made the island of Nahneeni out of their own molten interiors, looked down on him and on the baking street and buildings. It was near noon.

A few of the local people ceased their chatter of French as he passed, to stare at him. He paid no obvious attention to their looks. He was used to being stared at. At the same time, inside him, he felt the impact of their eyes like burning points of light against him. This trip was another failure.

He had thought that, as a tourist he would have been lost, lumped in with the other tourists, indistinguishable. It had not worked out that way. In San Francisco, before the boat sailed—in Hawaii, where they had made their first stop—on the boat with other passengers like Peter Toupil, he had already been recognized and set apart in others' minds as something different.

—Admit it, he told himself bitterly, pacing down the main street of Nahneeni's only decent town; you're a freak.

It was a cruel joke of fate that had been played on him. Nature had seen fit to give Barton Louis Dybig a good mind and a sensitive soul. Then, with razor-sharp humor, it had placed these attributes inside a body that might have been the envy of a caveman, back when the world was young. Even now, walking down the street dressed in a white suit purposely cut too loose for him, Bart was impressive enough to gather glances. He was not an exceptionally big man—he stood about five feet ten. Nor was he unusually wide-shouldered or bunchy-armed. But his face with its heavy bones was like the face of some ancient savage, crudely hacked from granite. His thick fingers and wide hands were like paws emerging from the white coat sleeves. And the peculiar balance with which he walked was like a banner proclaiming the power of his flesh.

It had always been like this. No clothes Bart had ever found, no mannerisms—no stooping of shoulders, shuffling of the feet, loosening of the belt, could hide the message of his appearance. Yet, bad as it was even then, Bart often silently thanked the first inventors of clothing. If he was impressive clothed, he was overwhelming stripped. Without undershirt, shirt and suitcoat to hide the fact, his upper body revealed itself like an anatomical drawing. Great flat, thick bands and slabs of muscle sculptured his chest and flowed into his shoulders and arms; each one unhidden by fat and distinct from its neighbors. Nor was their appearance an illusion.

At twelve, young Bart had bent horseshoes and torn telephone books for the amusement of his friends. And then, one day he had discovered that it no longer amused them. He had gone a little too far in the matter of being stronger than his friends; and he began then, for the first time, to taste the loneliness that the fourteen years that had followed had brought him in full measure.

Now, thinking of it, he saw a woman carrying a child, both wrapped in the same flowered robe, shrink back from him into a doorway. And he knew it was his savage mask of a face, reflecting his inner sorrow in a scowl. He forced himself to smile at her, but she drew back even farther, and he stalked on alone.

The market was all but deserted as he entered it. The thatched roofs threw light shadow on the open booths and the piles of fruit and produce displayed in them. But the proprietors of the booths—generally women, children, or old men—were gathered in lounging groups apart from their stock.

There were only two other obvious non-natives moving among the booths. They were a short, somewhat stocky man in a mustache and some sort of French-looking uniform, and a slim auburn-headed girl in a thin summer dress that had all the simplicity and elegance of great expense and high fashion. For a moment, as she turned to look at something in the booth by which the two were passing, the girl's glance crossed the row of booths between them and met Bart's; and he had time to see both that she was very beautiful and that her brown eyes caught at his for a second with a strange and almost desperate look. Then the officer, or whatever he was, beside her had said something and she turned away as they moved on. Without knowing quite what good it would do to do so, Bart moved off after them.

He followed, at a little distance, down the double row of booths to its end, keeping them in sight on its far side. As he rounded the far end, they also did so from their side, turning toward him. Just at that moment, the officer turned toward the end booth they had just passed, and Bart found himself once more face to face with the girl.

For a second he thought she was about to say something—something urgent. And then her glance went by him; and her eyes widened in a glance at something behind him that brought a sudden twist of sick horror to her features. Bart checked in mid-stride and spun around.

Behind him, and about fifteen feet away in the shadow

of the end booth of another row, a man squatted, surrounded by natives, who were standing back at some little distance so that Bart saw it all clearly. The man was dressed in soiled canvas trousers and an ancient flowered shirt, open at the neck to reveal a squat, bronze throat. In his thick hands he held one of the white gulls from the sea—and he was torturing the bird by bending its wings back. As he looked, Bart heard the bird cry out hoarsely.

The market wavered around Bart, like a scene viewed through heatwaves. A great hand seemed to reach into him to seize and turn his stomach. And before he realized what he was doing, he was striding toward the man.

"Stop that!" he said, thickly, halting over the native. He had spoken English, unthinkingly, but the other either knew that language or Bart's tone was clear enough. He tilted his face upward, grinning—a dish-face, blunt-boned, vaguely oriental in feature, brown and hard. With one quick movement he rose to his feet, revealing himself in his own way as much a freak as Bart. Half a head shorter than Bart he stood, but his shoulders were wider, his upper body enormous and flat as a plank door. Grinning into Bart's face, he twitched his hands; and tore the bird apart.

Bart hit him.

—And then it was as if the whole population of the market rose like a wave about Bart, and bore him under.

It was four days later. Above Nahneeni, the air was thick and still. The early afternoon held its clammy breath like a prisoner a moment before the second of execution. And, all over the island, the hurricane shutters were being put up on the buildings.

In a whitewashed cell of the island's small, concrete-block jail, Bart clung to the bars walling him off from the corridor. A little way down the corridor was the officer and the girl he had seen in the market. They had come, it seemed, to the jail on some other errand, and now were delaying about passing in the narrow corridor until the man talking with Bart through the bars should have finished his hushed, private conversation.

The man in question was the U. S. Consul from a neighboring island. He was a slim, nervous middle-aged man wearing a wristwatch below one neatly-pressed white suit-coat cuff, that had an expandable gold band. The yellow metal of it flashed sullenly to Bart's eyes in the muggy air of the cells.

"—You hit too hard, Dybig," the consul was saying. "—If the man hadn't died—" he raised his hands helplessly.

Bart's mind was a whirl with his arrest and the sudden sentencing. His paw-like hands gripped the bars, but his civilized mind still reeled under the thought that he had killed a fellow human being.

"How long?" he whispered hoarsely. The consul shrugged wearily.

"You heard the sentence," he said. "Fifteen years. I've talked to the French Governor, here. Ordinarily we can get a suspended sentence and have you deported. But he says the local people are too worked up. You'll have to serve your sentence for a while."

"How long?" husked Bart.

"—Six months—a year. Maybe even a little longer. Who knows? Until the excitement dies down and the governor can commute your sentence and have you deported. —We'll keep trying, of course."

"I can't—" Bart's hands closed convulsively on the bars. "I can't stand being locked up a year. Let alone more—"

"You won't be locked up." The consul took out a handkerchief and mopped his sweating forehead under the brim of his hat. "You'll be working up in the gravel pits or on the roads. It's not bad. They don't really push their prisoners here. It'll be more a matter of waiting than anything else."

"Waiting—on a chain gang—"

"Nothing so melodramatic. There'll be an armed guard, of course, but outside of that, it'll be like an easy day's labor anywhere. And, as I say, we'll keep trying—"

"You'll keep trying!" Bart leaned against the bars. "If it was you, here—"

"*I* didn't put you in there, Mr. Dybig." For the first time there was an edge in the consul's voice. "Remember— *the man died!* What did you expect—a scolding?"

"I—God!" Bart sagged against the bars, turning his head aside. Down the corridor he saw suddenly that the girl was looking at him, and for one further time, their eyes met. In hers was that same unreadable expression of strange desperation he had seen at first. The consul's voice brought Bart's eyes back to the man on the other side of the bars.

"—I understand you're fairly well off, back home?"

"I've got my own trucking firm. Why?" said Bart, dully.

"Just—if you've been thinking of trying a bit of bribery, don't. You'd likely spoil all our efforts to help you."

"I wasn't thinking of it," said Bart.

"I just thought I'd warn you." The consul mopped his brow again. "Well, I'll get going. The wind'll be starting up pretty quick now, according to the weather forecast. Don't worry about the jail, here. It's hurricane proof."

"Thanks," said Bart, almost inaudibly.

"Sorry I couldn't do more." The consul turned and went. Bart stayed where he was, still gripping the bars. A few seconds later, the officer and the girl came past. They had both testified as witnesses, Bart had learned—although he had not seen them do so, himself. On the advice of the consul, he had pleaded guilty, and only gone briefly before the governor and the island's two judges for sentencing in the governor's office. Now, as the two in the corridor passed him, only inches away, neither looked in his direction. He followed them with his eyes, through the steel door at the end of the corridor, that closed with a clash behind them.

Outside, the sound of the hurricane shutters going up over the barred windows, continued. Abruptly, the light from the window to Bart's cell was shut off. His swelling hands clenched suddenly and strained at the bars they held with all the massive strength of his arms. And the bars bent.

—But not enough.

That night, during the height of the hurricane, Bart went wild. No one came to interrupt him in his frenzy; but when morning came and the blow was over, his cell was a shambles, the door to it was hanging open, askew on its hinges; and Bart himself was found in unconscious exhaustion before the heavier bars of the door that shut off the corridor of cells from the jail office. Even these were somewhat twisted and bent.

Sunk in a stupor, he neither resisted nor spoke as heavy manacles were placed on his wrists and ankles, and the two linked by a short length of chain that allowed him to walk only at a shuffle. Dazedly, he allowed himself to be prodded onto the bed of a truck with a dozen or so other, unchained, prisoners; and was trucked off along a road that wound up the side of the Greater Volcanic cone. It came at last to a camp of thatch-roofed grass huts among the trees. Here they were all herded out of the truck, and his ankle-chains were taken off.

Food was served to the prisoners—bananas fried in oil and a fish stew. Bart did not eat. He remained, sunk in his own numbness, until they were once more herded on— this time on foot, up a steep foot-trail, over a hill, and down into some extensive gravel pits—a series of them pockmarked in the slope of the hill.

The other prisoners had shown no eagerness to get close to him, ever since the night of the hurricane. Now, it seemed, he was not even going to be working with them. He was prodded off into a little side-pit, whose sloping gravelly walls hid him from the rest of the prisoners. He was shown sacks and a shovel; and tethered by a long chain around his waist to an iron rod sunk deep in a rock that stuck up like a monolith out of the floor of the pit. Then, they left him. Still, he dreamed. It took the sudden sound of a voice addressing him in cultivated English to snap him out of his stupor.

"Sorry to bother you," said the voice, "but you'd better shovel a little gravel, at least. Otherwise they'll be forced to take some kind of action out of sheer need to save face."

Bart looked up—and found himself staring into the face of Peter Toupil. The slim, yellow-headed young Englishman was wearing a white shirt open at the neck and suit trousers. The trousers were unpressed; and the suit coat, folded over one arm, was rumpled and stained. But Peter himself looked cheerful and more sober than Bart had ever seen him. The fog began to clear from Bart's brain.

"What are you doing here?" he said.

"I'm your partner in this digging. I hold the sacks—you shovel. Then we change about— Oh, I see!" Peter chuckled. "You mean, how'd I get *here?* Same old story. One drink too many. Only this time I did something impolite to the French Flag, in front of the governor's house, I understand. Never did find out exactly what." He chuckled again. "Got on my high horse about principle and rights in court, and lost out on the chance to get quietly put back aboard ship as persona non grata. Got thirty days."

Slowly, Bart got to his feet. The chain clanked.

"Thirty days?" he said.

"Long enough to make me miss the boat, same as you." Peter nodded at the shovel and sacks. "Shall we fill a couple?"

Unthinkingly, Bart bent down and picked up the shovel. Peter took up a sack, and held it open. They began to work.

By the end of the first week, Bart had begun to recover from the shock. But something had happened to him in the jail that night of the hurricane. He had discovered in himself a deep, atavistic, animal hate and fury of the shackle and the cage. His wildness the night of the hurricane had not evaporated, but sunk untraceably into the deep waters of his soul changed their basic nature. Secretly, when ever Peter's back was turned in the privacy of their solitary pit, he tested the chains that linked his wrists and tied him to the boulder—and a deep red satisfaction stirred in him as he felt the links give to his grasp. When the time came, these could be broken; but with new cunning, he was content to wait until the time was right.

Meanwhile, above the primitive cauldron of his new feelings, he carried on a normal, civilized process of getting acquainted with Peter. Peter, sober, was far easier to take than Peter, drunk, he discovered. Also, there was something more to the yellow-haired young Englishman than he had suspected, Bart realized one day. It had suddenly struck Bart that in the past week he had told Peter all about himself—the fact that he was an orphan, raised by foster parents who claimed they could tell him nothing of himself—

"—Should have waited and asked again when you were older—" Peter had commented.

"They were killed when I was fifteen," Bart had scowled at the shovel in his hand. "No reason for it. It was a bright, moonlit night and Dad drove into a concrete railroad bridge abutment at sixty. They both died instantly."

"Drop too much—?"

"They didn't drink. Neither of them. I took over the trucking business."

"At fifteen?" Peter had lifted his almost invisible eyebrows.

"At fifteen. With the help of the bank. —This sacks' full. Get me another."

—At the same time, it came home to Bart now, that he could remember Peter telling him nothing about the Englishman's background or past history. The night of his seventh day on the road gang, as he lay chained to his cot in one of the grass huts to which they were marched back at night, Bart made up his mind to ask. And the next day he did, bluntly.

"—I?" Peter, holding the mouth of a sack open to Bart's shovel, smiled at the gravel that was going into it. "Nothing to me worth telling. Ordinary childhood. Bit too much of a taste for whisky—and last year I inherited a little money. Thought I'd try drinking in new places for a change."

"What was that—" Bart stopped and leaned for a second on his shovel, suddenly remembering. "In the bar that day— You were asking me something about Seats of something—Seats of Hell?"

"Oh—that," said Peter, glancing at him. "One of the local legends, I suppose." His eyes rested briefly on Bart. "Something about any man around here who becomes too proud of his strength getting spirited away to be a slave to Devils."

"Why ask me about it?"

"Well, you aren't the weakest man in the world, are you?" replied Peter, meeting him eye to eye. "I thought you might have heard more about it than I had."

Bart scowled. Since the chains had been put upon him, he had ceased to make any effort to hide the savage expressions his face was capable of showing in even mild emotion.

"Something damn funny about this island," he growled.

"You can say that two or three times," agreed Peter. "Look at this, right here."

"What?" Bart glanced around the pit, and saw nothing he had not seen before.

"Gravel," said Peter. "Now where would gravel come from naturally halfway up the side of a volcano?"

"It shouldn't?" Bart frowned.

"It takes water action to make gravel by breaking up larger rocks. We're eighteen hundred feet above sea-level here, on a young—geologically speaking—volcanic island that built itself up out of the sea-bottom by pouring lava out of a hole in the earth's crust. Makes you think, doesn't it?"

"There must be some reason for it," said Bart, impatiently. He had been shoveling in one spot until he had scooped out most of the gravel within easy reach of his shovel. He took a step forward and upward, and sank his shovel into the wall of gravel at about chest height before him. His shovel plunged forward, checking itself for a second as it hit the loose rock and then all but burying itself from sight.

Bart stared. He yanked the shovel backward. It came loose, starting a little avalanche of gravel that poured down around his ankles, and was still. He found himself staring into a hole in the slope—a hole rimmed by black basaltic rock.

For a long second, there was no movement in the pit. Only the blazing sun beating down and the little sound of a few last crumbs of light gravel sliding to rest. Both men stood looking and motionless. The sun hit the black rock and seemed to be absorbed by it, but there was enough light to see into a tunnel big enough for a man to walk upright and curving away up and to the left out of sight. From it came a cool breath, like the air under the forested slopes beyond the pits. It dried the sweat on Bart's face.

Suddenly he threw down his shovel and sucked in his hard belly. Seizing the now-slack chain around his belly with both fists, he bent one link against the next. There was a moment's swelling breath of silence, and then the sharp sound of the chain snapping. It fell from around him, to the gravel at his feet; and with a second violent gesture he flung both arms wide. The chain that bound his wrist manacles together twanged in its breaking like a guitar string. He took a step toward the hole. Peter spoke behind him.

"You could be acting like a damn fool, you know," said Peter.

Bart turned his head. Peter stood a short ways off. He had dropped the sack he had been holding, and stood with arms folded.

Bart grunted, turned away and started toward the hole, up the slippery gravel.

"In that case, wait for me," said Peter's voice behind him. But Bart was already into the darkness of the black rock tunnel. A second later, he heard Peter's footstep on the stone behind him. Bart did not turn his head. He went on into the hole, squinting against the darkness ahead and guiding himself with one powerful hand along the right hand wall.

He had not gone more than a short distance before he found himself in complete lightlessness. He stopped and looked behind him, but he could not see even the outline of Peter against the light of the entrance. A second later, the other man ran into him from behind.

"Bart?" Peter's voice came at him eerily out of nothingness.

"Go slow," growled Bart. "I've got to feel my way." He went on again. After a while the tunnel made a sharp turn and his right hand slipped off rock into thin air.

"Hold it," he said to Peter.

He felt around himself cautiously. His fingers gradually told him that he and Peter stood at a point where the tunnel forked. He told Peter.

"Let's go left," he said, to the Englishman. Peter did not object; and they started off again.

For a short while the left fork of the tunnel seemed no different from the entrance section. Then it began to grow smaller. It pressed in upon them; and gradually it acquired a downslope that became progressively steeper.

"Hold up," said Peter's voice behind him, suddenly, "—I'm slipping!" and a second later he bumped into Bart from behind. Only the strength of Bart's arms, braced against the rock walls on either side, kept them both from losing their footing. "We better go back and try that other fork."

Bart grinned humorlessly in the darkness, feeling the smooth rock underfoot.

"Try it," he suggested.

Behind him, he felt the weight of Peter's body removed; and then he heard the sound of panting and a scramble, ending in a sliding sound. He braced himself once more against the rock walls just in time before Peter's body caromed into him again.

"Too slippery in these shoes," gasped Peter. "I'll take them off—"

"It levels off ahead," interrupted Bart. "I'm not going back anyway." And he moved forward, onto the less precipitous tunnel floor he had just placed one foot on when Peter bumped into him.

"There's a blessing," murmured Peter, following him. "All the same, Bart—" he said behind Bart's shoulder. "We don't want to end up in the belly of the volcano. If you—"

Without warning, Bart's advancing foot trod suddenly on nothing at all. He never heard the end of Peter's sentence, which a second later was cut off as the Englishman behind him also walked off the edge of whatever it was. A sliding fall onto a slope too steep to brace against took the breath out of Bart's body. He shot downward, tumbling and turning. It was like being beaten to death by clubs of iron. For all his steel-hardness of body, Bart felt himself losing consciousness. He was aware of a red glow beginning to grow far below him, a waxing light beyond the edge of a cliff far below him to which he was falling with fantastic speed. But the multiple poundings made his head swim. The world reeled about him, and swallowed him, down into the black maw of unconsciousness. And he did not even remember reaching the edge of the cliff.

He awoke in hell.

He could never remember afterward just when he first returned to consciousness. It was a slow, gradual awakening that left him with the feeling that he had been unaware of his surroundings for some time—days, perhaps. Certainly the scene he opened his eyes on was not one he had just a few moments before tumbled into.

He found himself lying on a hard ledge in what appeared to be an enormous room or cavern with walls and floor cut out of unfaulted rock. He was a little above the main floor of the room, so that he could look down on several lower levels filled with crude wooden benches and tables, about which moved men clad only in a sort of grey-green trousers. But to call them men was to give them the benefit of naming them less brute than human.

All his life Bart had been, by reason of his freakish strength and musculature, like a giant among the pigmies of ordinary humanity. Now, here, in this cave-like scene lit by flaring, openly-burning black iron torches along the walls, he found himself at last in the society of his physical peers.

They were all shapes and sizes, moving down there below him; but there was not one naked torso among them that could not have called a gorilla "cousin" and made the beast think twice. Great cable-muscled arms, bunched shoulders, heavy bones, were common to all of them. They ate and drank at the tables, they even moved about with the half-slouch of the anthropoid.

So savage and bestial a group were they—and they must have numbered in the several hundreds—that Bart should have felt the same kind of sudden alarm that an ordinary man might feel on finding himself suddenly thrown into a bear-pit. Instead, for reasons he could not at the time understand, his nostrils widened, a half-inarticulate growl formed in his throat and he felt the stiff hairs on the back of his neck stir and erect themselves as a red tide of savage excitement thrilled suddenly through the whole length of him.

He sat up, quickly and easily, dropping his legs over the edge of the niche in which he had been lying. A nearby wall torch flamed redly upon him and he saw that he was dressed like the rest, in the grey-green trousers, with heavy grey-green boots coming up over them. Wonderingly, he flexed his arms and stretched. He was a little stiff and heavy-limbed, like someone who has overslept; but the results of the brutal pounding he had taken in his fall before he was knocked unconscious seemed to have evaporated. Looking himself over, he could find no bruises. But this was not as unusual as the other. Since he could remember, he had never been bruised visibly.

A sudden lulling of the voices and sounds from below him attracted his attention back to the crowd on the main floor of the place. He looked down to find faces upturned to him. The men below had discovered his conscious presence; and one by one they were turning to stare at him.

Like a wave the silence and the lifted heads moved up the floor, until it reached a great, hunch-shouldered individual sitting at one end of a long table. Slowly, his hairless skull tilted back to lift his face to Bart, and as the gleam of the naked head moved back, Bart for the first time realized that every one of the beings below was bald as well. His own hand went instinctively to his head—and felt it clean as if freshly shaven.

But the great, gargoyle face of the man at the end of the table was lifted to Bart now. A dead silence had fallen throughout the place, a silence that seemed to echo in the dark upper reaches above the torches, so profound it was. Then, hoarse and flat, and so guttural that any accent it might have had was hidden, the one at the table spoke. And his words carried as clearly as in a whispering gallery across eighty yards of distance to Bart's ears.

"You! Come down here!"

Bart grinned, and rose. He walked along the terrace below his niche, and dropped to the terrace six feet below. Steadily he approached the table.

The crowd made way for him when he reached the main floor. And as he came, the man at the head of the table stirred and rose to his own feet. He stepped out from behind the table to face Bart's approach, revealing himself a monster.

His face was like some ancient stone carving of a demon on a ruined castle. Big-boned as he was, the bones of his head were so much bigger as to be out of proportion. His cheekbones pushed out the skin of his face like bars of wood; his nose, broken as it was, was like the prow of a boat in miniature. His lower lip drooped over a gnarled, prothagonous jaw, revealing great horse-teeth. Half a head taller than Bart, he stood; and this, even though his enormous shoulders and spine were so bent and clouted with muscle that he looked like a hunchback. His arms hung like clubs at his side, and the outsize hands at the ends of them opened and closed hungrily at Bart's coming, like the grasping claws of a crab. For the first time in his life Bart felt the growing of a coldness inside him as he continued forward, and realized into what he was walking. It took him a moment to realize that the coldness was fear, for never before had he known what it was to be physically afraid of another human being.

The sudden recognition of the emotion in him made him tense himself internally, ready for combat. And it was a good thing he did, for the half-man, half-monster waiting for him wasted no time in talk, but launched himself immediately and without warning at Bart, as soon as Bart was within half a dozen feet.

Bart found himself slammed back against a table, those huge hands snatching at his throat. All he knew about fighting was what he had read on occasion; but he remembered enough to fling up his wrists and knock the other's reaching arms apart, while dodging to one side. The other plunged past him into the table, which splintered apart under the impact. Bart took a step backward and found himself hemmed in by a solid circle of bodies, gleaming in the torchlight. Then his opponent was charging him again.

Bart sidestepped once more, and struck out with his fist. The blow was considerably harder than the one that had landed him in the island jail and it checked the other, but only for a moment. Then he was coming on again, apparently untouched.

Once more, Bart ducked those reaching arms. The pattern of battle was becoming obvious to him. It was with a bitter sort of humor that he recognized that he, who had always been stronger than any other human being he had ever met, was now having to rely on his agility to stay alive. He was a little faster than the awesome mass of bone and muscle that confronted him; and he could only hope to stay at arms length until the other started to tire. His opponent, obviously, wanted nothing but to get those monster arms around Bart and start squeezing. Bart ducked once more out of reach.

But the other was becoming more cunning. He paid no attention to Bart's punches, although not even his massive features were built to take the punishment fists like Bart's could hand out. Gradually his face was being pounded out of recognition. But, ignoring this, he had begun to sidle after Bart around the small circle, arms outstretched to either side, to hem the smaller man in. Well over seven feet those pole-like arms must have measured; and Bart's margin of escape became smaller and smaller, each time he slipped aside.

Nor was the man he was fighting showing the signs of tiring Bart had hoped for. Tirelessly, almost patiently, he continued to pursue Bart while the brute-men around them watched silently. Instead, Bart began to feel his own wind growing short. In desperation, he made up his mind to gamble. And the next time the other swept in on him, arms outstretched, Bart did not duck aside. Instead, he stepped straight forward, into the other's grasp; and with the full leverage of his arms, drove both fists home together, one on each side of his opponent's head.

The twin blow would have cracked the skull of an ox. And for a minute, even Bart's enemy was stunned. He checked, wavering, in the center of the ring; and blood sprang from nose, mouth and ears all at once. Incredibly, he did not go down.

—And then the moment was lost. Bart felt the great arms sweep around him, and himself caught up into their vise-like grip against the sweating, gargantuan chest of his adversary.

The arms about him closed with the slow, relentless action of a steel cold-press machine. Bart felt his spine beginning to be bent back, the breath going from his collapsing lungs. He surged against the muscles holding him, but he could not break loose. A red tide seemed to rise, fogging his eyesight; and behind it came cold fury. Fury rose, swamping him; the old, primitive centers of his brain took over as the forebrain lapsed into unconsciousness; and out of the murk emerged slowly the animal urge to kill.

He closed his own arms around the giant body opposing him, his left fingers found the wrist of his right hand and locked about it. All the abnormal strength of his body flowed up into his arms and shoulders, as he, himself, began to close his grip.

They stood, locked together. They might have been two gigantic figures carved out of marble for all the apparent movement they showed. And the circle about them also was silent, waiting the end. Then—slowly, almost imperceptibly—Bart felt his own grip gaining, and a faint slackening in that of his opponent. Impossible as it seemed, now that they were matched hold for hold, his own freak muscles were proving the stronger. The man he was locked with was half again his size and double his weight; but now Bart, putting the pressure on, felt the great torso collapsing, the other's grip slackening.

Then, Bart should have stopped. He had won the battle. But all the thinking part of him was drowned now in the animal instinct to kill. He heard himself growling softly in his throat and increased his pressure. . . .

"Hold it!" roared a voice in his ears. Bart scarcely heard

it. "Leave off, brother!" And a stunning blow on the back of the head sent his senses suddenly swimming and his arms loosening about his opponent. Staggering, he tried to turn about to face this new enemy; and another blow sent him to the ground.

On hands and knees, he shook his head to drive the fog from his brain. As it cleared he looked up. Looming over him he saw a brown, dish-shaped, vaguely-oriental face that was not unfamiliar.

"You—!" stuttered Bart. He scrambled to his feet. "—They said I killed you—" It was the man he had seen torturing the gull, the man he had hit in the market place. Bart launched himself at the wide-shouldered little man's throat.

An instant later he found himself slammed to the ground.

"Easy, brother, easy," said the little man, conversationally, squatting beside him. "I knew what you knew about fighting eight hundred years ago and more. What were you trying to bust up old Horse, for?"

Bart wiped his hand across his lips. It came away bloody.

"He came at me." He looked at the little man sharply, and got to his feet. "I *didn't* kill you?"

"Do I look dead, brother?" the small man extended a square slab of a hand. "Chandt's the name." He had been speaking English almost without an accent, but as he mentioned his own name, it came out with a strange, almost sing-song, ring to it. "I was just part of the chain to bind you and drag you down to the Hall of The Dead here, with the rest of us. What do they call you, Brother?"

"Bart," said Bart. "Bart Dybig." He reached out with his own hand and felt the little man's catch him on the forearm. They shook hands in the ancient Roman fashion, grasping above the wrist. "Was it your idea to do that to the bird?"

"No—I was told." Chandt's eyes rested a second shrewdly on Bart's face. "It still bothers you? What is a bird, brother? A waving of wings in the sky for a second, and then nothing. Man at least lives a season; and we here in the Hall of the Dead live forever."

"What do you mean—Hall of the Dead?" demanded Bart. "Where is this place?"

"There are many halls," said Chandt. "More than I could tell you in one rest period. More—maybe—than even I know, brother. But you—" He broke off suddenly. A high, clear note like that made by an instrument combining the finest of violins and the finest of bells, had just rung through the place. Bart saw them all around him— even the brutish Horse, now struggling back to consciousness and his feet—turning to look at him. "That's for you," said Chandt, sharply. "Come on."

He led Bart back to the shadows at a far end of the hall. They mounted a flight of stone steps and came into what appeared to be a dressing room. From one of these Chandt extracted a long-sleeved upper garment of the same greygreen cloth as the trousers; and a heavy padded collar, with heavy hooks protruding from it in back and what looked like a metal pipe about eight inches in diameter and ten in length dangling from a chain in front. Chandt threw the collar over Bart's head, as soon as Bart had the tunic on.

"Put your hands in the tube," he said. Wondering, Bart obeyed. Chandt led him to the back of the dressing room, to a tall metal door. As they approached the door, it swung open, revealing a paved space beyond lit not by torches, but by some clear, light that was not daylight. "See you later, brother."

He shoved Bart through the door. Bemused, Bart took a step forward, and found himself face to face with the girl he had seen in the market place—and later, again, in the jail.

The door slammed to with a clash of metal behind him. At the same time he felt clamps inside the pipe snap shut upon his wrists, trapping them, helpless, inside a sort of double handcuff.

At the first bite of the handcuffs on his flesh, Bart checked. He stood brace-legged and saw the girl shrink back. From this he guessed the look of savagery upon his own face. But though she shrank from him, she did not actually retreat.

"Please—" she said. "Come with me."

Her voice betrayed only the slightest flavor of French. Other than that, her accent was as English as Peter's had been.

"Why?" snarled Bart.

"Please," she said. She reached out an uncertain hand

toward him, but without touching him. "If you don't, you will suffer. We all do what we have to do, down here."

She turned and walked off, glancing back at him over her shoulder. After a second, he followed.

They moved off across the paved space. Bart, glancing around, tried to decide what manner of place he had gotten into. His first and best impression of the Hall of the Dead had been that it was a cave. If that was so, what was he in now? A larger cave? Overhead the air became a white, all-encompassing area of illumination that gave no clue to what lay above it. Around them were huge buildings that stretched away one behind the other at all angles, so that it was impossible to tell whether they grew out of cavern wall, or simply stood, clear and distinct upon the pavement underfoot. The buildings themselves were of all shapes and architecture, except that they were uniformly constructed of stone; and many had a soaring, cathedral-like appearance about them.

In the distance, Bart caught a glimpse far down one of the corridors, or what ever they were, between buildings of something too far away to see, but which seemed like some great unwieldly beast tottering on two legs. He paused and would have looked more closely, but the girl caught him by the arm; and, looking down, he saw that she was beside him once more, her face urgent, under her auburn hair.

"Please!" she said.

He looked and saw they had approached the center of the area of pavement, and that one of the blocks that composed it was now tilted up on end. She was urging him down a flight of steps. He descended. She followed, closing the pavement slab behind him, and he found they were standing in a tunnel with a single rail running through it, and on that rail a small, two-seater car or cab.

She urged him into the cab; and got in herself, taking the front seat. A second later they shot forward, gathering speed as they went. The ride was a violent one through several branching tunnels, not merely right and left, but up and down; until it stopped, as suddenly as it had started, before a small, gold-colored door set in the tunnel wall.

"Come!" she said again. The hand she placed on his arm trembled; he could feel it through the cloth of his sleeve.

She led him through the gold door and into a small room with what looked like a marble floor, black and white, and walled with silken-appearing hangings of all colors.

Barely had they stepped through the door than a new sound reached Bart's ears and made him stop instinctively. It was a voice he heard—singing. But it was no human voice.

The Sirens who tempted Ulysses in the Grecian legend, he thought involuntarily, might have sung like the voice he heard. There were no words to the music pouring into the room about him, but the sound alone was almost too pure and sweet for the human mind to bear.

The girl was tugging at him again.

"What is it?" he whispered, awed in spite of himself.

"His Starfish!" she said. "Oh, come! Please come, without any more delays!"

She tugged him forward. Together they pushed through the hangings. But then once more he stopped. Nor could anyone have blamed him. For the sight of the two beings waiting for him there were like nothing he had ever expected to see in the world above.

Sprawled on a miniature couch with an uparching back was a stomach-twisting distortion of a human being. A sort of violet lounging robe covered a body no larger than that of a twelve-year-old boy's; and one fragile little hand held a small silver goblet with a red liquid in it. Above this, two pupilless blue eyes turned to stare at Bart out of a head as big as a barrel, completely hairless, and equipped with a horribly outsize smiling face with the wrinkles of a kindly grandfather. It did not stop smiling, and the upturned lips drew Bart's gaze with a hideous fascination. From the very first second, something inside him waited agonizingly for the smile to be erased. But it went on, and on.

The music had also been going on, all this time; but just then the being on the couch lifted his goblet, and the voice stopped abruptly, as if it had been choked off. The sudden silence jerked Bart's gaze around to the other occupant of the room.

It was this creature who had been singing; and instantly, Bart understood why the girl had referred to it as "his Starfish." A starfish it was not; but something like a starfish must have been at one time in its ancestry.

It was about four feet tall, and its shape was that of a

conventional starfish. However, in this creature, two of
the boneless appendages had become legs, two arms, and
the fifth had come to house what passed for a head,
although there was little to identify it as that, except a slit
just above the circular central body to which the limbs
were attached. It was from this slit that the singing had
issued.

A rapid trill came suddenly from the lips of the over-
sized head, causing Bart to jerk his gaze back in that
direction. But a second after the starfish sang, but this
time in English, and to him.

"Bartholemew Dybig!" sang the inhumanly lovely voice.
"This is your Protector, your All-Father, your Keeper,
who has been waiting for you. Now, your All-Father needs
you to carry him on a trip of inspection. Oh, thank—give
thanks to the All-Father, who finds you occupation!"

Bart stared, and then wheeling about stared at the impossible creature on the couch, who continued to smile at
him. There was a rustle of hangings, and a dragging sound
behind Bart. He turned quickly and saw a man dragging
what looked like an upholstered basket into the room. The
man had yellow hair. For a moment Bart blinked in
disbelief.

"Peter!" he said.

"Hello there—" Peter glanced at him, but ducked his
eyes away as if embarrassed, almost at once. "Not the best
time to talk right now. Here, I'll give you a hand with
this."

He had continued to drag the basket along the floor
until it was beside the couch on which the so-called All-
Father lay.

"Aid the All-Father into the basket seat, oh Bartholemew
Dybig!" sang the starfish.

The All-Father had laid down his goblet on a small
round stone pedestal by his couch; and picked a small,
ridiculous-looking whip, like the toys sold at circuses. He
beamed at Bart. Bart felt himself washed by a sudden
surge of anger. He folded his arms and stood still.

"Bart! Don't be a fool!" he heard Peter hiss in his ear.
He ignored the man, keeping his eyes fixed on the pupilless
blue eyes of the All-Father. The great head smiled cease-
lessly back at him. For a long second nothing seemed to

happen; and then, unexpectedly, Bart felt a clammy sensation about his feet and ankles, and glanced down.

The floor about his feet had become viscous. More than that, it had become alive. Like some hungry jelly, it was sucking itself up about his feet, crawling up his ankles. It's touch was like the touch of something dead, yet avid for some meat cleaner than itself. Shuddering instinctively, he jerked away from it—but his feet did not move. Already it had him gripped, rooted to the spot. It was creeping up around his knees.

He snarled like a wild animal, fighting it instinctively with all the freak strength of his body. But the creeping life of the floor continued to rise, suckingly; and through the haze of his own sweat he could see the All-Father, still smiling at him.

It was around his waist now, and now his chest. It had caught and imprisoned his arms and it laid its first cold, sticky touch on his naked throat. *It will smother me,* was the thought that rose to the surface of his mind; and with it, suddenly his thoughts cleared with a snap and understanding came to him.

Of course, he thought coolly, looking the great smiling face in the eye—it's hypnotism.

—And suddenly he was free. The floor underfoot was a floor again, patterned slabs of white and black rock. And still the smile of the creature on the couch did not waver. Bart smiled back—and a second later the cramp struck.

It was a great spasm of pain, a convulsion of the body that sent him rolling upon the floor, huddled over. —And then, rapidly, in swift succession, it was added to by cramps in his arms, his legs, his neck—all parts of his body. The pain was too much for any man to bear. He felt the room swim and fade about him as his tortured body fled into the refuge of unconsciousness.

—He awoke to find Peter bending over him, rubbing some life back into his arms and legs.

"Will you learn?" hissed Peter. "You can't fight him—not that way, in any case!" He helped Bart to his feet. "Come on—I'll give you a hand."

They went back to the basket, in which the All-Father was already seated. His smile washed Bart with tender forgiveness.

"This fastens to the hooks on your collar," said Peter. "Turn around."

Bart turned. Five seconds later he had become a loaded beast of burden.

The chains of a slave weigh as much as he thinks they do. The creature in the basket on Bart's back weighed no more than a hundred and twenty pounds; and the basket and collar was ideally designed to spread the load fairly upon Bart's powerful shoulders. But as he carried his master that first work period with the starfish scurrying before, and with the girl and Peter running attendance on either side; every so often a red haze would rise before Bart's gaze, so that he staggered drunkenly with fury and shame. Then, the little toy whip would flick about his ears, neither more wounding or less infuriating than the bite of a mosquito; and the sanity of his civilized mind would come to the rescue of his savage emotions, and he would continue to carry and obey.

It was a strange trip he carried his rider on. Through corridors, in the little railed cars, down escalators, along moving walkways that rippled behind balconies overlooking hidden depths, in and out of strange, high-ceilinged buildings. Eventually, they came out on a final balcony that overlooked a fantastic pit whose floor was easily a quarter mile below where they stood and whose further limits were lost in a haze of light. On that floor stood a blimp-shaped vessel of titanic proportions. That it was a vessel, Bart could hardly doubt, in view of the rows of windows along its sides and the transparent roofed blister amidships, through which could be faintly seen—not controls, but what seemed to be a long banqueting table set with innumerable chairs, tiny-appearing from the balcony's height.

As they stood looking down, and after a long moment of silence, Bart's ears caught the sound of a faint sigh, such as a child might have made—rapidly followed by a trilling from the lips of his rider.

"Back!" sang the starfish. "Back now to the quarters of the All-Father." And they turned away from the pit and the ship within it.

After they had returned to the room where Bart had first come upon the starfish and his rider, Bart hoped for a chance to speak to Peter, alone. But—almost as if the eternally smiling All-Father had read his mind—he was dismissed and sent back to the Hall of the Dead by himself. The little car outside the gold door took him back to where he had first boarded it, without his touching any controls—as if, in fact, it was controlled by someone somewhere else. And when he emerged once more into the area outside the Hall of the Dead, there seemed little choice but to reenter that strange den of beast-like men. In the maze of buildings around him he was free to run— but to what purpose? And his intelligent, unbrutelike mind told him that there would have been little point in the All-Father leaving him free to try and escape if there was any hope of his succeeding.

Accordingly, he strode back to the door of the Hall of the Dead. It opened before him, and he stepped inside. As it clashed shut behind him, he felt the clamps inside the pipe that held his hands, release his wrists; and saw the broad little man, Chandt, waiting for him.

"Had a busy first period, brother?" grinned Chandt, helping him off with the collar. He laid the collar aside, and caught up one of Bart's fists in his own. "Ah, you're one of those who don't take to it lightly." Around the wrist he held, where the clamp had fastened it, Bart's skin was scored to a bloody wound. Chandt caught up the other hand, which was similar. "Let me bind those, brother."

As the little man wrapped strips of cloth around the wrists, Bart gazed down at him curiously.

"Why do you do this?" Bart asked, finally.

"Why?" Chandt flashed a grin up at him. "Why, I'm boss-man in the Hall here, sort of."

"Boss? Why?"

Chandt shrugged.

"I'm oldest," he said, "for one thing. Near as old as one of the Heads. Eight hundred and forty-three, give or take a few years—we didn't keep much track of birthdays, when I was born."

"Eight hundred and forty-three!" Bart's lip curled.

"Believe it or not, all one to me," said Chandt. He finished wrapping the last dressing around Bart's left wrist. "Next time don't fight the cuffs, and then they won't cut you. —Cuts can lead to poison—then they've got to amputate." He spread his hands before Bart. "Look at me!" he said. "Over eight hundred years; and nothing missing. And there won't ever be, brother!"

The last words were said so grimly that Bart felt a shiver run down his back.

"What makes you so sure?" he asked curiously.

"I won't let it, brother." Chandt's eyes were as hard as flint. "The way I believe, all of me's Chandt. I'm no worm, to go crawling off in two directions when I'm cut apart. You try to take a piece of me, you'd better figure on taking all of me; because I don't aim to live as less than a man." He took a deep breath and some of the violence went out of him. "The Heads know that," he said. "They know me. I know them. We get along."

"Heads," said Bart. "You mean that—what I carried today?"

"Zonas," supplied Chandt. "They've got names like everyone else—though you'll never hear them mentioned. Come and eat, brother. You can be called back to work at any time after six hours from now—Zonas is a six-hour sleeper."

He led the way to one of the tables on which a harsh red wine sat in tall metal jugs amidst loaves of bread, plates of cooked meat—beef, pork, and chicken mixed indiscriminately—and huge chunks of cheese and loaves of bread.

Bart found himself ravenous. He had always been a large eater and now he found himself voracious. As he ate, he asked questions.

"—the girl?" Chandt answered. "She's been in the Hall of the Heads two years now, maybe three. Zonas'll probably keep her for handmaiding another four or five years; then she'll be sent down to us."

"Us?" Bart stopped eating.

"We get the leftovers," grinned Chandt. "When the Heads get tired of having their foreheads rubbed by the same set of dainty fingers, they send the old wench downstairs, to the Hall of the Women. We got a connecting door into it—want me to show you the way?"

"Not now," said Bart, harshly. "And Peter?"

"That his name?" Chandt grabbed a piece of pork and chewed on it reflectively with hard, white teeth worn down nearly to the gumline. "He's a new one. Came in

with you, so you ought to know more about him than I do.
—Though they weren't hunting *him*."

"They were hunting me?" Bart felt a cold shiver down
his back.

"For a couple of years anyway. Maybe they've had their
eyes on you all your life. Who knows? Hell, you're a
collector's item."

"Collector's item!"

"Prize bull." Chandt swallowed the last of his pork and
wiped greasy fingers across his bronze chest. "Zonas had
to be high up on the table, to rate something like you—
table, that's the way they rank among themselves. The
higher up the table you sit when they all sit together, the
more weight you swing. Zonas sits next to the Father of
Fathers, who sits at the table's head."

Bart himself had finished eating. He reached across the
table and caught at the little man's arm.

"How do I get out of here?" he whispered harshly.

Chandt made no effort to pull his arm away. His black
eyes met Bart's thoughtfully and appraisingly.

"Like that, eh?" he murmured. "Don't you want to live
forever? Light work, and no sickness, and everything taken
care of—and all you can eat and drink and the best-looking
women in the world delivered practically to your doorstep?"

"Tell me!" snarled Bart. His hand was closing on Chandt's
wrist.

"Turn me loose," replied Chandt in a low, even voice.
"You've got more strength than old Horse, but I know
how to break your arm without getting up from this table.
Turn me loose!"

Bart let go of the wrist.

"That's better." Chandt looked with interest at the marks
Bart's fingers had left on his own teak-like forearm. "You'll
be a boy to tangle with, someday." He looked back up at
Bart. "Well, now, I'll tell you. You being you, and me
being me, you came at the right time to ask me that." He
stood up from the table. "Come on."

Bart rose and followed him.

Chandt led Bart back to the end of the Hall of the Dead
that was opposite the metal door of the entrance. Bart had
assumed that back here the hall naturally closed off. Instead, to his wonderment, he found it split up into a

variety of corridors or tunnels. Chandt led him down one of these, past what appeared to be steam rooms, exercise and locker rooms, until the small man came to a bend in the tunnel. When this happened, Chandt stopped, glanced quickly in both directions, then stepped to the wall just at the bend. He leaned against one of the stone slabs that seemed to wall these tunnels. Bart could not make out exactly what he did; but suddenly the slab tilted inward and upward.

"Come on!" said Chandt sharply. Together they crawled through into darkness, and the slab closed behind them.

"Now what?" asked Bart. He heard Chandt grunt in the obscurity and then illumination from some hidden source burst on all around them. Bart blinked his eyes against the sudden light. When his vision had readjusted, he saw they stood in a tunnel identical to the one they had just left; but as empty as if it had never been used.

"This way," said Chandt. He led off. It was a strange route they followed, up and down and round about—and always by corridors and stairs that showed no sign of another living person. If it had not been for the fact that they were free of dust, Bart would have had to conclude that these passages had been forgotten for centuries.

"Who comes through here?" he asked Chandt.

"No one," said the little man, going on before. "Only the sweepers. They were spy passages once."

"Once?"

"Back when the Heads could still navigate on their own. Now, no one comes, and they think no one knows." Chandt chuckled. "But *I* remember when. I, alone."

A little further on they passed a mechanical thing composed mainly of whirring brushes, that was working down along one wall. Behind it the corridor gleamed.

"Sweeper," said Chandt briefly.

"The Heads ought to ride those sort of things," growled Bart. Chandt flashed him a twisted grin.

"They can't," he said. "Time you learned something, Brother. They can't touch anything mechanical. It robs them of their power."

"Power?" said Bart. "What power?"

"Power to make people like you and I believe things. Power to make your muscles cramp, or your head imagine things that aren't so. Power to think you to death, brother—

don't think they haven't got it." He paused significantly. "Tell me. Anyone watching you or listening to you, right now?"

Bart stopped suddenly; and Chandt stopped with him.

"No!" said Bart suddenly and explosively. But he had looked for a moment around him.

"That's right," said Chandt. "But some people they can hear and spy on. Only not me, brother. And not you. If they could, they'd have had an easier job getting you down here. I checked on you when I found all the trouble they were going to get you. You're like me—you're the first like me in many years. There's something about those that won't give in. They don't have the power over them they have over the rest." He stopped suddenly. They had walked some distance. He turned to the wall of the corridor behind him and again leaned against the stone. A panel tilted in; and Chandt gestured through it.

"Look—" he invited. "The Hall of the Mayflies."

Bart stepped to the opening and gazed through. He looked out and down the opening to see a small multitude of men and women; the men in the version of the grey-green uniform that he had seen Peter wearing in the All-Father's quarters, and the women in all kinds of colorful dress—most of it had a filmy, silken look, like ancient Grecian robes.

Physically, the Hall of the Mayflies was much like the Hall of the Dead; except that from where Bart was standing, he could see that an almost pathetic attempt had been made to dress it up and disguise its harsh interior. Paints had been used to brighten up the walls. The tables were not long benches, but smaller, more individual matters. Here and there, a bit of decoration, such as a woman's scarf, artistically draped, had been hung or tacked in place about table or wall. Men and women moved about, or sat at the tables.

"Mayflies," said Chandt, deep in his throat. "We live, brother. You and I, though we are dead, we may live forever. But these—a year, two years at the most. They down there are the gaudy ones, the weak ones. A twitch of a Head's eyelid can wake them from their dreams; and the breath of a moment's anger on the part of a Head can freeze them to death."

Bart heard him with only half an ear. His eyes were

busy searching the crowd below; and abruptly he found what he looked for. He lifted a finger and pointed it at Peter and the girl sitting alone together at the table.

"I want to talk to them," he said. There was no immediate answer from Chandt. He spun around to find the little man staring at him.

"Would you now?" said Chandt, softly. "And why, brother? Why?"

Bart opened his mouth and then closed it again. He could not say that from the first moment—when her brown eyes had met his in the market place—he had not been able to get her out of his mind. And Peter— Why should they be talking together like that now? It could be that merely their work had brought them together like this, in off-duty hours; but something like jealousy kindled its sullen spark in Bart.

"He's a friend of mine," growled Bart, lamely.

"But no friend of mine," said Chandt. He paused, looking closely at Bart. "But—I'm no enemy of friendliness. Maybe later, I'll fix it so you can see him."

He let the panel drop back into position, and led off again. Bart followed, scowling and thinking. A little farther on, several corridors and a couple of levels away, Chandt stopped suddenly and opened another panel.

"Now look!" he said.

Bart stepped to the opening and looked—down into something like a rock-strewn, watery cave. It was alive with the creatures he had come to know as starfish. They lay on the rocks, they swam in the water, they moved about together, the whole scene of their gathering lit not by the flaring torches, nor yet by the strange artificial light of the world outside the halls, and the quarters of the Heads. Instead, a white, phosphorescent glow covered the ceiling and half the walls, giving the whole place an illumination like moonlight.

"The Hall of the Starfish," said Chandt. He seemed about to drop the panel back into place, but he hesitated. For a moment his voice had a touch of something different in it—something between wonder and emotion. "Have you heard one sing?"

Bart nodded.

"Today," he said. "In the place of that Head I—work for."

Chandt nodded to himself.

"The Heads made them," he said. "When—don't ask me. It was even before my time. How—don't ask me. What—" His voice ran down. "The Heads are Gods to them; and yet it's the Heads who couldn't live without them, now. The Heads can't touch mechanical things without losing their powers of the mind; so the starfish do it for them. All this—" his broad hand swept out in a circle, "all of it, the starfish built. They worship, they serve, they—sing. And what do they get for it?"

"What?" asked Bart, when the little man did not answer his own question. Chandt let the panel fall heavily back into place.

"Death," said the little man softly. "They die to amuse Heads." He turned and led off once more down the corridor. Bart followed. After a few minutes, Bart caught up with him.

"Tell me something—" he began. Chandt turned on him in sudden fury.

"I'll tell you nothing!" he flared. His hands flashed up to hang, palm-upward, fingers crooked before Bart. "I could kill you now," he whispered. "Even you—I could touch you once or twice, and you'd be dead. Don't ask me questions, brother." As quickly as it appeared, the fury vanished. "Come on," he said mildly.

He led the way through several more corridors. Finally, he stopped and opened another panel. Bart looked through and down onto the ship he had seen from the balcony earlier. They were much closer above it than the time before, and he looked down into the enormously long blister on the hull, through the transparent roof of which he could see the long table with its rows of seats around them. The seats were of a size for children.

"There it is," said Chandt. "Your home and mine forever more. The table of the Heads. And the Seats of Hell."

Bart turned his head slowly to look down at the little man. Chandt's face set like rock as he gazed down through the transparent roof.

"Seats of Hell?" Bart said.

"When the Heads sit around that table all together, they can split the earth wide open and fly that ship out—that ship with you and me, the Mayflies and the Starfish, all aboard her. When they sit together around that table, anything that gets in their way burns like the tinder of Hell. This whole island above us was made when they sat around the table one day." He drew a deep breath. "And on another day they sat together and brought in topsoil, and plants, and trees and animals—and people."

"Why show me all this?" said Bart, bluntly.

"Because they're not going to get away with it!" the little man whirled on him, slamming his wide chest with one hard hand. "I—Chandt! I'm no slave to them, brother. They captured me many years ago, but no living thing makes Chandt work against his will. There was a deal between us, between myself and the Father of Fathers, who I carried all these hundreds of years—if they kept me whole and uncrippled, I'd serve them; and the deal was to hold as long as the grass grew in summer!"

"What's that got to do with it?" Bart asked.

"That!" Chandt jabbed a furious forefinger at the ship below him. "You were the last to be added. They say the world's getting too mechanical for them. They've built this ship and it's ready to fly now—to eternity among the stars. In two weeks they'll load us all aboard and take off. You— and me, brother—*away from the grass!*"

Bart felt himself shaken by the fury of the little man's emotion. Chandt was half-gathered to spring, his fingers hooked, and there were tears in his eyes. He sighed suddenly and the tension went out of him.

"Come on," he said. "It's time you were getting back. I'll show you a short cut."

He was gone almost before Bart could follow, the panel sliding down as he let go of it. Bart hurried after, and found him stepping through a panel in the opposite side of the corridor. Bart followed, and found they were standing by one of the little cars in a tunnel with the single rail running through it.

Chandt piled in without a word. Bart followed. Moments later, they stepped once more through the panel that let them back into the Hall of the Dead.

"You'll be called in a few minutes," said Chandt, putting a hand on Bart's arm. "But listen—I had to wait for someone like you, someone too new and too strong for the Heads to have in power yet. You and I together can do it, what nobody else can do. We can get out of here; and away from the Heads. Are you with me?"

"I'm with you," said Bart.

"Brother!" Chandt caught his forearm in the old Roman salute. Then he turned and went quickly down the corridor. Bart followed more slowly, his eyes hooded, and his mind thinking.

It was a dozen more work periods before Chandt said anything more, or anything at all came to introduce a sharp breath of freedom's hope into the unchanging underground air. Meanwhile the life to Bart became increasingly unbearable. He carried his particular Head about the subterranean world and through its many buildings. He saw great storehouses, museum-like buildings holding a plunder of the world's art. He saw tool shops and factories manned by the starfish—though his Head trilled with anger and beat him with the little whip when he got too close. And every day, he carried the creature back and forth in the Great Hall, a vast, domed interior with green and yellow striped floors and windows that reflected some fiery exterior pit which must have been a still glowing pocket of the original volcano. This place seemed to be an exercise ground for the Heads—if riding about in their baskets could be called exercise; for there were always a number of them about there, moving hither and yon and occasionally trilling across to each other.

It was here that Bart witnessed the death sentence of his Head's starfish; and for the first time realized the truth in Chandt's words about their relationship to the Heads. For no particular reason that Bart could understand, the creature in the basket on Bart's shoulders suddenly decided to have his starfish sing to all the Heads in the Great Hall. The starfish, who like Peter and the girl, was always in attendance, immediately opened its slit of a mouth and poured forth a melody which might have charmed the ears of angels. It did not charm the Heads for long. They clustered around to listen at first, but soon became restless and wandered off. After a while, the Head on Bart's shoulders forced him away, as if in a fit of pique—and without ordering the starfish to stop singing.

Abandoned, alone in the Great Hall, the starfish sang on and on, while the Heads paraded about it. Finally, Bart's Head rode him back to the Head's quarters. Bart could hear the song grow faint with distance behind them as they left.

Back at the quarters, the Head, almost petulantly, waved them out of the room. They stepped out into the little car of the monorail together; and for the first time found themselves with an opportunity to talk.

"Bart!" said Peter, wringing Bart's hand. Bart wrung back, forgetting how used he was becoming to his own strength, until he saw the other man wince. "I've been trying to get to talk to you ever since we came here. I—" suddenly he stopped, put his finger to his lips; and led them down the tunnel a short distance. There, to Bart's surprise, he activated a panel just as Chandt had done; and ushered them through. When the panel was closed behind them and they found themselves in one of the deserted corridors, he leaned against a wall and sighed with relief.

"They've lost us," he said. "Feel it?"

"Feel what?" said Bart, frowning. Peter looked startledly at him.

"Doesn't the Head have a rapport with you—" Peter broke off suddenly, and his face lit up. "Of course!" he said. "That explains the chains and handcuffs! I wondered why they had to chain you human horses when they had mental control over people. You must be immune."

"Anyway, I and—" Bart broke off, suddenly cautious. "You act like you know more than just a little about all this, Peter? You and—" he turned to the girl.

"Maria Reynaud," said Peter. "My cousin, as it happens. And more important, a fellow agent."

"Agent?" said Bart. "For what?"

"Can't tell you that, laddie," said Peter. "If we don't get out of this alive, it won't make any difference; and if we do, it's just as well for Maria and I you don't know. —Say hello, Maria. Least you can do."

"I said hello—a long time ago," said Maria, looking up at Bart.

"Yes," said Bart. His voice came from deep in his chest; but it was not his usual growl. "In the market place."

"I'm sorry about my part in that. I—"

"It doesn't matter," growled Bart. "The thing is to get us out of here, now."

"I'm afraid Maria and I still have a job to do," said Peter. "You've seen that ship of the Heads?"

Bart nodded.

"Maria was sent first to let herself be gathered in by the Heads just so we could find out about the starfish. The body of one of them was washed up on the shore of a Pacific island two years ago," said Peter. "Certain international powers—don't look so sullen, Bart, they're ones you'd agree with—decided to look into the matter. When we found out about the Heads, there was a furor. The Heads were too hot to handle and too dangerous to leave alone. It cost us eighteen top agents to even learn this place existed."

"Why?" asked Bart.

"Because the Heads found them out," said Peter. "Then we discovered a little device which, surgically implanted, gives Maria and I some measure of immunity to mental snooping. With it, Maria let herself be captured first, and found out about the ship. She yelled for help, and I came. But the Heads weren't, it seemed, interested in making any more captures. Then, Maria learned one of them was after you, so I latched on to you."

"What about the ship?" said Bart. "You don't want to let them get away, is that it?"

"That, and more than that," said Peter. "You've seen the table of the Heads, and the so-called Seats of Hell. Sitting around that table, the Heads can lift that ship by sheer mental power clear out into space. But it's hard work to go any distance, astronomically speaking, that way. So the Heads and the starfish together have come up with a warp engine."

"What's a warp engine?"

"Don't ask me, laddie," said Peter. "I'm not that much of a physical engineer. All I know is, if that engine were turned on down here, goodby ship—and goodby planet Earth. On the other hand, turn it on a few million miles out in space, and it's only goodby Earth."

Bart stared.

"You mean that?" he said at last.

"Our best scientists tell us so," said Peter. "We were working on the same sort of device ourselves. In fact, certain manifestations down here attracted our attentions to this island even before the starfish was washed up."

"Now," said Maria. "It's up to us—to destroy that engine." She looked at Bart. "We're too well protected underground here for even a nuclear blast to be sure of getting that ship before the Heads could take it up."

Bart's face set itself in grim lines. He was thinking of the little whip biting at his head and ears and of the brutemen in the Hall of the Dead—but mostly about a certain starfish who would be singing still in the Great Hall, singing itself to death.

"I've got a man I think you ought to meet," he said.

Six rest periods later, they met in one of the deserted tunnels. They made a strange group. The slim, almost fragile-looking young Englishman, the beautiful auburn-haired girl, the powerful dwarf that was Chandt, and the giant in ordinary man's shape that was Bart—his superhuman upper body, like Chandt's, revealed by the fact that they wore their rest-period dress of trousers and boots alone.

"How'd you know about the tunnels?" was Chandt's first word to Peter, delivered in the tone of a challenge.

Peter extended a closed right fist, knuckles up, and then opened it. In his palm lay something that looked like a small compass.

"I'm loaded down with these sorts of gadgets," he said. "When I was sent, I was sent equipped."

Chandt grunted.

"And you think you can wreck the ship?" he said.

"Not the ship—only the warp engine. But they won't try to leave without it."

"And then what?" said Chandt.

"And then an international police force will move in," said Peter. "Under French authority—since this is a French island."

Chandt grunted again.

"If!" he said. "If any of us gets out. I was for leaving quietly, with Bart. The two of us had a chance. But to spoil their ship, brother—after they broke faith with me—!" The small man's black eyes glowed like hot coals.

"There's two sides to that, you know, too," said Peter. "If revenge is all you do it for, how do we know—"

"Revenge!" Chandt's voice was a warning growl. "Why do you think I swore by the grass, brother? I was born in a cloth yurt and had the bare earth for bed and mother for the first forty years of my life. And this warp engine would kill earth and grass together—!" His voice dropped, and became thoughtful. "I wish I'd known that earlier. But it's like them. They can't bear the sun and the wind, and they hate what they can't bear."

"The point is," broke in Bart, "how're we going to do it?"

"Peter has to get into the ship," said Maria. "If Peter—"

Chandt's eyes hooded. He listened to them talk for a moment, then gave a short, harsh bark of a laugh, that silenced them all. Bart turned toward him, scowling.

"Smile, brother!" said Chandt, with a hard grin. "You're a child, after all. All of you are children, compared to me. Did you think I bothered to meet with you without having all planned and ready?" He stepped to the nearby wall and opened the panel that stood there. They had met in a corridor that ran alongside and all but under the belly of the ship. The view he exposed to them showed its monster side swelling above them; and, a short distance away, an entry port and a ramp leading up and into it. A starfish was scurrying up the ramp.

"That's for you, Peter," said Chandt, pointing to the ramp. "You'll find nothing but starfish aboard there. But you'll have to find the engine yourself. I've no way of knowing where it is. The starfish won't stop you. They only work and sing—they can't fight."

"Right," said Peter, looking out through the panel. "But it can't be that easy." Again, Chandt gave his hard grin.

"It wouldn't be," he said. "—But listen." He cocked his head.

The others listened also. But they heard nothing. The silence seemed to stretch out between them—and then, just as Bart was opening his mouth to speak, a faint distant ringing began to sound in their ears. It was not ringing like the ringing of a bell, but like the clear, high-pitched note of a fine wineglass when a finger is rubbed gently around its rim. And it grew.

"The call of the Heads!" said Chandt, in a low, fierce tone. "The call to assemble in the Great Hall." He flashed a glance at the rest of them. "Did you think I'd leave anything to chance, or to the planning of any of you, when all together you know less than I knew five hundred years ago? The Heads are calling all their slaves at once. The Mayflies are turning out. The Hall of the Dead is being emptied. It's time to go."

"They're going to board the ship!" It was Maria, crying out.

"Yes, woman!" Chandt whirled on her. "They will be all together in their strength—and their weakness. That's why we have a chance now—where otherwise, we'd have had none at all."

Bart took a step toward the little man, his rock-like fists clenching.

"Talk sense!" he said.

"I am." Chandt threw him a glance. "On the other side of the ship are the tubes—the tunnels for air, water, and fire. One leads to the surface, where it splits into little holes like you fell into, Bart, for ventilation. And that's the way out. One leads to the ocean, which is just a little below us here. And one leads to the old fires that the Heads kindled or called up long ago to build this island. If the air is shut off—the tubes interconnect to give us light and power, brother—we'll start to strangle swiftly on the fumes from below." And he looked at them with his burning black eyes.

"So?" said Bart. "And the Heads can't take the fumes?"

"Who knows?" Chandt shrugged. "But one thing I know—the Heads can control men and women—and animals, one by one. But when panic starts, when a normal thing goes mad with fear, not even the Head can control him. And if a panic should start in the Great Hall—"

He left the rest to their imaginations.

"You and I, brother," he said to Bart, "will go now and shut off the air—it's no task for weaklings. And you—" he turned to Peter, "you take your chance at the motor. If it should be possible, meet us in twenty minutes at the air shaft; and we'll all try to make the surface. The girl—" he turned to look at Maria.

"I'm going to help Peter," said Maria, swiftly.

"Good girl," said Peter softly; and for a moment the three of them exchanged a glance that seemed to contain a secret knowledge from which Bart was excluded. Bart frowned and opened his mouth; but before he could say anything, Chandt had grabbed him by one arm and swung him around.

"Come on. Time's short!" said the little man; and took off down the corridor at a run. Peter was already slipping out through the opened panel.

Bart turned and followed Chandt.

They went at a dead run down the corridor, through a cross-route, down two levels, and through another long corridor. Without warning, Chandt checked himself and pushed open a wall panel.

"Through, brother!" he said, breathing heavily. Bart slipped through, and found himself in a great, shadowy chamber.

Chandt followed. And he led Bart still at a run through the semidarkness, around a great, unrailed pit, from which came reeking waves of almost visible heat. Then they were beyond it. They skirted another pit from which a damp air came blowing—and then they were at the edge of a tunnel mouth that rose from the floor of the place like some dragon's maw—was open for a little ways,—and then became a hole in the wall of the chamber, a hole with a monorail slanting on up a further tunnel. Little cars waited on the monorail.

"Here!" said Chandt. He had stepped through the gap between the floor tunnel's mouth and the monorail tunnel. Bart followed and felt a perceptible wind blowing. On the far side, he found Chandt beside something that had been hidden in the darkness. It was an enormous stone disc which was pivoted to be cranked across the lower opening of the air tunnel by a gear and rachet arrangement. The disc was fully twelve feet in diameter and inches thick—and the rachet was missing.

"They close this only to clean the tube—and then others have to be closed as well," said Chandt. "Where the crank is, only the starfish know. But if any two men can move it without the crank, it's you and I, brother."

The little man crawled down under the bulge of the disc, and Bart put his shoulder against the curved edge away from the opening. They pushed together, against the hundreds of pounds of dead weight.

The disc did not move. In the silence, Bart heard their muscles creak and the labored strain of Chandt's hard breathing. He blinked away the sweat rolling into his eyes, to sting saltily there. With the stubbornness of inanimate objects, the disc held firm—and suddenly the ready fury in Bart's soul flamed up in opposition.

He snarled aloud. A black haze seemed to come between him and the rock and strength exploded into his arms. The disc stirred, it lifted—and with a sudden crash, rolled over, slamming into place across the tube.

"Well done, brother!" said Chandt, as dust settled about them. He grinned across at Bart. "It'll be only minutes now. The fumes will hit the furthest room first. Feel!" He held out his hand toward the upper opening of the tube. But Bart did not have to hold out his hand. Already he could feel the air in the chamber beginning to be sucked up past the little cars on the monorail. The current of air moving past them was steadily increasing in pressure and volume.

"Come on!" said Chandt. "This, we've earned the right to see." He ran toward a far wall, and thrust open a door. Following him, Bart discovered beyond the door, another monorail, and several of the little cars.

"Climb in," said Chandt, leading the way.

"Where to?" Bart demanded, looking down at his hard-twisted face.

"The Great Hall. Quick!"

Bart hesitated. Then, moved by that same strange stirring of the blood that had begun the night of the hurricane, and come to its first flowering when he awoke in the Hall of the Dead, he stepped into the car. A second later they were hurtling through the monorail tunnels.

It was merely moments before Chandt stopped the car at their destination. He led the way to a small red door, and opened it. They stepped out together onto a small balcony overlooking the Great Hall. Fumes bit sulphurously at their lungs and made them cough.

They looked down on chaos.

The hall was aswarm with the dying, the dead—and those who had murdered them. Who had panicked first, it was impossible to know, now. A surging, fighting mob was stampeding for the heavy main exit doors. As Bart watched, the doors swung open and the first of the mob poured out. But behind them hundreds were jammed, struggling to escape. Mayfly, Head, and man-brute, trampling and being trampled. Bart looked away, sickened.

"Come on," he said, reaching out to pull Chandt away. The little man jerked away from him and leaped up onto the railing of the balcony. Like a tightrope artist, he balanced there; and he beat his breast like an ape.

"Look!" he roared at the mob below. "Look up at who did this to you. I did it! I, Chandt! Look and see!"

He thumped his fists against his bare chest; and Bart saw, far below, a Head who looked—and lifted his hand in which something winked for a second before he was beaten down by the club-like arm of a basket-carrier.

Chandt fell backwards off the railing. As he caught him, Bart saw the little man's right hand was burnt off at the wrist. Chandt howled with rage; and fought to get away and leap over the railing. He was almost mindless with fury, or else Bart could not have handled him so easily. Bart dragged him back through the door, dumped him in the car, and pressed the small button that started it, hoping that the controls were set to take him back to the place where they had started.

As the car leaped forward, all the fight seemed to go out of Chandt. He collapsed on the floor of the car and lay there without moving. When they came to their destination, Bart had to all but lift him out of the car. He moved like a sleep-walker. But he followed Bart back to the air tube, up which now a young gale seemed to be blowing.

Bart looked around. But there was no sign of Peter and Maria.

"They aren't here!" he said urgently to Chandt.

"Wha'—" Chandt's voice was thick, like a drunken man's; and his eyes were glazed. But they cleared slowly as Bart's words penetrated. He shook his head. "No use," he said. "Knew it themselves. Go on, brother. Alone."

"No use!" Bart turned blazingly upon him. "What's no use? What'd you mean?" Chandt grinned weakly at him.

"Wreck the engine, they'd wreck themselves at the same time. No other way. Anybody but a big fool like you'd know that, brother."

Bart stared. Suddenly he spun about and sprinted back toward the corridor that would take him to the ship. He heard Chandt cry out behind him, but he paid no attention. When he arrived, panting at the ship, there was no one to be seen, human or starfish, or Head. But the ship itself was canted to one side, a great gap blown out of it. Bart wasted no time hunting an entrance, but leaped twisted girders into the hole the explosion had made.

Climbing, squirming, he burrowed his way back and up. After a short distance he no longer knew where he was, but he continued to hurl himself onward. After a while, he broke through a bent and jammed door into a corridor.

The corridor was blocked both ways, but a ladder led up. Where he was now must have been right on the edge of the explosion. If there was anyone alive, they would be above him. He threw himself at the ladder and began to climb. After a while he came to an opening and pulled himself up through it.

He found himself in the blister of the ship, facing the table of the Heads; and a fantastic sight met his eyes. Around the head of the table, in several dozen of the chairs, were lashed and propped wounded or dying Heads, starfish—even in one chair a small rhesus monkey. And, directly in front of where Bart had emerged, the All-Father, the eternal smile still on his face, was trying to drag a half-conscious Maria to one of the two empty chairs at the top of the table.

"You!" Bart snarled. In two long strides, he was on the pair, and had scooped Maria up in his arms. The Head, tottering on his tiny legs, turned his great face up to Bart and a trill issued from his lips.

"Go to Hell!" roared Bart, turning away. But he had not made more than one step when he heard a piping voice behind him.

"Bart—Bart, my son—"

Bart spun around, Maria still in his grasp. The head was tottering toward him, arms outstretched. For the first time the smile was gone from the huge features. Sorrow cut its deep lines there, and tragedy; and tears glistened in the great eyes.

"My son—come back. Come back—"

"Stand away!" snarled Bart. "I've had enough of that father business."

But the Head took another tottering step forward.

"Bart—you are my son," the piping words in English

rang on Bart's ear. "My real son—my only son. I should have told you. Sometimes it happens—as with your friend Chandt. But our sons must be put outside in the world to grow, or else they won't live."

"I don't believe it!" cried Bart, backing away in horror. The monstrous creature tottered after him.

"—Come back, son. Why do you think our minds had so little power over you? You have the strength yourself—the strength that Alokides, the Father-of-Fathers, discovered in marble-white Athens, twenty-three thousand years ago. My son—"

"Stand back!" cried Bart, backing up.

"Why do you shrink from me?" wept the Head, continuing to advance. "I was a man like you, once. My legs were straight and long, my arms had strength in them. It's the centuries, all the centuries that have made me like this! Drop that woman—come sit in one of the seats of strength, with me. Together, we can still lift what's left of this ship out of the earth, and save ourselves. We can use these little minds about the table and lift—"

"No!" shouted Bart. He had retreated clear across the end of the blister. He felt chill panes of glass press against his shoulder blades. "Even if it's true—no! You made this place for yourself—get yourself out of it!"

Holding Maria with one hand, he snatched up one of the chairs with the other; and, turning, clubbed the glass behind him with it, smashing a wide hole in the blister. Then, holding Maria, he leaped through.

"My son—" he heard the despairing cry fade behind him as he slid, Maria in his arms, down the gentle slope of the ship's side, braking with his feet as he went. It was a dozen yards before he could halt that slide.

Stopped at last, he looked around for some entry hatch to the ship. There was none in sight, but he spotted a heavy cable dangling down toward the floor below. He worked his way toward it. Seconds after his hands closed on it, he and Maria were safely on the floor.

The fumes were thick even here, now. He coughed as he ran with Maria in his arms, staggering down the corridors and back to the chamber where he had left Chandt. When he burst into it at last, he found the little man fighting for his life against five of the brutes from the Hall of the Dead.

Bart laid down Maria and staggered into the fight. But the five were down to three by the time he got there; and between himself and Chandt the other three died quickly. Without wasting time on words, Bart turned back and lifted Maria once more in his arms. She stirred against him and moaned, half-consciously.

"Just in time, brother," croaked Chandt. He pointed to something between his back and the wall. "One car left. The others blew up the tunnel." His reddened eyes searched Bart's face as he dragged the car into the blast and lifted it onto the rails. "What ails you?"

"My father," coughed Bart. "I just found out who he was."

"In!" snapped Chandt, hoarsely. He held the car as Bart laid Maria inside, and then climbed in himself. Bart turned to hold the car by the edge of the tube so that Chandt could climb in; but Chandt delayed.

"Come on!" coughed Bart. "What're you waiting for?"

"Half man—half animal!" croaked Chandt, pushing his face close to Bart. "Half man—half animal, that's what you've got to look out for."

"What're you talking about?" Bart choked, wheezing.

"I'm that mixture myself. I know. If you give it a chance, brother, the animal'll run away with you. It did for me, all these centuries down here. The man in me hated it, but the animal in me—the beast life called it. It liked being a beast—"

"Will you get in!"

Chandt pulled away from his hand that reached out after the little man.

"Not me—look!" he pointed across the chamber to the door. Just inside it Bart saw a line of tiny flames spring up, waver and start to advance toward the tube. "The Heads're dying now—and without their table and their seats, they're simply taking as many as they can along to Hell. Those flames are looking—and they've got to find some one here, or they'll follow you up the tube."

"Are you crazy?" shouted Bart. "I'm not leaving you behind."

"No time—" Chandt ducked away from him. "You think I want to live like this?" He held up his seared wrist. "I'm missing a hand now—no more for me." The flames were halfway across the floor to them now, turning about and searching like small red ferrets. "So long and good luck—one thing—!" He leaned toward the car. "Was it that Head of yours said he was your father?"

Bart nodded.

"He lied," husked Chandt. "I knew your father. Now, go!" His hand chopped down on Bart's wrist; and Bart's fingers, suddenly numbed and helpless, let go of the rim of the tube. Instantly the wind took them, and they went whirling up, up, up into nothingness. The gale roared in their ears, faster and faster. The car battered and slammed against the sides of the tube, uncontrollably. Bart gathered Maria to him, protecting her with his own body as best he could. Even over the roaring of the gale, he began to hear a distant and ominous rumble, as of millions of gallons of water pouring into the furnace of the earth itself.

—And then, the world exploded.

Bart awoke to find himself swaying in the litter of an ambulance. A bearded face bent over him.

"Coming to, are you?" inquired a voice with a French accent overlaying an English one. "How you could get that close to a volcanic eruption and still survive, beats me. But then, they say you tourists all have nine lives. I'd say it's true of both of you."

Bart turned his head weakly.

"Both of us?" he whispered. The bearded face across from him smiled and moved aside. On the other litter of the ambulance, he saw Maria. She was conscious.

And she, also, smiled at him. But her smile was by far the more beautiful.

LISTEN

Reru did not like to see humans eat. So he was waiting in the living room while Taddy and his parents finished breakfast.

"And quite right, too," boomed Taddy's father. "He has as much right to his own ways as we have to ours. Remember that, Taddy, when you grow up. The only reason humans have been successful conquerors throughout the galaxy is because they have always respected the attitudes and opinions of the people they conquered."

"Oh, Harry!" said Taddy's mother. "He's too young to understand all that."

"I am not young," said Taddy defensively, through a mouthful of breakfast food. "I'm four years old."

"See there, Celia," said Taddy's father, laughing. "He's four years old—practically grown up. But seriously, honey, he's going to be growing up into a world in which the great majority of thinking beings are Mirians like Reru. He should start to understand the natives early."

"Well, I don't know," said Taddy's mother, worriedly. "After all, he was born in space on the way here and he's a delicate child——"

"Delicate, nonsense!" boomed Taddy's father. "He comes from the toughest race in the galaxy. Look at these Mirians, chained to their planet by a symbiosis so extensive that our biologists haven't reached the end of the chain yet. Look at Reru himself, gentle, noncombative, unenergetic, a stalwart example of the Mirian race, and therefore the ideal nursemaid for our son."

"Oh, I don't have a word of complaint to say against Reru," answered Taddy's mother. "He's been just wonderful with Taddy. But I can't help it—when he cocks his head on one side and starts *listening* the way they all do, I get a little bit scared of him."

"Damn it, Celia!" said Taddy's father. "I've told you a thousand times that he's just hearing one of their cows calling that it wants to be milked."

Taddy squirmed in his chair. He knew all about the cows. They were six-legged Mirian animals that roamed around much as Reru and his mind roamed around. When they were full of milk they would start making a high, whistling sound, and Reru or some other Mirian would come along and attach his suckers to them and drink the milk. But the cows were no longer interesting. Reru was, and Taddy had finished his breakfast food.

"I'm all through," he broke in suddenly on his parents' conversation. "Can I go now? Can I?"

"I guess so," said Taddy's mother, and Taddy scrambled from the chair and ran off toward the living room.

"Don't go too far!" his mother's voice floated after him, followed by his father's deep bass.

"Let him go. Reru will bring him back all right. And, anyway, what on this planet of vegetarians could harm him?"

But Taddy had already forgotten his mother's words. For Reru was waiting for him, and Reru was fascinating.

He looked, at first glance, like a miniature copy of an old Chinese mandarin, with robe, bald head, and little wispy beard. It was only when you got to know him that you realized that there were tentacles beneath the robe, that he had never had hair on his head, and that the wispy beard hid and protected the suckers with which he milked the cows that were his source of food.

But Taddy liked him very much, and Taddy didn't think that there was anything the least bit strange about him.

"Where are we going today, Reru?" demanded Taddy, bouncing up and down before the little Mirian who was not quite twice as tall as he was.

Reru's voice was like the voice of a trilling bird, and it sang more than it spoke.

"Good morning, Taddy," it trilled. "Where would you like to go?"

"I want to go to the silver-and-green place," cried Taddy. "Can we go?"

Reru's dark little mandarin face did not smile because it did not have the muscles to do so. But the mouth opened and the Mirian gave a short wordless trill expressive of happiness and pleasure.

"Yes, small Taddy," Reru answered. "We can go." And, turning with a kind of stately dignity, he led the way out of the dwelling and into the soft yellow Mirian sunlight.

"Oh, good, good, good!" sang Taddy, skipping along beside him.

They went away from the buildings of the humans, out across the low rolling grassland of Miria, Taddy bounding and leaping in the light gravity and Reru gliding along with effortless ease. And if that dignified glide was the result of twisting tentacles hidden beneath the robe, what of it? Where older humans might have felt squeamish at the thought of the twisting ropes of white muscle, Taddy took it entirely for granted. To him, Reru was beautiful.

They went on across the grasslands. Several times Reru stopped to *listen* and each time Taddy tried to imitate him, standing with his tousled head cocked on one side and an intent expression on his baby face. After one of these stops his brow furrowed and he seemed to be thinking. The little Mirian noticed him.

"What is it, Taddy?" he trilled.

"Daddy says that when you listen, you're listening to the cows," Taddy answered. "You hear more than that, don't you, Reru?"

"Yes, Taddy," said Reru, "I am listening to all my brothers."

"Oh," said the boy, wisely. "I thought so."

As they went on, the grassland began to dip, and after a while a patch of deeper green came into sight in the distance.

"There it is," trilled the Mirian. Taddy broke into a run.

"Let's hurry, Reru," cried the boy, pulling at the mandarin robe. "Come *on*, Reru!"

Reru increased his glide and they hurried forward until they came to the silver-and-green place.

It was like a storybook land in its beauty. Little green islands and clumps of vegetation were interspersed with flashing slivers of water, so that no matter where you stood some small reflective surface caught the yellow light of the sun and sent it winking into your eyes. It looked like a toy landscape on which some giant had broken his mirror and left the bits to sparkle and shine in the daytime brightness. Reru squatted and Taddy sat down on the edge of one of the pools.

"What does it say?" asked the boy. "Tell me what it says, Reru."

The Mirian trilled again his little trill of pleasure; then composed himself. For a long time he sat silent, *listening*, while the boy squirmed, impatient, yet not daring to say anything that might interrupt or delay what Reru was about to say. Finally, the Mirian spoke.

"I can hear my brother the cow down in the tall grass at the edge of a pool. I can hear him as he moves among the grass; and I hear what he hears, his little brother, the dweller in the ground who stores up rich food for my brother the cow. And I can hear still further to all the other little brothers of the world as they go about their appointed tasks, until the air is thick with the sound of their living and their memories are my memories and their thoughts my thoughts.

"So the green-and-silver place is filled with a mighty thought, and this is what that thought says:

" 'The green-and-silver place is a coming together of waters that have traveled a long way. Our brothers in the earth have told us that there are three waters that come together here, and none flow in the light of day. Our brothers of the waters have told us that these waters run far, for they have traveled the waters.

" 'One comes from the south, but the other two from the north. And the ones from the north travel side by side for a long way, with the dark and silent earth between and around them, until they come out in a colder land to the far north of here. And, in the far north, the two come together and their source is a single river that comes from a high mountain where the winds blow over bare rock. And in that place there is a brother who lives on the stones of the hillside and watches the stars at night. He has listened along the water and heard us down here in the warm grasslands; and he dreams of the green-and-silver place as he lies at night on the bare rock, watching the stars.

" 'But the water that comes from the south comes from deep beneath the mountains of the south, from a silent lake in the heart of the rock. The lake is filled by the water that trickles down the veins of the mountains, and in it lives another brother who is blind and has never seen the yellow sun. But he lies in the dark on a rock shelf above the silent lake and listens to the grumbling of the world as it talks to itself deep in the heart of the planet. And he, too, has heard us here in the warm grasslands, under the light of the yellow sun, and he dreams of the green-and-silver place as he lies on his rock ledge listening to the grumbling of the world.' "

Reru ceased talking and opened his eyes.

"That is only one story, Taddy," he said, "of the green-and-silver place."

"More," begged the boy. "Tell me more, Reru."

And he looked up into the alien face with eyes glowing in the wonder and excitement of what he had just heard. And Reru told him more.

The morning was nearly gone when they returned to Taddy's home, and Taddy's father and mother were already seated at the table eating lunch.

"Late again, Taddy," said his mother.

"No, I'm not," Taddy retorted, sliding into his place. "You're early."

"You *are* a little early at that, Celia," said Taddy's father. "How come?"

"Oh, I promised to go over to visit Julia this afternoon," answered Taddy's mother. "Taddy! Did you wash your hands?"

"Uh-huh," said Taddy with a vigorous nod, his mouth already full. "Look!" He displayed them at arms' length.

"Where did you go today, anyway?" asked his mother.

"To the green-and-silver place," answered Taddy.

"Green-and-silver place?" She looked across at her husband. "Where's that, Harry?"

"Darned if I know," answered Taddy's father. "Where is it, son?"

Taddy pointed in a southwesterly direction.

"Out there," he said. "There's lots of little pieces of water and lots of little bushes and things."

"Why," said Harry, "he must mean the swamp."

"The swamp!" echoed Taddy's mother. "He spent the whole morning out at a swamp! Harry, you have to do something. It isn't healthy for a boy to go mooning around like these Mirians."

"Now, Celia," grumbled Taddy's father. "The Mirians put their planet before everything else. It's almost a form of worship with them. But that can't possibly affect Taddy. Humans are just too big and strong to be seduced into that dead-end sort of philosophy. Anyway, that swamp's going to be drained shortly and they're going to put a building in its place."

He leaned across the table toward Taddy.

"You'd like that better, now, wouldn't you, son?" he said. "A big new building to run around in instead of that water and muck!"

The boy's face had gone completely white and his mouth was open.

"You can get Reru to take you over and watch it go up," his father went on.

"No!" said the boy, suddenly and violently.

"Why, Taddy!" said his mother. "Is that any way to talk to your father? You apologize right now!"

"I won't," said Taddy.

"Taddy!" his father's big voice rumbled dangerously.

"I don't care!" cried Taddy. Suddenly the words were tumbling out of him all at once. "I hate you! I hate your old buildings. When I grow up I'm going to tear down that old building and put all the water and things back." He was crying now, and his words came interspersed with sobs. "I don't like you here. Nobody else likes you, either. Why don't you go 'way? Why don't you all go 'way?"

Taddy's father sat dumbfounded. But Taddy's mother got quickly up from her chair and around to Taddy's. She took him by the arm and pulled him away from the table.

"It's his nerves," she said. "I knew all this running around was bad for him." And she led him off in the direction of his room, his wails diminishing with distance and the closing of a door.

After a little while she came back.

"You see?" she said triumphantly to her husband. "Now he'll have to stay in bed all afternoon and I can't go over to Julia's because I'll have to stay here and watch him."

But Taddy's father had recovered his composure.

"Nonsense, Celia," he said. "It's just a case of nerves, like you said. Every boy has them one time or another. We can let the young pioneer kick up a few fusses without worrying too much about it. It won't hurt his character any. Now, you go on over to Julia's as you planned. He'll stay put."

"Well," said Taddy's mother slowly, wanting to be convinced, "if you say so. . . . I don't suppose it would do any harm to run over for a few minutes. . . ."

Up in his room, Taddy's sobs diminished until they no longer racked his small body. He got up and went to the window and looked out at the rolling grasslands.

"I will, too," he said to himself, "I will too tear down all their old buildings when I grow up."

And, immediately as he said it, a strange thing seemed to happen. A wave of peace flooded over him and he stopped crying. It was as if all the brothers that Reru had been talking about were here in the room and just outside his window, comforting him. He felt them all around him; and at the same time he sensed that they were all waiting for him to say something, waiting and listening. For just a few seconds he could feel all of Miria listening to him, to Taddy.

And he knew what they wanted, for he stretched both his arms out the window to them, a love filling his heart like no love he had ever felt before, as he spoke the two words they were waiting to hear.

"I promise," said Taddy.

SOLDIER, ASK NOT

Soldier, ask not—now or ever—
Where to war your banners go . . .

I

As I got off the spaceliner on St. Marie, the little breeze from the higher pressure of the ship's atmosphere at my back was like a hand from the darkness behind me, shoving me into the dark day and the rain. My Newsman's cloak covered me. The wet chill of the day wrapped around me but did not enter me. I was like the naked claymore of my own early ancestors, wrapped and hidden in the plaid—sharpened on a stone—and carried now at last to the meeting for which it had been guarded over three years of waiting.

A meeting in the cold rain of spring. I felt it, cold as old blood on my hands and tasteless on my lips. Above, the sky was low and clouds flowing to the east. The rain fell steadily.

The sound of it was like a rolling of drums as I went down the outside landing stairs, the multitude of raindrops sounding their own end against the unyielding concrete all around. The concrete stretched far from the ship in every direction, hiding the earth, as bare and clean as the last page of an account book before the final entry. At its far edge, the spaceport terminal stood like a single gravestone. The curtains of falling water between it and me

117

thinned and thickened like the smoke of battle, but could not hide it entirely from my sight.

It was the same rain that falls in all places and on all worlds. It had fallen like this on Athens of Old Earth, when I was only a boy, on the dark, unhappy house of the uncle who brought me up after my parents' death, on the ruins of the Parthenon as I saw it from my bedroom window.

I listened to it now as I went down the landing stairs, drumming on the great ship behind me which had shifted me free between the stars—from Old Earth to this second smallest of the worlds, this small terraformed planet under the Procyon suns—and drumming hollowly upon the Credentials case sliding down the conveyor belt beside me. That case now meant nothing to me—neither my papers or the Credentials of Impartiality I had carried six years and worked so long to earn. Now I thought less of these than of the name of the man I should find dispatching groundcars at the edge of the field. If, that was, he was actually the man my Earth informants had named to me. And if they had not lied . . .

". . . Your luggage, sir?"

I woke from my thoughts and the rain. I had reached the concrete. The debarking officer smiled at me. He was older than I, though he looked younger. As he smiled some beads of moisture broke and spilled like tears from the brown visor-edge of his cap onto the tally sheet he held.

"Send it to the Friendly compound," I said. "I'll take the Credentials case."

I took it up from the conveyor belt and turned to walk off. The man standing in a dispatcher's uniform by the first groundcar in line did fit the description.

"Name, sir?" he said. "Business on St. Marie?"

If he had been described to me, I must have been described to him. But I was prepared to humor him.

"Tam Olyn," I said. "Old Earth resident and Interworld News Network representative. I'm here to cover the Friendly-Exotic conflict." I opened my case and gave him my papers.

"Fine, Mr. Olyn." He handed them back to me, damp from the rain. He turned away to open the door of the car beside him and set the automatic pilot. "Follow the highway straight to Joseph's Town. Put it on automatic at the city limits and the car'll take you to the Friendly compound."

"All right," I said. "Just a minute."

He turned back. He had a young, good-looking face with a little mustache and he looked at me with a bright blankness. "Sir?"

"Help me get in the car."

"Oh, I'm sorry, sir." He came quickly over to me. "I didn't realize your leg—"

"Damp stiffens it," I said. He adjusted the seat and I got my left leg in behind the steering column. He started to turn away.

"Wait a minute," I said again. I was out of patience. "You're Walter Imera, aren't you?"

"Yes, sir," he said softly.

"Look at me," I said. "You've got some information for me, haven't you?"

He turned slowly back to face me. His face was still blank.

"No, sir."

I waited a long moment, looking at him.

"All right," I said then, reaching for the car door. "I guess you know I'll get the information anyway. And they'll believe you told me."

His little mustache began to look like it was painted on.

"Wait—" he said.

"What for?"

"Look," he said, "you've got to understand. Information like that's not part of your news, is it? I've got a family—"

"And I haven't," I said. I felt nothing for him.

"But you don't understand. They'd kill me. That's the sort of organization the Blue Front is now, here on St. Marie. What d'you want to know about them for? I didn't understand you meant—"

"All right," I said. I reached for the car door.

"Wait—" He held out a hand to me in the rain. "How do I know you can make them leave me alone if I tell you?"

"They may be back in power here some day," I said. "Not even outlawed political groups want to antagonize the Interplanetary News Network." I started to close the door once more.

"All right—" he said quickly. "All right. You go to New San Marcos. The Wallace Street Jewelers there. It's just beyond Joseph's Town, where the Friendly compound is you're going to." He licked his lips. "You'll tell them about me?"

"I'll tell them." I looked at him. Above the edge of the blue uniform collar on the right side of his neck I could see an inch or two of fine silver chain, bright against winter-pale skin. The crucifix attached to it would be down under his shirt. "The Friendly soldiers have been here two years now. How do people like them?"

He grinned a little. His color was coming back.

"Oh, like anybody," he said. "You just have to understand them. They've got their own ways."

I felt the ache in my stiff leg where the doctors on New Earth had taken the needle from the spring rifle out of it three years before.

"Yes, they have," I said. "Shut the door."

He shut it. I drove off.

There was a St. Christopher's medal on the car's instrument panel. One of the Friendly soldiers would have ripped it off and thrown it away, or refused the car. And so it gave me a particular pleasure to leave it where it was, though it meant no more to me than it would to him. It was not just because of Dave, my brother-in-law, and the other prisoners they had shot down on New Earth. It was simply because there are some duties that have a small element of pleasure. After the illusions of childhood are gone and there is nothing left but duties, such pleasures are welcome. Fanatics, when all is said and done, are no worse than mad dogs.

But mad dogs have to be destroyed; it is a simple common sense.

And you return to common sense after a while in life, inevitably. When the wild dreams of justice and progress are all dead and buried, when the painful beatings of feeling inside you are finally stilled, then it becomes best to be still, unliving, and unyielding as—the blade of a sword sharpened on a stone. The rain through which such a blade is carried to its using does not stain it, any more than the blood in which it is bathed at last. Rain and blood are alike to sharpened iron.

I drove for half an hour past wooded hills and plowed meadows. The furrows of the fields were black in the rain. I thought it a kinder black than some other shades I had seen; and at last I reached the outskirts of Joseph's Town.

The autopilot of the car threaded me through a small, neat, typical St. Marie City of about a hundred thousand people. We came out on the far side into a cleared area, beyond which lifted the massive, sloping concrete walls of a military compound.

A Friendly non-com stopped my car at the gate with his black spring rifle, and opened the car door at my left.

"Thee have business here?"

His voice was harsh and high in his nose. The cloth tabs of a groupman edged his collar. Above them his forty-year-old face was lean and graven with lines. Both face and hands, the only uncovered parts of him, looked unnaturally white against the black cloth and rifle.

I opened the case beside me and handed him my papers.

"My Credentials," I said. "I'm here to see your acting Commander of Expeditionary Forces, Commandant Jamethon Black."

"Move over, then," he said nasally. "I must drive thee."

I moved.

He got in and took the stick. We drove through the gate and turned down an approach alley. I could see an interior square at the alley's far end. The close concrete walls on either side of us echoed the sound of our passage as we went. I heard drill commands growing louder as we approached the square. When we rolled out into it, soldiers were drawn up in ranks for their midday service, in the rain.

The groupman left me and went in the entrance of what seemed to be an office inset in the wall on one side of the square. I looked over the soldiers standing in formation. They stood at present-arms, their position of worship under field conditions; and as I watched, the officer standing facing them, with his back to a wall, led them into the words of their Battle Hymn.

Soldier, ask not—now or ever,
Where to war your banners go.
Anarch's legions, all surround us.
Strike! And do not count the blow!

I sat trying not to listen. There was no musical accompaniment, no religious furniture or symbols except the thin shape of the cross whitewashed on the gray wall behind the officer. The massed male voices rose and fell slowly in the dark, sad hymn that promised them only pain, and suffering, and sorrow. At last, the final line mourned its harsh prayer for a battle death, and they ordered arms.

A groupman dismissed the ranks as the officer walked back past my car without looking at me, and passed in through the entrance where my non-commissioned guide had disappeared. As he passed I saw the officer was young.

A moment later the guide came for me. Limping a little on my stiffened leg, I followed him to an inner room with the lights on above a single desk. The young officer rose and nodded as the door closed behind me. He wore the faded tabs of a commandant on his uniform lapels.

As I handed my credentials across the desk to him, the glare of the light over the desk came full in my eyes, blinding me. I stepped back and blinked at his blurred face. As it came back into focus I saw it for a moment as if it was older, harsher, twisted and engraved with the lines of years of fanaticism.

Then my eyes refocused completely, and I saw him as he actually was. Dark-faced, but thin with the thinness of youth rather than that of self-starvation. He was not the face burned in my memory. His features were regular to the point of being handsome, his eyes tired and shadowed; and I saw the straight, weary line of his mouth above the still, self-controlled stiffness of his body, smaller and slighter than mine.

He held the credentials without looking at them. His mouth quirked a little, dryly and wearily, at the corners. "And no doubt, Mr. Olyn," he said, "you've got another pocket filled with authorities from the Exotic Worlds to interview the mercenary soldiers and officers they've hired from the Dorsai and a dozen other worlds to oppose God's Chosen in War?"

I smiled. Because it was good to find him as strong as that, to add to my pleasure of breaking him.

II

I looked across the ten feet or so of distance that separated us. The Friendly non-com who had killed the prisoners on New Earth had also spoken of God's Chosen.

"If you'll look under the papers directed to you," I said, "you'll find them. The News Network and its people are impartial. We don't take sides."

"Right," said the dark young face opposing me, "takes sides."

"Yes, Commandant," I said. "That's right. Only sometimes it's a matter of debate where Right is. You and your troops here now are invaders on the world of a planetary system your ancestors never colonized. And opposing you are mercenary troops hired by two worlds that not only belong under the Procyon suns but have a commitment to defend the smaller worlds of their system—of which St. Marie is one. I'm not sure right *is* on your side."

He shook his head slightly and said, "We expect small understanding from those not Chosen." He transferred his gaze from me to the papers in his hand.

"Mind if I sit down?" I said. "I've got a bad leg."

"By all means." He nodded to a chair beside his desk and, as I sat down, seated himself. I looked across the papers on the desk before him and saw, standing to one side, the solidograph of one of the windowless high-peaked churches the Friendlies build. It was a legitimate token for him to own—but there just happened to be three people, an older man and woman and a young girl of about fourteen, in the foreground of the image. All three of them bore a family resemblance to Jamethon Black. Glancing up from my credentials he saw me looking at them; and his gaze shifted momentarily to the graph and away again, as if he would protect it.

"I'm required, I see," he said, drawing my eyes back to him, "to provide you with cooperation and facilities. We'll find quarters for you here. Do you need a car and driver?"

"Thanks," I said. "That commercial car outside will do. And I'll manage my own driving."

"As you like." He detached the papers directed to him, passed the rest back to me and leaned toward a grill in his desktop. "Groupman."

"Sir," the grill answered promptly.

"Quarters for a single male civilian. Parking assignment for a civilian vehicle, personnel."

"Sir."

The voice from the grill clicked off. Jamethon Black

looked across his desk at me. I got the idea he was waiting for my departure.

"Commandant," I said, putting my credentials back in their case, "two years ago your Elders of the United Churches on Harmony and Association found the planetary government of St. Marie in default of certain disputed balances of credit, so they sent an expedition in here to occupy and enforce payment. Of that expedition, how much in the way of men and equipment do you have left?"

"That, Mr. Olyn," he said, "is restricted military information."

"However—" and I closed the case "—you, with the regular rank of commandant, are acting Commander of Forces for the remnants of your expedition. That position calls for someone about five ranks higher than you. Do you expect such an officer to arrive and take charge?"

"I'm afraid you'd have to ask that question of Headquarters on Harmony, Mr. Olyn."

"Do you expect reinforcements of personnel and more supplies?"

"If I did—" his voice was level "—I would have to consider that restricted information, too."

"You know that it's been pretty widely mentioned that your General Staff on Harmony has decided that this expedition to St. Marie is a lost cause? But that to avoid loss of face they prefer you here to be cut up, instead of withdrawing you and your men."

"I see," he said.

"You wouldn't care to comment?"

His dark, young, expressionless face did not change. "Not in the case of rumors, Mr. Olyn."

"One last question then. Do you plan to retreat westward, or surrender when the spring offensive of the Exotic mercenary forces begins to move against you?"

"The Chosen in War never retreat," he said. "Neither do they abandon, or suffer abandonment by, their Brothers in the Lord." He stood up. "I have work I must get back to, Mr. Olyn."

I stood up, too. I was taller than he was, older, and heavier-boned. It was only his almost unnatural composure that enabled him to maintain his appearance of being my equal or better.

"I'll talk to you later, perhaps, when you've got more time," I said.

"Certainly." I heard the office door open behind me. "Groupman," he said, speaking past me, "take care of Mr. Olyn."

The groupman he had turned me over to found me a small concrete cubicle with a single high window, a camp bed and a uniform cabinet. He left me for a moment and returned with a signed pass.

"Thanks," I said as I took it. "Where do I find the Headquarters of the Exotic Forces?"

"Our latest advice, sir," he said, "is that they're ninety kilometers east of here. New San Marcos." He was my height, but, like most of them, half a dozen years younger than I, with an innocence that contrasted with the strange air of control they all had.

"San Marcos." I looked at him. "I suppose you enlisted men know your General Headquarters on Harmony has decided against wasting replacements for you?"

"No, sir," he said. I might have commented on the rain for all the reaction he showed. Even these boys were still strong and unbroken. "Is there something else?"

"No," I said. "Thanks."

He went out. And I went out, to get in my car and head ninety kilometers east through the same sort of country to New San Marcos. I reached it in about three-quarters of an hour. But I did not go directly to find the Exotic Field Headquarters. I had other fish to fry.

These took me to the Wallace Street Jewelers. There, three shallow steps down from street level and an opaqued door let me in to a long, dim-lighted room filled with glass cases. There was a small elderly man at the back of the store behind the final case and I saw him eyeing my correspondent's cloak and badge as I got closer.

"Sir?" he said, as I stopped across the case from him. He raised gray, narrow old eyes in a strangely smooth face to look at me.

"I think you know what I represent," I said. "All worlds know the News Services. We're not concerned with local politics."

"Sir?"

"You'll find out how I learned your address anyway," I

kept on smiling at him. "So I'll tell you it was from a spaceport autodispatcher named Imera. I promised him protection for telling me. We'd appreciate it if he remains well and whole."

"I'm afraid—" He put his hands on the glass top of the case. They were veined with the years. "You wanted to buy something?"

"I'm willing to pay in good will," I said, "for information."

His hands slid off the countertop.

"Sir." He sighed a little. "I'm afraid you're in the wrong store."

"I'm sure I am," I said. "But your store'll have to do. We'll pretend it's the right store and I'm talking to someone who's a member of the Blue Front."

He shook his head slowly and stepped back from the case.

"The Blue Front is illegal," he said. "Good-by, sir."

"In a moment. I've got a few things to say first."

"Then I'm sorry." He retreated toward some drapes covering a doorway. "I can't listen. No one will come into this room with you, sir, as long as you talk like that."

He slipped through the drapes and was gone. I looked around the long, empty room.

"Well," I said, a little more loudly, "I guess I'll have to speak to the walls. I'm sure the walls can hear me."

I paused. There was no sound.

"All right," I said. "I'm a correspondent. All I'm interested in is information. Our assessment of the military situation here on St. Marie—" and here I told the truth— "shows the Friendly Expeditionary Forces abandoned by their home headquarters and certain to be overrun by the Exotic Forces as soon as the ground dries enough for heavy equipment to move."

There was still no answer, but the back of my neck knew they were listening, and watching me.

"As a result," I went on—and here I lied, though they would have no way of knowing—"we consider it inevitable that the Friendly Command here will have got in contact with the Blue Front. Assassination of enemy commanders is expressly in violation of the Mercenaries' Code and the Articles of Civilized Warfare—but civilians could do what soldiers could not."

Still there was no sound or movement beyond the drapes.

"A news representative," I said, "carries Credentials of Impartiality. You know how highly these are held. I only want to ask a few questions. And the answers will be kept confidential . . ."

For a last time I waited, and there was still no answer. I turned and went up the long room and out. It was not until I was well out on to the street that I let the feeling of triumph within spread out and warm me.

They would take the bait. People of their sort always did. I found my car and drove to Exotic Headquarters.

These were outside the town. There a mercenary commandant named Janol Marat took me in charge. He conducted me to the bubble structure of their HQ building. There was a feel of purpose, there, a sure and cheerful air of activity. They were well armed, well trained. After the Friendlies it jumped at me. I said so to Janol.

"We've got a Dorsai Commander and we outnumber the opposition." He grinned at me. He had a deeply tanned, long face that went into deep creases as his lips curved up. "That makes everybody pretty optimistic. Besides, our commander gets promoted if he wins. Back to the Exotics and staff rank—out of field combat for good. It's good business for us to win."

I laughed and he laughed.

"Tell me more, though," I said. "I want reasons I can use in the stories I send back to News Network."

"Well—" he answered the snappy salute of a passing groupman, a Cassidan, by the look of him—"I guess you might mention the usual—the fact our Exotic employers don't permit themselves to use violence and consequently they're always rather generous than otherwise when it comes to paying for men and equipment. And the Out-Bond—that's the Exotic Ambassador to St. Marie, you know— "

"I know."

"He replaced the former OutBond here three years ago. Anyway, he's something special, even for someone from Mara or Kultis. He's an expert in ontogenic calculations. If that means much to you. It's all over my head." Janol pointed. "Here's the Field Commander's office. He's Kensie Graeme."

"Graeme?" I said, frowning. I had spent a day at the

Hague looking up Kensie Graeme before I came, but I wanted Janol's reactions to him. "Sounds familiar." We approached the office building. "Graeme . . ."

"You're probably thinking of another member of the same family." Janol took the bait. "Donal Graeme. A nephew. The one who pulled that wild stunt not long ago, attacking Newton with just a handful of Freiland ships. Kensie is Donal's uncle. Not as spectacular as the young Graeme, but I'll bet you'll like him better than you would the nephew. Kensie's got two men's likeableness." He looked at me, grinning slightly again.

"That supposed to mean something special?" I said.

"That's right," said Janol. "His own likeableness and his twin brother's, too. Meet Ian Graeme sometime when you're in Blauvain. That's where the Exotic embassy is, east of here. Ian's a dark man."

We walked into the office.

"I can't get used," I said, "to how so many Dorsai seem related."

"Neither can I. Actually, I guess it's because there really aren't so many of them. The Dorsai's a small world, and those that live more than a few years—" Janol stopped by a commandant sitting at a desk. "Can we see the Old Man, Hari? This is a News Network man."

"Why, I guess so." The other looked at his desk signal board. "The OutBond's with him, but he's just leaving now. Go on in."

Janol led me between the desks. A door at the back of the room opened before we reached it and a calm-faced man of middle age wearing a blue robe and close-cropped white hair came out. He looked strange but not ridiculous—particularly after you met his odd, hazel-colored eyes.

He was an Exotic.

I knew of Padma, as I knew the Exotics. I had seen them on their own home worlds of Mara and Kultis. A people committed to non-violence, mystics but very practical mystics, masters of what were known as the "strange sciences"—a dozen wizardic step-children of early psychology, sociology and the humanistic fields of research.

"Sir," said Janol to Padma, "this is—"

"Tam Olyn. I know," said Padma softly. He smiled up at me, and those eyes of his seemed to catch light for a moment and blind me. "I was sorry to learn about your brother-in-law, Tam."

I went quite cool all over. I had been ready to walk on, but now I stood stock still and looked at him.

"My brother-in-law?" I said.

"The young man who died near Castlemain, on New Earth."

"Oh, yes," I said, between stiff lips. "I'm surprised that you'd know."

"I know because of you, Tam." Once more the hazel eyes of Padma seemed to catch light. "We have a science called ontogenics, by which we calculate the probabilities of human actions in present and future situations. You've been an important factor in those calculations for some time." He smiled. "That's why I was expecting to meet you here, and now. We've calculated you into our present situation here on St. Marie, Tam."

"Have you?" I said. "Have you? That's interesting."

"I thought it would be," said Padma softly. "To you, especially. Someone like a newsman, like yourself, would find it interesting."

"It is," I said. "It sounds like you know more than I do about what I'm going to be doing here."

"We've got calculations," said Padma in his soft voice, "to that effect. Come see me in Blauvain, Tam; and I'll show you."

"I'll do that," I said.

"You'll be very welcome." Padma inclined his head. His blue robe whispered on the floor as he turned, and went out of the room.

"This way," said Janol, touching my elbow. I started as if I had just wakened from a deep sleep. "The commander's in here."

I followed him automatically into a further office. The individual I had come to see stood up as we came through the door. He was a great, lean man in field uniform, with a heavy-boned, but open, smiling face under black, slightly curly hair. A sort of golden warmth of personality—a strange thing in a Dorsai—seemed to flow out from him as he rose to meet me and his long-fingered, powerful hand swallowed mine in a handshake.

"Come on in," he said. "Let me fix you up with a drink. Janol," he added to my mercenary commandant from New

Earth, "no need for you to stick around. Go on to chow. And tell the rest of them in the outer office to knock off."

Janol saluted and went. I sat down as Graeme turned to a small bar cabinet behind his desk. And for the first time in three years, under the magic of the unusual fighting man opposite me, a little peace came into my soul. With someone like this on my side, I could not lose.

III

"Credentials?" asked Graeme, as soon as we were settled with drinks of Dorsai whisky—which is a fine whisky— in our hands.

I passed my papers over. He glanced through them, picking out the letters from Sayona, the Bond of Kultis, to *"Commander—St. Marie Field Forces."* He looked these over and put them aside. He handed me back the credentials folder.

"You stopped at Joseph's Town first?" he said.

I nodded. I saw him looking at my face, and his own sobered.

"You don't like the Friendlies," he said.

His words took my breath away. I had come prepared to fence for an opening to tell him. It was too sudden. I looked away.

I did not dare answer right away. I could not. There was either too much or too little to say if I let it come out without thinking. Then I got a grip on myself.

"If I do anything at all with the rest of my life," I said, slowly, "it'll be to do everything in my power to remove the Friendlies and all they stand for from the community of civilized human beings."

I looked back up at him. He was sitting with one massive elbow on his desktop, watching me.

"That's a pretty harsh point of view, isn't it?"

"No harsher than theirs."

"Do you think so?" he said seriously. "I wouldn't say so."

"I thought," I said, "you were the one who was fighting them."

"Why, yes." He smiled a little. "But we're soldiers on both sides."

"I don't think they think that way."

He shook his head a little.

"What makes you say that?" he said.

"I've seen them," I answered. "I got caught up front in the lines on Castlemain on New Earth, three years ago." I tapped my stiff knee. "I got shot and I couldn't navigate. The Cassidans around me began to retreat—they were mercenaries, and the troops opposing them were Friendlies hired out as mercenaries."

I stopped and took a drink of the whisky. When I took the glass away, Graeme had not moved. He sat as if waiting.

"There was a young Cassidan, a buck soldier," I said. "I was doing a series on the campaign from an individual point of view. I'd picked him for my individual. It was a natural choice. You see—" I drank again, and emptied the glass—"my younger sister went out on contract as an accountant to Cassida two years before that, and she'd married him. He was my brother-in-law."

Graeme took the glass from my hand and silently replenished it.

"He wasn't actually a military man," I said. "He was studying shift mechanics and he had about three years to go. But he stood low on one of the competitive examinations at a time when Cassida owed a contractual balance of troops to New Earth." I took a deep breath. "Well, to make a long story short, he ended up on New Earth in this same campaign I was covering. Because of the series I was writing, he was assigned to me. We both thought it was a good deal for him, that he'd be safer that way."

I drank some more of the whisky.

"But," I said, "you know, there's always a better story a little deeper in the combat zone. We got caught up front one day when the New Earth troops were retreating. I picked up a needle through the kneecap. The Friendly armor was moving up and things were getting hot. The soldiers around us took off toward the rear in a hurry, but Dave tried to carry me, because he thought the Friendly armor would fry me before they had time to notice I was a non-combatant. Well," I took another deep breath, "the Friendly ground troops caught us. They took us to a sort of clearing where they had a lot of prisoners and kept us there for a while. Then a Groupman—one of their fanatic types, a tall, starved-looking soldier about my age—came up with orders they were to reform for a fresh attack."

I stopped and took another drink. But I could not taste it.

"That meant they couldn't spare men to guard the prisoners. They'd have to turn them loose back of the Friendly lines. The Groupman said that wouldn't work. They'd have to make sure the prisoners couldn't endanger them."

Graeme was still watching me.

"I didn't understand. I didn't even catch on when the other Friendlies—none of them were non-coms like the Groupman—objected." I put my glass on the desk beside me and stared at the wall of the office, seeing it all over again, as plainly as if I looked through a window at it. "I remember how the Groupman pulled himself up straight. I saw his eyes. As if he'd been insulted by the others, objecting.

" *'Are they Chosen of God?'* he shouted at them. *'Are they of the Chosen?'* "

I looked across at Kensie Graeme and saw him still motionless, still watching me, his own glass small in one big hand.

"You understand?" I said to him. "As if because the prisoners weren't Friendlies, they weren't quite human. As if they were some lower order it was all right to kill." I shook, suddenly. "And he did it! I sat there against a tree, safe because of my News Correspondent's uniform and watched him shoot them down. All of them. I sat there and looked at Dave, and he looked at me, sitting there, as the Groupman shot him!"

I quit all at once. I hadn't meant to have it all come out like that. It was just that I'd been able to tell no one who would understand how helpless I had been. But something about Graeme had given me the idea he would understand.

"Yes," he said after a moment, and took and filled my glass again. "That sort of thing's very bad. Was the Groupman found and tried under the Mercenaries Code?"

"After it was too late, yes."

He nodded and looked past me at the wall. "They aren't all like that, of course."

"There's enough to give them a reputation for it."

"Unfortunately, yes. Well"—he smiled slightly at me—"we'll try and keep that sort of thing out of this campaign."

"Tell me something," I said, putting my glass down. "Does that sort of thing—as you put it—ever happen to the Friendlies, themselves?"

Something took place then in the atmosphere of the room. There was a little pause before he answered. I felt my heart beat slowly, three times, as I waited for him to speak.

He said at last, "No, it doesn't."

"Why not?" I said.

The feeling in the room became stronger. And I realized I had gone too fast. I had been sitting talking to him as a man and forgetting what else he was. Now I began to forget that he was a man and become conscious of him as a Dorsai—an individual as human as I was, but trained all his life, and bred down the generations to a difference. He did not move or change the tone of his voice, or any such thing; but somehow he seemed to move off some distance from me, up into a higher, colder, stonier land into which I could venture only at my peril.

I remembered what was said about his people from that small, cold stony-mountained world: that if the Dorsai chose to withdraw their fighting men from the services of all the other worlds, and challenge those other worlds, not the combined might of the rest of civilization could stand against them. I had never really believed that before. I had never even really thought much about it. But sitting there just then, becuase of what was happening in the room, suddenly it became real to me. I could feel the knowledge, cold as a wind blowing on me off a glacier, that it was true; and then he answered my question.

"Because," said Kensie Graeme, "anything like that is specifically prohibited by Article Two of the Mercenaries' Code."

Then he broke out abruptly into a smile and what I had just felt in the room withdrew. I breathed again.

"Well," he said, putting his glass down empty on the desk, "how about joining us in the Officers' Mess for something to eat?"

I had dinner with them and the meal was very pleasant.

They wanted to put me up for the night—but I could feel myself being pulled back to that cold, joyless compound near Joseph's Town, where all that waited for me was a sort of cold and bitter satisfaction at being among my enemies.

I went back.

It was about 11 PM when I drove through the gate of the compound and parked, just as a figure came out of the entrance to Jamethon's headquarters. The square was dim-lighted with only a few spotlights about the walls, their light lost in the rain-wet pavement. For a moment I did not recognize the figure—and then I saw it was Jamethon.

He would have passed by me at some little distance, but I got out of my car and went to meet him. He stopped when I stepped in front of him.

"Mr. Olyn," he said evenly. In the darkness I could not make out the expression of his face.

"I've got a question to ask," I said, smiling in the darkness.

"It's late for questions."

"This won't take long." I strained to catch the look on his face, but it was all in shadow. "I've been visiting the Exotic camp. Their commander's a Dorsai. I suppose you know that?"

"Yes." I could barely see the movement of his lips.

"We got to talking. A question came up and I thought I'd ask you, Commandant. Do you ever order your men to kill prisoners?"

An odd, short silence came between us. Then he answered.

"The killing or abuse of prisoners of war," he said without emotion, "is forbidden by Article Two of the Mercenaries' Code."

"But you aren't Mercenaries here, are you? You're native troops in service to your own True Church and Elders."

"Mr. Olyn," he said, while I still strained without success to make out the expression of his shadowed face—and it seemed that the words came slowly, though the tone of the voice that spoke them remained as calm as ever. "My Lord has set me to be His servant and a leader among men of war. In neither of those tasks will I fail Him."

And with that he turned, his face still shadowed and hidden from me, and passed around me and went on.

*   *   *

Alone, I went back inside to my quarters, undressed and lay down on the hard and narrow bed they had given me. The rain outside had stopped at last. Through my open, unglazed window I could see a few stars showing.

I lay there getting ready to sleep and making mental notes on what I would need to do tomorrow. The meeting with Padma the OutBond had jolted me sharply. I took his so-called calculations of human actions with reservation—but I had been shaken to learn of them. I would have to find out more about how much his science of ontogenics knew and could predict. If necessary, from Padma himself. But I would start first with ordinary reference sources.

No one, I thought, would ordinarily entertain the fantastic thought that one man like myself could destroy a culture involving the populations of two worlds. No one, except perhaps a Padma. What I knew, he with his calculations might have discovered. And that was that the Friendly worlds of Harmony and Association were facing a decision that would mean life or death to their way of living. A very small thing could tip the scales they weighed on.

For there was a new wind blowing between the stars.

Four hundred years before we had all been men of Earth—Old Earth, the mother planet which was my native soil. One people.

Then, with the movement out to new worlds, the human race had "splintered," to use an Exotic term. Every small social fragment and psychological type had drawn apart by itself, and joined others like it and progressed toward specialized types. Until we had half a dozen fragments of human types—the warrior on the Dorsai, the philosopher on the Exotic worlds, the hard scientist on Newton, Cassida and Venus, and so forth . . .

Isolation had bred specific types. Then a growing intercommunication between the younger worlds, now established, and an ever-increasing rate of technological advance had forced specialization. The trade between the worlds was the trade of skilled minds. Generals from the Dorsai were worth their exchange rate in psychiatrists from the Exotics. Communications men like myself from Old Earth bought spaceship designers from Cassida. And so it had been for the last hundred years.

But now the worlds were drifting together. Economics was fusing the race into one whole, again. And the struggle on each world was to gain the advantages of that fusion while holding on to as much as possible of their own ways.

Compromise was necessary—and the harsh, stiff-necked Friendly religion forbade compromise and had made many enemies. Already public opinion moved against the Friendlies on other worlds. Discredit them, smear them publicly here in this campaign, and they would not be able to hire out their soldiers. They would lose the balance of trade they needed to hire the skilled specialists trained by the special facilities of other worlds, and which they needed to keep their own two poor-in-natural-resources worlds alive. They would die.

As young Dave had died. Slowly. In the dark.

. . . In the darkness now, as I thought of it, it rose up before me once again. It had been only noon when we were taken prisoner, but by the time the Groupman came with his orders for our guards to move up, the sun was almost down.

After they left, after it was all over and I was left alone, I crawled to the bodies in the clearing. And I found Dave among them; and he was not quite gone.

He was wounded in the body and I could not stop the bleeding.

It would not have helped if I had, they told me afterwards. But then it seemed that it would have. So I tried. But finally I gave up and by that time it was quite dark. I only held him and did not know he was dead until he began to grow cold. And then was when I had begun to change into what my uncle had always tried to make me. I felt myself die inside. Dave and my sister were to have been my family, the only family I had ever had hopes of keeping. Instead, I could only sit there in the darkness, holding him and hearing the blood from his red-soaked clothing, falling drop by drop, slowly on the dead variform oak leaves beneath us.

I lay there now in the Friendly compound, not able to sleep and remembering. And after a while I heard the soldiers marching, forming in the square for midnight service.

I lay on my back, listening to them. Their marching feet

stopped at last. The single window of my room was over my bed—high in the wall against which the left side of my cot was set. It was unglazed and the night air with its sounds came freely through it along with the dim light from the square which painted a pale rectangle on the opposite wall of my room. I lay watching that rectangle and listening to the service outside; and I heard the duty officer lead them in a prayer for worthiness. After that they sang their battle hymn again, and I lay hearing it, this time, all the way through.

> Soldier, ask not—now, or ever,
> Where to war your banners go.
> Anarch's legions all surround us.
> Strike—and do not count the blow.

> Glory, honor—praise and profit,
> Are but toys of tinsel worth.
> Render up your work, unasking,
> Leave the human clay to earth.

> Blood and sorrow—pain unending,
> Are the portion of us all.
> Grasp the naked sword, opposing,
> Gladly in the battle fall.

> So shall we, anointed soldiers,
> Stand at last before the Throne.
> Baptized in our wounds, red-flowing,
> Sealed unto our Lord—alone!

After that they dispersed to cots no different from mine. I lay there listening to the silence in the square and the measured dripping of a rain-spout outside by my window, its slow drops falling after the rain, one by one, uncounted in the darkness.

IV

After the day I landed, there was no more rain. Day by day the fields dried. Soon they would be firm underneath the weight of heavy surface-war equipment, and everyone knew that then the Exotic spring offensive would get under way. Meanwhile both Exotic and Friendly troops were in training.

During the next few weeks, I was busy about my newswork. Mostly feature and small stories on the soldiers and the native people. I had dispatches to send and I sent them faithfully. A correspondent is only as good as his contacts; I made contacts everywhere but among the Friendly troops. These remained aloof, though I talked to many of them. They refused to show fear or doubt.

I had heard these Friendly soldiers were generally undertrained because the suicidal tactics of their officers kept their ranks always filled with green replacements. But the ones here were the remnants of an Expeditionary Force six times their present numbers. They were all veterans, though most of them were in their teens. Only here and there, among the non-coms, and more often among the commissioned officers, I saw the prototype of the non-com who had ordered the prisoners shot on New Earth. Here, the men of this type looked like rabid, gray wolves mixed among polite, well-schooled young dogs just out of puppyhood.

It was a temptation to think that they alone were what I had set out to destroy.

To fight that temptation I told myself that Alexander the Great had led expeditions against the hill tribes and ruled in Pella, capital of Macedonia, and ordered men put to death when he was sixteen. But still the Friendly soldiers looked young to me. I could not help contrasting them with the adult, experienced mercenaries in Kensie Graeme's forces. For the Exotics, in obedience to their principles, would hire no drafted troops or soldiers who were not in uniform of their own free will.

Meanwhile I had heard no word from the Blue Front. But by the time two weeks had gone, I had my own connections in New San Marcos, and at the beginning of the third week one of these brought me word that the jewelers shop in Wallace Street there had closed its door—had pulled its blinds and emptied the long room of stock and fixtures, and moved or gone out of business. That was all I needed to know.

For the next few days, I stayed in the vicinity of Jamethon Black himself, and by the end of the week my watching him paid off.

At ten o'clock that Friday night I was up on a catwalk just above my quarters and under the sentry-walk of the walls, watching as three civilians with Blue Front written all over them drove into the square, got out and went into Jamethon's office.

They stayed a little over an hour. When they left, I went back down to bed. That night I slept soundly.

The next morning I got up early, and there was mail for me. A message had come by spaceliner from the director of News Network back on Earth, personally congratulating me on my dispatches. Once, three years before, this would have meant a great deal to me. Now, I only worried that they would decide I had made the situation here newsworthy enough to require extra people being sent out to help me. I could not risk having other news personnel here now to see what I was doing.

I got in my car and headed east along the highway to New San Marcos and the Exotic Headquarters. The Friendly troops were already out in the field; eighteen kilometers east of Joseph's Town, I was stopped by a squad of five young soldiers with no non-com over them. They recognized me.

"In God's name, Mr. Olyn," said the first one to reach my car, bending down to speak to me through the open window at my left shoulder. "You cannot go through."

"Mind if I ask why?" I said.

He turned and pointed out and down into a little valley between two wooded hills at our left.

"Tactical survey in progress."

I looked. The little valley or meadow was perhaps a hundred yards wide between the wooded slopes, and it wound away from me and curved to disappear to my right. At the edge of the wooded slopes where they met open meadow, there were lilac bushes with blossoms several days old. The meadow itself was green and fair with the young chartreuse grass of early summer and the white and purple of the lilacs, and the variform oaks behind the lilacs were fuzzy in outline, with small, new leaves.

In the middle of all this, in the center of the meadow, were black-clad figures moving about with computing devices, measuring and figuring the possibilities of death from every angle. In the very center of the meadow for some reason they had set up marking stakes—a single stake, then a stake in front of that with two stakes on either side of it, and one more stake in line before these. Farther on was another single stake, down, as if fallen on the grass and discarded.

I looked back up into the lean young face of the soldier.

"Getting ready to defeat the Exotics?" I said.

He took it as if it had been a straightforward question, with no irony in my voice at all.

"Yes sir," he said seriously. I looked at him and at the taut skin and clear eyes of the rest.

"Ever think you might lose?"

"No, Mr. Olyn." He shook his head solemnly. "No man loses who goes to battle for the Lord." He saw that I needed to be convinced, and he went about it earnestly. "He hath set His hand upon His soldiers. And all that is possible to them is victory—or sometimes death. And what is death?"

He looked to his fellow soldiers and they all nodded.

"What is death?" they echoed.

I looked at them. They stood there asking me and each other what was death as if they were talking about some hard but necessary job.

I had an answer for them, but I did not say it. Death was a Groupman, one of their own kind, giving orders to soldiers just like themselves to assassinate prisoners. That was death.

"Call an officer," I said. "My pass lets me through here."

"I regret, sir," said the one who had been talking to me. "We cannot leave our posts to summon an officer. One will come soon."

I had a hunch what "soon" meant, and I was right. It was high noon before a Force Leader came by to order them to chow and let me through.

As I pulled into Kensie Graeme's Headquarters, the sun was low, patterning the ground with the long shadows of trees. Yet it was as if the camp was just waking up. I did not need experience to see the Exotics were beginning to move at last against Jamethon.

I found Janol Marat, the New Earth commandant.

"I've got to see Field Commander Graeme," I said.

He shook his head, for all that we now knew each other well.

"Not now, Tam. I'm sorry."

"Janol," I said, "this isn't for an interview. It's a matter of life and death. I mean that. I've got to see Kensie."

He stared at me. I stared back.

"Wait here," he said. We were standing just inside the headquarters office. He went out and was gone for perhaps five minutes. I stood, listening to the wall clock ticking away. Then he came back.

"This way," he said.

He led me outside and back between the bubble roundness of the plastic buildings to a small structure half-hidden in some trees. When we stepped through its front entrance, I realized it was Kensie's personal quarters. We passed through a small sitting room into a combination bedroom and bath. Kensie had just stepped out of the shower and was getting into battle clothes. He looked at me curiously, then turned his gaze back on Janol.

"All right, Commandant," he said, "you can get back to your duties, now."

"Sir," said Janol, without looking at me.

He saluted and left.

"All right, Tam," Kensie said, pulling on a pair of uniform slacks. "What is it?"

"I know you're ready to move out," I said.

He looked at me a little humorously as he locked the waistband of his slacks. He had not yet put on his shirt, and in that relatively small room he loomed like a giant, like some irresistible natural force. His body was tanned like dark wood and the muscles lay in flat bands across his chest and shoulders. His belly was hollow and the cords in his arms came and went as he moved them. Once more I felt the particular, special element of the Dorsai in him. It was not just his physical size and strength. It was not even the fact that he was someone trained from birth to war, someone bred for battle. No, it was something living but untouchable—the same quality of difference to be found in the pure Exotic like Padma the OutBond, or in some Newtonian or Cassidan researchist. Something so much above and beyond the common form of man that it was like a serenity, a sense of conviction where his own type of thing was concerned that was so complete it made him beyond all weaknesses, untouchable, unconquerable.

I saw the slight, dark shadow of Jamethon Black in my mind's eye, standing opposed to such a man as this; and the thought of any victory for Jamethon was unthinkable, an impossibility.

But there was always danger.

"All right, I'll tell you what I came about," I said to Kensie. "I've just found out Black's been in touch with the Blue Front, a native terrorist political group with its headquarters in Blauvain. Three of them visited him last night. I saw them."

Kensie picked up his shirt and slid a long arm into one sleeve.

"I know," he said.

I stared at him.

"Don't you understand?" I said. "They're assassins. It's their stock in trade. And the one man they and Jamethon Black both could use out of the way is you."

He put his other arm in a sleeve.

"I know that," he said. "They want the present government here on St. Marie out of the way and themselves n power—which isn't possible with Exotic money hiring us to keep the peace here."

"They haven't had Jamethon Black's help."

"Have they got it now?" he asked, sealing the shirt closure between thumb and forefinger.

"The Friendlies are desperate," I said. "Even if reinforcements arrived tomorrow, Jamethon knows what his chances are with you ready to move. Assassins may be outlawed by the Conventions of War and the Mercenaries' Code, but you and I know the Friendlies."

Kensie looked at me oddly and picked up his jacket.

"Do we?" he said.

I met his eyes. "Don't we?"

"Tam." He put on the jacket and closed it. "I know the men I have to fight. It's my business to know. But what makes you think you know them?"

"They're my business too," I said. "Maybe you'd forgotten. I'm a newsman. People are my business, first, last and always."

"But you've got no use for the Friendlies."

"Should I?" I said. "I've been on all the worlds. I've

seen the Cetan entrepreneur—and he wants his margin, but he's a human being. I've seen the Newtonian and the Cassidan with their heads in the clouds, but if you yanked on their sleeves hard enough, you could pull them back to reality. I've seen Exotics like Padma at their mental parlor tricks, and the Freilander up to his ears in his own red tape. I've seen them from my own world of Old Earth, and Coby, and Venus and even from the Dorsai, like you. And I tell you they've all got one thing in common. Underneath it all they're human. Every one of them's human—they've just specialized in some one, valuable way."

"And the Friendlies haven't?"

"Fanaticism," I said. "Is that valuable? It's just the opposite. What's good—what's even permissible about blind, deaf, dumb, unthinking faith that doesn't let a man reason for himself?"

"How do you know they don't reason?" Kensie asked. He was standing facing me now.

"Maybe some of them do," I said. "Maybe the young ones, before the poison's had time to work in. What good does that do, as long as the culture exists?"

A sudden silence came into the room.

"What are you talking about?" said Kensie.

"I mean you want the assassins," I said. "You don't want the Friendly troops. Prove that Jamethon Black has broken the Conventions of War by arranging with them to kill you; and you can win St. Marie for the Exotics without firing a shot."

"And how would I do that?"

"Use me," I said. "I've got a pipeline to the political group the assassins represent. Let me go to them as your representative and outbid Jamethon. You can offer them recognition by the present government, now. Padma and the present St. Marie government heads would have to back you up if you could clean the planet of Friendlies that easily."

He looked at me with no expression at all.

"And what would I be supposed to buy with this?" he said.

"Sworn testimony they'd been hired to assassinate you. As many of them as needed could testify."

"No Court of Interplanetary Inquiry would believe people like that," Kensie said.

"Ah," I said, and I could not help smiling. "But they'd believe me as a News Network Representative when I backed up every word that was said."

There was a new silence. His face had no expression at all.

"I see," he said.

He walked past me into the salon. I followed him. He went to his phone, put his finger on a stud and spoke into an imageless, gray screen.

"Janol," he said.

He turned away from the screen, crossed the room to an arms cabinet and began putting on his battle harness. He moved deliberately and neither looked nor spoke in my direction. After a few long minutes, the building entrance slid aside and Janol stepped in.

"Sir?" said the Freilander officer.

"Mr. Olyn stays here until further orders."

"Yes sir," said Janol.

Graeme went out.

I stood numb, staring at the entrance through which he had left. I could not believe that he would violate the Conventions so far himself as not only to disregard me, but to put me essentially under arrest to keep me from doing anything further about the situation.

I turned to Janol. He was looking at me with a sort of wry sympathy on his long, brown face.

"Is the OutBond here in camp?" I asked him.

"No." He came up to me. "He's back in the Exotic Embassy in Blauvain. Be a good fella now and sit down, why don't you? We might as well kill the next few hours pleasantly."

We were standing face to face; I hit him in the stomach.

I had done a little boxing as an undergraduate on the college level. I mention this not to make myself out a sort of muscular hero, but to explain why I had sense enough not to try for his jaw. Graeme could probably have found the knockout point there without even thinking, but I was no Dorsai. The area below a man's breastbone is relatively large, soft, handy and generally just fine for amateurs. And I did know something about how to punch.

For all that, Janol was not knocked out. He went over

on the floor and lay there doubled up with his eyes still
open. But he was not ready to get up right away. I turned
and went quickly out of the building.

The camp was busy. Nobody stopped me. I got back
into my car, and five minutes later I was free on the
darkening road for Blauvain.

V

From New San Marcos to Blauvain and Padma's Embassy
was fourteen hundred kilometers. I should have made it in
six hours, but a bridge was washed out and I took fourteen.

It was after eight the following morning when I burst
into the half-park, half-building that was the embassy.

"Padma—" I said. "Is he still—"

"Yes, Mr. Olyn," said the girl receptionist. "He's expecting you."

She smiled above her purple robe. I did not mind. I was
too busy being glad Padma had not already taken off for
the fringe areas of the conflict.

She took me down and around a corner and turned me
over to a young male Exotic, who introduced himself as
one of Padma's secretaries. He took me a short distance
and introduced me to another secretary, a middle-aged
man this time, who led me through several rooms and
then directed me down a long corridor and around a
corner, beyond which he said was the entrance to the
office area where Padma worked at the moment. Then he
left me.

I followed his direction. But when I stepped through
that entrance it was not into a room, but into a further
short corridor. And I checked, stopping myself dead. For
what I suddenly thought I saw coming at me was Kensie
Graeme—Kensie with murder on his mind.

But the man who looked like Kensie merely glanced at
me and dismissed me, continuing to come on. Then I
knew.

Of course, he was not Kensie. He was Kensie's twin
brother, Ian, commander of Garrison Forces for the Exotics, here in Blauvain. He strode on toward me; and I
began once more to walk toward him, but the shock stayed
with me until we had passed one another.

I do not think anyone could have come on him like that, in

my position and not been hit the same way. From Janol, at different times, I had gathered how Ian was the converse of Kensie. Not in a military sense—they were both magnificent specimens of Dorsai officers—but in the matter of their individual natures.

Kensie had had a profound effect on me from the first moment, with his cheerful nature and the warmth of being that at times obscured the very fact that he was a Dorsai. When the pressure of military affairs was not directly on him he seemed all sunshine; you could warm yourself in his presence as you might in the sun. Ian, his physical duplicate, striding toward me like some two-eyed Odin, was all shadow.

Here at last was the Dorsai legend come to life. Here was the grim man with the iron heart and the dark and solitary soul. In the powerful fortress of his body, what was essentially Ian dwelt as isolated as a hermit on a mountain. He was the fierce and lonely Highlandman of his distant ancestry, come to life again.

Not law, not ethics, but the trust of the given word, clan-loyalty and the duty of the blood feud held sway in Ian. He was a man who would cross hell to pay a debt for good or ill; and in that moment when I saw him coming toward me and recognized him at last, I suddenly thanked whatever gods were left, that he had no debt with me.

Then we had passed each other, and he was gone around a corner.

Rumor had it, I remembered then, that the blackness around him never lightened except in Kensie's presence. That he was truly his twin brother's other half. And that if he should ever lose the light that Kensie's bright presence shed on him, he would be doomed to his own lightlessness forever.

It was a statement I was to remember at a later time, as I was to remember seeing him come toward me in that moment.

But now I forgot him as I went forward through another entrance into what looked like a small conservatory and saw the gentle face and short-cropped white hair of Padma, the OutBond, wearing a pale yellow robe.

"Come in, Mr. Olyn," he said, getting up. "And come along with me."

He turned and walked out through an archway of purple clematis blooms. I followed him, and found a small courtyard, all but filled with the elliptical shape of a sedan aircar. Padma was already climbing into one of the seats facing the controls. He held the door for me.

"Where are we going?" I asked as I got in.

He touched the autopilot panel; the ship rose in the air. He left it to its own navigation, and pivoted his chair about to face me.

"To Commander Graeme's headquarters in the field," he answered.

His eyes were a light hazel color, but they seemed to catch and swim with the sunlight striking through the transparent top of the aircar, as we reached altitude and began to move horizontally. I could not read them, or the expression on his face.

"I see," I said. "Of course, I know a call from Graeme's HQ could get to you much faster than I could by groundcar from the same spot. But I hope you aren't thinking of having him kidnap me or something like that. I have Credentials of Impartiality protecting me as a Newsman, as well as authorizations from both the Friendly and the Exotic worlds. And I don't intend to be held responsible for any conclusions drawn by Graeme after the conversation the two of us had earlier this morning—*alone*."

Padma sat still in his aircar seat, facing me. His hands were folded in his lap together, pale against the yellow robe, but with strong sinews showing under the skin of their backs.

"You're coming with me now by my decision, not Kensie Graeme's."

"I want to know why," I said tensely.

"Because," he said slowly, "you are very dangerous." And he sat still, looking at me with unwavering eyes.

I waited for him to go on, but he did not. "Dangerous?" I said. "Dangerous to who?"

"To the future of all of us."

I stared at him, then I laughed. I was angry.

"Cut it out!" I said.

He shook his head slowly, his eyes never leaving my face. I was baffled by those eyes. Innocent and open as a child's, but I could not see through them into the man himself.

"All right," I said. "Tell me, why am I dangerous?"

"Because you want to destroy a race of people. And you know how."

There was a short silence. The aircar fled on through the skies without a sound.

"Now that's an odd notion," I said slowly and calmly. "I wonder where you got it?"

"From our ontogenic calculations," said Padma, as calmly as I had spoken. "And it's not a notion, Tam. As you know yourself."

"Oh, yes," I said. "Ontogenics. I was going to look that up."

"You did look it up, didn't you, Tam?"

"Did I?" I said. "I guess I did, at that. It didn't seem very clear to me, though, as I remember. Something about evolution."

"Ontogenics," said Padma, "is the study of the effect of evolution upon the interacting forces of human society."

"Am I an interacting force?"

"At the moment and for the past several years, yes," said Padma. "And possibly for some years into the future. But possibly not."

"That sounds almost like a threat."

"In a sense it is." Padma's eyes caught the light as I watched them. "You're capable of destroying yourself as well as others."

"I'd hate to do that."

"Then," said Padma, "you'd better listen to me."

"Why, of course," I said. "That's my business, listening. Tell me all about ontogenics—and myself."

He made an adjustment in the controls, then swung his seat back to face mine once more.

"The human race," said Padma, "broke up in an evolutionary explosion at the moment in history when interstellar colonization became practical." He sat watching me. I kept my face attentive. "This happened for reasons stemming from racial instinct which we haven't completely charted yet, but which was essentially self-protective in nature."

I reached into my jacket pocket.

"Perhaps I'd better take a few notes," I said.

"If you want to," said Padma, unperturbed. "Out of that

explosion came cultures individually devoted to single facets of the human personality. The fighting, combative facet became the Dorsai. The facet which surrendered the individual wholly to some faith or other became the Friendly. The philosophical facet created the Exotic culture to which I belong. We call these Splinter Cultures."

"Oh, yes," I said. "I know about Splinter Cultures."

"You know about them, Tam, but you don't know them."

"I don't?"

"No," said Padma, "because you, like all our ancestors, are from Earth. You're old, full-spectrum man. The Splinter peoples are evolutionarily advanced over you."

I felt a little twist of bitter anger knot suddenly inside me.

"Oh? I'm afraid I don't see that."

"Because you don't want to," said Padma. "If you did, you'd have to admit that they were different from you, and had to be judged by different standards."

"Different? How?"

"Different in a sense that all Splinter people, including myself, understand instinctively, but full-spectrum man has to extrapolate to imagine." Padma shifted a little in his seat. "You'll get some idea, Tam, if you imagine a member of a Splinter culture to be a man like yourself, only with a monomania that shoves him wholly toward being one type of person. But with this difference: Instead of all parts of his mental and physical self outside the limits of that monomania being ignored and atrophied as, they would be with you—"

I interrupted, "Why specifically with me?"

"With any full-spectrum man, then," said Padma calmly. "These parts, instead of being atrophied, are altered to agree with and support the monomania, so that we don't have a sick man—but a healthy, different one."

"Healthy?" I said, seeing the Friendly non-com on New Earth again in my mind's eye.

"Healthy as a culture. Not as occasional crippled individuals of that culture. But as a culture."

"Sorry," I said. "I don't believe it."

"But you do, Tam," said Padma, softly. "Unconsciously you do. Because you're planning to take advantage of the weakness such a culture must have to destroy it."

"And what weakness is that?"

"The obvious weakness that's the converse of any strength," said Padma. "The Splinter Cultures are not viable."

I must have blinked. I was honestly bewildered.

"Not viable? You mean they can't live on their own?"

"Of course not," said Padma. "Faced with an expansion into space, the human race reacted to the challenge of a different environment by trying to adapt to it. It adapted by trying out separately all the elements of its personality, to see which could survive best. Now that all elements— the Splinter Cultures—have survived and adapted, it's time for them to breed back into each other again, to produce a more hardy, universe-oriented human."

The aircar began to descend. We were nearing our destination.

"What's that got to do with me?" I said, at last.

"If you frustrate one of the Splinter Cultures, it can't adapt on its own as full-spectrum man would do. It will die. And when the race breeds back to a whole, that valuable element will be lost to the race."

"Maybe it'll be no loss," I said, softly in my turn.

"A vital loss," said Padma. "And I can prove it. You, a full-spectrum man, have in you an element from every Splinter Culture. If you admit this you can identify even with those you want to destroy. I have evidence to show you. Will you look at it?"

The ship touched ground; the door beside me opened. I got out with Padma and found Kensie waiting.

I looked from Padma to Kensie, who stood with us and a head taller than I—two heads taller than OutBond. Kensie looked back down at me with no particular expression. His eyes were not the eyes of his twin brother—but just then, for some reason, I could not meet them.

"I'm a newsman," I said. "Of course my mind is open."

Padma turned and began walking toward the headquarters building. Kensie fell in with us and I think Janol and some of the others came along behind, though I didn't look back to make sure. We went to the inner office where I first met Graeme—just Kensie, Padma and myself. There was a file folder on Graeme's desk. He picked it up, extracted a photocopy of something and handed it to me as I came up to him.

I took it. There was no doubting its authenticity.

It was a memo from Eldest Bright, ranking elder of the joint government of Harmony and Association, to the Friendly War Chief at the Defense X Center, on Harmony. It was dated two months previously. It was on the single-molecule sheet, where the legend cannot be tampered with, or removed once it is on.

Be Informed, in God's Name—

—That since it does seem the Lord's Will that our Brothers on St. Marie make no success, it is ordered that henceforth no more replacements or personnel or supplies be sent them. For if our Captain does intend us the victory, surely we shall conquer without further expenditure. And if it be His will that we conquer not, then surely it would be an impiety to throw away the substance of God's Churches in an attempt to frustrate that Will.

Be it further ordered that our Brothers on St. Marie be spared the knowledge that no further assistance is forthcoming, that they may bear witness to their faith in battle as ever, and God's Churches be undismayed.

Heed this Command, in the Name of the Lord:

> *By order of he who is called . . .*
> *Bright*
> *Eldest Among The Chosen*

I looked up from the memo. Both Graeme and Padma were watching me.

"How'd you get hold of this?" I said. "No, of course you won't tell me." The palms of my hands were suddenly sweating so that the slick material of the sheet in my fingers was slippery. I held it tightly, and talked fast to keep their eyes on my face. "But what about it? We already knew this, everybody knew Bright had abandoned them. This just proves it. Why even bother showing it to me?"

"I thought," said Padma, "it might move you just a

little. Perhaps enough to make you take a different view of things."

I said, "I didn't say that wasn't possible. I tell you a Newsman keeps an open mind at all times. Of course," I picked my words carefully, "if I could study it—"

"I'd hoped you'd take it with you," said Padma.

"Hoped?"

"If you dig into it and really understand what Bright means there, you might understand all the Friendlies differently. You might change your mind about them."

"I don't think so," I said. "But—"

"Let me ask you to do that much," said Padma. "Take the memo with you."

I stood for a moment, with Padma facing me and Kensie looming behind him, then shrugged and put the memo in my pocket.

"All right," I said. "I'll take it back to my quarters and think about it. —I've got a groundcar here somewhere, haven't I?" And I looked at Kensie.

"Ten kilometers back," said Kensie. "You wouldn't get through anyway. We're moving up for the assault and the Friendlies are maneuvering to meet us."

"Take my aircar," said Padma. "The Embassy flags on it will help."

"All right," I said.

We went out together toward the aircar. I passed Janol in the outer office and he met my eyes coldly. I did not blame him. We walked to the aircar and I got in.

"You can send the aircar back whenever you're through with it," said Padma, as I stepped in through the entrance section of its top. "It's an Embassy loan to you, Tam. I won't worry about it."

"No," I said. "You needn't worry."

I closed the section and touched the controls.

It was a dream of an aircar. It went up into the air as lightly as thought, and in a second I was two thousand feet up and well away from the spot. I made myself calm down, though, before I reached into my pocket and took the memo out.

I looked at it. My hand still trembled a little as I held it.

Here it was in my grasp at last. What I had been after from the start. And Padma himself had insisted I carry it away with me.

It was the lever, the Archimedes pry-bar which would move not one world but fourteen. And push the Friendly Peoples over the edge to extinction.

VI

They were waiting for me. They converged on the aircar as I landed it in the interior square of the Friendlies compound, all four of them with black rifles at the ready.

They were apparently the only ones left. Black seemed to have turned out every other man of his remnant of a battle unit. And these were all men I recognized, case-hardened veterans. One was the Groupman who had been in the office that first night when I had come back from the Exotic camp and stepped in to speak to Black, asking him if he ever ordered his men to kill prisoners. Another was a forty-year-old Force Leader, the lowest commissioned rank, but acting Major—just as Black, a Commandant, was acting as Expeditionary Field Commander—a position equivalent to Kensie Graeme's. The other two soldiers were non-commissioned, but similar. I knew them all. Ultra-fanatics. And they knew me.

We understood each other.

"I have to see the commandant," I said, as I got out, before they could begin to question me.

"On what business?" said the Force-Leader. "This aircar hath no business here. Nor thyself."

I said, "I must see Commandant Black immediately. I wouldn't be here in a car flying the flags of the Exotic Embassy if it wasn't necessary."

They could not take the chance that my reason for seeing Black wasn't important, and I knew it. They argued a little, but I kept insisting I had to see the Commandant. Finally, the Force-Leader took me across into the same outer office where I had always waited to see Black.

I faced Jamethon Black alone in the office.

He was putting on his battle harness, as I had seen Graeme putting on his earlier. On Graeme, the harness and the weapons it carried had looked like toys. On Jamethon's slight frame they looked almost too heavy to bear.

"Mr. Olyn," he said.

I walked across the room toward him, drawing the memo

from my pocket as I came. He turned a little to face me, his fingers sealing the locks on his harness, jingling slightly with his weapons and his harness as he turned.

"You're taking the field against the Exotics," I said.

He nodded. I had never been this close to him before. From across the room I would have believed he was holding his usual stony expression, but standing just a few feet from him now I saw the tired wraith of a smile touch the corners of his straight mouth in that dark, young face, for a second.

"That is my duty, Mr. Olyn."

"Some duty," I said. "When your superiors back on Harmony have already written you off their books."

"I've already told you," he said, calmly. "The Chosen are not betrayed in the Lord, one by another."

"You're sure of that?" I said.

Once more I saw that little ghost of a weary smile.

"It's a subject, Mr. Olyn, on which I am more expert than you."

I looked into his eyes. They were exhausted but calm. I glanced aside at the desk where the picture of the church, the older man and woman and the young girl stood still.

"Your family?" I asked.

"Yes," he said.

"It seems to me you'd think of them in a time like this."

"I think of them quite often."

"But you're going to go out and get yourself killed just the same."

"Just the same," he said.

"Sure!" I said. "You would!" I had come in calm and in control of myself. But now it was as if a cork had been pulled on all that had been inside me since Dave's death. I began to shake. "Because that's the kind of hypocrites you are—all of you Friendlies. You're so lying, so rotten clear through with your own lies, if someone took them away from you there'd be nothing left. Would there? So you'd rather die now than admit committing suicide like this isn't the most glorious thing in the universe. You'd rather die than admit you're just as full of doubts as anyone else, just as afraid."

I stepped right up to him. He did not move.

"Who're you trying to fool?" I said. "Who? I see through

you just like the people on all the other worlds do! I know you know what a mumbo-jumbo your United Churches are. I know you know the way of life you sing of through your nose so much isn't what you claim it is. I know your Eldest Bright and his gang of narrow-minded old men are just a gang of world-hungry tyrants that don't give a damn for religion or anything as long as they get what they want. I know you know it—and I'm going to make you admit it!"

And I shoved the memo under his nose.

"Read it!"

He took it from me. I stepped back from him, shaking badly as I watched him.

He studied it for a long minute, while I held my breath. His face did not change. Then he handed it back to me.

"Can I give you a ride to meet Graeme?" I said. "We can get across the lines in the OutBond's aircar. You can get the surrender over with before any shooting breaks out."

He shook his head. He was looking at me in a particularly level way, with an expresison I could not understand.

"What do you mean—no?"

"You'd better stay here," he said. "Even with ambassadorial flags, that aircar may be shot at over the lines." And he turned as if he would walk away from me, out the door.

"Where're you going?" I shouted at him. I got in front of him and pushed the memo before his eyes again. "That's real. You can't close your eyes to that!"

He stopped and looked at me. Then he reached out and took my wrist and put my arm and hand with the memo aside. His fingers were thin, but much stronger than I thought, so that I let the arm go down in front of him when I hadn't intended to do so.

"I know it's real. I'll have to warn you not to interfere with me any more, Mr. Olyn. I've got to go now." He stepped past me and walked toward the door.

"You're a liar!" I shouted after him. He kept on going. I had to stop him. I grabbed the solidograph from his desk and smashed it on the floor.

He turned like a cat and looked at the broken pieces at my feet.

"That's what you're doing!" I shouted, pointing at them.

He came back without a word and squatted down and carefully gathered up the pieces, one by one. He put them into his pocket and got back to his feet, and raised his face at last to mine. And when I saw his eyes I stopped breathing.

"If my duty," he said, in a low, controlled voice, "were not in this minute to—"

His voice stopped. I saw his eyes staring into me; and slowly I saw them change and the murder that was in them soften into something like wonder.

"Thou—" he said, softly—"Thou hast *no* faith?"

I had opened my mouth to speak. But what he said stopped me. I stood as if punched in the stomach, without the breath for words. He stared at me.

"What made you think," he said, "that that memo would change my mind?"

"You read it!" I said. "Bright wrote you were a losing proposition here, so you weren't to get any more help. And no one was to tell you for fear you might surrender if you knew."

"Is that how you read it?" he said. "Like that?"

"How else? How else can you read it?"

"As it is written." He stood straight facing me now and his eyes never moved from mine. "You have read it without faith, leaving out the Name and the will of the Lord. Eldest Bright wrote not that we were to be abandoned here—but that since our cause was sore tried, we be put in the hands of our Captain and our God. And further he wrote that we should not be told of this, that none here should be tempted to a vain and special seeking of the martyr's crown. Look, Mr. Olyn. It's down there in black and white."

"But that's not what he meant! *That's not what he meant!*"

He shook his head. "Mr. Olyn, I can't leave you in such delusion."

I stared at him, for it was sympathy I saw in his face. For me.

"It's your own blindness that deludes you," he said. "You see nothing, and so believe no man can see. Our Lord is not just a name, but all things. That's why we have no ornament in our churches, scorning any painted screen between us and our God. Listen to me, Mr. Olyn. Those churches themselves are but tabernacles of the earth. Our

Elders and Leaders, though they are Chosen and Anointed, are still but mortal men. To none of these things or people do we hearken in our faith, but to the very voice of God within us."

He paused. Somehow I could not speak.

"Suppose it was even as you think," he went on, even more gently. "Suppose that all you say was a fact; and that our Elders were but greedy tyrants, ourselves abandoned here by their selfish will and set to fulfill a false and prideful purpose. No." Jamethon's voice rose. "Let me attest as if it were only for myself. Suppose that you could give me proof that all our Elders lied, that our very Covenant was false. Suppose that you could prove to me—" his face lifted to mine and his voice drove at me—"that all was perversion and falsehood, and nowhere among the Chosen, not even in the house of my father, was there faith or hope! If you could prove to me that no miracle could save me, that no soul stood with me—and that opposed were all the legions of the universe—still I, I *alone*, Mr. Olyn, would go forward as I have been commanded, to the end of the universe, to the culmination of eternity. For without my faith I am but common earth. But with my faith, there is no power can stay me!"

He stopped speaking and turned about. I watched him walk across the room and out the door.

Still I stood there, as if I had been fastened in place— until I heard from outside, in the square of the compound, the sound of a military aircar starting up.

I broke out of my stasis then and ran out of the building.

As I burst into the square, the military aircar was just taking off. I could see Black and his four hard-shell subordinates in it. And I yelled up into the air after them.

"That's all right for you, but what about your men?"

They could not hear me. I knew that. Uncontrollable tears were running down my face, but I screamed up into the air after him anyway—

"You're killing your men to prove your point! Can't you listen? You're murdering helpless men!"

Unheeding, the military aircar dwindled rapidly to the west and south, where the converging battle forces waited. And the heavy concrete walls and buildings about the empty compound threw back my words with a hollow, wild and mocking echo.

VII

I should have gone to the spaceport. Instead, I got back into the aircar and flew back across the lines looking for Graeme's Battle Command Center.

I was as little concerned about my own life just then as a Friendly. I think I was shot at once or twice, in spite of the ambassadorial flags on the aircar, but I don't remember exactly. Eventually I found the Command Center and descended.

Enlisted men surrounded me as I stepped out of the aircar. I showed my credentials and went up to the battle screen, which had been set up in open air at the edge of shadow from some tall variform oaks. Graeme, Padma and his whole staff were grouped around it, watching the movements of their own and the Friendly troops reported on it. A continual low-voiced discussion of the movements went on, and a steady stream of information came from the communications center fifteen feet off.

The sun slanted steeply through the trees. It was almost noon and the day was bright and warm. No one looked at me for a long time; and then Janol, turning away from the screen, caught sight of me standing off at one side by the flat-topped shape of a tactics computer. His face went cold. He went on about what he was doing. But I must have been looking pretty bad, because after a while he came by with a canteen cup and set it down on the computer top.

" Drink that," he said shortly, and went off. I picked it up, found it was Dorsai whisky and swallowed it down. I could not taste it; but evidently it did me some good, because in a few minutes the world began to sort itself out around me and I began to think again.

I went up to Janol. "Thanks."

"All right." He did not look at me, but went on with the papers on the field desk before him.

"Janol," I said. "Tell me what's going on."

"See for yourself," he said, still bent over his papers.

"I can't see for myself. You know that. Look—I'm sorry

about what I did. But this is my job, too. Can't you tell me what's going on now and fight with me afterwards?"

"You know I can't brawl with civilians." Then his face relaxed. "All right," he said, straightening up. "Come on."

He led me over to the battle screen, where Padma and Kensie were standing, and pointed to a sort of small triangle of darkness between two snakelike lines of light. Other spots and shapes of light ringed it about.

"These—" he pointed to the two snakelike lines—"are the Macintok and Sarah Rivers, where they come together—just about ten miles this side of Joseph's Town. It's fairly high ground, hills thick with cover, fairly open between them. Good territory for setting up a stubborn defense, bad area to get trapped in."

"Why?"

He pointed to the two river lines.

"Get backed up in here and you find yourself hung up on high bluffs over the river. There is no easy way across, no cover for retreating troops. It's nearly all open farmland the rest of the way, from the other sides of the rivers to Joseph's Town."

His finger moved back out from the point where the river lines came together, past the small area of darkness and into the surrounding shapes and rings of light.

"On the other hand, the approach to this territory from our position is through open country, too—narrow strips of farmland interspersed with a lot of swamp and marsh. It's a tight situation for either commander, if we commit to a battle here. The first one who has to backpedal will find himself in trouble in a hurry."

"Are you going to commit?"

"It depends. Black sent his light armor forward. Now he's pulling back into the high ground, between the rivers. We're far superior in strength and equipment. There's no reason for us not to go in after him, as long as he's trapped himself—" Janol broke off.

"No reason?" I asked.

"Not from a tactical standpoint." Janol frowned at the screen. "We couldn't get into trouble unless we suddenly had to retreat. And we wouldn't do that unless he suddenly acquired some great tactical advantage that'd make it impossible for us to stay there."

I looked at his profile.

"Such as losing Graeme?" I said.

He transferred his frown to me. "There's no danger of that."

There was a certain change in the movement and the voices of the people around us. We both turned and looked.

Everybody was clustering around a screen. We moved in with the crowd and, looking between the soldiers of two of the officers of Graeme's staff, I saw on the screen the image of a small grassy meadow enclosed by wooded hills. In the center of the meadow, the Friendly flag floated its thin black cross on white background beside a long table on the grass. There were folding chairs on each side of the table, but only one person—a Friendly officer, standing on the table's far side as if waiting. There were the lilac bushes along the edge of the wooded hills where they came down in variform oak and ash to the meadow's edge; and the lavender blossoms were beginning to brown and darken for their season was almost at an end. So much difference had twenty-four hours made. Off to the left of the screen I could see the gray concrete of a highway.

"I know that place—" I started to say, turning to Janol.

"Quiet!" he said, holding up a finger. Around us, everybody else had fallen still. Up near the front of our group a single voice was talking.

"—it's a truce table."

"Have they called?" said the voice of Kensie.

"No, sir."

"Well, let's go see." There was a stir up front. The group began to break up and I saw Kensie and Padma walking off toward the area where the aircars were parked. I shoved myself through the thinning crowd like a process server, running after them.

I heard Janol shout behind me, but I paid no attention. Then I was up to Kensie and Padma, who turned.

"I want to go with you," I said.

"It's all right, Janol," Kensie said, looking past me. "You can leave him with us."

"Yes, sir." I could hear Janol turn and leave.

"So you want to come with me, Mr. Olyn?" Kensie said.

"I know that spot," I told him. "I drove by it just earlier

today. The Friendlies were taking tactical measurements all over that meadow and the hills on both sides. They weren't setting up truce talks."

Kensie looked at me for a long moment, as if he was taking some tactical measurements himself.

"Come on, then," he said. He turned to Padma. "You'll be staying here?"

"It's a combat zone. I'd better not." Padma turned his unwrinkled face to me. "Good luck, Mr. Olyn," he said, and walked away. I watched his yellow-robed figure glide over the turf for a second, then turned to see Graeme halfway to the nearest military aircar. I hurried after him.

It was a battle car, not luxurious like the OutBond's, and Kensie did not cruise at two thousand feet, but snaked it between the trees just a few feet above ground. The seats were cramped. His big frame overfilled his, crowding me where I sat. I felt the butt-plate of his spring pistol grinding into my side with every movement he made on the controls.

We came at last to the edge of the wooded and hilly triangle occupied by the Friendlies and mounted a slope under the cover of the new-leaved variform oaks.

They were massive enough to have killed off most ground cover. Between their pillar-like trunks the ground was shaded, and padded with the brown shapes of dead leaves. Near the crest of the hill, we came upon a unit of Exotic troops resting and waiting the orders to advance. Kensie got out of the car and returned the Force-Leader's salute.

"You've seen these tables the Friendlies set up?" Kensie asked.

"Yes, Commander. That officer they've got is still standing there. If you go just up over the crest of the slope here, you can see him—and the furniture."

"Good," said Kensie. "Keep your men here, Force. The Newsman and I'll go take a look."

He led the way up among the oak trees. At the top of the hill we looked down through about fifty yards more of trees and out into the meadow. It was two hundred yards across, the table right in the middle, the unmoving black figure of the Friendly officer standing on its far side.

"What do you think of it, Mr. Olyn?" asked Kensie, looking down through the trees.

"Why hasn't somebody shot him?" I asked.

He glanced sideways at me.

"There's plenty of time to shoot him," he said, "before he can get back to cover on the far side. If we have to shoot him at all. That wasn't what I wanted to know. You've seen the Friendly commander recently. Did he give you the impression he was ready to surrender?"

"No!" I said.

"I see," said Kensie.

"You don't really think he means to surrender? What makes you think something like that?"

"Truce tables are generally set up for the discussion of terms between opposing forces," he said.

"But he hasn't asked you to meet him?"

"No," Kensie watched the figure of the Friendly officer, motionless in the sunlight. "It might be against his principles to call for a discussion, but not to discuss—if we just happened to find ourselves across a table from one another."

He turned and signaled with his hand. The Force-Leader, who had been waiting down the slope behind us, came up.

"Sir?" he said to Kensie.

"Any Friendly strength in those trees across the way?"

"Four men, that's all, sir. Our scopes pick out their body heats clear and sharp. They aren't attempting to hide."

"I see." He paused. "Force."

"Sir?"

"Be good enough to go down there in the meadow and ask that Friendly officer what this is all about."

"Yes, sir."

We stood and watched as the Force-Leader went stiff-legging it down the steep slope between the trees. He crossed the grass—it seemed very slowly—and came up to the Friendly officer.

They stood facing each other. They were talking but there was no way to hear their voices. The flag with its thin black cross whipped in the little breeze that was blowing there. Then the Force-Leader turned and climbed back toward us.

He stopped in front of Kensie, and saluted. "Commander," he said, "the Commander of the Chosen Troops of God will meet with you in the field to discuss a surrender." He stopped to draw a fresh breath. "If you'll show yourself at the edge of the opposite woods at the same time; and you can approach the table together."

"Thank you, Force-Leader," said Kensie. He looked past his officer at the field and the table. "I think I'll go down."

"He doesn't mean it," I said.

"Force-Leader," said Kensie. "Form your men ready, just under the crown of the slope on the back side, here. If he surrenders, I'm going to insist he come back with me to this side immediately."

"Yes, sir."

"All this business without a regular call for parley may be because he wants to surrender first and break the news of it to his troops afterwards. So get your men ready. If Black intends to present his officers with an accomplished fact, we don't want to let him down."

"He's not going to surrender," I said.

"Mr. Olyn," said Kensie, turning to me. "I suggest you go back behind the crest of the hill. The Force-Leader will see you're taken care of."

"No," I said. "I'm going down. If it's a truce parley to discuss surrender terms, there's no combat situation involved and I've got a perfect right to be there. If it isn't, what're you doing going down yourself?"

Kensie looked at me strangely for a moment.

"All right," he said. "Come with me."

Kensie and I turned and went down the sharply pitched slope between the trees. Our bootsoles slipped until our heels dug in, with every step downward. Coming through the lilacs I smelled the faint, sweet scent—almost gone now—of the decaying blossoms.

Across the meadow, directly in line with the table, four figures in black came forward as we came forward. One of them was Jamethon Black.

Kensie and Jamethon saluted each other.

"Commandant Black," said Kensie.

"Yes, Commander Graeme. I am indebted to you for meeting me here," said Jamethon.

"My duty and a pleasure, Commandant."

"I wished to discuss the terms of a surrender."

"I can offer you," said Kensie, "the customary terms

extended to troops in your position under the Mercenaries' Code."

"You misunderstand me, sir," said Jamethon. "It was your surrender I came here to discuss."

The flag snapped.

Suddenly I saw the men in black measuring the field here, as I had seen them the day before. They had been right where we were now.

"I'm afraid the misunderstanding is mutual, Commandant," said Kensie. "I am in a superior tactical position and your defeat is normally certain. I have no need to surrender."

"You will not surrender?"

"No," said Kensie strongly.

All at once I saw the five stakes, in the position the Friendly non-coms, officers and Jamethon were now, and the stake up in front of them fallen down.

"Look out!" I shouted at Kensie—but I was far too late.

Things had already begun to happen. The Force-Leader had jerked back in front of Jamethon and all five of them were drawing their sidearms. I heard the flag snap again, and the sound of its rolling seemed to go on for a long time.

For the first time then I saw a man of the Dorsai in action. So swift was Kensie's reaction that it was eerily as if he had read Jamethon's mind in the instant before the Friendlies began to reach of their weapons. As their hands touched their sidearms, he was already in movement forward over the table and his spring pistol was in his hand. He seemed to fly directly into the Force-Leader and the two of them went down together, but Kensie kept travelling. He rolled on off the Force-Leader who now lay still in the grass. He came to his knees, fired, and dived forward, rolling again.

The Groupman on Jamethon's right went down. Jamethon and the remaining two were turned nearly full about now, trying to keep Kensie before them. The two that were left shoved themselves in front of Jamethon, their weapons not yet aimed. Kensie stopped moving as if he had run into a stone wall, came to his feet in a crouch, and fired twice more. The two Friendlies fell apart, one to each side.

Jamethon was facing Kensie now, and Jamethon's pistol

was in his hand and aimed. Jamethon fired, and a light blue streak leaped through the air, but Kensie had dropped again. Lying on his side on the grass, propped on one elbow, he pressed the firing button on his spring pistol twice.

Jamethon's sidearm sagged in his hand. He was backed up against the table now, and he put out his free hand to steady himself against the table top. He made another effort to lift his sidearm but he could not. It dropped from his hand. He bore more of his weight on the table, half-turning around, and his face came about to look in my direction. His face was as controlled as it had ever been, but there was something different about his eyes as he looked into mine and recognized me—something oddly like the look a man gives a competitor whom he had just beaten, and who was no real threat to begin with. A little smile touched the corners of his thin lips. Like a smile of inner triumph.

"Mr. Olyn . . ." he whispered. And then the life went out of his face and he fell beside the table.

Nearby explosions shook the ground under my feet. From the crest of the hill behind us the Force-Leader whom Kensie had left there was firing smoke bombs between us and the Friendly side of the meadow. A gray wall of smoke was rising between us and the far hillside, to screen us from the enemy. It towered up the blue sky like some impassable barrier, and under the looming height of it, only Kensie and I were standing.

On Jamethon's dead face there was a faint smile.

VIII

In a daze I watched the Friendly troops surrender that same day. It was the one situation in which their officers felt justified in doing so.

Not even their Elders expected subordinates to fight a situation set up by a dead Field Commander for tactical reasons unexplained to his officers. And the live troops remaining were worth more than the indemnity charges for them that the Exotics would make.

I did not wait for the settlements. I had nothing to wait for. One moment the situation on this battlefield had been poised like some great, irresistable wave above all our heads, cresting, curling over and about to break downward with an impact that would reverberate through all the worlds of Man. Now, suddenly, it was no longer above us. There was nothing but a far-flooding silence, already draining away into the records of the past.

There was nothing for me. Nothing.

If Jamethon had succeeded in killing Kensie—even if as a result he had won a practically bloodless surrender of the Exotic troops—I might have done something damaging with the incident of the truce table. But he had only tried; and died, failing. Who could work up emotion against the Friendlies for that?

I took ship back to Earth like a man walking in a dream, asking myself why.

Back on Earth, I told my editors I was not in good shape physically; and they took one look at me and believed me. I took an indefinite leave from my job and sat around the News Network Center Library, at the Hague, searching blindly through piles of writings and reference material on the Friendlies, the Dorsai and the Exotic worlds. For what? I did not know. I also watched the news dispatches from St. Marie concerning the settlement, and drank too much while I watched.

I had the numb feeling of a soldier sentenced to death for failure on duty. Then in the news dispatches came the information that Jamethon's body would be returned to Harmony for burial; and I realized suddenly it was this I had been waiting for: The unnatural honoring by fanatics of the fanatic who with four henchmen had tried to assassinate the lone enemy commander under a truce flag. Things could still be written.

I shaved, showered, pulled myself together after a fashion and went to see my superiors about being sent to Harmony to cover the burial of Jamethon, as a wrap-up.

The congratulations of the Director of News Network, that had reached me on St. Marie earlier, stood me in good stead. It was still fresh in the minds of the men just over me. I was sent.

Five days later I was on Harmony, in a little town called Remembered-of-the-Lord. The buildings in the town were of concrete and bubble plastic, though evidently they had been up for many years. The thin, stony soil about the town had been tilled as the fields on St. Marie had been tilled when I got to that other world—for Harmony now was just entering the spring of its northern hemisphere. And it was raining as I drove from the spaceport of the town, as it had on St. Marie that first day. But the Friendly fields I saw did not show the rich darkness of the fields of St. Marie. Only a thin, hard blackness in the wet that was like the color of Friendly uniforms.

I got to the church just as people were beginning to arrive. Under the dark, draining skies, the interior of the church was almost too dim to let me see my way about— for the Friendlies permit themselves no windows and no artificial lighting in their houses of worship. Gray light, cold wind and rain entered the doorless portal at the back of the church. Through the single rectangular opening in the roof watery sunlight filtered over Jamethon's body, on a platform set up on trestles. A transparent cover had been set up to protect the body from the rain, which was channeled off the open space and ran down a drain in the back wall. But the elder conducting the Death Service and anyone coming up to view the body was expected to stand exposed to sky and weather.

I got in line with the people moving slowly down the central aisle and past the body. To right and left of me the barriers at which the congregation would stand during the service were lost in gloom. The rafters of the steeply pitched roof were hidden in darkness. There was no music, but the low sound of voices individually praying to either side of me in the ranks of barriers and in the line blended into a sort of rhythmic undertone of sadness. Like Jamethon, the people were all very dark here, being of North African extraction. Dark into dark, they blended, and were lost about me in the gloom.

I came up and passed at last by Jamethon. He looked as I remembered him. Death had had no power to change him. He lay on his back, his hands at his sides, and his lips were as firm and straight as ever. Only his eyes were closed.

I was limping noticeably because of the dampness, and as I turned away from the body, I felt my elbow touched. I turned back sharply. I was not wearing my correspondent's uniform. I was in civilian clothes, so as to be inconspicuous.

I looked down into the face of the young girl in Jamethon's solidograph. In the gray rainy light her unlined face was like something from the stained glass window of an ancient cathedral back on Old Earth.

"You've been wounded," she said in a soft voice to me. "You must be one of the mercenaries who knew him on Newton, before he was ordered to Harmony. His parents, who are mine as well, would find solace in the Lord by meeting you."

The wind blew rain down through the overhead opening all about me, and its icy feel sent a chill suddenly shooting through me, freezing me to my very bones.

"No!" I said. "I'm not. I didn't know him." And I turned sharply away from her and pushed my way into the crowd, back up the aisle.

After about fifteen feet, I realized what I was doing and slowed down. The girl was already lost in the darkness of the bodies behind me. I made my way more slowly toward the back of the church, where there was a little place to stand before the first ranks of the barriers began. I stood watching the people come in. They came and came, walking in in their black clothing with their heads down and talking or praying in low voices.

I stood where I was, a little back from the entrance, half numbed and dull-minded with the chill about me and the exhaustion I had brought with me from Earth. The voices droned about me. I almost dozed, standing there. I could not remember why I had come.

Then a girl's voice emerged from the jumble, bringing me back to full consciousness again.

"—he did deny it, but I am sure he is one of those mercenaries who was with Jamethon on Newton. He limps and can only be a soldier who hath been wounded."

It was the voice of Jamethon's sister, speaking with more of the Friendly cant on her tongue than she had used speaking to me, a stranger. I woke fully and saw her standing by the entrance only a few feet from me, half-facing two elder people who I recognized as the older couple in Jamethon's solidograph. A bolt of pure, freezing horror shot through me.

"No!" I nearly shouted at them. "I don't know him. I never knew him—I don't understand what you're talking about!" And I turned and bolted out through the entrance of the church into the concealing rain.

I all but ran for about thirty or forty feet. Then I heard no footsteps behind me; I stopped.

I was alone in the open. The day was even darker now and the rain suddenly came down harder. It obscured everything around me with a drumming, shimmering curtain. I could not even see the groundcars in the parking lot toward which I was facing; and for sure they could not see me from the church. I lifted my face up to the downpour and let it beat upon my cheeks and my closed eyelids.

"So," said a voice from behind me. "You did not know him?"

The words seemed to cut me down the middle, and I felt as a cornered wolf must feel. Like a wolf I turned.

"Yes, I knew him!" I said.

Facing me was Padma, in a blue robe the rain did not seem to dampen. His empty hands that had never held a weapon in their life were clasped together before him. But the wolf part of me knew that as far as I was concerned, he was armed and a hunter.

"You?" I said. "What are you doing here?"

"It was calculated you would be here," said Padma, softly. "So I am here, too. But why *are* you here, Tam? Among those people in there, there's sure to be at least a few fanatics who've heard the camp rumors of your responsibility in the matter of Jamethon's death and the Friendlies' surrender."

"Rumors!" I said. "Who started them?"

"You did," Padma said. "By your actions on St. Marie." He gazed at me. "Didn't you know you were risking your life, coming here today?"

I opened my mouth to deny it. Then I realized I had known.

"What if someone should call out to them," said Padma, "that Tam Olyn, the St. Marie campaign Newsman, is here incognito?"

I looked at him with my wolf-feeling, grimly.

"Can you square it with your Exotic principles if you do?"

"We are misunderstood," answered Padma calmly. "We hire soldiers to fight for us not because of some moral commandment, but because our emotional perspective is lost if we become involved."

There was no fear left in me. Only a hard, empty feeling.

"Then call them," I said.

Padma's strange, hazel eyes watched me through the rain.

"If that was all that was needed," he said. "I could have sent word to them. I wouldn't have needed to come myself."

"Why did you come?" My voice tore at my throat. "What do you care about me, or the Exotics?"

"We care for every individual," said Padma. "But we care more for the race. And you remain dangerous to it. You're an idealist, Tam, warped to destructive purpose. There is a law of conservation of energy in the pattern of cause-and-effect as in other sciences. Your destructiveness was frustrated on St. Marie. Now it may turn inward to destroy you, or outward against the whole race of man."

I laughed, and heard the harshness of my laughter.

"What're you going to do about it?" I said.

"Show you how the knife you hold cuts the hand that holds it as well as what you turn it against. I have news for you, Tam. Kensie Graeme is dead."

"Dead?" The rain seemed to roar around me suddenly and the parking lot shifted unsubstantially under my feet.

"He was assassinated by three men of the Blue Front in Blauvain five days ago."

"Assassinated . . ." I whispered. "Why?"

"Because the war was over," said Padma. "Because Jamethon's death and the surrender of the Friendly troops without the preliminary of a war that would tear up the countryside left the civilian population favorably disposed toward our troops. Because the Blue Front found themselves farther from power than ever, as a result of this favorable feeling. They hoped by killing Graeme to provoke his troops into retaliation against the civilian population, so that the St. Marie government would have to order them home to our Exotics, and stand unprotected to face a Blue Front revolt."

I stared at him.

"All things are interrelated," said Padma. "Kensie was slated for a final promotion to a desk command back on

Mara or Kultis. He and his brother Ian would have been out of the wars for the rest of their professional lives. Because of Jamethon's death, that allowed the surrender of his troops without fighting, a situation was set up which led the Blue Front to assassinate Kensie. If you and Jamethon had not come together on St. Marie, and Jamethon had won, Kensie would still be alive. So our calculations show."

"Jamethon and I?" The breath went dry in my throat without warning, and the rain came down harder.

"You were the factor," said Padma, "that helped Jamethon to his solution."

"I helped him!" I said. "*I* did?"

"He saw through you," said Padma. "He saw through the revenge-bitter, twisted surface you thought was yourself, to the idealistic core that was so deep in the bone of you that even your uncle hadn't been able to eradicate it."

The rain thundered between us. But Padma's every word came clearly through it to me.

"I don't believe you!" I shouted. "I don't believe he did anything like that!"

"I told you," said Padma, "you didn't fully appreciate the evolutionary advances of our Splinter Cultures. Jamethon's faith was not the kind that can be shaken by outer things. If you had been in fact like your uncle, he would not even have listened to you. He would have dismissed you as a soulless man. As it was, he thought of you instead as a man possessed. A man speaking with what he would have called Satan's voice."

"I don't belive it!" I yelled.

"You do believe it," said Padma. "You've got no choice except to believe it. Because only because of it could Jamethon find his solution."

"Solution!"

"He was a man ready to die for his faith. But as a commander he found it hard his men should go out to die for no other reasonable cause." Padma watched me, and the rain thinned for a moment. "But you offered him what he recognized as the devil's choice—his life in this world, if he would surrender his faith and his men, to avoid the conflict that would end in his death and theirs."

"What crazy thinking was that?" I said. Inside the church,

the praying had stopped, and a single strong, deep voice was beginning the burial service.

"Not crazy," said Padma. "The moment he realized this, his answer became simple. All he had to do was begin by denying whatever the Satan offered. He must start with the absolute necessity of his own death."

"And that was a solution?" I tried to laugh but my throat hurt.

"It was the only solution," said Padma. "Once he decided that, he saw immediately that the one situation in which his men would permit themselves to surrender was if he was dead and they were in an untenable position for reasons only he had known."

I felt the words go through me with a soundless shock.

"But he didn't mean to die!" I said.

"He left it to his God," said Padma. "He arranged it so only a miracle could save him."

"What're you talking about?" I stared at him. "He set up a table with a flag of truce. He took four men—"

"There was no flag. The men were overage, martyrdom-seekers."

"He took four!" I shouted. "Four and one made five. The five of them against one man. I stood there by that table and saw. Five against—"

"Tam."

The single word stopped me. Suddenly I began to be afraid. I did not want to hear what he was about to say. I was afraid I knew what he was going to tell me. That I had known it for some time. And I did not want to hear it, I did not want to hear him say it. The rain grew even stronger, driving upon us both and mercilessly on the concrete, but I heard every word relentlessly through all its sound and noise.

Padma's voice began to roar in my ears like the rain, and a feeling came over me like the helpless floating sensation that comes in high fever. "Did you think that Jamethon for a minute fooled himself? He was a product of a Splinter Culture. He recognized another in Kensie. Did you think that for a minute he thought that barring a miracle he and four overage fanatics could kill an armed, alert and ready man of the Dorsai—*a man like Kensie*

Graeme? Before they were gunned down and killed themselves?"

Themselves . . . themselves . . . themselves . . .

I rode off a long way on that word from the dark day and the rain. Like the rain and the wind behind the clouds it lifted me and carried me away at last to that high, hard and stony land I had glimpsed when I had asked Kensie Graeme that question about his ever allowing Friendly prisoners to be killed. It was this land I had always avoided, but to it I was come at last.

And I remembered . . .

From the beginning I had known inside myself that the fanatic who had killed Dave and the others was not the image of all Friendlies. Jamethon was no casual killer. I had tried to make him into one in order to hide my own shame, my own self-destruction. For three years I had lied to myself. It had not been with me as I claimed, at Dave's death.

I had sat there under that tree watching Dave and the others die, watching the black-clad Groupman killing them with his machine rifle. And, in that moment, the thought in my mind had not been the one with which I justified three years of hunting for an opportunity to ruin someone like Jamethon and destroy the Friendly peoples.

It had not been me, thinking, *what is he doing there, what is he doing to those helpless, innocent men!* I had thought nothing so noble. Only one thought had filled all my mind and body in that instant. It had been simply—*after he's done, is he going to turn that gun on me?*

I came back to the day and to the rain. The rain was slackening and Padma was holding me upright. As with Jamethon, I was amazed at the strength of his hands.

"Let me go," I mumbled.

"Where would you go, Tam?" said Padma.

"Any place," I muttered. "I'll get out of it. I'll go hole up somewhere and get out of it. I'll give up."

"An action," said Padma, letting me go, "goes on reverberating for ever. Cause never ceases its effects. You can't let go now, Tam. You can only change sides."

"Sides!" I said. The rain was dwindling fast. "What sides?" I stared at him drunkenly.

"You uncle's side which is one," said Padma. "And the

opposing side, which is yours—which is ours as well." The rain was falling only lightly now, and the day was lightening. A little pale sunlight worked through thin clouds and illuminated the space between us. "In addition there are two strong influences besides we Exotics concerned with the attempt of man to evolve. We can't calculate or understand them yet, beyond the fact they act almost as single powerful individual wills. One seems to try to aid, one to frustrate, the evolutionary process; and their influences can be traced back at least as far as man's first venture into space from Earth."

I shook my head.

"I don't understand it," I muttered. "It's not my business."

"It is. It has been all your life." Padma eyes caught light for a moment. "A force intruded on the pattern on St. Marie, in the shape of a unit warped by personal loss and oriented toward violence. That was you, Tam."

I tried to shake my head again, but I knew he was right.

"You are blocked in your effort," said Padma. "But the law of conservation of energies could not be denied. When you were frustrated by Jamethon, your force, transmuted, left the pattern in the unit of another individual, warped by personal loss and oriented toward violent effect on the fabric."

I stared at him and wet my lips. "What other individual?"

"Ian Graeme."

I stared at him.

"Ian found his brother's three assassins hiding in a hotel room in Blauvain. He killed them with his hands—and in doing that he calmed the mercenaries and frustrated the Blue Front. But then he resigned and went home to the Dorsai. He's charged now with the sense of loss and bitterness you were charged with when you came to St. Marie." Padma paused and added softly. "Now he has great causal potential for some purpose we can't yet calculate."

"But—" I looked at Padma. "You mean I'm free!"

Padma shook his head.

"You're only charged with a different force instead," he said. "You received the full impact and charge of Jamethon's self-sacrifice."

He looked at me almost with sympathy, and in spite of the sunlight I began to shiver.

It was so. I could not deny it. Jamethon, in giving his life up for a belief, when I had thrown away all belief before the face of death, had melted and changed me as lightning melts and changes the uplifted sword-blade that it strikes. I could not deny what had happened to me.

"No," I said, shivering, "I can't do anything about it."

"You can," said Padma, calmly. "You will."

He unclasped his hands that he had held together earlier.

"The purpose for which we calculated I should meet you here is accomplished now," he said. "The idealism which was basic in you remains. Even your uncle couldn't take it from you. He could only attack it so that the threat of death on New Earth could twist it for a while against itself. Now you've been hammered straight in the forge of events on St. Marie."

I laughed, and the laugh hurt my throat still.

"I don't feel straight," I said.

"Give yourself time," said Padma. "Healing takes time. New growth has to harden, like muscle, before it becomes useful. Now you understand much more about the faith of the Friendlies, the courage of the Dorsai—and something of the philosophical strength for man we work toward on the Exotics."

He stopped and smiled at me. Almost an impish smile.

"It should have been clear to you a long while ago, Tam," he said. "Your job's the job of translator—between the old and the new. Your work will prepare the minds of the people on all the worlds—full-spectrum and Splinter Culture alike—for the day when the talents of the race will combine into the new breed." The smile softened, his face saddened. "You'll live to see more of it than I. Good-by, Tam."

He turned. Through the still misty, but brightening air, I saw him walking alone toward the church, from which came the voice of the speaker within, now announcing the number of the final hymn.

Dazedly, I turned away myself, went to my car and got in. Now the rain was almost over and the sky was brightening fast. The faint moisture fell, it seemed, more kindly; and the air was fresh and new.

I put the car windows open as I pulled out of the lot onto the long road back to the spaceport. And through the open window beside me I heard them beginning to sing the final hymn inside the church.

It was the Battle Hymn of the Friendly Soldiers that they sang. As I drove away down the road the voices seemed to follow me strongly. Not sounding slowly and mournfully as if in sadness and farewell, but strongly and triumphantly, as in a marching song on the lips of those taking up a route at the beginning of a new day.

> Soldier, ask not—now or ever!—
> Where to war your banners go!

The singing followed me as I drove away. And as I got farther into the distance, the voices seemed to blend until they sounded like one voice alone, powerfully singing. Ahead, the clouds were breaking. With the sun shining through, the patches of blue sky were like bright flags waving—like the banners of an army, marching forever forward into lands unknown.

I watched them, as I drove forward toward where they blended into open sky; and for a long time I heard the singing behind me, as I drove to the spaceport and the ship for Earth that waited in the sunlight.

STRICTLY CONFIDENTIAL

To: Interstellar Bureau of Criminal Apprehension
From: Jake Hall
      Hall Detective Service "BEHIND
      THE EIGHT BALL? CALL HALL!"

My connection with the Topla Pong caper began at approximately 3:15 P.M. of August 3rd, 1965. I was sitting at my desk, cleaning the dried blood from the front sight of my forty-five and having a couple of eye-openers from the office bottle. Both of the windows in the office were open.

The windows are at right angles to each other, since the dump is a corner office. As I finished the shot and poured myself another, a large green and purple butterfly came fluttering in one window, picked up the forty-five and flew out the other.

I don't mind admitting this made me sore. That was a sweet little gun and I had conceived a sentimental attachment for it, due to having many memories attached to it. I ripped open the right hand bottom drawer of my desk, grabbed my second best gun—a .38 police special—and got to my feet determined to track down the butterfly that had taken it. Unfortunately, I made the mistake of turning my back to one of the windows as I rose. I caught a glimpse of green and purple out of the corner of my eye and the ceiling fell in.

"What the hell—" I thought, and passed out.

* * *

When I woke up, a short, hefty individual in a grey business suit was splashing water in my face.

"Lay off, buster," I said. "This is my best and only tie." And I struggled to my feet. He stopped splashing water and stood back. My head was killing me. I located the bottle and poured myself a triple shot. Then I took a second look at him.

"Who're you?" I said, picking up the thirty-eight, which was still on the desk top. I was sore enough to let him have it. I'm glad now I didn't. Some guys are sensitive and I know enough now to realize it would have hurt his feelings.

"IBCA Agent Dobuk," he answered me. "I am a Memnian from Pesh—formerly of the Plagiarism Section."

"Listen," I said. "The last time I copied anything was in the third grade. State your business, or blow."

"I am an agent of the Interstellar Bureau of Criminal Apprehension," he said sadly. "An emergency has caused me to be transferred to the Violent Crimes Section. That same emergency has brought me to your office. Although it is ordinarily against Interstellar Commision Rules to admit the existence of other races to backward natives, events have forced my hand."

I turned away from him and picked up my hat from the desk.

"See me later," I said. "I got a date with a butterfly."

"Wait," he said; and closed his fist around a handful of my suitcoat. "Let me explain first."

I tried to walk away from him, but it was like being held in a steel vise. Experimentally, I chopped his wrist with the barrel of the thirty-eight and bent it—the barrel of the thirty-eight, that is.

"Okay, bud," I said. "You talked me into it. I'll listen."

He let me go. I went back to the desk, put the bent thirty-eight away and got out my thirty-two from the filing case.

I felt better with that in my shoulder holster. I sat down.

"Take a chair," I said.

"Thank you," he answered. "I'll have to adjust my weight first. What should a human my size weigh?"

"I'd guess you at about a hundred and eighty," I said.

He fiddled with his belt and sat down. The chair took it all right. "Sorry," he added. "I didn't want to take chances."

"Well, what's the dope?" I asked. He looked at me.

"What I have to say," he said, lowering his voice impressively, "must never go beyond this room."

"I'll shut the windows," I said, starting to get up.

"Never mind," he said, "I trust you."

"In that case," I said, "my fees are thirty bucks a day and expenses. If you feel like paying a retainer—"

He tossed me a thousand dollar bill. I stuffed it carelessly in my hip pocket. "Go ahead," I said. He looked at me grimly.

"You have just been visited by an interstellar criminal," he told me, lowering his voice. "In fact by one of *the* interstellar criminals."

"You mean the butterfly?" I asked.

"That butterfly, as you call him," he nodded. "He is, in reality, none other than Topla Pong, a Sngrian from Jchok." I shrugged. He was paying for the time.

"You're paying for the time," I said. "If you say so, okay. To me he's still a butterfly."

"A most dangerous butterfly," replied Dobuk. "A butterfly of the worst order. Not more than two weeks ago, sidereal time, he engaged a battle cruiser of the second class in the Coal Sack Area and destroyed it utterly. He is one of the great criminal minds of our present galactic era and one of the few great crime organizers."

"Crime organizers?" I asked.

"Criminal executives," he told me. "They do not belong to any particular branch of the criminal world, but to all. In two weeks he is capable of organizing the population of this planet and so infecting it with criminal ideas that the Interstellar Fleet will have no choice but to sterilize the globe by wiping out all intelligent life upon it."

"I get you," I said. "He's dangerous."

"We must stop him," Dobuk nodded. "You and I together must do what the IBCA has been trying to do for centuries."

"Why us?" I asked.

"The situation is critical," he answered. "Topla Pong has cropped up here where there is no one trained to stop him."

"What about you?" I said. He shook his head.

"I have the basic training, of course," he said mournfully. "But I'm strictly a plagiarism expert. I have no experience in violence. Also I'm too heavy for this world."

"Come again?" I asked. He gestured toward his belt.

"I have a gravity nullifier," he explained. "I adjusted it to one hundred and eighty of your pounds. Without it I would weigh approximately two of your tons."

He looked to me like a guy on short leave from a straitjacket, but he handed out thousand dollar bills. I picked up my hat.

"Okay," I said. "Let's go."

We went down the stairs and out into the street to where my battered forty-eight Chev was parked. It looked like a heap but things had been done to the motor and it was capable of a hundred and twenty if pushed. Detective Lieutenant Joe Haggerty was standing beside it. He glowered at me as I came up.

"Still clipping fruit stands for free apples, Haggerty?" I greeted him. His glower became a snarl.

"Listen, shamus," he said. "The fact that you saved the Governor's life last year isn't going to protect you forever. One of these days I'll find something to connect you with these hoods that are being found dead around town with a forty-five, a thirty-eight, a thirty-two, or some other size slug in them. And when I do—"

He left the threat hanging in the air. We got in the Chev and pulled off. Dobuk was looking at me in awe.

"How can you stand to have anyone dislike you that much?"

"I manage," I said. Dobuk shook his head in disbelief.

"You humans have such tough emotions," he said. "There was a note on that in the IBCA guidebook to this planet, but I could hardly believe it."

"Live and learn, buster," I said. I pulled out into the traffic.

"Where are we going?" asked Dobuk.

"To the Platinum Wheel," I told him.

"But shouldn't we start trying to trace—"

"Look, bud," I said. "You hire me, you do things my way. Arson, gut-shooting, little things like that, I'll maybe cover up for a client. But if I find you're the guilty party,

I'll throw you to the badges. After all, I'm in business in this town."

"What?" he said. He sounded bewildered.

We pulled up in front of the Platinum Wheel, the plushest nightclub in the territory—run by the Syndicate, of course. We left the car and walked inside.

"Jake!" screamed a gorgeous, long-legged, red-haired cigarette girl the minute she saw me. "What are you doing here? Don't you know the Syndicate is out for your blood?"

"It's worth a couple of quarts just to see you, baby," I said, clutching her. We kissed. It was like drowning in a sunset colored sea. She was a good kid. I kissed her every time I saw her.

When I finally let her go, she stepped back revealing a hard-looking character in a head-waiter's outfit.

"Who let you in, Hall?" he grated.

"The pest exterminators," I said. "They got the small lice, but they wanted some help with the rats."

"A wise guy, huh?" he sneered and let fly a left with all of his two hundred and twenty pounds behind it. I ducked; and there was a nasty, splintering sound just behind my neck.

He had hit Dobuk.

"Oh, I'm so sorry!" said Dobuk, bending over him.

"Forget it and come on," I said. We left the hard guy writhing on the emerald green carpet, clutching his mashed mitt; and walked back toward the office in the rear of the building.

"Are you sure we're going about this in the right way?" asked Dobuk.

"In this territory, when you talk about organized crime, you talk about the Syndicate," I said.

"I just thought—a careful investigation of probabilities—a calculation of—"

"Let me give you a piece of advice," I said.

"What?" he asked.

"Don't think," I said.

"But that's impossible," said Dobuk.

We had reached the door of the office. I opened it and led the way in without bothering to knock. Inside, Mikey McGwendon sat wearing a tux, his nails smoothly manicured, behind a large desk on the front edge of which perched a platinum blonde—a knockout. Also present was a large gorilla-like character and a small weasel-faced character. They were wearing Brooks Bros. suits; but they weren't fooling me any. After you've been in this business as long as I have you can spot the type a mile off.

Mikey gave me a mechanical smile as Dobuk and I advanced to his desk. I thought to myself he had taken us for a couple of his well-heeled sucker patrons. But I was wrong.

"Well, if it isn't Jake Hall, the wonder boy shamus," he greeted me. "What can I do for you?"

"That depends," I said. Reaching out, I snagged the platinum blonde off the desk and crushed her in my arms. Our lips met. It was like drowning in a sea of black flame. This was a no good kid. I had never kissed her before, but one touch of her lips told me that. Holding her off at arms length, I saw I was right. Her green eyes were as cold as ice on a go-light.

"Care to try that again, shamus?" she inquired, throatily.

I pushed her away while I still had my strength left. I turned back to Mikey. I could tell he hadn't liked my little byplay with his girl friend, but he hadn't got where he was in the rackets without learning some self-control—I'll give him that. He took his hand out of his desk drawer, closed the desk drawer and gave me that same mechanical smile.

"I don't think I know your friend," he said.

"Client, Mikey, client," I answered. "We got a little something to talk over with you. How about some privacy?"

Not a muscle in his face twitched. He flicked his hand at the door.

"Beat it," he growled.

The blonde pouted, but undulated out. The two characters hesitated. But they wouldn't have been Mikey's boys unless they'd learned some self-control. They took their hands out from under their left armpits and went out.

"Well, shamus?" said Mikey, turning to me as the door slammed.

"Well, it's like this," began Dobuk, behind me. "We're looking for—"

"Can it!" I growled. I perched on Mikey's desk myself and helped myself to a cigar from his humidor and a stiff slug from a decanter that stood handy on the desk top. "I thought you had this town organized, Mikey."

"Who says I haven't?" he retorted.

"Nobody said it yet," I told him. "What if I told you there's rumors of a freelance character running around with a forty-five?"

"There's no free guns in this town, Hall. If there is, I'll have the boys take care of him. What's he look like?"

"About eight inches long," I said. "Two and a half ounces, green with purple patches and about two feet across the wings."

He was writing the particulars down on a note pad.

"Eight inches long—" he repeated and stopped suddenly, looking up at me. "Who you trying to kid, Hall?"

I reached over, grabbed him by the lapels and hauled him to me. He clanked a little coming across the desk and I reached in to grab what I figured was a gun in his inside pocket. I never made it. Before I could close my hand, the lights went out.

I came to lying on a couch. Raising my head, I saw a large room with dark wooden rafters overhead. I was in somebody's hunting lodge. Looking down, I saw a fireplace and the platinum blonde in something filmy curled up on a polar-bear skin in front of it.

"Where am I?" I said.

"In my hunting lodge," she answered, throatily. "Don't you like me on a polar-bear skin, shamus?"

I reached for a bottle of bourbon on an end table nearby and poured myself a healthy slug. It made me feel a little better. My head was killig me.

"Save the routine for Mikey," I growled.

"But I can't stand Mikey," she answered. "I want to run away from him. Oh, he buys me presents and things—like this hunting lodge. But I can't stand him." Suddenly she was up in a swirl of something filmy and had flung herself into my arms. "Oh, Jake, Jake," she sobbed. "You don't know what it's like, living the kind of life I lead."

Looking down at her platinum blonde head, I almost felt sorry for her. Poor kid, it was the old story, I thought. Miss Podunk Corners of nineteen sixty-three, a knockout at sixteen, chased by all the local punks, but with stars in her eyes. A beauty contest win, Hollywood, a contract as a starlet at two hundred a week—and then nothing. Nothing to do, week after week, but sit around drawing her two hundred and killing time. Never a part. In desperation, marriage—to a wealthy, handsome, older man, who, however, turned out to have no time for anything but his aircraft plant. Six weeks of this, and disillusionment. Reno, divorce, a modest hunk of alimony. Then—one day she had woken up to look in the mirror and see herself—twenty, no longer a kid.

In desperation, she had begun to live for kicks, started running with a tougher and tougher crowd. Finally, she had ended up with Mikey. Oh, I'd no doubt, he had attracted her at first, with his crude, unsophisticated ways; and then it had begun to dawn on her that she was trapped.

It was the sort of thing I saw all the time in my business. But that was neither here nor there. I was here, and where was Dobuk?

"Where's the guy that was with me?" I demanded.

She choked back her sobs.

"He's out back," she said. We got up and went out. In a shed at the rear of the building we found a stack of hickory logs piled up like so much cordwood. On top was Dobuk, out cold.

I shook him out of it, got him moving and we all went back into the lodge.

"How'd they ever knock you out?" I asked him, when we were back inside. He shook his head.

"This is more serious than I thought," he said, shaking his head. "The only thing that could so affect a Peshniam Memnian like myself—"

"A what?" said the blonde.

"A Peshniam—I am a Memnian from Pesh, Miss," said Dobuk. "I and Mr. Hall are in quest of a Jchoknian Sngrian, or a Sngrian from Jchok. I was pointing out that since I am a Memnian Peshnian, unlike a Zumnian Omnian, that is, an Omnian from Zumn, a lighter gravity world to which one branch of our Memnian race has adapted—"

"Get to the point," I interrupted.

"Well," said Dobuk, "the point is that about the only thing on this planet which could render me unconscious would be a jolt of Emirnian nerve gas, one capsule of which Topla Pong was known to have in his possession after his encounter with the cruiser in the Coal Sack. I sadly fear that the Sngrian we are seeking has already joined forces with your Earthly underworld."

"Could be—" I said, frowning. I turned to the blonde. "What's your name, baby?" I demanded.

"It's Sheila," she answered, shyly. "Sheila Coombes."

"I'll bet it is," I snapped. She colored.

"How did you guess?" she murmured. "The name of my husband in my first unhappy marriage was Swinebender, but after I got my divorce I took back my maiden name— only changing it a little from the original, which was Gumbs."

"I thought so," I said. "I been in the business too long to be fooled by a name like Coombes. Now listen, Sheila, baby. If you want help to get away from Mikey, now's your time to level with us. First, how'd we get here?"

Her lower lip trembled.

"Gorilla and Weasel brought you out," she said. "You were all tied up but, when they went back to town, I took a chance and untied you."

"What were they going to do with us here?"

"Keep you on ice, they said, until Mikey had time to figure out how to dispose of you. I was supposed to keep an eye on you. Mikey said he wanted Gorilla and Weasel back in town for something."

"Yeah?" I said. Things were beginning to make sense to me. "Got a radio anyplace around the dump, Sheila?"

"There's one in the bedroom," she said. We went into the bedroom. Between drapes of flaming pink, a Capehart stood under one window. On top of it was a small table model radio in black leather inlaid with brilliants. Sheila turned it on.

"Get the news," I told her.

She fiddled with the dial. We got music, sports, a lecture by a professor at UCLA, more music—but no news.

"It's no use," said Sheila.

"No, wait," said Dobuk. "I believe I sense—"

The moaner sobbing his tune at us out of the loud-speaker got suddenly cut off in mid-howl. The dry-toast

voice of an on-the-spot announcer came crackling out at
us.

"—we interrupt this program to bring you a special
announcement. It has just been learned that the govern-
ments of the world's leading nations have received a communication from some organization calling itself the
Syndicate and believed in some circles to be the criminal
ring behind much of the illegal activities in this country.
The communication gives the world's law enforcement
agencies twenty-four hours to, quote—get out of business—
unquote. In the event that the law enforcement agencies
do not comply within the stated time, the Syndicate an-
nounces its intention of dropping one atomic bomb each
on every major city on the face of the globe. The letter is
thought to be a hoax; and if this is so, the hoax will soon be
exposed. For it has just been learned that although the
news was just now released to the news agencies, the
ultimatums were delivered yesterday and the deadline is
less than four hours away. We now return to Tommy
Mugwu—"

I switched off the set.

"Yesterday!" I said. "How long were we out?"

"Almost twenty hours," said Sheila. Dobuk turned pale.

"Sure it's a hoax," I said. "Where would they get atomic
bombs?"

Dobuk turned paler.

"You don't know Sngrians," he said. " 'Snfle beh jkt
Sngrian' as the native saying goes. Or, to translate roughly
into English, 'Sngrians are all natural-born scientists.' Give
Topla Pong a few pinches of middle to heavyweight elements and he can turn out atomic bombs like bjiks—or as
you would say—hot rolls."

"But why would he want to blow up all the big cities?"
cried Sheila. "That won't help the Syndicate, any."

"The Syndicate itself must be helpless in his grasp," said
Dobuk. "Remember, he is not merely an ordinary criminal, but a criminal executive with the very best of up-to-
date galactic methods of criminal organization at his
antennae-tips. To take over your Syndicate would be pu-
pa's play to the Sngrian who once held undisputed sway
over four systems before the IBCA broke his power."

"But the cities—"

"Ah, but there you are," said Dobuk. "He has no scruples. So he destroys the cities today. Slave labor will build them back up again for him tomorrow—and with newer, bigger, better gambling houses and vice dens. No doubt he plans something like criminal conscription where every adult will be forced into some sort of criminal activity, no matter how minor. Ordinary values mean nothing to him. Remember he is a creature of great natural genius and tremendous talent which he gets his greatest happiness from utilizing. To him there is something creative and artistic about building a criminal empire. He does it not for the material, but for the spiritual rewards."

"Dress it up in fancy clothes if you want," I said. "To me, he's still nothing more than a two-bit butterfly with delusions of grandeur. I've met the biggest of them; and when the chips are down they're all punks who think they can make it the easy way."

"No, no," said Dobuk, earnestly, "you don't understand."

"I understand all right," I told him. I reached for my shoulder holster. It was empty. "They took my gun," I said. I turned on Sheila. "Got a gun around the house, baby?"

"Well, let me see—" she frowned and thought. "I have a twenty-five automatic and a ladies purse model twenty-two. But they're both out being fixed. I know, I've got a little .12 caliber automatic. Will that do?"

"It'll have to," I growled.

"Not a toy," she said. "Built in imitation of one of Germany's most famous firearms. Not an air or a CO_2 gun, this is a small-bore gun that actually shoots a clip of six .12 caliber lead bullets." She extracted it from the center drawer of her dressing table and handed it to me. "Excellent for small game, target work, and scaring prowlers."

I picked the twelve up between two fingers and dropped it carefully into my shoulder holster. I felt more natural with a gun on me.

"What are you going to do?" asked Dobuk.

"Time's running short," I grated. "There's only one thing to do. Go to Mikey's town house and get to the bottom of things."

Sheila turned pale.

"The Syndicate West Coast headquarters?" she cried.

"Oh, no, no! I won't let you, Jake. They'll kill you. An army couldn't get into that place."

I shrugged.

"Who's using the army?" I said.

"Then I'll go with you," cried Sheila.

"And I, of course, also," said Dobuk.

We went out and hopped into Sheila's gold and black Cad convertible and lit out for L.A. I was behind the wheel and I kept the needle crowding a hundred and ten all the way in. It was tense driving, especially through the business districts along the way.

We made it in three hours. It had been about five o'clock when we left the lodge; and night had fallen by the time I skidded to a stop at the rear of the estate grounds of Mikey's town residence. I switched off the lights and sat for a minute listening to see if our approach had been noticed. But everything was quiet inside the high stone fence with the broken bottles set in concrete on the top and the electric wire running above them. Through the dark stillness, we could hear the mutters of the hoods on the front gate changing guard, and see the white ghost of the searchlight on top of the mansion sweeping the grounds.

"Perhaps," suggested Dobuk, "perhaps we should inform the local law enforcement agency of our mission?"

"In this suburb of L.A.?" I said. "Don't make me laugh. Mikey's always been careful to play the good, solid home owner in this neighborhood. He gives to the charities and sits on the local committees. They're sold on him. The local law would laugh in our faces."

I got out of the car. Dobuk got out on the other side.

"I'm coming with you!" cried Sheila.

"No," I said.

"Yes!"

"No."

"Yes!"

I hated to have to do it. But I slugged her. Glass jaw—she went out like a light.

"All right," I said to Dobuk. "Now, follow me."

"Where?" inquired Dobuk.

"Over the wall," I said.

"Why not through?" he asked; and walked through the wall. He made a fair-sized hole. I followed.

But the noise of the smashing wall had alarmed the

mansion. From the front gate came startled cries; and the searchlight stopped roaming about at random and began a personal hunt in our area of the grounds. I ducked behind some fir trees, dragging Dobuk with me. He was shaking like a leaf.

"What's wrong?" I snapped.

"Oh, these violent emotions!" he groaned. "The place quivers with them. Pesh, why did I ever leave you? I am impaled living on darting shafts of fear and hatred."

"Snap out of it!" I whispered. "If you can't take it from these hoods, how'll you be able to stand up to The Butterfly?"

"He's nowhere near so savage," said Dobuk. "Evil, yes— but as violent, no. You humans!"

I looked at him in the sudden glare of the searchlight that flickered over us without stopping. He was a sad sight. These amateurs are never any good.

"Here, take a jolt of this," I said, handing him the pint I always carry in my hip pocket.

His trembling hand took it and there was a splintering, crunching sound.

"Hey! You nuts?" I yelped in a loud whisper. He had just chewed the neck off the bottle and was about to take a bite out of the rest of it. "You drink it, you don't eat it."

"I'm sorry," he said, humbly, "a little bit of silicon is good for my nerves."

"To hell with your nerves," I said. "I need something to carry my whisky in." I grabbed the bottle back. It was already ruined. "Oh, well," I said; and drank it off. My head was killing me anyway. I handed the bottle back to Dobuk. "Here, finish it off."

"Thank you," he said. There was a little more crunching, a quiet gulp, and we were ready to roll.

We headed for the dim outline of the house, running bent over double. We came up against the back of the building. There was a basement window. Rapidly, I criss-crossed it with scotch tape and broke it open with the butt of the twelve. I reached it, unlatched it, opened it, and we crawled in.

The basement was dark and silent. Suddenly the lights went on.

"Who's there?" snarled a voice; and a rough-looking

character came galloping down the stairs. I let him have it between the eyes with the twelve.

"Pick up his body," I said to Dobuk. "Stack it out of sight behind the furnace."

"Whuzzat?" he said. His eyes were glazed. All of a sudden it hit me. He was drunk as a skunk. I should never have let him have the rest of that bottle.

I backhanded him a couple of times across the face, bruising my knuckles.

"Snap out of it," I growled.

He whimpered and cringed away from me.

"If there's anything I hate," I snarled. 'It's a lush. Particularly during business hours."

"Don't," he whimpered. "Don't hate me. I'll be all right."

He looked so bad, I relented.

"Okay, come on then," I said. He followed me upstairs.

In the kitchen were five more hoods playing Hollywood gin at five cents a point. I let them all have it between the eyes. The little twelve was empty. I checked the shoulder holsters of the hoods. They were all carrying thirty-twos. I took one.

"Come on," I said to Dobuk. We moved out through the kitchen door. As I stepped through, I had a glimpse of someone swinging at me. I ducked, but not quickly enough. For a moment the room went black; and then I had staggered to my feet and let the man who tried to slug me have it between the eyes. He was dressed in a monkey suit; and for a second I didn't get it. Then I realized he must be the butler.

On the dining table was a tray he had evidently been carrying upstairs when he heard me. It held a bottle, ice, and glasses. I poured myself a stiff shot and downed it. My head was killing me.

I searched the butler. He was carrying a thirty-eight and I traded my thirty-two for it. While I was doing this, someone shot at us from the living room, but missed because I was bent over; and the bullet hit nobody but Dobuk, who, of course, it didn't hurt.

"There's someone in the living room," said Dobuk, looking down at the flattened slug where it lay on the chartreuse carpet before him.

"I know," I said.

I sprayed the living room with bullets and we advanced. Inside, Gorilla and Weasel lay dead with bullet holes between the eyes. Gorilla had my forty-five clutched in his ham-like mitt. Here, at last, was proof positive of the hookup between Topla Pong and the Syndicate. I pointed this out to Dobuk. He agreed.

I led the way on up the stairs toward the second floor, the forty-five clutched in my hand. It felt good to have it back again, though I noticed Gorilla hadn't been taking good care of it. There was dried blood on the front sight at least twenty-four hours old.

At the top of the stairs, we entered a wide hallway. On the plum-colored carpet lay Sheila, her platinum blonde hair tumbled back from her pale face and a spreading stain on the front of her dress. She was dying.

"What are you doing here?" I asked. "I thought I left you in the car."

"You did—" she gasped. "I went to the front gate after I came to and one of the hoods on duty there brought me in to Mikey. I was going to double-cross you, but when I looked at him and thought of you I couldn't do it. He shot me." She choked suddenly on a rush of blood. "Kiss me once more, Jake."

I crushed her in my arms. It was like drowning in a sea of black flame for the last time. Halfway through the clinch, the flame flickered and went out. Gently, I laid her down on the plum-colored carpet. Her eyes were already closed in death, her face peaceful. She looked like a little girl again—a wayward kid, who at the last minute had found a spark of unexpected decency in herself—a spark that had cost her her life.

Now I was really mad. Dobuk yelped and backed off from me.

"What's the matter with you?" I growled.

"You burnt me," he said. Then I got it. I was in a red hot rage after seeing Sheila, and the poor guy had been standing too close.

"Keep behind me," I said. Sheila's outstretched hand on the carpet seemed to be pointing toward a closed door at the end of the hall. I had a hunch that what Dobuk and I were both looking for would be behind the door. I headed for it, gun in hand.

I kicked the door open. It was a library; and behind a desk stood Mikey, faultlessly attired in evening clothes, a highball in one hand and a gun in the other. He gave me a mechanical smile.

"Drop the rod, Mikey," I said. "I got you covered."

"Nuts," he said, oilily, "drop yours, Jake. I got you covered."

Without lowering my forty-five, I glanced at the gun in his hand. It was true. He was holding a forty-eight. I was outgunned.

Helplessly, I dropped the forty-five on the maroon carpet. Moving with piston-like efficiency, he stalked around the desk and scooped it up.

"Come in and shut the door," he said. "You too, Dobuk."

Dobuk! I had forgotten him. Dobuk was immune to bullets.

"Grab the gun from him, Dobuk!" I yelled.

Dobuk stepped around me and advanced on Mikey. Mikey flashed his vicious, mechanical smile at him.

"I've got the solution to you," he said. "To coin a phrase—'bye, bye, Dobuk!' "

His hand flashed out with piston-like efficiency and ripped Dobuk's belt from his pants. There was a splintering crash and Dobuk disappeared. A gaping hole marred the carpet where he had stood a minute before. Suddenly deprived of his gravity nullifier, Dobuk had reverted to his normal weight of two tons and dropped through two floors down into the basement.

"And now," said Mikey, pointing the forty-eight at me. "For you."

"Hold it!" I said, sharply. "I can see I'm not going to get out of this alive, so you better tell me how you did it."

"Very well," said Mikey. I could almost see the gears grinding in his head as he mulled over various plans for disposing of me. "Sheila was actually a third cousin of my aunt-by-marriage. Although she did not know it herself, she stood to inherit a large share of Syndicate voting stock, following my aunt's recent death. I was planning to maneuver for a position on the Syndicate Executive Board and needed her stock. The killing of Weasel was actually an accident. I was cleaning that forty-five of yours when it went off of its own accord, letting him have it between the eyes. I realized then that it was not safe to have a gun trained by you around the house. I handed it over to Gorilla without even finishing the job of taking the dried blood off the front sight. . . ."

So that was why the dried blood was still on the front sight. Even the little things checked now. If only I'd put two and two together earlier.

". . . and told Gorilla to take it and Weasel out and bury them. You must have run into them as Gorilla was carrying them out of the living room front door."

That explained why there had been only one shot from the living room—and why the bullet had missed me, only bruising Dobuk slightly between the eyes.

"The rest of it," wound up Mikey, "you know. With Sheila's stock and the know-how of The Butterfly, I saw my way clear to take over the Syndicate Executive Board."

"Where's Topla Pong now?" I demanded.

His eyes had a hard, metallic glint in them.

"Where you'll never find him," he said. He lifted his gun and aimed it at me. The hole in the muzzle looked big enough to crawl into. "And now, to coin a phrase—"

"But *I* will find him!" announced Dobuk suddenly, rising up through the hole in the floor beneath us.

"Dobuk!" I yelled. "But how—? Your gravity nullifier—"

"Though only a plagiarism agent," he replied, "I have had the basic IBCA training. I built a new gravity nullifier out of parts from the thermostat on the basement furnace. And now," he said, turning toward Mikey, "to wind up the case."

"Then you know where Topla Pong is?" I asked.

"Exactly!" replied Dobuk. Striding across the carpet, he picked up Mikey and unscrewed his head. Reaching down inside Mikey's body, he hauled out by one wing the struggling green and purple figure of Topla Pong. The headless body of Mikey dropped to the carpet with a thump. Now I saw why his smiles and so many of his actions had been so mechanical.

"A robot!" I said.

"Exactly," repeated Dobuk. "Controlled from inside by Topla Pong, whom I will now return to interstellar justice."

"No, you won't!" shouted The Butterfly, speaking up now for the first time. "I've done nothing on this planet that the real Mikey wouldn't have done. In my proper person I have committed no crimes. I claim sanctuary on this planet in accordance with Interstellar Law; and there are no courts here in which you can bring a case for extraplanetary extradition."

Dobuk looked stunned. He turned to me in consternation.

"Is this true?" he asked. "Has he actually done no more than the real Mikey would have done?"

"I hate to say yes," I said. "But it's a fact."

Topla Pong began to laugh wickedly.

"Then—then I'm helpless," said Dobuk, his shoulders dropping. "I felt sure he would have committed at least one crime here in his proper person."

"But he has!" I shouted. "What about Mikey, himself? He had to get rid of Mikey before he could pose as Mikey."

"True!" cried Dobuk. He turned to Topla Pong. "Where's Mikey?"

"Dissolved," retorted Topla Pong. " 'Snfle beh jkt Sngrian' as the old saying goes, or in English—'All Sngrians are natural born scientists.' I dissolved him in acid and evaporated the acid. You'll never get me on that. As I need hardly point out—no corpus delecti."

"That does it," groaned Dobuk.

"No, no. wait—" I said. "We're forgetting the one crime he did that there's a living witness to. Right after he got here, he slugged me and stole my forty-five."

"My word against yours," smirked Topla Pong.

"I—I'm afraid—" stamamered Dobuk.

"What?" I shouted. "You don't mean you aren't going to get him on that?"

"Well—after all—" fumbled Dobuk. "There were no other witnesses—were there?"

"But you came in and found me unconscious, yourself."

"Oh, yes," said Dobuk. "But consider the business you're in. Almost anybody is liable to knock you unconscious. Perhaps it was another would-be client. Inference is not evidence, you know. Short of an out and out confession—"

"Do you mean," I demanded, "that this butterfly is going to be turned loose to build more criminal empires, to conscript more honest citizens into the ranks of the underworld, to start anew his career of blood and dope-soaked organizing?"

"Yes."

"We'll see about that!" I snapped. There was a newspaper lying on the desk. I rolled it up and slammed Topla Pong with it.

"Help!" he shouted. "Dobuk, help!"

"Jake—no!" cried Dobuk.

"Stay out of this," I snarled. "Stand back before I hate you."

"No, no, not that—" said Dobuk. "I—I'll go outside. I can't stand this."

He turned and staggered out of the room. I swatted Topla Pong again.

"Confess!" I snarled.

I gritted my teeth and steeled myself. My stomach was going queasy on me and for a minute I thought I couldn't go through with it. Then I thought of what this insect had done to Sheila and knew I could. Luckily, there was something that made it easier for me. I hate bugs.

I continued. Within a few seconds, Topla Pong broke.

"Stop it!" he yelled. "I'll confess. Get Dobuk back in here." I went out in the hall and got Dobuk, who was shaking like a leaf.

"He broke," I said, bringing him back into the room.

"So I see," said Dobuk. "Luckily I have my first aid kit here with me. I'll fix you up, Pong. There! That was a bad break."

"It sure was. Thanks," said The Butterfly. "Naturally, I put on a complete nerve block when this human started batting me around; but this is my second best body and I'd hate to have a lot of regrowth scars. I confess."

"In that case I hereby put you under hypnotic compulsion to return to Sngr and go on trial for your interstellar crimes."

"I go," said Topla Pong, and flew out a window.

Dobuk turned to me.

"You will, of course," he said, "submit a full report of this in writing?"

"Count on me," I said. "There's just one thing, though. What was it that tipped you off to the fact that Mikey was really a robot with Topla Pong inside?"

"I'll tell you," said Dobuk. "Like every master criminal, it was the fact that he could not resist the commission of one minor crime that tripped him up. Before depriving me of my nullifier belt he spoke the words—*to coin a phrase—bye, bye, Dobuk.* He forgot that I am essentially a Plagiarism Expert; and as such I immediately recognized his words for the Interstellar Misdemeanor (non-extraditable) that they were. The original of that phrase, which could not conceivably be known to a human like Mikey, is found in A TOUCH OF WELIGIAN POISON by A. Zzanzr Lllg, protected by total Interstellar copyright, covering all known verbal and non-verbal reproductions in all languages, including thought—copyright number 8274390-6645382—569. It is found on spool thirty, eight hundred and forty-three syllables from the end and goes, correctly—*to coin a phrase—bye, bye, Ugluck!*"

"I get it," I said.

POWERWAY EMERGENCY!

The high speed mid-afternoon traffic on the eight north-bound lanes of 16N by Station 11 was light enough so that the whine of it sounded almost gentle in the March afternoon sunlight. Ben Audette dropped the company's two-seater aircopter toward the white box of Station 11, sitting back on the open hillside less than a hundred meters from the reddish stick-and wire snow fence that had held back the hillside's winter drifts from the taller chain-link fence protecting the powerway itself. Ben frowned a little. The maintenance crews should have taken that snow fence down by now.

Spring had already been starting to tinge with green the fields he had flown over on his way out from the Powerway Vehicle Pool at Anoka; and the canal alongside the powerway was thick with traffic headed north from the Twin Cities to Duluth and the Great Lakes. It was, he thought, a good time to take a short break. He had eight days coming after the first of next month. He could take Robby fishing off the Alaskan coast . . .

Still thinking about the fishing trip, he set the two-seater down on the station landing pad and made his way into the building. Alden Marine, powerman on duty for D-shift, Station 11, was seated at the main console in the glare of the sunlight from the windows, running his final check on the controls. Ben sat down in the stand-by chair to wait for Alden to finish. The polished metal front of the computer cabinet reflected his own lean, block-shouldered image in the blue duty coveralls.

". . . and Substation 119, clear and steady," said Al into the recorder mike, punching the last keys in the check sequence. He looked at Ben. "All substations are clear for takeover at 1558 hours."

"Powerman Ben Audette taking over E-shift, Station 11 at 1558 hours," said Ben, pitching his own deep voice up for the recorder. He traded seats with Al and clicked off the recorder since the next question was off the record. "Anything?"

"Your wife called. Wants you to call back right away." Al was already moving toward the station door. "Two-seater outside? I've got to travel. Due in Kansas City at six p.m. and I've still got to check out and dress first."

He disappeared through the gap of the closing door.

"Kansas City's a long way to go for a date!" Ben shouted after him.

"You're old-fashioned," Al's voice floated back. "Old, and married. Kansas City's just next door, and besides—"

The closing of the door shut off his voice. Ben turned to run his own incoming check on the console, but for the thirty kilometers of eight-lane northbound, full-power roadway that was now his responsibility until eight p.m., all signals glowed a steady, reassuring red. He flipped on the switch of the automatic monitor and then turned to the telephone to punch out his own home number.

There were a few seconds of ringing at the far end of the line, and then the phone screen lit up with the face of Marlie, a faint frown line between her blue eyes.

"Al said you phoned," Ben told her.

"It's Robby," she said. "I have to rush out and buy him a new packframe and some other things, so I won't be home for dinner. Can you get a bite somewhere and go right to the PTA party? I'll bring your magic equipment and meet you there."

"Magic . . . ?" he began. Then he remembered. Almost, he had managed to forget tonight. It had been years since he had monkeyed around as an amateur magician. But apparently Robby had been boasting about him at school . . . "Sure. I can meet you at the party."

He noticed then that the frown line was still there.

"Anything else?" he said.

"Well," she said. "Of course, Robby's going to hate missing your act—"

"Robby's not going to be at the PTA party?"

"That's why I have to go shopping. His ecology study group got its chance early for an overnight canoe trip in the Boundary Waters area."

"Now, wait a minute," said Ben. "Wait just a minute! You know how I feel about putting on a top hat and making a fool of myself in front of a couple hundred kids and grownups. I only agreed so Robby could see me on stage. Now you tell me he isn't even going to be there."

"Now, Ben!" she said.

"Ben, my eye!" he growled. "I don't—"

Sharp as the whir of a rattlesnake and equally as frightening, the sudden, high-pitched shrilling of the automatic alarm sliced across their conversation.

"Trouble on the line!" he snapped at Marlie. "Call you later. Leave a tracer on the phone."

He cut the connection to the phone with his left hand. His right was already flying over the controls of the console, testing, requesting a pinpoint on the trouble and a computer printout.

Along the console's schematic of the powerway section controlled and fed by Station 11 the trouble lights were blinking red-to-green, red-to-green, in Substations 116 through 119, showing a struggle by the automatic equipment of those substations to share the burden of an overload somewhere within the stretch of powerway they controlled.

An overload? Traffic was not even normally heavy at this hour through the thirty kilometer distance of Station 11—it was light. Ben punched up a composite view from the overhead cameras along the powerway to show him the twelve-kilometer stretch of Substations 116 through 119. There were no more than a dozen passenger vehicles—no trucks at all—cruising at this moment in the gently curving, woods-enclosed length of that stretch. Each was in its own lane, and moving under automatic power and control from Station 11 at the standard cruising speed of 300 kph—180 miles an hour on the old scale. No sign of trouble.

Abruptly the lights stopped flashing into green. They went back to a steady red. The station computer's printout whirred, typing out a coded response at the same time as its message appeared in clear on the computer screen.

"Temporary overload. Substations 116-119 inclusive. Malfunction terminated. The point of overload not established."

There it was. Ben chewed his lower lip. Computers were a great help—except when they weren't. Like now. He hesitated a moment, then punched the phone button directly under the blue light of the direct line to the Traffic Flow Office back at Twin City Powerways HQ. The screen lit up with the traffic coordination desk and the long-jawed face of Harley Gregson. Ben breathed a small sigh of relief. Harley was himself a powerways engineer with station experience, a coordinator Ben had known and worked with over a period of years.

"What's up?" asked Harley. He glanced down, obviously at a just-arrived copy of the report printed out moments before by Ben's station computer. "Trouble on the system?"

"Not now," Ben answered. "But there was a flutter for a good eighty seconds there. Now . . . nothing."

Harley frowned.

"What do you want us to do?" he asked. As traffic coordinator, his responsibility was to provide everything from emergency repair crews to relief powerway stationmen, on request from stationmen like Ben, himself. But, just as Ben knew that Harley understood his own position out on Station 11 with an undiagnosed trouble rearing its ugly head, so also Harley knew that Ben understood Harley's. Like every other department backing up the overloaded powerways nowadays, Harley's had to worry about tying up emergency personnel at a spot where the trouble might turn out to be nothing at all, and then finding itself shorthanded to meet a real emergency somewhere else along the line.

"Better alert a substation repair group—but to stand by only," Ben said. "A backup stationman, too. How does the four o'clock rush seem to be building up?"

"Just a second. I'll check." Harley turned his attention a little away from the screen.

Ben waited. This was the large fear raised by any problem that might halt or even slow down traffic on 16N—the possibility of a traffic jam at rush hour, with cars backed up unmoving, bumper to bumper, for eighty or ninety miles.

At four p.m.—1600 hours—as Ben had been taking over

the station, the day shift of office workers in the Twin Cities metropolitan area had been starting to leave their offices and head homeward. Northbound commuters from as far away as Thunder Bay and Winnipeg in Canada would right now be picking up their vehicles from the parking towers and heading into 16N from more than two hundred ramps between Buffalo and the St. Croix River. From that point on, the worries of their drivers ceased and became the worries of people like Ben and Harley.

As the incoming car entered the admittance lane of the powerway, his controls would go dead and a blue light would come on in the center of his control panel, announcing the fact that the computers and other equipment of the powerway had taken over command of the vehicle. The driver would push his control stick up into neutral position and swivel his chair around to face the other seats, or the single, sofa-like curving seat at the back of some cars. He could sit back, put his feet up and open his evening newspaper, or even play a game of cards with any of the other commuters riding in the car.

Meanwhile, their car would be accelerating. The battery power pack under its rear section was only capable of producing speeds of forty miles an hour when the vehicle was driver-controlled on city and suburban streets. But now the stripe down the center of the powerway lane in which the car was traveling was beginning to feed extra power to the auxiliary drive unit underneath the front part of the car. Gradually, so gradually that the passengers would be hardly aware of it, the speed of the now auto-controlled vehicle would begin to climb, to eighty . . . a hundred and twenty . . . a hundred and fifty . . . a hundred and eighty miles an hour, sliding the car along with hardly a sound on the aircushion that floated its ton of glass and metal eight inches above the clean surface of the powerway lane in which it was travelling.

"Estimate is that by the time the front of the four o'clock rush reaches your station," Harley said now, turning back to face into the screen, "we'll have a near-saturation overload. One hundred and eighty-two per cent of the maximum traffic load 16N is designed for. Over 150,000 cars on the powerway between you and the Twin Cities in case of a jam. No hope of taking a substation out and spreading the load if you have to, I guess?"

Ben punched the figure Harley had just given him into his own station computer and watched as the readout chattered forth on its strip of paper.

"Not a chance," he said softly. "At 182 per cent load input at your end, my estimate computes at 103 vehicles per kilometer, per lane, here, twenty-six minutes from now—which means I've got to cut the speed of cars passing my station down to 132 miles per hour—excuse me, I mean 220 kilometers. Take out one substation on top of that and I lose a fifth of my individual vehicle control units. I'd have to cut speed to less than thirty miles an hour."

"Right," said Harley bleakly.

They both knew what reducing the speed of cars passing Station 11 to that snail's pace could mean. It was not a case of having too little power to move the vehicles at proper speed. With the great fusion plants now in operation there was no lack of available raw power. The problem was simply a matter of a lack of individual car-control equipment to move that many extra cars safely, when overloading the powerway jammed the vehicles that closely together.

Once 16N had been opened, eight years ago, people had flocked in unexpected thousands to build their homes farther and farther from their jobs, counting on the powerway to get them to work and back each day. As with all the other great powerways of the nation, the traffic increases on 16N far exceeded the estimates of its builders. Reduce traffic speed to thirty miles an hour at Station 11, and cars farther back would be entering the powerway faster than those already on it could reach their destination and get off. There would be created an eighty-to-ninety-mile-long traffic jam that could take eight to ten hours to disperse. Luckily it was not the middle of winter now, with twenty below temperatures or a blizzard coming on—though the power strips of the lanes could keep the vehicles heated and safe in any case—but that did not mean such a traffic jam could be harmless. The grim tale of statistics from past powerway halts told otherwise. When a couple hundred thousand people became stranded, statistics became an enemy. For every hundred thousand men, women and children stranded, there would be so many pregnant women who could not be gotten to a hospital in time; there would be so many people dependent on some special medication who would run out of it before they could replenish their supply; there would be so many human-initiated accidents or crimes that would not otherwise have taken place . . .

A half hour's delay could be bad. An hour's delay could be tragic. The six-to-ten-hours delay necessary to clear the powerway of vehicles moving on self-power at no more than forty miles an hour could be catastrophic.

"Give me five minutes," said Ben. "I'll take the hopper and go have a look at those substations. Keep your phone open and emergency help on stand-by."

He got to his feet, keying in the automatic controls of the station. Going out the door, he glanced once more at the console. All lights red—and then it happened again. Red-to-green, red-to-green, red-to-green . . .

Ben bolted out of the station to the hopper shed.

The hopper was little more than an air-going motorcycle, only one step more complex than the strap-on, individual copter-harnesses used for sport touring of inaccessible areas from the air. He sat on a saddle, straddling a battery-driven power plant which activated the single-foiled rotor blade over his head. Ben flipped the motor switch the moment he touched the seat and he took off straight up into the air with a sudden jerk.

He swung the hopper toward the northern end of his section of the powerway and the computer remote chattered to life between the hopper control bars in his fists.

"Malfunction terminated. Malfunction terminated. All operations red. Malfunction traced to Substation 118."

118? Ben swung the hopper a little away from the sun, heading past Sub-stations 116 and 117 toward 118. What could be going on there that would threaten malfunction for moments at a stretch like this, then suddenly cease? There was almost something deliberate about the way the trouble was happening. A small coldness made itself felt at the back of Ben's neck. There had been attempts before this, by deranged individuals, to sabotage powerways. If someone was actually trying to wreck Substation 118 . . .

Like all stationmen, Ben held a State Peace Officer's commission, giving him authority comparable to that of a highway patrolman. But the sidearm that went with that commission was back at the station behind him. He glanced at the carrier rack below the handlebars of the hopper.

There was nothing there but the flare pistol provided for emergency signaling in the highly unlikely event of all power, including lights, failing to a section of the powerway.

Well, a flare pistol could look like a handgun at least, although the safety flares in its cartridges would not do noticeable damage to any saboteur much larger than a squirrel, at more than ten feet from the flare pistol's muzzle.

At about 180 feet of altitude, he swung the hopper over the tops of a band of spruce trees crowning the crest of a rise and looked down on the cleared hillside where Substation 118 sat overlooking the powerway.

At first glance, as he dropped the hopper down towards the substation, everything seemed to be in order. Ben's stationkeeper's eye noticed with approval that, at least at this substation, maintenance had taken down the snow fence. He could see the one that had been up, now rolled into a reddish-brown bundle beside the power-pack supercharger in one corner of the chain-link fence that enclosed the powerway substation.

Traffic was still light on the powerway in front of the substation. Only five cars were in sight, each gliding along in its own lane, automatically following the dark power-control stripe down the center of its lane. Nothing seemed in any way out of order—and then, as Ben dropped the hopper closer, he caught sight of a black figure charging at one section of the chain-link fence around the substation.

The figure hit. The fence sagged deeply inward, revealing that at least one of its posts had been broken off and the fence itself had been partially dug under at that point. The casing of a buried low-voltage control cable, now partly exposed by the digging, glinted in the sun. A wild, animal bawl of rage drifted up on the air and the black figure rebounded to reveal itself as a black bear about three hundred pounds in weight.

The voice of the computer remote on the hopper jabbered to life.

"Malfunction: Substation 118. Malfunction: Substation 118 . . . Malfunction terminated . . ."

The voice ceased as the fence fell back outwards from the exposed control cable. Ben swung the hopper in low over the station and the black bear stood upright on hind legs to chop her jaws at him. Staying prudently up out of reach, Ben stared about below him. He had grown up near Yellowstone National Park where black bears were very common, and he had heard—and seen—them do some odd things. But he had never heard of a black bear attacking a powerway substation for no obvious reason.

Then, he saw the reason.

Down at one corner of the fence enclosing the substation, spring drainage on the hill had evidently washed some earth away, so that there was a gap, small indeed, but evidently big enough, because Ben now spotted a bear cub, hardly bigger than a teddy bear, inside the fence.

So, he thought, balancing the hopper against the slight breeze blowing up the slope of the hill from the freeway, that was the answer. Junior had gotten inside the fence and lacked the sense to find his way out again. Mama bear was determined to rescue him, and those three hundred pounds of hers were something to reckon with, even in the case of a heavy-duty, eight foot, chain-link fence. A few more charges like that and she would break through the fence. The cub was small enough to run about safely under the conductors in the substation, but Mama was not—once she got inside the fence. The result could be not only a dead bear, but a dead substation, resulting in the sort of powerway breakdown and traffic jam Ben had been fearing.

He thumbed the switch on the hopper's phone remote.

"Harley?" he said.

"Right here," Harley's voice came back at him.

"The trouble's at 118. You probably got copy on that yourself from my station computer. It's being caused by a black bear trying to get inside the fence. She's dug down to a control cable and partly broken down the fence already. Got a cub inside that can't get out."

"I see." There was a moment's pause before Harley went on. "Should I send out a tranquilizer gun, or a rifle? Or have you got a rifle there?"

"Only a sidearm," said Ben, "and it's not with me. But I'll tell you something, Harley. It'll take you twenty-five minutes to get someone up here with a weapon, and that mother bear's going to be through the fence in less than half that time."

"Well," said Harley, "all we can do is try. You better not take any chances there yourself."

"Me?" said Ben. "Why would I want to take chances with a wound-up wild sow bear?"

"That's what I said," said Harley, "there's no good reason. But you've taken chances before. It makes better sense to wait for help."

A click over the phone signalized Harley's final word on the subject. Ben looked down below him once more.

The cub had now gotten up on the supercharger by the gate and was trying to climb the fence from the inside, with Mama's nose just beyond the chain links, following it anxiously. All went well until the young bear got to the top wire of the fence. This, unlike the rest of it—as Ben but not the cub knew—was a thin rod powered to vibrate rapidly when it was touched and so scare off squirrels and other small animals who might try to get over the fence into the substation. At the first feel of the rod buzzing against the pads of his forepaws, the cub squalled in alarm and fell back to the ground inside the fence.

Mama bear snarled, dealt the fence a couple of lightning punches and backed off with the plain intention of making another charge. Ben had a sudden mental picture of an electrocuted sow bear and miles on miles of backed-up traffic with numerous potential emergencies along every kilometer of the way.

"Hey! Hey! Stop!" he shouted downward. Mama stopped backing off and stood up, snarling, waving her paws and clearly inviting him to come down to face her on the level, man-to-bear. Ben felt cold. He had known mother bears to run for safety on being shouted at, leaving their cubs without a second thought. This one was evidently made of much sterner stuff.

He glanced at his wristwatch. 4:23. Where had the time gone? Already most of the nearly 200,000 vehicles in the evening traffic rush out of the Twin Cities would be committed to the powerway south of here. Another ten minutes and the first of their numbers would be passing Station 11. Already—he glanced down at the powerway—all eight of the northbound lanes were occupied, although the speed of the visible cars was still at the 160-180 mph of cruising normal.

The sound of Mama bear below him slamming into the fence once more, and the shrill, temporary protest of the station computer over his hopper's radio, as the control cable shorted momentarily, drew his attention back to the substation. There was no choice in the matter. He had to solve the problem at 118 and solve it by himself. There was no time to wait for anybody.

The obvious answer was to get the cub back outside the substation fence. There should be no difficulty to that if Ben could just get into the substation himself. But there was no room to land the hopper among the equipment inside the fence. And to land outside so that he could open the gate in the fence was to invite attack by Mama. He had nothing to defend himself in case of such attack but the flare pistol . . . Ben became suddenly thoughtful.

He took the pistol from its holding clip, adjusted the first flare in the chamber to go off on contact and maneuvered the hopper over towards Mama, who was snarling and punching at the weakened section of fence. She stopped this and rose up on her hind legs to face him as he brought the hopper closer. He lifted the flare pistol and fired into the spring-soft earth just before her.

The flare went off in a soundless explosion of white light. Mama gave one startled bawl and literally fell over backwards. A second later she was back on all four paws and humping for the protection of the spruce trees on the hill crest as if all memory of the cub had been washed from her mind.

With a small sigh of relief, Ben shoved the pistol back into its clip, swung the hopper about, and set it down in front of the gate in the substation fence. He got off the saddle and fished out his authorization card. As he took it from his pocket something half-heard, half-sensed, made him look around. It was a good thing for him he did so. Mama bear had gotten over her fright at the flare and was returning at top speed, headed straight toward him.

He fumbled with the card at the lock slot, then tore his gaze away from the charging bear long enough to look at the lock and slide the card in properly. Luckily it was an electronic lock. The second that the card was inserted, the bolt snicked back. He jerked the gate open, dived through, and pulled it shut and locked behind him just as Mama hit it from the other side with enough force to send him sprawling.

Mama woofed and grunted with fury on her side of the

fence. Ben scrambled to his feet and headed in search of the bear cub.

The cub was not hard to find. In fact, he had been standing less than a dozen feet away, watching. But as Ben came after him, he turned and skittered off among the equipment. Ben followed.

It was almost as bad, Ben found, as trying to catch a greased pig. The cub was young enough so that it was barely beyond being wobbly on his legs, but it was fast, nonetheless, and it could get through narrow spaces where Ben could not follow. Ben scrambled about after it, barking his shins and skinning his elbows as he ducked and dodged around the maze of equipment in the substation, and, after a few minutes of unsuccessful chase, he found himself getting short of wind.

He paused, leaning on the roll of snow fence with one hand to get his breath back, in a corner of the substation. In the excitement of chasing the cub he had forgotten about Mama bear. Now, pausing to breathe, he looked about for her and suddenly chilled at what he saw.

The fence around the substation, for most of its distance, had been anchored below ground level to keep it from being burrowed under by any of the same small animals that were prevented from climbing it by the top vibratory wire. The gate to the fence, however, necessarily cleared the ground by several inches, and evidently this had given Mama ideas. She was now energetically digging her way underneath the gate's bottom bar . . . and her powerful forepaws were removing the wet earth of springtime with such success that she seemed to be sinking into the ground as Ben watched. She would be inside the gate, at this rate, in a few more minutes.

Ben looked around for something he could put in the way to stop her. There was nothing movable at hand but the snow fence. He bent down and with some difficulty got the tied-up fence rolling. He rolled it up against the inside of the gate, opposite the hole the bear was digging. As Mama dug underneath the gate, the fencing should drop down into the hole she was making, and block her way—only temporarily, of course. A bear her size could heave that sort of barrier out of the way without trouble.

Then, inspiration struck. Ben looked down at his hands, which were wet from handling the snow fence. The wood of its stakes had been soaked by exposure to damp weather during the past week. He put a wet finger to his tongue and tasted salt. Of course, the snow fence had been close enough to the powerway so that the salt spread there by the winter maintenance crews had been flung out over the fencing by passing vehicles.

Ben grinned suddenly, in spite of Mama bear digging industriously only a foot or so away. There were advantages to being old-fashoned, after all, and particularly to remembering when power lines were not all underground. The wet, salt-impregnated snow fencing was only a few feet from the supercharger, that small unit the bear cub had climbed up on earlier. The supercharger was within the substation fence for the purpose of recharging the power packs of hoppers like his own, or the self-powered vehicles and heavy power tools of repair crews. He stepped over to it now and flicked its motor to life. Taking the two charging cables, he carried them over and attached their heavy clips, one at each end of a slat of the snow fence.

For a second, nothing happened . . . Then little blue flames appeared on the slat to which the clips were clamped, racing out over the adjoining sticks until the whole, thick roll of fencing burst suddenly into a blaze.

"Woof!" said Mama bear in astonishment and alarm, sitting back on her haunches. For a second she stared at the flaring snow fence just beyond the gate, and then, hastily, she backed off.

Ben turned and saw the cub standing, watching, less than a dozen feet behind him. He bolted in pursuit, and the cub, panicking, tumbled over backwards, scrambled to its feet and galloped away in a straight line that finally led it into a blind alley between the computer house and the cement base of a rack pole.

Ben snatched up the cub, which growled high-pitched growls and squirmed angrily in his hands. Carrying the ten-to-fifteen-pound youngster, he ran awkwardly to the low spot under the fence where it had gotten in. It was a good thing, thought Ben fleetingly, that Mama had not thought to try to dig into the substation at that point. Or, maybe it wasn't. If Mama had tried to dig in there, the cub might have had the sense to go back out the way it had entered and saved them all trouble. Falling to his knees, he shoved the protesting little animal like a fur bundle under the chain links into the open.

The cub went—but not without leaving Ben something to remember it by. As he let it go, it managed to get one paw around and stick a claw into Ben's right thumb. Then it was out on the hillside, galloping toward the line of spruce trees, and, a second later, Mama was right behind it.

Ben was left leaning against the fence, oblivious to the blood dripping from his thumb, exhaustedly but triumphantly watching the two furry black rumps headed safely away from Substation 118.

It was not until the emergency help sent out by Harley had put out the fire, relieved Ben from station duty, and brought him back to Powerway HQ back in the Twin Cities, that he remembered he had not yet called Marlie back to explain the emergency that had interrupted his phone call to her. He waited impatiently through the attentions of the nurse at HQ clinic, who was binding up his thumb while Harley asked questions.

"But what made you so sure that snow fence would catch fire?" Harley demanded. "You said it was wet."

"Remember when powerlines used to be above ground on poles?" Ben said. "Once, away back in the spring of 1970, the Twin Cities had a rash of pole fires. The salt shoveled on the streets to clear them of ice had gotten kicked up on the poles by cars passing them, and the salt, plus water, formed an electrolytic solution that caused arcing on the lines, shorts and fires."

"Humph," said Harley. "All right. But you took a chance again."

"If I hadn't," retorted Ben, "118 would be out right now, and the traffic jam from that wouldn't be untangled until tomorrow morning."

"Hmph," said Harley again.

He went off. Ben finally escaped from the nurse and found a phone booth. It took the phone computer a few seconds to follow the tracer Marlie had left, but Ben finally got her at a sporting goods store.

"Ben!" she said, when he told her. "That bear could have killed you."

"Sure," he interrupted. "But look at it from the other side. What if you'd been someone in a car jammed on the powerway because 118 had gone out? Besides—" he added quickly, "I can't possibly do tricks with this."

He held up his thickly bandaged thumb to the phone screen.

"Oh, Ben!" she said, "I think you'd do almost anything to get out of performing tonight. But what are Robby's friends going to think? It won't sound very convincing to them to say you can't work magic because your thumb got scratched. What if they tease Robby about it?"

"I've thought of that," Ben said earnestly. "Don't just say I won't be there because of a scratch."

"But that's the reason, isn't it?" Marlie said. "What else can I tell them?"

"Tell them the truth," said Ben. "The plain, unvarnished truth. They can't tease Robby about that."

He leaned back in the phone booth, contemplating his bandaged thumb blissfully.

"Tell them," he said, "I was mauled by a bear."

IDIOT SOLVANT

The afternoon sun, shooting the gap of the missing slat in the Venetian blind on the window of Art Willoughby's small rented room, splashed fair in Art's eyes, blinding him.

"Blast!" muttered Art. "Got to do something about that sun."

He flipped one long, lean hand up as an eyeshield and leaned forward once more over the university news sheet, unaware that he had reacted with his usual gesture and litany to the sun in his eye. His mouth watered. He spread out his sharp elbows on the experiment-scarred surface of his desk and reread the ad.

Volunteers for medical research testing. $1.60 hr., rm., board. Dr. Henry Rapp, Room 432, A Bldg., University Hospital.

"Board—" echoed Art aloud, once more unaware he had spoken. He licked his lips hungrily. *Food,* he thought. Plus wages. And hospital food was supposed to be good. If they would just let him have all he wanted. . . .

Of course, it would be worth it for the $1.60 an hour alone.

"I'll be sensible," thought Art. "I'll put it in the bank and just draw out what I need. Let's see—one week's work, say—seven times twenty-four times sixteen. Two-six-eight-eight—to the tenth. Two hundred sixty-eight dollars and eighty cents. . . ."

212

That much would support him for—mentally, he totted up his daily expenses. Ordinary expenses, that was. Room, a dollar-fifty. One and a half pound loaf of day-old bread at half price—thirteen cents. Half a pound of peanut butter, at ninety-eight cents for the three-pound economy size jar—seventeen cents roughly. One all-purpose vitamin capsule—ten cents. Half a head of cabbage, or whatever was in season and cheap—approximately twelve cents. Total, for shelter with all utilities paid and a change of sheets on the bed once a week, plus thirty-two hundred calories a day—two dollars and two cents.

Two dollars and two cents. Art sighed. Sixty dollars and sixty cents a month for mere existence. It was heart-breaking. When sixty dollars would buy a fine double magnum of imported champagne at half a dozen of the better restaurants in town, or a 1954 used set of the Encyclopedia Britannica, or the parts from a mail order house so that he could build himself a little ocean-hopper shortwave receiver so that he could tune in on foreign language broadcasts and practice understanding German, French, and Italian.

Art sighed. He had long ago come to the conclusion that since the two billion other people in the world could not very well all be out of step at the same time, it was probably he who was the odd one. Nowadays he no longer tried to fight the situation, but let himself reel uncertainly through life, sustained by the vague, persistent conviction that somewhere, somehow, in some strange fashion destiny would eventually be bound to call on him to have a profound effect on his fellow men.

It was a good twenty-minute walk to the university. Art scrambled lankily to his feet, snatched an ancient leather jacket off the hook holding his bagpipes, put his slide rule up on top of the poetry anthologies in the bookcase so he would know where to find it again—that being the most unlikely place, Q.E.D.—turned off his miniature electric furnace in which he had been casting up a gold pawn for his chess set, left some bread and peanut butter for his pet raccoon, now asleep in the wastebasket, and hurried off, closing the door.

"There's one more," said Margie Hansen, Dr. Hank Rapp's lab assistant. She hesitated. "I think you'd better see him." Hank looked up from his desk, surprised. He was a short, cheerful, tough-faced man in his late thirties.

"Why?" he said. "Some difficulties? Don't sign him up if you don't want to."

"No. No . . . I just think maybe you'd better talk to him. He passed the physical all right. It's just . . . well, you have a look at him."

"I don't get it," said Hank. "But send him in."

She opened the door behind her and leaned out through it.

"Mr. Willoughby, will you come in now?" She stood aside and Art entered. "This is Dr. Rapp, Mr. Willoughby. Doctor, this is Art Willoughby." She went out rather hastily, closing the door behind her.

"Sit down," said Hank, automatically. Art sat down, and Hank blinked a little at his visitor. The young man sitting opposite him resembled nothing so much as an unbearded Abe Lincoln. A *thin* unbearded Abe Lincoln, if it was possible to imagine our sixteenth President as being some thirty pounds lighter than he actually had been.

"*Are* you a student at the university here?" asked Hank, staring at the decrepit leather jacket.

"Well, yes," said Art, hoping the other would not ask him what college he was in. He had been in six of them, from Theater Arts to Engineering. His record in each was quite honorable. There was nothing to be ashamed of—it was just always a little bit difficult to explain.

"Well—" said Hank. He saw now why Margie had hesitated. But if the man was in good enough physical shape, there was no reason to refuse him. Hank made up his mind. "Has the purpose of this test been explained to you?"

"You're testing a new sort of stay-awake pill, aren't you?" said Art. "Your nurse told me all about it."

"Lab assistant," corrected Hank automatically. "There's no reason you can think of yourself, is there, why you shouldn't be one of the volunteers?"

"Well, no. I . . . I don't usually sleep much," said Art, painfully.

"That's no barrier." Hank smiled. "We'll just keep you awake until you get tired. How much do you sleep?" he asked, to put the younger man at his ease at least a little.

"Oh . . . six or seven hours."

"That's a little less than average. Nothing to get in our way . . . why, what's wrong?" said Hank, sitting up suddenly, for Art was literally struggling with his conscience, and his Abe Lincoln face was twisted unhappily.

"A . . . a week," blurted Art.

"A week! Are you—" Hank broke off, took a good look at his visitor and decided he was not kidding. Or at least, believed himself that he was not kidding. "You mean, less than an hour a night?"

"Well, I usually wait to the end of the week—Sunday morning's a good time. Everybody else is sleeping then, anyway. I get it over all at once—" Art leaned forward and put both his long hands on Hank's desk, pleadingly. "But can't you test me, anyway, Doctor? I need this job. Really, I'm desperate. If you could use me as a control, or something——"

"Don't worry," said Hank, grimly. "You've got the job. In fact if what you say is true, you've got more of a job than the rest of the volunteers. This is something we're all going to want to see!"

"Well," said Hank, ten days later. "Willoughby surely wasn't kidding."

Hank was talking to Dr. Arlic Bohn, of the Department of Psychology. Arlic matched Hank's short height, but outdid him otherwise to the tune of some fifty pounds and fifteen years. They were sitting in Hank's office, smoking cigarettes over the remains of their bag lunches.

"You don't think so?" said Arlic, lifting blond eyebrows toward his half-bare, round skull.

"Arlie! Ten days!"

"And no hallucinations?"

"None."

"Thinks his nurses are out to poison him? Doesn't trust the floor janitor?"

"No. No. No!"

Arlie blew out a fat wad of smoke.

"I don' believe it," he announced.

"I beg your pardon!"

"Oh—not you, Hank. No insults intended. But this boy of yours is running some kind of a con. Sneaking some sort of stimulant when you aren't looking."

"Why would he do that? We'd be glad to give him all

the stimulants he wants. He won't take them. And even if he was sneaking something—ten days, Arlie! Ten days and he looks as if he just got up after a good eight hours in his own bed." Hank smashed his half-smoked cigarette out in the ash try. "He's not cheating. He's a freak."

"You can't be that much of a freak."

"Oh, can't you?" said Hank. "Let me tell you some more about him. Usual body temperature—about one degree above normal average."

"Not unheard of. You know that."

"Blood pressure a hundred and five systolic, sixty-five diastolic. Pulse, fifty-five a minute. Height, six feet four, weight when he came in here a hundred and forty-two. We've been feeding him upwards of six thousand calories a day since he came in and I swear he still looks hungry. No history of childhood diseases. All his wisdom teeth. No cavities in any teeth. Shall I go on?"

"How is he mentally?"

"I checked up with the university testing bureau. They rate him in the genius range. He's started in six separate colleges and dropped out of each one. No trouble with grades. He gets top marks for a while, then suddenly stops going to class, accumulates a flock of incompletes, and transfers into something else. Arlie," said Hank, breaking off suddenly, lowering his voice and staring hard at the other, "I think we've got a new sort of man here. A mutation."

"Hank," said Arlie, crossing his legs comfortably, "when you get to be my age, you won't be so quick to think that Gabriel's going to sound the last trump in your own particular back yard. This boy's got a few physical peculiarities, he's admittedly bright, and he's conning you. You know our recent theory about sleep and sanity."

"Of course I—"

"Suppose," said Arlie, "I lay it out for you once again. The human being deprived of sleep for any length of time beyond what he's accustomed to, begins to show signs of mental abnormality. He hallucinates. He exhibits paranoid behavior. He becomes confused, flies into reasonless rages, and overreacts emotionally to trifles."

"Arthur Willoughby doesn't."

"That's my point." Arlie held up a small, square slab of a hand. "Let me go on. How do we explain these reactions?

We theorize that possibly sleep has a function beyond that of resting and repairing the body. In sleep we humans, at least, dream pretty constantly. In our dreams we act out our unhappiness, our frustrations, our terrors. Therefore sleep, we guess, may be the emotional safety valve by which we maintain our sanity against the intellectual pressures of our lives."

"Granted," said Hank, impatiently. "But Art—"

"Now, let's take something else. The problem-solving mechanism—"

"Damn it, Arlie—"

"If you didn't want my opinion, why did you bring me in on this . . . what was that you just said, Hank?"

"Nothing. Nothing."

"I'll pretend I didn't hear it. As I was saying—the problem-solving mechanism. It has been assumed for centuries that man attacked his intellectual problems consciously, and consciously solved them. Recent attention to this assumption has caused us to consider an alternate viewpoint, of which I may say I"—Arlie folded his hands comfortably over his bulging shirtfront—"was perhaps the earliest and strongest proponent. It may well be—I and some others now think—that Man is inherently incapable of consciously solving any new intellectual problem."

"The point is, Art Willoughby—what?" Hank broke off suddenly and stared across the crumpled paper bags and wax paper on his desk, at Arlie's chubby countenance. "What?"

"Incapable. Consciously." Arlie rolled the words around in his mouth. "By which I mean," he went on, with a slight grin. "Man has no *conscious* mechanism for the solution of new intellectual problems." He cocked his head at Hank, and paused.

"All right. All right!" fumed Hank. "Tell me."

"There seems to be a definite possibility," said Arlie, capturing a crumb from the piece of wax paper that had enwrapped his ham sandwich, and chewing on it thoughtfully, "that there may be more truth than poetry to the words *inspiration, illuminating flash*, and *stroke of genius*. It may well turn out that the new-problem solving mechanism is not under conscious control at all. Hm-m-m, yes. Did I tell you Marta wants me to try out one of these new all-liquid reducing diets? When a wife starts that—"

"Never mind Marta!" shouted Hank. "What about no-body being consciously capable of solving a problem?"

Arlie frowned.

"What I'm trying to say," he said, "is that when we try to solve a problem consciously, we are actually only utilizing an attention-focusing mechanism. Look, let me define a so-called 'new problem' for you—"

"One that you haven't bumped into before."

"No," said Arlie. "No. Now you're falling into a trap." He waggled a thick finger at Hank; a procedure intensely irritating to Hank, who suffered a sort of adrenalin explosion the moment he suspected anybody of lecturing down to him. "Does every hitherto undiscovered intersection you approach in your car constitute a new problem in automobile navigation? Of course not. A truly new problem is not merely some variation or combination of factors from problems you have encountered before. It's a problem that for you, at least, previously, did not even exist. It is, in fact, *a problem created by the solution of a problem of equal value in the past.*"

"All right. Say it is," scowled Hank. "Then what?"

"Then," said Arlie, "a true problem must always pose the special condition that no conscious tools of education or experience yet exist for its solution. Ergo, it cannot be handled on the conscious level. The logic of conscious thought is like the limb structure of the elephant, which, though ideally adapted to allow seven tons of animal a six-and-a-half foot stride, absolutely forbids it the necessary spring to jump across a seven-foot trench that bars its escape from the zoo. For the true problem, you've got to get from hyar to thar without any stepping stone to help you across the gap that separates you from the solution. So, you're up against it, Hank. You're in a position where you can't fly but you got to. What do you do?"

"You tell me," glowered Hank.

"The answer's simple," said Arlie, blandly. "You fly."

"But you just said I couldn't!" Hank snapped.

"What I said," said Arlie, "was two things. One, you can't fly; two, you got to fly. What you're doing is clinging to one, which forces you to toss out two. What I'm pointing out is that you should cling to two, which tosses out one. Now, your conscious, experienced, logical mind *knows* you can't fly. The whole idea's silly. It won't even consider the problem. But your unconscious—aha!"

"What about my unconscious?"

"Why, your unconscious isn't tied down by any ropes of logical process like that. When it wants a solution, it just goes looking for it."

"Just like that."

"Well," Arlie frowned, "not just like that. First it has to fire up a sort of little donkey-engine of its own which we might call the intuitive mechanism. And that's where the trickiness comes in. Because the intuitive mechanism seems to be all power and no discipline. Its great usefulness comes from the fact that it operates under absolutely no restrictions—and of course this includes the restriction of control by the conscious mind. It's a sort of idiot savant . . . no, idiot solvant would be a better term." He sighed.

"So?" said Hank, after eyeing the fat man for a moment. "What's the use of it all? If we can't control it, what good is it?"

"What good is it?" Arlie straightened up. "Look at art. Look at science! Look at civilization. You aren't going to deny the existence of inspiration, are you? They exist—and one day we're going to find some better method of sparking them than the purely inductive process of operating the conscious, attention-focusing mechanism in hopes that something will catch."

"You think that's possible?"

"I know it's possible."

"I see," said Hank. There was a moment or so of silence in the office. "Well," said Hank, "about this little problem of my own, which I hate to bring you back to, but you did say the other day you had some ideas about this Art Willoughby. Of course, you were probably only speaking inspirationally, or perhaps I should say, without restriction by the conscious mind——"

"I was just getting to that," interrupted Arlie. "This Art Willoughby obviously suffers from what educators like to call poor work habits. Hm-m-m, yes. Underdevelopment of the conscious, problem-focusing mechanism. He tries to get by on a purely intuitive basis. When this fails him, he is helpless. He gives up—witness his transfers from college to college. On the other hand, when it works good, it works very, very good. He has probably come up with some way of keeping himself abnormally stimulated, either externally or internally. The only trouble will be that he probably isn't even conscious of it, and he certainly has no control over it. He'll fall asleep any moment now. And when he wakes up you'll want him to duplicate his feat of wakefulness but he won't be able to do it."

Hank snorted disbelievingly.

"All right," said Arlie. "All right. Wait and see."

"I will," said Hank. He stood up. "Want to come along and see him? He said he was starting to get foggy this morning. I'm going to try him with the monster."

"What," wondered Arlie, ingenuously, rising, "if it puts him to sleep?"

Hank threw him a glance of pure fury.

"Monster!" commanded Hank. He, Arlie, and Margie Hansen were gathered in Art's hospital room, which was a pleasant, bedless place already overflowing with books and maps. Art, by hospital rules deprived of such things as tools and pets, had discovered an interest in the wars of Hannibal of Carthage. At the present moment he was trying to pick the truth out of the rather confused reports following Hannibal's escape from the Romans, after Antiochus had been defeated at Magnesia and surrendered his great general to Rome.

Right now, however, he was forced to lay his books aside and take the small white capsule which Margie, at Hank's order, extended to him. Art took it; then hesitated.

"Do you think it'll make me very jittery?" he asked.

"It should just wake you up," said Hank.

"I told you how I am with things like coffee. That's why I never drink coffee, or take any stimulants. Half a cup and my eyes feel like they're going to pop out of my head."

"There wouldn't," said Hank a trifle sourly, "be much point in our paying you to test out the monster if you refused to take it, now would there?"

"Oh . . . oh, no," said Art, suddenly embarrassed. "Water?"

Margie gave him a full glass and threw an unkind glance at her superior.

"If it starts to bother you, Art, you tell us right away," she said.

Art gulped the capsule down. He stood there waiting as if he expected an explosion from the region of his stomach. Nothing happened, and after a second or two he relaxed.

"How long does it take?" he asked.

"About fifteen minutes," said Hank.

They waited. At the end of ten minutes, Art began to brighten up and said he was feeling much more alert. At fifteen minutes, he was sparkling-eyed and cheerful, almost, in fact, bouncy.

"Awfully sorry, Doctor," he said to Hank. "Awfully sorry I hesitated over taking the monster that way. It was just that coffee and things—"

"That's all right," said Hank, preparing to leave. "Margie'll take you down for tests now."

"Marvelous pill. I recommend it highly," said Art, going out the door with Margie. They could hear him headed off down the corridor outside toward the laboratory on the floor below, still talking.

"Well?" said Hank.

"Time will tell," said Arlie.

"Speaking of time," continued Hank. "I've got the plug-in coffee pot back at the office. Have you got time for a quick cup?"

". . . Don't deny it," Hank was saying over half-empty cups in the office a short while later. "I heard you; I read you loud and clear. If a man makes his mind up to it, he can fly, you said."

"Not at all. And besides, I was only speaking academically," retorted Arlie, heatedly. "Just because I'm prepared to entertain fantastic notions academically doesn't mean I'm going to let you try to shove them down my throat on a practical basis. Of course nobody can fly."

"According to your ideas, someone like Willoughby could if he punched the right buttons in him."

"Nonsense. Certainly he can't fly."

There was the wild patter of feminine feet down the hallway outside the office, the door was flung open, and Margie tottered in. She clung to the desk and gasped, too out of wind to talk.

"What's wrong?" cried Hank.

"Art . . ." Margie managed, "flew out—lab window."

Hank jumped to his feet, and pulled his chair out for her. She fell into it gratefully.

"Nonsense!" said Arlie. "Illusion. Or"—he scowled at Margie—"collusion of some sort."

"Got your breath back, yet? What happened?" Hank was demanding. Margie nodded and drew a deep breath.

"I was testing him," she said, still breathlessly. "He was talking a blue streak and I could hardly get him to stand still. Something about Titus Quintus Flamininius, the three-body problem, Sauce Countess Waleska, the family Syrphidae of the order Diptera—all mixed up. Oh, he was babbling! And all of a sudden he dived out an open window."

"Dived?" barked Arlie. "I thought you said he *flew*?"

"Well, the laboratory's on the third floor!" wailed Margie, almost on the verge of tears.

Further questioning elicited the information that when Margie ran to the window, expecting to see a shattered ruin on the grass three stories below, she perceived Art swinging by one arm from the limb of an oak outside the window. In response to sharp queries from Arlie, she asserted vehemently that the closest grabable limb of the oak was, however, at least eight feet from the window out which Art had jumped, fallen, or dived.

"And then what?" said Hank.

Then, according to Margie, Art had uttered a couple of Tarzanlike yodels, and swung himself to the ground. When last seen he had been running off across the campus through the cool spring sunlight, under the budding trees, in his slacks and shirt unbuttoned at the throat. He had been heading in a roughly northeasterly direction—*i.e.*, toward town—and occasionally bounding into the air as if from a sheer access of energy.

"Come on!" barked Hank, when he had heard this. He led the way at a run toward the hospital parking lot three stories below and his waiting car.

On the other side of the campus, at a taxi stand, the three of them picked up Art's trail. A cab driver waiting there remembered someone like Art taking another cab belonging to the same company. When Hank identified the passenger as a patient under his, Hank's, care, and further identified himself as a physician from the university hospital, the cab driver they were talking to agreed to call in for the destination of Art's cab.

The destination was a downtown bank. Hank, Arlie, and Margie piled back into Hank's car and went there.

When they arrived, they learned that Art had already come and gone, leaving some confusion behind him. A vice-president of the bank, it appeared, had made a loan to Art of two hundred and sixty-eight dollars and eighty cents; and was now, it seemed, not quite sure as to why he had done so.

"He just talked me into it, I guess," the vice-president was saying unhappily as Hank and the others came dashing up. It further developed that Art had had no collateral. The vice-president had been given the impression that the money was to be used to develop some confusing but highly useful discovery or discoveries concerning Hannibal, encylopedias, the sweat fly and physics—with something about champagne and a way of preparing trout for the gourmet appetite.

A further check with the cab company produced the information that Art's taxi had taken him on to a liquor store. They followed. At the liquor store they discovered that Art had purchased the single jeroboam of champagne (Moet et Chandon) that the liquor store had on hand, and had mentioned that he was going on to a restaurant. What restaurant, the cab company was no longer able to tell them. Art's driver had just announced that he would not be answering his radio for the next half hour.

They began checking the better and closer restaurants. At the fourth one, which was called the Calíce d'Or, they finally ran Art to ground. They found him seated alone at a large, round table, surrounded by gold-tooled leather volumes of a brand-new encyclopedia, eating and drinking what turned out to be Truite Sauce Countess Waleska and champagne from the jeroboam, now properly iced.

"Yahoo!" yelped Art, as he saw them approaching. He waved his glass on high, sloshing champagne liberally about. "Champagne for everybody! Celebrate Dr. Rapp's pill!"

"You," said Hank, "are coming back to the hospital."

"Nonsense! Glasses! Champagne for m'friends!"

"Oh, Art!" cried Margie.

"He's fried to the gills," said Arlie.

"Not at all," protested Art. "Illuminated. Blinding flash. Understand everything. D'you know all knowledge has a common point of impingement?"

"Call a taxi, Margie," commanded Hank.

"Encyclopedia. Champagne bubble. Same thing."

"Could I help you, sir?" inquired a waiter, approaching Hank.

"We want to get our friend here home—"

"All roads lead knowledge. Unnerstand ignorance, unnerstand everything—"

"I understand, sir. Yes sir, he paid the check in advance—"

"Would *you* like to speak three thousand, four hundred and seventy-one languages?" Art was asking Arlie.

"Of course," Arlie was saying, soothingly.

"My assistant has gone to get a taxi, now. I'm Dr. Rapp of the university hospital, and—"

"When I was child," announced Art, "thought as child, played child; now man—put away childish things."

"Here's the young lady, sir."

"But who will take care of pet raccoon?"

"I flagged a taxi down. It's waiting out front."

"Hoist him up," commanded Hank.

He and Arlie both got a firm hold on a Willoughby arm and maneuvered Art to his feet.

"This way," said Hank, steering Art toward the door.

"The universe," said Art. He leaned confidentially toward Hank, almost toppling the three of them over. "Only two inches across."

"That so?" grunted Hank.

"Hang on to Arlie, Art, and you won't fall over. There—" said Margie. Art blinked and focused upon her with some difficulty.

"Oh . . . there you are—" he said. "Love you. Naturally. Only real woman in universe. Other four point seven to the nine hundred seventeenth women in universe pale imitations. Marry me week Tuesday, three P.M. courthouse, wear blue." Margie gasped.

"Open the door for us, will you?"

"Certainly sir," said the waiter, opening the front door to the Calice d'Or. A pink and gray taxi was drawn up at the curb.

"Sell stock in Wehauk Cannery immediately," Art was

saying to the waiter. "Mismanagement. Collapse." The waiter blinked and stared. "News out in ten days."

"But how did you know I had—" the waiter was beginning as they shoved Art into the back seat of the cab. Margie got in after him.

"Ah, there you are," came Art's voice from the cab. "First son of Charles Jonas—blond hair, blue eyes. Second son, William—"

"I'll send somebody to pick up that encyclopedia and anything else he left," said Hank to the waiter and got into the taxi himself. The taxi pulled way from the curb.

"Well," said the waiter, after a long pause in which he stared after the receding cab, to the doorman who had just joined him on the sidewalk, "how do you like that? Ever see anything like that before?"

"No, and I never saw anyone with over a gallon of champagne in him still walking around, either," said the doorman.

". . . And the worst of it is," said Hank to Arlie, as they sat in Hank's office, two days later. "Margie *is* going to marry him."

"What's wrong with that?" asked Arlie.

"What's wrong with it? Look at that!" Hank waved his hand at an object in the center of his desk.

"I've seen it," said Arlie.

They both examined the object. It appeared to be an ordinary moveable telephone with a cord and wall plug. The plug, however, was plugged into a small cardboard box the size of a cheese carton, filled with a tangled mess of wire and parts cannibalized from a cheap portable radio. The box was plugged into nothing.

"What was that number again . . . oh yes," said Arlie. He picked up the phone and dialed a long series of numbers. He held the phone up so that they could both hear. There was a faint buzzing ring from the earphone and then a small, tinny voice filled the office.

". . . The time is eight forty-seven. The temperature is eighteen degrees above zero, the wind westerly at eight miles an hour. The forecast for the Anchorage area is continued cloudy and some snow with a high of twenty-two degrees, a low tonight of nine above. Elsewhere in Alaska—"

Arlie sighed, and replaced the phone in its cradle.

"We bring him back here," said Hank, "stewed to the gills. In forty minutes before he passed out, he builds this trick wastebasket of his that holds five times as much as it ought to. He sleeps seven hours and wakes up as good as ever. What should I do? Shoot him, or something? I must have some responsibility to the human race—if not to Margie."

"He seems sensible now?"

"Yes, but what do I do?"

"Hypnosis."

"You keep saying that. I don't see—"

"We must," said Arlie, "inhibit the connection of his conscious mind with the intuitive mechanism. The wall between the two—the normal wall—seems to have been freakishly thin in his case. Prolonged sleeplessness, combined with the abnormal stimulation of your monster, has caused him to break through—to say to the idiot-solvant, '*Solve!*' And the idiot solvant in the back of his head has provided him with a solution."

"I still think it would be better for me to shoot him."

"You are a physician——"

"You would remind me of that. All right, so I can't shoot him. I don't even want to shoot him. But, Arlie, what's going to happen to everybody? Here I've raised up a sort of miracle worker who can probably move the North American continent down to the South Pacific if he wants to—only it just happens he's also a featherheaded butterfly who never lit on one notion for more than five minutes at a time in his life. Sure, I've got a physician's responsibility toward him. But what about my responsibility to the rest of the people in the world?"

"There is no responsibility being violated here," said Arlie patiently. "Simply put him back the way you found him."

"No miracles?"

"None. At least, except accidental ones."

"It might be kinder to shoot him."

"Nonsense," said Arlie sharply. "It's for the good of everybody." Hank sighed, and rose.

"All right," he said. "Let's go."

They went down the hall to Art's room. They found him

seated thoughtfully in his armchair, staring at nothing, his books and maps ignored around him.

"Good morning, Art," said Arlie.

"Oh? Hello," said Art, waking up. "Is it time for tests?"

"In a way," said Arlie. He produced a small box surmounted by a cardboard disk on which were inked alternate spirals of white and black. He plugged the box in to a handy electric socket by means of the cord attached to it, and set it on a small table in front of Art. The disk began to revolve. "I want you to watch that," said Arlie.

Art stared at it.

"What do you see?" asked Arlie.

"It looks like going down a tunnel," said Art.

"Indeed it does," said Arlie. "Just imagine yourself going down that tunnel. Down the tunnel. Faster and faster. . . ." He continued to talk quietly and persuasively for about a minute and a half, at the end of which Art was limply demonstrating a state of deep trance. Arlie brought him up a bit for questioning.

". . . And how do these realizations, these answers come to you?" Arlie was asking a few minutes later.

"In a sort of a flash," replied Art. "A blinding flash."

"That is the way they have always come to you?"

"More lately," said Art.

"Yes," said Arlie, "that's the way it always is just before people outgrow these flashes—you know that."

There was a slight pause.

"Yes," said Art.

"You have now outgrown these flashes. You have had your last flash. Flashes belong to childhood. You have had a delayed growing-up, but from now on you will think like an adult. Logically. You will think like an adult. Repeat after me."

"I will think like an adult," intoned Art.

Arlie continued to hammer away at his point for a few more minutes; then he brought Art out of his trance, with a final command that if Art felt any tendency to a recurrence of his flashes he should return to Arlie for further help in suppressing them.

"Oh, hello, Doctor," said Art to Hank, as soon as he woke up. "Say, how much longer are you going to need me as a test subject?"

Hank made a rather unhappy grimace.

"In a hurry to leave?" he said.

"I don't know," said Art, enthusiastically, rubbing his long hands together as he sat up in the chair, "but I was just thinking maybe it's time I got to work. Settled down. As long as I'm going to be a married man shortly."

"We can turn you loose today, if you want," said Hank.

When Art stepped once more into his room, closing the door behind him and taking off his leather jacket to hang it up on the hook holding his bagpipes, the place seemed so little changed that it was hard to believe ten full days had passed. Even the raccoon was back asleep in the wastebasket. It was evident the landlady had been doing her duty about keeping the small animal fed—Art had worried a little about that. The only difference, Art thought, was that the room seemed to feel smaller.

He sighed cheerfully and sat down at the desk, drawing pencil and paper to him. The afternoon sun, shooting the gap of the missing slat on the Venetian blind at the window, splashed fair in Art's eyes, blinding him.

"Blast!" he said aloud. "Got to do something about that—"

He checked himself suddenly with one hand halfway up to shield his eyes, and smiled. Opening a drawer of the desk, he took out a pair of heavy kitchen scissors. He made a single cut into the rope slot at each end of the plastic slat at the bottom of the blind, snapped the slat out of position, and snapped it back in where the upper slat was missing.

Still smiling, he picked up the pencil and doodled the name *Margie* with a heart around it in the upper left-hand corner as he thought, with gaze abstracted. The pencil moved to the center of the piece of paper and hovered there.

After a moment, it began to sketch.

What it sketched was a sort of device to keep the sun out of Art's eyes. At the same time, however, it just happened to be a dome-shaped all-weather shield capable of protecting a city ten miles in diameter the year around. The "skin" of the dome consisted of a thin layer of carbon dioxide such as one finds in the bubbles of champagne, generated and maintained by magnetic lines of force emanating from three heavily charged bodies, in rotation about each other at the apex of the dome and superficially housed in a framework the design of which was reminiscent of the wing structure found in the family Syriphidae of the order Diptera.

Art continued to smile as the design took form. But it was a thoughtful smile, a mature smile. Hank and Arlie had been quite right about him. He had always been a butterfly, flitting from notion to notion, playing.

But then, too, he had always been a bad hypnotic subject, full of resistances.

And he was about to have a wife to care for. Consequently it is hard to say whether Arlie and Hank would have been reassured if they could have seen Art at that moment. His new thinking was indeed adult, much more so than the other two could have realized. Where miracles were concerned, he had given up *playing*.

Now, he was *working*.

ON MESSENGER MOUNTAIN

I

It was raw, red war for all of them, from the moment the two ships intercepted each other, one degree off the plane of the ecliptic and three diameters out from the second planet of the star that was down on the charts as K94. K94 was a GO type star; and the yelping battle alarm of the trouble horn tumbled sixteen men to their stations. This was at thirteen hours, twenty-one minutes, four seconds of the ship's day.

Square in the scope of the laser screen, before the Survey Team Leader aboard the *Harrier*, appeared the gray, lightedged silhouette of a ship unknown to the ship's library. And the automatic reflexes of the computer aboard, that takes no account of men not yet into their vacuum suits, took over. The *Harrier* disappeared into no-time.

She came out again at less than a quarter-mile's distance from the stranger ship and released a five-pound weight at a velocity of five miles a second relative to the velocity of the alien ship. Then she had gone back into no-time again—but not before the alien, with computer-driven reflexes of its own, had rolled like the elongated cylinder it resembled, and laid out a soft green-colored beam of radiation which opened up the *Harrier* forward like a hot knife through butter left long on the table. Then it too was gone into no-time. The time aboard the *Harrier* was thirteen hours, twenty-two minutes and eighteen seconds; and on both ships there were dead.

"There are good people in the human race," Cal Hartlett had written only two months before, to his uncle on Earth, *"who feel that it is not right to attack other intelligent beings without warning—to drop five-pound weights at destructive relative velocities on a strange ship simply because you find it at large in space and do not know the race that built it.*

"What these gentle souls forget is that when two strangers encounter in space, nothing at all is known—and everything must be. The fates of both races may hinge on which one is first to kill the other and study the unknown carcass. Once contact is made, there is no backing out and no time for consideration. For we are not out here by chance, neither are they, and we do not meet by accident."

Cal Hartlett was Leader of the Mapping Section aboard the *Harrier,* and one of those who lived through that first brush with the enemy. He wrote what he wrote as clearly as if he had been Survey Leader and in command of the ship. At any moment up until the final second when it was too late, Joe Aspinall, the Survey Leader, could have taken the *Harrier* into no-time and saved them. He did not; as no commander of a Survey Ship ever has. In theory, they could have escaped.

In practice, they had no choice.

When the *Harrier* ducked back into no-time, aboard her they could hear the slamming of emergency bulkheads. The mapping room, the fore weight-discharge room and the sleeping quarters all crashed shut as the atmosphere of the ship whiffed out into space through the wound the enemy's beam had made. The men beyond the bulkheads and in the damaged sections would have needed to be in their vacuum suits to survive. There had not been time for that, so those men were dead.

The *Harrier* winked back into normal space.

Her computer had brought her out of the far side of the second planet, which they had not yet surveyed. It was larger than Earth, with somewhat less gravity but a deeper atmospheric envelope. The laser screen picked up the enemy reappearing almost where she had disappeared, near the edge of that atmosphere.

The *Harrier* winked back all but alongside the other and laid a second five-pound weight through the center of the cylindrical vessel. The other ship staggered, disappeared into no-time and appeared again far below, some five miles above planetary surface in what seemed a desperation attempt to gain breathing time. The *Harrier* winked after her—and came out within five hundred yards, square in the path of the green beam which it seemed was waiting for her. It opened up the drive and control rooms aft like a red-hot poker lays open a cardboard box.

A few miles below, the surface stretched up the peaks of titanic mountains from horizon to horizon.

"Ram!" yelled the voice of Survey Leader Aspinwall, in warning over the intercom.

The *Harrier* flung itself at the enemy. It hit like an elevator falling ten stories to a concrete basement. The cylindrical ship broke in half in midair and bodies erupted from it. Then its broken halves and the ruined *Harrier* were falling separately to the surface below and there was no more time for anyone to look. The clock stood at 13 hours, 23 minutes and 4 seconds.

The power—except from emergency storage units—was all but gone. As Joe punched for a landing the ship fell angling past the side of a mountain that was a monster among giants, and jarred to a stop. Joe keyed the intercom of the control board before him.

"Report," he said.

In the Mapping Secton Cal Hartlett waited for other voices to speak before him. None came. He thumbed his audio.

"The whole front part of the ship's dogged shut, Joe," he said. "No use waiting for anyone up there. So—this is Number Six reporting. I'm all right."

"Number Seven," said anther voice over the intercom. "Maury. O.K."

"Number Eight. Sam. O.K."

"Number Nine. John. O.K. . . ."

Reports went on. Numbers Six through Thirteen reported themselves as not even shaken up. From the rest there was no answer.

In the main Control Section, Joe Aspinwall stared bleakly at his dead control board. Half of his team was dead.

The time was 13 hours, 30 minutes, no seconds.

He shoved that thought from his mind and concentrated

on the positive rather than the negative elements of the situation they were in. Cal Hartlett, he thought, was one. Since he could only have eight survivors of his Team, he felt a deep gratitude that Cal should be one of them. He would need Cal in the days to come. And the other survivors of the Team would need him, badly.

Whether they thought so at this moment or not.

"All right," said Joe, when the voices had ended. "We'll meet outside the main airlock, outside the ship. There's no power left to unseal those emergency bulkheads. Cal, Doug, Jeff—you'll probably have to cut your way out through the ship's side. Everybody into respirators and warmsuits. According to pre-survey—" he glanced at the instruments before him—"there's oxygen enough in the local atmosphere for the respirators to extract, so you won't need emergency bottles. But we're at twenty-seven thousand three hundred above local sea-level. So it'll probably be cold—even if the atmosphere's not as thin here as it would be at this altitude on Earth." He paused. "Everybody got that? Report!"

They reported. Joe unharnessed himself and got up from his seat. Turning around, he faced Maury Taller.

Maury, rising and turning from his own communications board on the other side of the Section, saw that the Survey Leader's lean face was set in iron lines of shock and sorrow under his red hair. They were the two oldest members of the Team, whose average age had been in the mid-twenties. They looked at each other without words as they went down the narrow tunnel to the main airlock and, after putting on respirators and warmsuits, out into the alien daylight outside.

The eight of them gathered together outside the arrowhead shape of their *Harrier*, ripped open fore and aft and as still now as any other murdered thing.

Above them was a high, blue-black sky and the peaks of mountains larger than any Earth had ever known. A wind blew about them as they stood on the side of one of the mountains, on a half-mile wide shelf of tilted rock. It narrowed backward and upward like a dry streambed up the side of the mountain in one direction. In the other it broke off abruptly fifty yards away, in a cliff-edge that hung over eye-shuddering depths of a clefted valley, down in which they could just glimpse a touch of something like jungle greenness.

Beyond that narrow clefted depth lifted the great mountains, like carvings of alien devils too huge to be completely seen from one point alone. Several thousand feet above them on their mountain, the white spill of a glacier flung down a slope that was too steep for ice to have clung to in the heavier gravity of Earth. Above the glacier, which was shaped like a hook, red-gray peaks of the mountain rose like short towers stabbing the blue-dark sky. And from these, even as far down as the men were, they could hear the distant trumpeting and screaming of winds whistling in the peaks.

They took it all in in a glance. And that was all they had time to do. Because in the same moment that their eyes took in their surroundings, something no bigger than a man but tiger-striped and moving with a speed that was more than human, came around the near end of the dead *Harrier,* and went through the eight men like a predator through a huddle of goats.

Maury Taller and even Cal, who towered half a head over the rest of the men, all were brushed aside like cardboard cutouts of human figures. Sam Cloate, Cal's assistant in the mapping section, was ripped open by one sweep of a clawed limb as it charged past, and the creature tore out the throat of Mike DeWall with a sideways slash of its jaws. Then it was on Joe Aspinall.

The Survey Team Leader went down under it. Reflex got metal cuffs on the gloves of his warmsuit up and crossed in front of his throat, his forearms and elbows guarding his belly, before he felt the ferocious weight grinding him into the rock and twisting about on top of him. A snarling, worrying noise sounded in his ears. He felt teeth shear through the upper part of his thigh and grate on bone.

There was an explosion. He caught just a glimpse of Cal towering oddly above him, a signal pistol fuming in one big hand.

Then the worrying weight pitched itself full upon him and lay still. And unconsciousness claimed him.

II

When Joe came to, his respirator mask was no longer on

his face. He was looking out, through the slight waviness of a magnetic bubble field, at ten mounds of small rocks and gravel in a row about twenty feet from the ship. Nine crosses and one six-pointed star. The Star of David would be for Mike DeWall. Joe looked up and saw the unmasked face of Maury Taller looming over him, with the dark outside skin of the ship beyond him.

"How're you feeling, Joe?" Maury asked.

"All right," he answered. Suddenly he lifted his head in fright. "My leg—I can't feel my leg!" Then he saw the silver anesthetic band that was clamped about his right leg, high on the thigh. He sank back with a sigh.

Maury said, "You'll be all right, Joe."

The words seemed to trip a trigger in his mind. Suddenly the implications of his damaged leg burst on him. He was the Leader!

"Help me!" he gritted, trying to sit up.

"You ought to lie still."

"Help me up, I said!" The leg was a dead weight. Maury's hands took hold and helped raise his body. He got the leg swung off the edge of the surface on which he had been lying, and got into sitting position. He looked around him.

The magnetic bubble had been set up to make a small, air-filled addition of breathable ship's atmosphere around the airlock entrance of the *Harrier*. It enclosed about as much space as a good-sized living room. Its floor was the mountain hillside's rock and gravel. A mattress from one of the ship's bunks had been set up on equipment boxes to make him a bed. At the other end of the bubble-enclosed space something as big as a man was lying zippered up in a gray cargo freeze-sack.

"What's that?" Joe demanded. "Where's everybody?"

"They're checking equipment in the damaged sections," answered Maury. "We shot you full of medical juices. You've been out about twenty hours. That's about three-quarters of a local day-and-night cycle here." He grabbed the wounded man's shoulders suddenly with both hands. "Hold it! What're you trying to do?"

"Have a look in that freeze-sack there," grunted the Team Leader between his teeth. "Let go of me, Maury. I'm still in charge here!"

"Sit still," said Maury. "I'll bring it to you."

He went over to the bag, taking hold of one of the carrying handles he dragged it back. It came easily in the lesser gravity, only a little more than eight-tenths of Earth's. He hauled the thing to the bed and unzipped it.

Joe stared. What was inside was not what he had been expecting.

"Cute, isn't it?" said Maury.

They looked down at the hard-frozen gray body of a biped, with the back of its skull shattered and burnt by the flare of a signal pistol. It lay on its back. The legs were somewhat short for the body and thick, as the arms were thick. But elbow and knee joints were where they should be, and the hands had four stubby gray fingers, each with an opposed thumb. Like the limbs, the body was thick— almost waistless. There were deep creases, as if tucks had been taken in the skin, around the body under the arm-pits, around the waist and around the legs and arms.

The head, though, was the startling feature. It was heavy and round as a ball, sunk into thick folds of neck and all but featureless. Two long slits ran down each side into the neck and shoulder area. The slits were tight closed. Like the rest of the body, the head had no hair. The eyes were little pockmarks, like raisins sunk into a doughball, and there were no visible brow ridges. The nose was a snout-end set almost flush with the facial surface. The mouth was lipless, a line of skin folded together, through which now glinted barely a glimpse of close-set, large, tridentated teeth.

"What's this?" said Joe. "Where's the thing that attacked us?"

"This is it," said Maury. "One of the aliens from the other ship."

Joe stared at him. In the brighter, harsher light from the star K94 overhead, he noticed for the first time a sprinkling of gray hairs in the black shock above Maury's spade-shaped face. Maury was no older than Joe himself.

"What're you talking about?" said Joe. "I saw that thing that attacked me. And this isn't it!"

"Look," said Maury and turned to the foot of the bed. From one of the equipment boxes he brought up eight by ten inch density photographs. "Here," he said, handing them to the Survey Team Leader. "The first one is set for bone density."

Joe took them. It showed the skeleton of the being at his feet . . . and it bore only a relative kinship to the shape of the being itself.

Under the flesh and skin that seemed so abnormally thick, the skull was high-forebrained and well developed. Heavy brown ridges showed over deep wells for the eyes. The jaw and teeth were the prognathous equipment of a carnivorous animal.

But that was only the beginning of the oddities. Bony ridges of gill structures were buried under a long fold on either side of the head, neck and shoulders. The rib cage was enormous and the pelvis tiny, buried under eight or nine inches of the gray flesh. The limbs were literally double-jointed. There was a fantastic double structure of ball and socket that seemed wholly unnecessary. Maury saw the Survey Leader staring at one hip joint and leaned over to tap it with the blunt nail of his forefinger.

"Swivel and lock," said Maury. "If the joint's pulled out, it can turn in any direction. Then, if the muscles surrounding it contract, the two ball joints interlace those bony spurs there and lock together so that they operate as a single joint in the direction chosen. That hip joint can act like the hip joint on the hind leg of a quadruped, or the leg of a biped. It can even adapt for jumping and running with maximum efficiency. —Look at the toes and the fingers."

Joe looked. Hidden under flesh, the bones of feet and hands were not stubby and short, but long and powerful. And at the end of finger and toe bones were the curved, conical claws they had seen rip open Sam Cloate with one passing blow.

"Look at these other pictures now," said Maury, taking the first one off the stack Joe held. "These have been set for densities of muscle—that's this one here—and fat. Here. And this one is set for soft internal organs—here." He was down to the last. "And this one was set for the density of the skin. Look at that. See how thick it is, and how great folds of it are literally tucked away underneath in those creases.

"Now," said Maury, "look at this closeup of a muscle. See how it resembles an interlocking arrangement of innumerable tiny muscles? Those small muscles can literally shift to adapt to different skeletal positions. They can take away beef from one area and add it to an adjoining area. Each little muscle actually holds on to its neighbors, and they have little sphincter-sealed tube-systems to hook on to whatever blood-conduit is close. By increased hookup they can increase the blood supply to any particular muscle that's being overworked. There's parallel nerve connections."

Maury stopped and looked at the other man.

"You see?" said Maury. "This alien can literally be four or five different kinds of animal. Even a fish! And no telling how many varieties of each kind. We wondered a little at first why he wasn't wearing any kind of clothing, but we didn't wonder after we got these pictures. Why would he need clothing when he can adapt to any situation— Joe!" said Maury. "You see it, don't you? You see the natural advantage these things have over us all?"

Joe shook his head.

"There's no body hair," he said. "The creature that jumped me was striped like a tiger."

"Pigmentation. In response to emotion, maybe," said Maury. "For camouflage—or for terrifying the victims."

Joe sat staring at the pictures in his hand.

"All right," he said after a bit. "Then tell me how he happened to get here three or four minutes after we fell down here ourselves? And where did he come from? We rammed that other ship a good five miles up."

"There's only one way, the rest of us figured it out," said Maury. "He was one of the ones who were spilled out when we hit them. He must have grabbed our hull and ridden us down."

"That's impossible!"

"Not if he could flatten himself out and develop suckers like a starfish," said Maury. "The skin picture shows he could."

"All right," said Joe. "Then why did he try a suicidal trick like that attack—him alone against the eight of us?"

"Maybe it wasn't so suicidal," said Maury. "Maybe he didn't see Cal's pistol and thought he could take the unarmed eight of us." Maury hesitated. "Maybe he could, too. Or maybe he was just doing his duty—to do as much damage to us as he could before we got him. There's no cover around here that'd have given him a chance to escape from us. He knew that we'd see him the first time he moved."

* * *

Joe nodded, looking down at the form in the freeze-sack. For the aliens of the other ship there would be one similarity with the humans—a duty either to get home themselves with the news of contact, at all costs; or failing that, to see their enemy did not get home.

For a moment he found himself thinking of the frozen body before him almost as if it had been human. From what strange home world might this individual now be missed forever? And what thoughts had taken place in that round, gray-skinned skull as it had fallen surfaceward clinging to the ship of its enemies, seeing the certainty of its own death approaching as surely as the rocky mountainside?

"Do we have record films of the battle?" Joe asked.

"I'll get them." Maury went off.

He brought the films. Joe, feeling the weakness of his condition stealing up on him, pushed it aside and set to examining the pictorial record of the battle. Seen in the film viewer, the battle had a remote quality. The alien ship was smaller than Joe had thought, half the size of the *Harrier*. The two dropped weights had made large holes in its midships. It was not surprising that it had broken apart when rammed.

One of the halves of the broken ship had gone up and melted in a sudden flare of green light like their weapons beam, as if some internal explosion had taken place. The other half had fallen parallel to the *Harrier* and almost as slowly—as if the fragment, like the dying *Harrier*, had had yet some powers of flight—and had been lost to sight at last on the opposite side of this mountain, still falling.

Four gray bodies had spilled from the alien ship as it broke apart. Three, at least, had fallen some five miles to their deaths. The record camera had followed their dwindling bodies. And Maury was right; these had been changing even as they fell, flattening and spreading out as if in an instinctive effort to slow their fall. But, slowed or not, a five-mile fall even in this lesser-than-Earth gravity was death.

Joe put the films aside and began to ask Maury questions.

The *Harrier*, Maury told him, would never lift again. Half her drive section was melted down to magnesium alloy slag. She lay here with food supplies adequate for the men who were left for four months. Water was no problem as long as everyone existed still within the ship's recycling system. Oxygen was available in the local atmosphere and respirators would extract it. Storage units gave them house-keeping power for ten years. There was no shortage of medical supplies, the tool shop could fashion ordinary implements, and there was a good stock of usual equipment.

But there was no way of getting off this mountain.

III

The others had come into the bubble while Maury had been speaking. They stood now around the bed. With the single exception of Cal, who showed nothing, they all had a new, taut, skinned-down look about their faces, like men who have been recently exhausted or driven beyond their abilities.

"Look around you," said Jeff Ramsey, taking over from Maury when Maury spoke of the mountain. "Without help we can't leave here."

"Tell him," said Doug Kellas. Like young Jeff, Doug had not shaved recently. But where Jeff's stubble of beard was blond, Doug's was brown-dark and now marked out the hollows under his youthful cheekbones. The two had been the youngest of the Team.

"Well, this is a hanging valley," said Jeff. Jeff was the surface man geologist and meterologist of the Team. "At one time a glacier used to come down this valley we're lying in, and over that edge there. Then the valley sub-sided, or the mountain rose or the climate changed. All the slopes below that cliff edge—any way down from here—brings you finally to a sheer cliff."

"How could the land raise that much?" murmured Maury, looking out and down at the green too far below to tell what it represented. Jeff shrugged.

"This is a bigger world than Earth—even if it's lighter," he said. "Possibly more liable to crustal distortion." He nodded at the peaks above them. "These are young mountains. Their height alone reflects the lesser gravity. That glacier up there couldn't have formed on that steep a slope on Earth."

"There's the Messenger," said Cal.

His deeper-toned voice brought them all around. He had been standing behind the rest, looking over their heads. He smiled a little dryly and sadly at the faint unanimous look of hostility on the faces of all but the Survey Leader's. He was unusual in the respect that he was so built as not to need their friendship. But he was a member of the Team as they were and he would have liked to have had that friendship—if it could have been had at any price short of changing his own naturally individualistic character.

"There's no hope of that," said Doug Kellas. "The Messenger was designed for launching from the ship in space. Even in spite of the lower gravity here, it'd never break loose of the planet."

The Messenger was an emergency device every ship carried. It was essentially a miniature ship in itself, with drive unit and controls for one shift through no-time and an attached propulsive unit to kick it well clear of any gravitic field that might inhibit the shift into no-time. It could be set with the location of a ship wishing to send a message back to Earth, and with the location of Earth at the moment of arrival—both figured in terms of angle and distance from the theoretical centerpoint of the galaxy, as determined by ship's observations. It would set off, translate itself through no-time in one jump back to a reception area just outside Earth's critical gravitic field, and there be picked up with the message it contained.

For the *Harrier* team, this message could tell of the aliens and call for rescue. All that was needed was the precise information concerning the *Harrier's* location in relation to Galactic Centerpoint and Earth's location.

In the present instance, this was no problem. The ship's computer log developed the known position and movement of Earth with regard to Centerpoint, with every shift and movement of the ship. And the position of the second planet of star K94 was known to the chartmakers of Earth recorded by last observation aboard the *Harrier*.

Travel in no-time made no difficulty of distance. In no-time all points coincided, and the ship was theoretically touching them all. Distance was not important, but location was. And a precise location was impossible—the very time taken to calculate it would be enough to render it impossibly inaccurate. What ships travelling by no-time operated on were calculations approximately as correct as possible—*and leave a safety factor*, read the rulebook.

Calculate not to the destination, but to a point safely short enough of it, so that the predictable error will not bring the ship out in the center of some solid body. Calculate safely short of the distance remaining . . . and so on by smaller and smaller jumps to a safe conclusion.

But that was with men aboard. With a mechanical unit like the Messenger, a one-jump risk could be taken.

The *Harrier* had the figures to risk it—but a no-time drive could not operate within the critical area of a gravitic field like this planet's. And, as Jeff had said, the propulsive unit of the Messenger was not powerful enough to take off from this mountainside and fight its way to escape from the planet.

"That was one of the first things I figured," said Jeff, now. "We're more than four miles above this world's sea-level, but it isn't enough. There's too much atmosphere still above us."

"The Messenger's only two and a half feet long put together," said Maury. "It only weighs fifteen pounds earthside. Can't we send it up on a balloon or something? Did you think of that?"

"Yes," said Jeff. "We can't calculate exactly the time it would take for a balloon to drift to a firing altitude, and we have to know the time to set the destination controls. We can't improvise any sort of a booster propulsion unit for fear of jarring or affecting the destination controls. The Messenger is meant to be handled carefully and used in just the way it's designed to be used, and that's all." He looked around at them. "Remember, the first rule of a Survey Ship is that it never lands anywhere but Earth."

"Still," said Cal, who had been calmly waiting while they talked this out, "we can make the Messenger work."

"How?" challenged Doug, turning on him. "Just how?"

Cal turned and pointed to the wind-piping battlemented peaks of the mountain looming far above.

"I did some calculating myself," he said. "If we climb up there and send the Messenger off from the top, it'll break free and go."

None of the rest of them said anything for a moment. They had all turned and were looking up the steep slope of the mountain, at the cliffs, the glacier where no glacier should be able to hang, and the peaks.

"Any of you had any mountain-climbing experience?" asked Joe.

"There was a rock-climbing club at the University I went to," said Cal. "They used to practice on the rock walls of the bluffs on the St. Croix River—that's about sixty miles west of Minneapolis and St. Paul. I went out with them a few times."

No one else said anything. Now they were looking at Cal.

"And," said Joe, "as our nearest thing to an expert, you think that—" he nodded to the mountain—"can be climbed carrying the Messenger along?"

Cal nodded.

"Yes," he said slowly. "I think it can. I'll carry the Messenger myself. We'll have to make ourselves some equipment in the tool shop, here at the ship. And I'll need help going up the mountain."

"How many?" said Joe.

"Three." Cal looked around at them as he called their names. "Maury, Jeff and Doug. All the able-bodied we've got."

Joe was growing paler with the effort of the conversation.

"What about John?" he asked looking past Doug at John Martin, Number Nine of the Survey Team. John was a short, rugged man with wiry hair—but right now his face was almost as pale as Joe's, and his warmsuit bulged over the chest.

"John got slashed up when he tried to pull the alien off you," said Cal calmly. "Just before I shot. He got it clear across the pectoral muscles at the top of his chest. He's no use to me."

"I'm all right," whispered John. It hurt him even to breathe and he winced in spite of himself at the effort of talking.

"Not all right to climb a mountain," said Cal. "I'll take Maury, Jeff and Doug."

"All right. Get at it then." Joe made a little, awkward gesture with his hand, and Maury stooped to help pull the pillows from behind him and help him lie down. "All of you—get on with it."

"Come with me," said Cal. "I'll show you what we're going to have to build ourselves in the tool shop."

"I'll be right with you," said Maury. The others went off. Maury stood looking down at Joe. They had been friends and teammates for some years.

"Shoot," whispered Joe weakly, staring up at him. "Get it off your chest, whatever it is, Maury." The effort of the last few minutes was beginning to tell on Joe. It seemed to him the bed rocked with a seasick motion beneath him, and he longed for sleep.

"You want Cal to be in charge?" said Maury, staring down at him.

Joe lifted his head from the pillow. He blinked and made an effort and the bed stopped moving for a moment under him.

"You don't think Cal should be?" he said.

Maury simply looked down at him without words. When men work and sometimes die together as happens with tight units like a Survey Team, there is generally a closeness amongst them. This closeness, or the lack of it, is something that is not easily talked about by the men concerned.

"All right," Joe said. "Here's my reasons for putting him in charge of this. In the first place he's the only one who's done any climbing. Secondly, I think the job is one he deserves." Joe looked squarely back up at the man who was his best friend on the Team. "Maury, you and the rest don't understand Cal. I do. I know that country he was brought up in and I've had access to his personal record. You all blame him for something he can't help."

"He's never made any attempt to fit in with the Team—"

"He's not built to fit himself into things. Maury—" Joe struggled up on one elbow. "He's built to make things fit him. Listen, Maury—he's bright enough, isn't he?"

"I'll give him that," said Maury, grudgingly.

"All right," said Joe. "Now listen. I'm going to violate Department rules and tell you a little bit about what made him what he is. Did you know Cal never saw the inside of a formal school until he was sixteen—and then the school was a university? The uncle and aunt who brought him up in the old voyageur's-trail area of the Minnesota-Canadian border were just brilliant enough and nutty enough to get Cal certified for home education. The result was Cal grew up in the open woods, in a tight little community that was the whole world, as far as he was concerned. And that world was completely indestructible, reasonable and handlable by young Cal Hartlett."

"But—"

"Let me talk, Maury. I'm going to this much trouble," said Joe, with effort, "to convince you of something important. Add that background to Cal's natural intellect and you get a very unusual man. Do you happen to be able to guess what Cal's individual sense of security rates out at on the psych profile?"

"I suppose it's high," said Maury.

"It isn't simply high—it just isn't," Joe said. "He's off the scale. When he showed up at the University of Minnesota at sixteen and whizzed his way through a special ordering of entrance exams, the psychology department there wanted to put him in a cage with the rest of the experimental animals. He couldn't see it. He refused politely, took his bachelor's degree and went into Survey Studies. And here he is." Joe paused. "That's why he's going to be in charge. These aliens we've bumped into could be the one thing the human race can't match. We've got to get word home. And to get word home, we've got to get someone with the Messenger to the top of that mountain."

He stopped talking. Maury stood there.

"You understand me, Maury?" said Joe. "I'm Survey Leader. It's my responsibility. And in my opinion if there's one man who can get the Messenger to the top of the mountain, it's Cal."

The bed seemed to make a slow half-swing under him suddenly. He lost his balance. He toppled back off the support of his elbow, and the sky overhead beyond the bubble began to rotate slowly around him and things blurred.

Desperately he fought to hold on to consciousness. He had to convince Maury, he thought. If he could convince Maury, the others would fall in line. He knew what was wrong with them in their feelings toward Cal as a leader. It was the fact that the mountain was unclimbable. Anyone could see it was unclimbable. But Cal was going to climb it anyway, they all knew that, and in climbing it he would probably require the lives of the men who went with him. They would not have minded that if he had been one of them. But he had always stood apart, and it was a cold way to give your life—for a man whom you have never understood, or been able to get close to.

"Maury," he choked. "Try to see it from Cal's—try to see it from his—"

The sky spun into a blur. The world blurred and tilted.

"Orders," Joe croaked at Maury. "Cal—command—"

"Yes," said Maury, pressing him back down on the bed as he tried blindly to sit up again. "All right. All right, Joe. Lie still. He'll have the command. He'll be in charge and we'll all follow him. I promise . . ."

IV

During the next two days, the Survey Leader was only intermittently conscious. His fever ran to dangerous levels, and several times he trembled and jerked as if on the verge of going into convulsions. John Martin also, although he was conscious and able to move around and even do simple tasks, was pale, high-fevered and occasionally thick-tongued for no apparent reason. It seemed possible there was an infective agent in the claw and teeth wounds made by the alien, with which the ship's medicines were having trouble coping.

With the morning of the third day when the climbers were about to set out both men showed improvement.

The Survey Leader came suddenly back to clear-headedness as Cal and the three others were standing, all equipped in the bubble, ready to leave. They had been discussing last-minute warnings and advices with a pale but alert John Martin when Joe's voice entered the conversation.

"What?" it said. "Who's alive? What was that?"

They turned and saw him propped up on one elbow on his makeshift bed. They had left him on it since the sleeping quarters section of the ship had been completely destroyed, and the sections left unharmed were too full of equipment to make practical places for the care of a wounded man. Now they saw his eyes taking in their respirator masks, packs, hammers, the homemade pitons and hammers, and other equipment including rope, slung about them.

"What did one of you say?" Joe demanded again. "What was it?"

"Nothing, Joe," said John Martin, coming toward him. "Lie down."

Joe waved him away, frowning. "Something about one being still alive. One what?"

Cal looked down at him. Joe's face had grown lean and fallen in even in these few days but the eyes in the face were sensible.

"He should know," Cal said. His calm, hard, oddly carrying baritone quieted them all. "He's still Survey Leader." He looked around at the rest but no one challenged his decision. He turned and went into the corridor of the ship, down to the main control room, took several photo prints from a drawer and brought them back. When he got back out, he found Joe now propped up on pillows but waiting.

"Here," said Cal, handing Joe the photos. "We sent survey rockets with cameras over the ridge up there for a look at the other side of the mountain. That top picture shows you what they saw."

Joe looked down at the top picture that showed a stony mountainside steeper than the one the *Harrier* lay on. On this rocky slope was what looked like the jagged, broken-off end of a blackened oil drum—with something white spilled out on the rock by the open end of the drum.

"That's what's left of the alien ship," said Cal. "Look at the closeup on the next picture."

Joe discarded the top photo and looked at the one beneath. Enlarged in the second picture he saw that the white something was the body of an alien, lying sprawled out and stiff.

"He's dead, all right," said Cal. "He's been dead a day or two anyway. But take a good look at the whole scene and tell me how it strikes you."

Joe stared at the photo with concentration. For a long moment he said nothing. Then he shook his head, slowly.

"Something's phony," he said at last, huskily.

"I think so too," said Cal. He sat down on the makeshift bed beside Joe and his weight tilted the wounded man a little toward him. He pointed to the dead alien. "Look at him. He's got nothing in the way of a piece of equipment he was trying to put outside the ship before he died. And that mountainside's as bare as ours. There was no place for him to go outside the ship that made any sense as a destination if he was that close to dying. And if you're dying on a strange world, do you crawl *out* of the one familiar place that's there with you?"

"Not if you're human," said Doug Kellas behind Cal's shoulder. There was the faintly hostile note in Doug's voice still. "There could be a dozen different reasons we don't know anything about. Maybe it's taboo with them to die inside a spaceship. Maybe he was having hallucinations at the end, that home was just beyond the open end of the ship. Anything."

Cal did not bother to turn around.

"It's possible you're right, Doug," he said. "They're about our size physically and their ship was less than half the size of the *Harrier*. Counting this one in the picture and the three that fell with the one that we killed here, accounts for five of them. But just suppose there were six. And the sixth one hauled the body of this one outside in case we came around for a look—just to give us a false sense of security thinking they were all gone."

Joe nodded slowly. He put the photos down on the bed and looked at Cal who stood up.

"You're carrying guns?" said Joe. "You're all armed in case?"

"We're starting out with sidearms," said Cal. "Down here the weight of them doesn't mean much. But up there . . ." He nodded to the top reaches of the mountain and did not finish. "But you and John better move inside the ship nights and keep your eyes open in the day."

"We will." Joe reached up a hand and Cal shook it. Joe shook hands with the other three who were going. They put their masks on.

"The rest of you ready?" asked Cal, who by this time was already across the bubble enclosure, ready to step out. His voice came hollowly through his mask. The others broke away from Joe and went toward Cal, who stepped through the bubble.

"Wait!" said Joe suddenly from the bed. They turned to him. He lay propped up, and his lips moved for a second as if he was hunting for words. "—Good luck!" he said at last.

"Thanks," said Cal for all of them. "To you and John, too. We'll all need it."

He raised a hand in farewell. They turned and went.

They went away from the ship, up the steep slope of the old glacier stream bed that became more steep as they climbed. Cal was in the lead with Maury, then Jeff, then Doug bringing up the rear. The yellow bright rays of K94 struck back at them from the ice-scoured granite surface of the slope, gray with white veinings of quartz. The warmsuits were designed to cool as well as heat their wearers, but they had been designed for observer-wearers, not working wearers. At the bend-spots of arm and leg joints, the soft interior cloth of the warmsuits soon became damp with sweat as the four men toiled upward. And the cooling cycle inside the suits made these damp spots clammy-feeling when they touched the wearer. The respirator masks also became slippery with perspiration where the soft, elastic rims of their transparent faceplates pressed against brow and cheek and chin. And to the equipment-heavy men the *feel* of the angle of the steep rock slope seemed treacherously less than eyes trained to Earth gravity reported it. Like a subtly tilted floor in a fun house at an amusement park.

They climbed upward in silence as the star that was larger than the sun of Earth climbed in the sky at their backs. They moved almost mechanically, wrapped in their own thoughts. What the other three thought were personal, private thoughts having no bearing on the moment. But Cal in the lead, his strong-boned, rectangular face expressionless, was wrapped up in two calculations. Neither of these had anything to do with the angle of the slope or the distance to the top of the mountain.

He was calculating what strains the human material walking behind him would be able to take. He would need more than their grudging cooperation. And there was something else.

He was thinking about water.

Most of the load carried by each man was taken up with items constructed to be almost miraculously light and compact for the job they would do. One exception was the fifteen Earth pounds of components of the Messenger, which Cal himself carried in addition to his mountain-climbing equipment—the homemade crampons, pitons and ice axe-piton hammer—and his food and the sonic pistol at his belt. Three others were the two-gallon containers of water carried by each of the other three men. Compact rations of solid food they all carried, and in a pinch they could go hungry. But to get to the top of the mountain they would need water.

Above them were ice slopes, and the hook-shaped glacier that they had been able to see from the ship below.

That the ice could be melted to make drinking water was beyond question. Whether that water would be safe to drink was something else. There had been the case of another Survey ship on another world whose melted local ice water had turned out to contain as a deposited impurity a small windborn organism that came to life in the inner warmth of men's bodies and attacked the walls of their digestive tracts. To play safe here, the glacier ice would have to be distilled.

Again, one of the pieces of compact equipment Cal himself carried was a miniature still. But would he still have it by the time they reached the glacier? They were all ridiculously overloaded now.

Of that overload, only the Messenger itself and the climbing equipment, mask and warmsuit had to be held on to at all costs. The rest could and probably would go. They would probably have to take a chance on the melted glacier ice. If the chance went against them—how much water would be needed to go the rest of the way?

Two men at least would have to be supplied. Only two men helping each other could make it all the way to the top. A single climber would have no chance.

Cal calculated in his head and climbed. They all climbed.

From below, the descending valley stream bed of the former glacier had looked like not too much of a climb. Now that they were on it, they were beginning to appreciate the tricks the eye could have played upon it by sloping distances in a lesser gravity, where everything was constructed to a titanic scale. They were like ants inching up the final stories of the Empire State Building.

Every hour they stopped and rested for ten minutes. And it was nearly seven hours later, with K94 just approaching its noon above them, that they came at last to the narrowed end of the ice-smoothed rock, and saw, only a few hundred yards ahead, the splintered and niched vertical rock wall they would have to climb to the foot of the hook-shaped glacier.

V

They stopped to rest before tackling the distance between them and the foot of the rock wall. They sat in a line on the bare rock, facing downslope, their packloads leaned back against the higher rock. Cal heard the sound of the others breathing heavily in their masks, and the voice of Maury came somewhat hollowly through the diaphragm of his mask.

"Lots of loose rock between us and that cliff," said the older man. "What do you suppose put it there?"

"It's talus," answered Jeff Ramsey's mask-hollowed voice from the far end of the line. "Weathering—heat differences, or maybe even ice from snowstorms during the winter season getting in cracks of that rock face, expanding, and cracking off the sedimentary rock it's constructed of. All that weathering's made the wall full of wide cracks and pockmarks, see?"

Cal glanced over his shoulder.

"Make it easy to climb," he said. And heard the flat sound of his voice thrown back at him inside his mask. "Let's get going. Everybody up!"

They got creakily and protestingly to their feet. Turning, they fell into line and began to follow Cal into the rock debris, which thickened quickly until almost immediately they were walking upon loose rock flakes any size up to that of a garage door, that slipped or slid unexpectedly under their weight and the angle of this slope that would not have permitted such an accumulation under Earth's great gravity.

"Watch it!" Cal threw back over his shoulder at the others. He had nearly gone down twice when loose rock under his weight threatened to start a miniature avalanche among the surrounding rock. He labored on up the talus slope, hearing the men behind swearing and sliding as they followed.

"Spread out!" he called back. "So you aren't one behind the other—and stay away from the bigger rocks."

These last were a temptation. Often as big as a small platform, they looked like rafts floating on top of the

smaller shards of rock, the similarity heightened by the
fact that the rock of the cliff-face was evidently planar in
structure. Nearly all the rock fragments split off had flat
faces. The larger rocks seemed to offer a temptingly clear
surface on which to get away from the sliding depth of
smaller pieces in which the boots of the men's warmsuits
went mid-leg deep with each sliding step. But the big
fragments, Cal had already discovered, were generally in
precarious balance on the loose rock below them and the
angled slope. The lightest step upon them was often enough
to make them turn and slide.

He had hardly called the warning before there was a
choked-off yell from behind him and the sound of more-
than-ordinary roaring and sliding of rock.

He spun around. With the masked figures of Maury on
his left and Doug on his right he went scrambling back
toward Jeff Ramsey, who was lying on his back, half-
buried in rock fragments and all but underneath a ten by
six foot slab of rock that now projected reeflike from the
smaller rock pieces around it.

Jeff did not stir as they came up to him, though he
seemed conscious. Cal was first to reach him. He bent
over the blond-topped young man and saw through the
faceplate of the respirator mask how Jeff's lips were sucked
in at the corners and the skin showed white in a circle
around his tight mouth.

"My leg's caught." The words came tightly and hollowly
through the diaphragm of Jeff's mask. "I think something's
wrong with it."

Carefully, Cal and the others dug the smaller rock away.
Jeff's right leg was pinned down under an edge of the big
rock slab. By extracting the rock underneath it piece by
piece, they got the leg loose. But it was bent in a way it
should not have been.

"Can you move it?"

Jeff's face stiffened and beaded with sweat behind the
mask faceplate.

"No."

"It's broken, all right," said Maury. "One down already," he added bitterly. He had already gone to work,
making a splint from two tent poles out of Jeff's pack. He
looked up at Cal as he worked, squatting beside Jeff.

"What do we do now, Cal? We'll have to carry him back down?"

"No," said Cal. He rose to his feet. Shading his eyes against the sun overhead he looked down the hanging valley to the *Harrier*, tiny below them.

They had already used up nearly an hour floundering over the loose rock, where one step forward often literally had meant two steps sliding backward. His timetable, based on his water supplies, called for them to be at the foot of the ice slope leading to the hook glacier before camping for the night—and it was already noon of the long local day.

"Jeff," he said. "You're going to have to get back down to the *Harrier* by yourself." Maury started to protest, then shut up. Cal could see the other men looking at him.

Jeff nodded. "All right," he said. "I can make it. I can roll most of the way." He managed a grin.

"How's the leg feel?"

"Not bad, Cal." Jeff reached out a warmsuited hand and felt the leg gingerly. "More numb than anything right now."

"Take his load off," said Cal to Doug. "And give him your morphine pack as well as his own. We'll pad that leg and wrap it the best we can, Jeff, but it's going to be giving you a rough time before you get it back to the ship."

"I could go with him to the edge of the loose rock—" began Doug, harshly.

"No. I don't need you. Downhill's going to be easy," said Jeff.

"That's right," said Cal. "But even if he did need you, you couldn't go, Doug. *I* need you to get to the top of that mountain."

They finished wrapping and padding the broken leg with one of the pup tents and Jeff started off, half-sliding, half-dragging himself downslope through the loose rock fragments.

They watched him for a second. Then, at Cal's order, they turned heavily back to covering the weary, struggle-some distance that still separated them from the foot of the rock face.

They reached it at last and passed into the shadow at its

base. In the sunlight of the open slope the warmsuits had struggled to cool them. In the shadow, abruptly, the process went the other way. The cliff of the rock face was about two hundred feet in height, leading up to that same ridge over which the weather balloon had been sent to take pictures of the fragment of alien ship on the other side of the mountain. Between the steep rock walls at the end of the glacial valley, the rock face was perhaps fifty yards wide. It was torn and pocked and furrowed vertically by the splitting off of rock from it. It looked like a great chunk of plank standing on end, weathered along the lines of its vertical grain into a decayed roughness of surface.

The rock face actually leaned back a little from the vertical, but, looking up at it from its foot, it seemed not only to go straight up, but—if you looked long enough—to overhang, as if it might come down on the heads of the three men. In the shadowed depths of vertical cracks and holes, dark ice clung.

Cal turned to look back the way they had come. Angling down away behind them, the hanging valley looked like a giant's ski-jump. A small, wounded creature that was the shape of Jeff was dragging itself down the slope, and a child's toy, the shape of the *Harrier*, lay forgotten at the jump's foot.

Cal turned back to the cliff and said to the others, "Rope up."

He had already shown them how this was to be done, and they had practiced it back at the *Harrier*. They tied themselves together with the length of sounding line, the thinness of which Cal had previously padded and thickened so that a man could wrap it around himself to belay another climber without being cut in half. There was no worry about the strength of the sounding line.

"All right," said Cal, when they were tied together— himself in the lead, Maury next, Doug at the end. "Watch where I put my hands and feet as I climb. Put yours in exactly the same places."

"How'll I know when to move?" Doug asked hollowly through his mask.

"Maury'll wave you on, as I'll wave him on," said Cal. Already they were high enough up for the whistling winds up on the mountain peak to interfere with mask-impeded conversations conducted at a distance. "You'll find this cliff is easier than it looks. Remember what I told you about handling the rope. And don't look down."

"All right."

Cal had picked out a wide rock chimney rising twenty feet to a little ledge of rock. The inner wall of the chimney was studded with projections on which his hands and feet could find purchase. He began to climb.

When he reached the ledge he was pleasantly surprised to find that, in spite of his packload, the lesser gravity had allowed him to make the climb without becoming winded. Maury, he knew, would not be so fortunate. Doug, being the younger man and in better condition, should have less trouble, which was why he had put Doug at the end, so that they would have the weak man between them.

Now Cal stood up on the ledge, braced himself against the rock wall at his back and belayed the rope by passing it over his left shoulder, around his body and under his right arm.

He waved Maury to start climbing. The older man moved to the wall and began to pull himself up as Cal took in the slack of the rope between them.

Maury climbed slowly but well, testing each hand and foothold before he trusted his weight to it. In a little while he was beside Cal on the ledge, and the ascent of Doug began. Doug climbed more swiftly, also without incident. Shortly they were all on the ledge.

Cal had mapped out his climb on this rock face before they had left, studying the cliff with powerful glasses from the *Harrier* below. Accordingly, he now made a traverse, moving horizontally across the rock face to another of the deep, vertical clefts in the rock known as chimneys to climbers. Here he belayed the rope around a projection and, by gesture and shout, coached Maury along the route.

Maury, and then Doug, crossed without trouble.

Cal then led the way up the second chimney, wider than the first and deeper. This took them up another forty-odd feet to a ledge on which all three men could stand or sit together.

Cal was still not winded. But looking at the other two, he saw that Maury was damp-faced behind the faceplate of his mask. The older man's breath was whistling in the respirator. It was time, thought Cal, to lighten loads. He had never expected to get far with some of their equipment in any case, but he had wanted the psychological advantage of starting the others out with everything needful.

"Maury," he said, "I think we'll leave your sidearm here, and some of the other stuff you're carrying."

"I can carry it," said Maury. "I don't need special favors."

"No," said Cal. "You'll leave it. I'm the judge of what's ahead of us, and in my opinion the time to leave it's now." He helped Maury off with most of what he carried, with the exception of a pup tent, his climbing tools and the water container and field rations. Then as soon as Maury was rested, they tackled the first of the two really difficult stretches of the cliff.

This was a ten-foot traverse that any experienced climber would not have found worrisome. To amateurs like themselves it was spine-chilling.

The route to be taken was to the left and up to a large, flat piece of rock wedged in a wide crack running diagonally up the rock face almost to its top. There were plenty of available footrests and handholds along the way. What would bother them was the fact that the path they had to take was around a boss, or protuberance of rock. To get around the boss it was necessary to move out over the empty atmosphere of a clear drop to the talus slope below.

Cal went first.

He made his way slowly but carefully around the outcurve of the rock, driving in one of his homemade pitons and attaching an equally homemade snap-ring to it, at the outermost point in the traverse. Passing the line that connected him to Maury through this, he had a means of holding the other men to the cliff if their holds should slip and they had to depend on the rope on their way around. The snap-ring and piton were also a psychological assurance.

Arrived at the rock slab in the far crack, out of sight of the other two, Cal belayed the rope and gave two tugs. A second later a tug came back. Maury had started crossing the traverse.

He was slow, very slow, about it. After agonizing minutes Cal saw Maury's hand come around the edge of the boss. Slowly he passed the projecting rock to the rock slab. His face was pale and rigid when he got to where Cal stood. His breath came in short, quick pants.

Cal signaled on the rope again. In considerably less time than Maury had taken Doug came around the boss. There was a curious look on his face.

"What is it?" asked Cal.

Doug glanced back the way he had come. "Nothing, I guess," he said. "I just thought I saw something moving back there. Just before I went around the corner. Something I couldn't make out."

Cal stepped to the edge of the rock slab and looked as far back around the boss as he could. But the ledge they had come from was out of sight. He stepped back to the ledge.

"Well," he said to the others, "the next stretch is easier."

VI

It was. The crack up which they climbed now slanted to the right at an almost comfortable angle.

They went up it using hands and feet like climbing a ladder. But if it was easy, it was also long, covering better than a hundred feet of vertical rock face. At the top, where the crack pinched out, there was the second tricky traverse across the rock face, of some eight feet. Then a short climb up a cleft and they stood together on top of the ridge.

Down below, they had been hidden by the mountain walls from the high winds above. Now for the first time, as they emerged onto the ridge they faced and felt them.

The warmsuits cut out the chill of the atmosphere whistling down on them from the mountain peak, but they could feel the pressure of it molding the suits to their bodies. They stood now once more in sunlight. Behind them they could see the hanging valley and the *Harrier*. Ahead was a cwm, a hollow in the steep mountainside that they would have to cross to get to a further ridge leading up to the mountain peak. Beyond and below the further ridge, they could see the far, sloping side of the mountain and, black against it, the tiny, oil-drum-end fragment of alien ship with a dot of white just outside it.

"We'll stay roped," said Cal. He pointed across the steep-sloping hollow they would need to cross to reach the further rocky ridge. The hollow seemed merely a tilted area with occasional large rock chunks perched on it at angles that to Earth eyes seemed to defy gravity. But there was a high shine where the sun's rays struck.

"Is that ice?" said Maury, shading his eyes.

"Patches of it. A thin coating over the rocks," said Cal. "It's time to put on the crampons."

They sat down and attached the metal frameworks to their boots that provided them with spiked footing. They drank sparingly of the water they carried and ate some of their rations. Cal glanced at the descending sun, and the blue-black sky above them. They would have several hours yet to cross the cwm, in daylight. He gave the order to go, and led off.

He moved carefully out across the hollow, cutting or kicking footholds in patches of ice he could not avoid. The slope was like a steep roof. As they approached the deeper center of the cwm, the wind from above seemed to be funnelled at them so that it was like a hand threatening to push them into a fall.

Some of the rock chunks they passed were as large as small houses. It was possible to shelter from the wind in their lees. At the same time, they often hid the other two from Cal's sight, and this bothered him. He would have preferred to be able to watch them in their crossings of the ice patches, so that if one of them started to slide he would be prepared to belay the rope. As it was, in the constant moan and howl of the wind, his first warning would be the sudden strain on the rope itself. And if one of them fell and pulled the other off the mountainside, their double weight could drag Cal loose.

Not for the first time, Cal wished that the respirator masks they wore had been equipped with radio intercom. But these were not and there had been no equipment aboard the *Harrier* to convert them.

They were a little more than halfway across when Cal felt a tugging on the line.

He looked back. Maury was waving him up into a shelter of one of the big rocks. He waved back and turned off from the direct path, crawling up into the ice-free overhang. Behind him, as he turned, he saw Maury coming toward him, and behind Maury, Doug.

"Doug wants to tell you something!" Maury shouted against the wind noise, putting his mask up close to Cal's.

"What is it?" Cal shouted.

"—Saw it again!" came Doug's answer.

"Something moving?" Doug nodded. "Behind us?" Doug's mask rose and fell again in agreement. "Was it one of the aliens?"

"I think so!" shouted Doug. "It could be some sort of animal. It was moving awfully fast—I just got a glimpse of it!"

"Was it—" Doug shoved his masked face closer, and Cal raised his voice—"was it wearing any kind of clothing that you could see?"

"No!" Doug's head shook back and forth.

"What kind of life could climb around up here without freezing to death—unless it had some protection?" shouted Maury to them both.

"We don't know!" Cal answered. "Let's not take chances. If it is an alien, he's got all the natural advantages. Don't take chances. You've got your gun, Doug. Shoot anything you see moving!"

Doug grinned and looked harshly at Cal from inside his mask.

"Don't worry about me!" he shouted back. "Maury's the one without a gun."

"We'll both keep an eye on Maury! Let's get going now. There's only about another hour or so before the sun goes behind those other mountains—and we want to be in camp underneath the far ridge before dark!"

He led off again and the other two followed.

As they approached the far ridge, the wind seemed to lessen somewhat. This was what Cal had been hoping for—that the far ridge would give them some protection from the assault of the atmosphere they had been enduring in the open. The dark wall of the ridge, some twenty or thirty feet in sudden height at the edge of the cwm, was now only a hundred yards or so away. It was already in shadow from the descending sun, as were the downslope sides of the big rock chunks. Long shadows stretched toward a far precipice edge where the cwm ended, several thousand feet below. But the open icy spaces were now ruddy and brilliant with the late sunlight. Cal thought wearily of the pup tents and his sleeping bag.

Without warning a frantic tugging on the rope roused

him. He jerked around, and saw Maury, less than fifteen
feet behind him, gesturing back the way they had come.
Behind Maury, the rope to Doug led out of sight around
the base of one of the rock chunks.

Then suddenly Doug slid into view.

Automatically Cal's leg muscles spasmed tight, to take
the sudden jerk of the rope when Doug's falling body
should draw it taut. But the jerk never came.

Sliding, falling, gaining speed as he descended the rooftop-
steep slope of the cwm, Doug's body no longer had the
rope attached to it. The rope still lay limp on the ground
behind Maury. And then Cal saw something he had not
seen before. The dark shape of Doug was not falling like a
man who finds himself sliding down two thousand feet to
eternity. It was making no attempt to stop its slide at all.
It fell limply, loosely, like a dead man—and indeed, just at
that moment, it slid far upon a small, round boulder in his
path which tossed it into the air like a stuffed dummy,
arms and legs asprawl, and it came down indifferently
upon the slope beyond and continued, gaining speed as
it went.

Cal and Maury stood watching. There was nothing else
they could do. They saw the dark shape speeding on and
on, until finally it was lost for good among the darker
shapes of the boulders farther on down the cwm. They
were left without knowing whether it came eventually to
rest against some rock, or continued on at last to fall from
the distant edge of the precipice to the green, unknown
depth that was far below them.

After a little while Maury stopped looking. He turned
and climbed on until he had caught up with Cal. His eyes
were accusing as he pulled in the loose rope to which
Doug had been attached. They looked at it together.

The rope's end had been cut as cleanly as any knife
could have cut it.

The sun was just touching the further mountains. They
turned without speaking and climbed on to the foot of the
ridge wall.

Here the rocks were free of ice. They set up a single
pup tent and crawled into it with their sleeping bags
together, as the sun went down and darkness flooded their
barren and howling perch on the mountainside.

VII

They took turns sitting up in their sleeping bags, in the darkness of their tiny tent, with Cal's gun ready in hand.

Lying there in the darkness, staring at the invisible tent roof nine inches above his nose, Cal recognized that in theory the aliens could simply be better than humans—and that was that. But, Cal, being the unique sort of man he was, found that he could not believe such theory.

And so, being the unique sort of man he was, he discarded it. He made a mental note to go on trying to puzzle out the alien's vulnerability tomorrow . . . and closing his eyes, fell into a light doze that was the best to be managed in the way of sleep.

When dawn began to lighten the walls of their tent they managed, with soup powder, a little of their precious water and a chemical thermal unit, to make some hot soup and get it into them. It was amazing what a difference this made, after the long, watchful and practically sleepless night. They put some of their concentrated dry rations into their stomachs on top of the soup and Cal unpacked and set up the small portable still.

He took the gun and his ice-hammer and crawled outside the tent. In the dawnlight and the tearing wind he sought ice which they could melt and then distill to replenish their containers of drinking water. But the only ice to be seen within any reasonable distance of their tent was the thin ice-glaze—*verglas*, mountaineers back on Earth called it—over which they had struggled in ~~erossing~~ the cwm the day before. And Cal dared not take their only gun too far from Maury, in case the alien made a sudden attack on the tent.

There was more than comradeship involved. Alone, Cal knew, there would indeed be no hope of his getting the Messenger to the mountaintop. Not even the alien could do that job alone—and so the alien's strategy must be to frustrate the human party's attempt to send a message.

It could not be doubted that the alien realized what their reason was for trying to climb the mountain. A race whose spaceships made use of the principle of no-time in their drives, who was equipped for war, and who responded to attack with the similarities shown so far, would not have a hard time figuring out why the human party was carrying the equipment on Cal's pack up the side of a mountain.

More, the alien, had he had a companion, would probably have been trying to get message equipment of his own up into favorable dispatching position. Lacking a companion his plan must be to frustrate the human effort. That put the humans at an additional disadvantage. They were the defenders, and could only wait for the attacker to choose the time and place of his attempt against them.

And it would not have to be too successful an attempt, at that. It would not be necessary to kill either Cal or Maury, now that Doug was gone. To cripple one of them enough so that he could not climb and help his companion climb, would be enough. In fact, if one of them were crippled Cal doubted even that they could make it back to the *Harrier*. The alien then could pick them off at leisure.

Engrossed in his thoughts, half-deafened by the ceaseless wind, Cal woke suddenly to the vibration of something thundering down on him.

He jerked his head to stare upslope—and scrambled for his life. It was like a dream, with everything in slow motion—and one large chunk of rock with its small host of lesser rocks roaring down upon him.

Then—somehow—he was clear. The miniature avalanche went crashing by him, growing to a steady roar as it grew in size sweeping down alongside the ridge. Cal found himself at the tent, from which Maury was half-emerged, on hands and knees, staring down at the avalanche.

Cal swore at himself. It was something he had been told, and had forgotten. Such places as they had camped in last night were natural funnels for avalanches of loose rock. So, he remembered now, were wide cracks like the sloping one in the cliff face they had climbed up yesterday—as, indeed, the cwm itself was on a large scale. And they had crossed the cwm in late afternoon, when the heat of the day would have been most likely to loosen the frost that held precariously balanced rocks in place.

Only fool luck had gotten them this far!

"Load up!" he shouted to Maury. "We've got to get out of here."

Maury had already seen that for himself. They left the pup-tent standing. The tent in Cal's load would do. With that, the Messenger, their climbing equipment, their sleeping bags and their food and water, they began to climb the steeply sloping wall of the ridge below which they had camped. Before they were halfway up it, another large rock with its attendant avalanche of lesser rocks came by below them.

Whether the avalanches were alien-started, or the result of natural causes, made no difference now. They had learned their lesson the hard way. From now on, Cal vowed silently, they would stick to the bare and open ridges unless there was absolutely no alternative to entering avalanche territory. And only after every precaution.

In the beginning Cal had kept a fairly regular check on how Maury was doing behind him. But as the sun rose in the bluish-black of the high altitude sky overhead the weariness of his body seemed to creep into his mind and dull it. He still turned his head at regular intervals to see how Maury was doing. But sometimes he found himself sitting and staring at his companion without any real comprehension of why he should be watching over him.

The blazing furnace of K94 overhead, climbing toward its noontime zenith, contributed to this dullness of the mind. So did the ceaseless roaring of the wind which had long since deafened them beyond any attempt at speech. As the star overhead got higher in the sky this and the wind noise combined to produce something close to hallucinations . . . so that once he looked back and for a moment seemed to see the alien following them, not astraddle the ridge and hunching themselves forward as they were, but walking along the knife-edge of rock like a monkey along a branch, foot over foot, and grasping the rock with toes like fingers, oblivious of the wind and the sun.

Cal blinked and, the illusion—if that was what it was— was gone. But its image lingered in his brain with the glare of the sun and the roar of the wind.

His eyes had fallen into the habit of focusing on the rock only a dozen feet ahead of him. At last he lifted them and saw the ridge broaden, a black shadow lying sharply across it. They had come to the rock walls below the hanging glacier they had named the Hook.

They stopped to rest in the relative wind-break shelter of the first wall, then went on.

Considering the easiness of the climb they made remarkably slow progress. Cal slowly puzzled over this until, like the slow brightening of a candle, the idea grew in him to check the absolute altimeter at his belt.

They were now nearly seven thousand feet higher up than they had been at the wreck of the *Harrier*. The mask respirators had been set to extract oxygen for them from the local atmosphere in accordance with the *Harrier* altitude. Pausing on a ledge, Cal adjusted his mask controls.

For a minute there seemed to be no difference at all. And then he began to come awake. His head cleared. He became sharply conscious, suddenly of where he stood—on a ledge of rock, surrounded by rock walls with, high overhead, the blue-black sky and brilliant sunlight on the higher walls. They were nearly at the foot of the third, and upper, battlement of the rock walls.

He looked over the edge at Maury, intending to signal the man to adjust his mask controls. Maury was not even looking up, a squat, lumpish figure in the warmsuit totally covered, with the black snout of the mask over his face. Cal tugged at the rope and the figure raised its face. Cal with his gloved hands made adjusting motions at the side of his mask. But the other's face below, hidden in the shadow of the faceplate, stared up without apparent comprehension. Cal started to yell down to him—here the wind noise was lessened to the point where a voice might have carried—and then thought better of it.

Instead he tugged on the rope in the signal they had repeated an endless number of times; and the figure below, foreshortened to smallness stood dully for a moment and then began to climb. His eyes sharpened by the fresh increase in the oxygen flow provided by his mask, Cal watched that slow climb almost with amazement carefully taking in the rope and belaying it as the other approached.

There was a heaviness, an awkwardness, about the warmsuited limbs, as slowly—but strongly enough—they pulled the climber up toward Cal. There was something abnormal about their movement. As the other drew closer, Cal stared more and more closely until at last the gloves of the climber fastened over the edge of the ledge.

Cal bent to help him. But, head down not looking, the other hoisted himself up alongside Cal and a little turned away.

Then in that last instant the combined flood of instinct and a lifetime of knowledge cried certainty. And Cal knew.

The warmsuited figure beside him was Maury no longer.

VIII

Reflexes have been the saving of many a man's life. In this case, Cal had been all set to turn and climb again, the moment Maury stood beside him on the edge. Now recognizing that somewhere among these rocks, in the past fumbling hours of oxygen starvation, Maury had ceased to live and his place had been taken by the pursuing alien, Cal's reflexes took over.

If the alien had attacked the moment he stood upright on the ledge, different reflexes would have locked Cal in physical combat with the enemy. When the alien did not attack, Cal turned instinctively to the second prepared response of his body and began automatically to climb to the next ledge.

There was no doubt that any other action by Cal, any hesitation, any curiosity about his companion would have forced the alien into an immediate attack. For then there would have been no reason not to attack. As he climbed, Cal felt his human brain beginning to work again after the hours of dullness. He had time to think.

His first thought was to cut the line that bound them together, leaving the alien below. But this would precipitate the attack Cal had already instinctively avoided. Any place Cal could climb at all, the alien could undoubtedly climb with ease. Cal's mind chose and discarded possibilities. Suddenly he remembered the gun that hung innocently at his hip.

With that recollection, the situation began to clear and settle in his mind. The gun evened things. The knowledge that it was the alien on the other end of the rope, along with the gun, more than evened things. Armed and prepared, he could afford to risk the present situation for a while. He could play a game of pretense as well as the alien could, he thought.

That amazing emotional center of gravity, Cal's personal sense of security and adequacy that had so startled the psychology department at the university was once more in command of the situation. Cal felt the impact of the question—why was the alien pretending to be Maury? Why had he adapted himself to man-shape, put on man's clothes and fastened himself to the other end of Cal's climbing rope?

Perhaps the alien desired to study the last human that opposed him before he tried to destroy it. Perhaps he had some hope of rescue by his own people, and wanted all the knowledge for them he could get. If so it was a wish that cut two ways. Cal would not be sorry of the chance to study a living alien in action.

And when the showdown came—there was the gun at Cal's belt to offset the alien's awesome physical natural advantage.

They continued to climb. Cal watched the other figure below him. What he saw was not reassuring.

With each wall climbed, the illusion of humanity grew stronger. The clumsiness Cal had noticed at first—the appearance of heaviness—began to disappear. It began to take on a smoothness and a strength that Maury had never shown in the climbing. It began in fact, to look almost familiar. Now Cal could see manlike hunching and bulgings of the shoulder muscles under the warmsuit's shapelessness, as the alien climbed and a certain trick of throwing the head from right to left to keep a constant watch for a better route up the face of the rock wall.

It was what he did himself, Cal realized suddenly. The alien was watching Cal climb ahead of him and imitating even the smallest mannerisms of the human.

They were almost to the top of the battlements, climbing more and more in sunlight. K94 was already far down the slope of afternoon. Cal began to hear an increase in the wind noise as they drew close to the open area above. Up there was the tumbled rock-strewn ground of a terminal moraine and then the snow slope to the hook glacier.

Cal had planned to camp for the night above the moraine at the edge of the snow slope. Darkness was now only about an hour away and with darkness the showdown must come between himself and the alien. With the gun, Cal felt a fair amount of confidence. With the showdown, he would probably discover the reason for the alien's impersonation of Maury.

Now Cal pulled himself up the last few feet. At the top of the final wall of the battlements the windblast was strong. Cal found himself wondering if the alien recognized the gun as a killing tool. The alien which had attacked them outside the *Harrier* had owned neither weapons nor clothing. Neither had the ones filmed as they fell from the enemy ship, or the one lying dead outside the fragment of that ship on the other side of the mountain. It might be that they were so used to their natural strength and adaptability they did not understand the use of portable weapons. Cal let his hand actually brush against the butt of the sidearm as the alien climbed on to the top of the wall and stood erect, faceplate turned a little from Cal.

But the alien did not attack.

Cal stared at the other for a long second, before turning and starting to lead the way through the terminal moraine, the rope still binding them together. The alien moved a little behind him, but enough to his left so that he was within Cal's range of vision, and Cal was wholly within his. Threading his way among the rock rubble of the moraine, Cal cast a glance at the yellow orb of K94, now just hovering above the sharp peaks of neighboring mountains around them.

Night was close. The thought of spending the hours of darkness with the other roped to him cooled the back of Cal's neck. Was it darkness the alien was waiting for?

Above them, as they crossed the moraine the setting sun struck blazing brilliance from the glacier and the snow slope. In a few more minutes Cal would have to stop to set up the pup-tent, if he hoped to have enough light to do so. For a moment the wild crazy hope of a notion crossed Cal's mind that the alien had belatedly chosen life over duty. That at this late hour, he had changed his mind and was trying to make friends.

Cold logic washed the fantasy from Cal's mind. This being trudging almost shoulder to shoulder with him was the same creature that had sent Doug's limp and helpless body skidding and falling down the long ice-slope to the edge of an abyss. This companion alongside was the creature that had stalked Maury somewhere among the rocks of the mountainside and disposed of him, and stripped his clothing off and taken his place.

Moreover, this other was of the same race and kind as the alien who had clung to the hull of the falling *Harrier* and, instead of trying to save himself and get away on landing, had made a suicidal attack on the eight human survivors. The last thing that alien had done, when there was nothing else to be done was to try to take as many humans as possible into death with him.

This member of the same race walking side by side with Cal would certainly do no less.

But why was he waiting so long to do it? Cal frowned hard inside his mask. That question had to be answered. Abruptly he stopped. They were through the big rubble of the moraine, onto a stretch of gravel and small rock. The sun was already partly out of sight behind the mountain peaks. Cal untied the rope and began to unload the pup tent.

Out of the corner of his eyes, he could see the alien imitating his actions. Together they got the tent set up and their sleeping bags inside. Cal crawled in the tiny tent and took off his boots. He felt the skin between his shoulder blades crawl as a second later the masked head of his companion poked itself through the tent opening and the other crept on hands and knees to the other sleeping bag. In the dimness of the tent with the last rays of K94 showing thinly through its walls, the shadow on the far tent wall was a monstrous parody of a man taking off his boots.

The sunlight failed and darkness filled the tent. The wind moaned loudly outside. Cal lay tense, his left hand gripping the gun he had withdrawn from its holster. But there was no movement.

The other had gotten into Maury's sleeping bag and lay with his back to Cal. Facing that back, Cal slowly brought the gun to bear. The only safe thing to do was to shoot the alien now, before sleep put Cal completely at the other's mercy.

Then the muzzle of the gun in Cal's hand sank until it pointed to the fabric of the tent floor. To shoot was the only safe thing—and it was also the only impossible thing.

Ahead of them was the snow-field and the glacier, with its undoubted crevasses and traps hidden under untrustworthy caps of snow. Ahead of them was the final rock climb to the summit. From the beginning, Cal had known no one man could make this final stretch alone. Only two climbers roped together could hope to make it safely to the top.

Sudden understanding burst on Cal's mind. He quietly reholstered the gun. Then, muttering to himself, he sat up suddenly without any attempt to hide the action, drew a storage cell lamp from his pack and lit it. In the sudden illumination that burst on the tent he found his boots and stowed them up alongside his bag.

He shut the light off and lay down again, feeling cool and clear-headed. He had had only a glimpse in turning, but the glimpse was enough. The alien had shoved Maury's pack up into a far corner of the tent as far away from Cal as possible. But the main pockets of that pack now bulked and swelled as they had not since Cal had made Maury lighten his load on the first rock climb.

Cal lay still in the darkness with a grim feeling of humor inside him. Silently, in his own mind he took his hat off to his enemy. From the beginning he had assumed that the only possible aim one of the other race could have would be to frustrate the human attempt to get word back to the human base—so that neither race would know of the two ships' encounter.

Cal had underestimated the other. And he should not have, for technologically they were so similar and equal. The aliens had used a no-time drive. Clearly, they had also had a no-time rescue signalling device like the Messenger, which needed to be operated from the mountaintop.

The alien had planned from the beginning to join the human effort to get up into Messenger-firing position, so as to get his own device up there.

He too, had realized—in spite of his awesome natural advantage over the humans—that no single individual could make the last stage of the climb alone. Two, roped together, would have a chance. He needed Cal as much as Cal needed him.

In the darkness, Cal almost laughed out loud with the irony of it. He need not be afraid of sleeping. The showdown would come only at the top of the mountain.

Cal patted the butt of the gun at his side and smiling, he fell asleep.

But he did not smile, the next morning when, on waking, he found the holster empty.

IX

When he awoke to sunlight through the tent walls the form beside him seemed not to have stirred, but the gun was gone.

As they broke camp, Cal looked carefully for it. But there was no sign of it either in the tent, or in the immediate vicinity of the camp. He ate some of the concentrated rations he carried and drank some of the water he still carried. He made a point not to look to see if the alien was imitating him. There was a chance, he thought, that the alien was still not sure whether Cal had discovered the replacement.

Cal wondered coldly where on the naked mountainside Maury's body might lie—and whether the other man had recognized the attacker who had killed him, or whether death had taken him unawares.

Almost at once they were on the glacier proper. The glare of ice was nearly blinding. Cal stopped and uncoiled the rope from around him. He tied himself on, and the alien in Maury's warmsuit, without waiting for a signal, tied himself on also.

Cal went first across the ice surface, thrusting downward with the forearm-length handle of his homemade ice axe. When the handle penetrated only the few inches of top snow and jarred against solidity, he chipped footholds like a series of steps up the steep pitch of the slope. Slowly they worked their way forward.

Beyond the main length of the hook rose a sort of tower of rock that was the main peak. The tower appeared to have a cup-shaped area or depression in its center—an ideal launching spot for the Messenger, Cal had decided, looking at it through a powerful telescopic viewer from the wreck of the *Harrier*. A rare launching spot in this landscape of steeply tilted surfaces.

Without warning a shadow fell across Cal's vision. He started and turned to see the alien towering over him. But, before he could move, the other had begun chipping at the ice higher up. He cut a step and moved up ahead of Cal. He went on, breaking trail, cutting steps for Cal to follow.

A perverse anger began to grow in Cal. He was aware of the superior strength of the other, but there was something contemptuous about the alien's refusal to stop and offer Cal his turn. Cal moved up close behind the other and abruptly began chipping steps in a slightly different direction. As he chipped, he moved up them, and gradually the two of them climbed apart.

When the rope went taut between them they both paused and turned in each other's direction—and without warning the world fell out from underneath Cal.

He felt himself plunging. The cruel and sudden jerk of the rope around his body brought him up short and he dangled, swaying between ice-blue walls.

He craned his head backward and looked up. Fifteen feet above him were two lips of snow, and behind these the blue-black sky. He looked down and saw the narrowing rift below him plunge down into darkness beyond vision.

For a moment his breath caught in his chest.

Then there was a jerk on the rope around him, and he saw the wall he was facing drop perhaps eighteen inches. He had been lifted. The jerk came again, and again. Steadily it progressed. A strength greater than that of any human was drawing him up.

Slowly, jerk by jerk, Cal mounted to the edge of the crevasse—to the point where he could reach up and get his gloved hands on the lip of ice and snow, to the point where he could get his forearms out on the slope and help lift his weight from the crevasse.

With the aid of the rope he crawled out at last on the downslope side of the crevasse. Just below him, he saw the alien in Maury's clothing, buried almost to his knees in loose snow, half-kneeling, half-crouching on the slope with the rope in his grasp. The alien did not straighten up at once. It was as if even his great strength had been taxed to the utmost.

Cal, trembling, stared at the other's crouched immobility. It made sense. No physical creature was possessed of inexhaustible energy—and the alien had also been climbing a mountain. But, the thought came to chill Cal's sudden hope, if the alien had been weakened, Cal had been weakened also. They stood in the same relationship to each other physically that they had to begin with.

After a couple of minutes, Cal straightened up. The alien straightened up also, and began to move. He stepped out and took the lead off to his left, circling around the crevasse revealed by Cal's fall. He circled wide, testing the surface before him.

They were nearing the bend of the hook—the point at

which they could leave the glacier for the short slope of bare rock leading up to the tower of the main peak and the cup-shaped spot from which Cal had planned to send off the Messenger. The hook curved to their left. Its outer bulge reached to the edge of a ridge on their right running up to the main peak, so that there was no avoiding a crossing of this final curve of the glacier. They had been moving closer to the ice-edge of the right-hand ridge, and now they were close enough to see how it dropped sheer, a frightening distance to rocky slopes far below.

The alien, leading the way, had found and circled a number of suspicious spots in the glacier ice. He was now a slack thirty feet of line in front of Cal, and some fifty feet from the ice-edge of the rim.

Suddenly, with almost no noise—as if it had been a sort of monster conjuring feat—the whole edge of the ice disappeared.

The alien and Cal both froze in position.

Cal, ice axe automatically dug in to anchor the other, was still on what seemed to be solid ice-covered rock. But the alien was revealed to be on an ice-bridge, all that was left of what must have been a shelf of glacier overhanging the edge of the rocky ridge. The rock was visible now—inside the alien's position. The ice-bridge stretched across a circular gap in the edge of the glacier, to ice-covered rock at the edge of the gap ahead and behind. It was only a few feet thick and the sun glinted on it.

Slowly, carefully, the masked and hidden face of the alien turned to look back at Cal, and the darkness behind his face-plate looked square into Cal's eyes.

For the first time there was direct communication between them. The situation was their translator and there was no doubt between them about the meanings of their conversation. The alien's ice-bridge might give way at any second. The jerk of the alien's fall on the rope would be more than the insecure anchor of Cal's ice-hammer could resist. If the alien fell while Cal was still roped to him, they would both go.

On the other hand, Cal could cut himself loose. Then, if the ice-bridge gave way, Cal would have lost any real chance of making the peak. But he would still be alive.

The alien made no gesture asking for help. He merely looked.

Well, which is it to be? the darkness behind his face-plate asked. If Cal should cut loose, there was only one thing for the alien to do, and that was to try to crawl on across the ice-bridge on his own—an attempt almost certain to be disastrous.

Cal felt a cramping in his jaw muscles. Only then did he realize he was smiling—a tight-lipped, sardonic smile. Careful not to tauten the rope between them, he turned and picked up the ice axe, then drove it into the ice beyond and to his left. Working step by step, from anchor point to anchor point, he made his way carefully around the gap, swinging well inside it, to a point above the upper end of the ice-bridge. Here he hammered and cut deeply into the ice until he stood braced in a two-foot hole with his feet flat against a vertical wall, lying directly back against the pull of the rope leading to the alien.

The alien had followed Cal's movements with his gaze. Now, as he saw Cal bracing himself, the alien moved forward and Cal took up the slack in the rope between them. Slowly, carefully, on hands and knees like a cat stalking in slow motion a resting butterfly, the alien began to move forward across the ice-bridge.

One foot—two feet—and the alien froze suddenly as a section of the bridge broke out behind him.

Now there was no way to go but forward. Squinting over the lower edge of his faceplate and sweating in his warmsuit, Cal saw the other move forward again. There were less than ten feet to go to solid surface. Slowly, the alien crept forward. He had only five feet to go, only four, only three—

The ice-bridge went out from under him.

X

The shock threatened to wrench Cal's arms from their shoulder-sockets—but skittering, clawing forward like a cat in high gear, the alien was snatching at the edge of the solid ice. Cal suddenly gathered in the little slack in the line and threw his weight into the effort of drawing the alien forward.

Suddenly the other was safe, on solid surface. Quickly, without waiting, Cal began to climb.

He did not dare glance down to see what the alien was

doing; but from occasional tautenings of the rope around his shoulders and chest, he knew that the other was still tied to him. This was important, for it meant that the moment of their showdown was not yet. Cal was gambling that the other, perhaps secure in the knowledge of his strength and his ability to adapt, had not studied the face of this tower as Cal had studied it through the telescopic viewer from the *Harrier*.

From that study, Cal had realized that it was a face that he himself might be able to climb unaided. And that meant a face that the alien certainly could climb unaided. If the alien should realize this, a simple jerk on the rope that was tied around Cal would settle the problem of the alien as far as human competition went. Cal would be plucked from his meager hand and footholds like a kitten from the back of a chair, and the slope below would dispose of him. He sweated now, climbing, trying to remember the path up the towerside as he had planned it out, from handhold to handhold, gazing through the long-distance viewer.

He drew closer to the top. For some seconds and minutes now, the rope below him had been completely slack. He dared not look down to see what that might mean. Then finally he saw the edge of the cup-shaped depression above him, bulging out a little from the wall.

A second more and his fingers closed on it. Now at last he had a firm handhold. Quickly he pulled himself up and over the edge. For a second perspiration blurred his vision. Then he saw the little, saucer sloping amphitheater not more than eighteen feet wide, and the further walls of the tower enclosing it on three sides.

Into the little depression the light of K94 blazed from the nearly black sky. Unsteadily Cal got to his feet and turned around. He looked down the wall he had just climbed.

The alien still stood at the foot of the wall. He had braced himself there, evidently to belay Cal against a fall that would send him skidding down the rock slope below. Though what use to belay a dead man, Cal could not understand, since the more than thirty feet of fall would undoubtedly have killed him. Now, seeing Cal upright and in solid position, the alien put his hands out toward the tower wall as if he would start to climb.

Cal immediately hauled taut on the line, drew a knife from his belt and, reaching as far down as possible, cut the line.

The rope end fell in coils at the alien's feet. The alien was still staring upward as Cal turned and went as quickly as he could to the center of the cup-shaped depression.

The wind had all but died. In the semi-enclosed rock depression the reflected radiation of the star overhead made it hot. Cal unsnapped his pack and let it drop. He stripped off the gloves of his warmsuit and, kneeling, began to open up the pack. His ears were alert. He heard nothing from outside the tower, but he knew that he had minutes at most.

He laid out the three sections of the silver-plated Messenger, and began to screw them together. The metal was warm to his touch after being in the sun-warmed backpack, and his fingers, stiff and cramped from gripping at handholds, fumbled. He forced himself to move slowly, methodically, to concentrate on the work at hand and forget the alien now climbing the tower wall with a swiftness no human could have matched.

Cal screwed the computer-message-beacon section of the nose tight to the drive section of the middle. He reached for the propulsive unit that was the third section. It rolled out of his hand. He grabbed it up and began screwing it on to the two connected sections.

The three support legs were still in the pack. He got the first one out and screwed it on. The next stuck for a moment, but he got it connected. His ear seemed to catch a scratching noise from the outside of the tower where the alien would be climbing. He dug in the bag, came out with the third leg and screwed it in. Sweat ran into his eyes inside the mask face-plate, and he blinked to clear his vision.

He set the Messenger upright on its three legs. He bent over on his knees, facemask almost scraping the ground to check the level indicator.

Now he was sure he heard a sound outside on the wall of the tower. The leftmost leg was too long. He shortened it. Now the middle leg was off. He lengthened that. He shortened the leftmost leg again . . . slowly . . . there, the Messenger was leveled.

He glanced at the chronometer on his wrist. He had set it with the ship's chronometer before leaving. Sixty-six ship's hours thirteen minutes, and . . . the sweep second hand was moving. He fumbled with two fingers in the breast pocket of his warmsuit, felt the small booklet he had made up before leaving and pulled it out. He flipped through the pages of settings, a row of them for each second of time. Here they were . . . sixty-three hours, thirteen minutes—

A gust of wind flipped the tiny booklet from his stiffened fingers. It fluttered across the floor of the cup and into a crack in the rock wall to his right. On hands and knees he scrambled after it, coming up against the rock wall with a bang.

The crack reached all the way through the further wall, narrowing until it was barely wide enough for daylight to enter—or a booklet to exit. The booklet was caught crossways against the unevenness of the rock sides. He reached in at arm's length. His fingers touched it. They shoved it a fraction of an inch further away. Sweat rolled down his face.

He ground the thickness of his upper arm against the aperture of the crack. Gently, gently, he maneuvered two fingers into position over the near edge of the booklet. The fingers closed. He felt it. He pulled back gently. The booklet came.

He pulled it out.

He was back at the Messenger in a moment, finding his place in the pages again. Sixteen hours—fourteen minutes—the computer would take four minutes to warm and fire the propulsive unit.

A loud scratching noise just below the lip of the depression distracted him for a second.

He checked his chronometer. Sixty-three hours, sixteen minutes plus . . . moving on toward thirty seconds. Make it sixty-three hours sixteen minutes even. Setting for sixty-three hours, sixteen minutes plus four minutes—sixty-three hours, twenty minutes.

His fingers made the settings on the computer section as the second hand of his chronometer crawled toward the even minute . . .

There.

His finger activated the computer. The Messenger began to hum faintly, with a soft internal vibration.

The sound of scraping against rock was right at the lip of the depression, but out of sight.

He stood up. Four minutes the Messenger must remain undisturbed. Rapidly, but forcing himself to calmness, he unwound the rest of the rope from about him and unclipped it. He was facing the lip of the depression over which the alien would come, but as yet there was no sign. Cal could not risk the time to step to the depression's edge and make sure.

The alien would not be like a human being, to be dislodged by a push as he crawled over the edge of the lip. He would come adapted and prepared. As quickly as he could without fumbling, Cal fashioned a slipknot in one end of the rope that hung from his waist.

A gray, wide, flat parody of a hand slapped itself over the lip of rock and began to change form even as Cal looked. Cal made a running loop in his rope and looked upward. There was a projection of rock in the ascending walls on the far side of the depression that would do. He tossed his loop up fifteen feet toward the projection. It slipped off—as another hand joined the first on the lip of rock. The knuckles were becoming pale under the pressure of the alien's great weight.

Cal tossed the loop again. It caught. He drew it taut.

He backed off across the depression, out of line with the Messenger, and climbed a few feet up the opposite wall. He pulled the rope taut and clung to it with desperate determination.

And a snarling tiger's mask heaved itself into sight over the edge of rock, a tiger body following. Cal gathered his legs under him and pushed off. He swung out and downward, flashing toward the emerging alien, and they slammed together, body against fantastic body.

For a fraction of a second they hung together, toppling over space while the alien's lower extremities snatched and clung to the edge of the rock.

Then the alien's hold loosened. And wrapped together, still struggling, they fell out and down toward the rock below accompanied by a cascade of rocks.

XI

"Waking in a hospital," Cal said later, "when you don't expect to wake at all, has certain humbling effects."

It was quite an admission for someone like himself, who had by his very nature omitted much speculation on either humbleness or arrogance before. He went deeper into the subject with Joe Aspinall when the Survey Team Leader visited him in that same hospital back on Earth. Joe by this time, with a cane, was quite ambulatory.

"You see," Cal said, as Joe sat by the hospital bed in which Cal lay, with the friendly and familiar sun of Earth making the white room light about them, "I got to the point of admiring that alien—almost of liking him. After all, he saved my life, and I saved his. That made us close, in a way. Somehow, now that I've been opened up to include creatures like him, I seem to feel closer to the rest of my own human race. You understand me?"

"I don't think so," said Joe.

"I mean, I needed that alien. The fact brings me to think that I may need the rest of you, after all. I never really believed I did before. It made things lonely."

"I can understand that part of it," said Joe.

"That's why," said Cal, thoughtfully, "I hated to kill him, even if I thought I was killing myself at the same time."

"Who? The alien?" said Joe. "Didn't they tell you? You didn't kill him."

Cal turned his head and stared at his visitor.

"No, you didn't kill him!" said Joe. "When the rescue ship came they found you on top of him and both of you halfway down that rock slope. Evidently landing on top of him saved you. Just his own natural toughness saved him— that and being able to spread himself out like a rug and slow his fall. He got half a dozen broken bones—but he's alive right now."

Cal smiled. "I'll have to go say hello to him when I get out of here."

"I don't think they'll let you do that," said Joe. "They've got him guarded ten deep someplace. Remember, his people still represent a danger to the human race greater than anything we've ever run into."

"Danger?" said Cal. "They're no danger to us."

It was Joe who stared at this. "They've got a definite weakness," said Cal. "I figured they must have. They seemed too good to be true from the start. It was only in trying to beat him out to the top of the mountain and get the Messenger off that I figured out what it had to be, though."

"What weakness? People'll want to hear about this!" said Joe.

"Why, just what you might expect," said Cal. "You don't get something without giving something away. What his race had gotten was the power to adapt to any situation. Their weakness is that same power to adapt."

"What're you talking about?"

"I'm talking about my alien friend on the mountain," said Cal, a little sadly. "How do you suppose I got the Messenger off? He and I both knew we were headed for a showdown when we reached the top of the mountain. And he had the natural advantage of being able to adapt. I was no match for him physically. I had to find some advantage to outweigh that advantage of his. I found an instinctive one."

"Instinctive . . ." said Joe, looking at the big, bandaged man under the covers and wondering whether he ought not to ring for the nurse.

"Of course, instinctive," said Cal thoughtfully, staring at the bed sheet. "His instincts and mine were diametrically opposed. He adapted to fit the situation. I belonged to a people who adapted situations to fit *them*. I couldn't fight a tiger with my bare hands, but I could fight something half-tiger, half something else."

"I think I'll just ring for the nurse," said Joe, leaning forward to the button on the bedside table.

"Leave that alone," said Cal calmly. "It's simple enough. What I had to do was force him into a situation where he would be between adaptations. Remember, he was as exhausted as I was, in his own way; and not prepared to quickly understand the unexpected."

"What unexpected?" Joe gaped at him. "You talk as if you thought you were in control of the situation all the way."

"Most of the way," said Cal. "I knew we were due to have a showdown. I was afraid we'd have it at the foot of the tower—but he was waiting until we were solidly at the top. So I made sure to get up to that flat spot in the tower first, and cut the rope. He had to come up the tower by himself."

"Which he was very able to do."

"Certainly—in one form. He was in one form coming up," said Cal. "He changed to his fighting form as he came over the edge—and those changes took energy. Physical and nervous, if not emotional energy, when he was pretty exhausted already. Then I swung at him like Tarzan as he was balanced, coming over the edge of the depression in the rock."

"And had the luck to knock him off," said Joe. "Don't tell me with someone as powerful as that it was anything but luck. I was there when Mike and Sam got killed at the *Harrier*, remember."

"Not luck at all," said Cal, quietly. "A foregone conclusion. As I say, I'd figured out the balance sheet for the power of adaptation. It had to be instinctive. That meant that if he was threatened, his adaptation to meet the threat would take place whether consciously he wanted it to or not. He was barely into tiger-shape, barely over the edge of the cliff, when I hit him and threatened to knock him off into thin air. He couldn't help himself. He adapted."

"Adapted!" said Joe, staring.

"Tried to adapt—to a form that would enable him to cling to his perch. That took the strength out of his tiger-fighting form, and I was able to get us both off the cliff together instead of being torn apart the minute I hit him. The minute we started to fall, he instinctively spread out and stopped fighting me altogether."

Joe sat back in his chair. After a moment, he swore.

"And you're just now telling me this?" he said.

Cal smiled a little wryly.

"I'm surprised you're surprised," he said. "I'd thought people back here would have figured all this out by now. This character and his people can't ever pose any real threat to us. For all their strength and slipperiness, their reaction to life is passive. They adapt to it. Ours is active—we adapt it to us. On the instinctive level, we can always choose the battlefield and the weapons, and win every time in a contest."

He stopped speaking and gazed at Joe, who shook his head slowly.

"Cal," said Joe at last, "you don't think like the rest of us."

Cal frowned. A cloud passing beyond the window dimmed the light that had shown upon him.

"I'm afraid you're right," he said quietly. "For just a while, I had hopes it wasn't so."

UNTITLED

And if it should not be you, after all—
Down the long passage, turning in the hall;
Or slipping at a distance through the light
Of streetlamped corners just within my sight;
I will not then turn back into my room,
Chilled and disheartened, wrapped in angry gloom;
But warm myself to think the mind should send
So many shades of you to be my friend . . .